ALSO BY MICHAEL PRYOR

10 Futures

The EXTRAORDINAIRES series
Book Two: The Subterranean Stratagem

The LAWS OF MAGIC series
Book One: Blaze of Glory
Book Two: Heart of Gold
Book Three: Word of Honour
Book Four: Time of Trial
Book Five: Moment of Truth
Book Six: Hour of Need

For younger readers

The CHRONICLES OF KRANGOR series
Book One: The Lost Castle
Book Two: The Missing Kin
Book Three: The King in Reserve

The
EXTINCTION Gambit

one

THE EXTRAORDINAIRES

MICHAEL PRYOR

RANDOM HOUSE AUSTRALIA

A Random House book
Published by Random House Australia Pty Ltd
Level 3, 100 Pacific Highway, North Sydney NSW 2060
www.randomhouse.com.au

First published by Random House Australia in 2011

Addresses for companies within the Random House Group can be found at
www.randomhouse.com.au/offices.

National Library of Australia
Cataloguing-in-Publication Entry

Author: Pryor, Michael
Title: The extinction gambit / Michael Pryor
ISBN: 978 1 86471 820 1 (pbk.)
Series: Pryor, Michael. Extraordinaires; 1
Target audience: For secondary school age
Dewey number: A823.3

Cover photograph courtesy Getty Images
Chain illustration © iStockphoto/pixhook
Cover design by Astred Hicks, www.designcherry.com
Internal design by Midland Typsetters
Typeset in Bembo by Midland Typsetters, Australia
Printed and bound in Australia by Griffin Press, an accredited ISO AS/NZ
14001:2004 Environmental Management System printer

For Dora, Erina, Nadia, Kor, Stephen, Tarran, Kate, Zahri, Rebecca, Meelsie, Shane, Raphael, Yu-Jie, Ellise and all the other Loyal Readers out there.

Was he not the Friend of the Stars as well as of all the World, crammed to the teeth with dreadful secrets?
—Rudyard Kipling, *Kim*

ONE

Kingsley Ward's wolfishness was a problem. If it weren't the howling, it was the occasional desire to bite boorish people, which was rarely acceptable, no matter how boorish the boor.

If 1908 were going to be a good year, however, he would have to maintain his control when it was his turn to walk onto the stage of the Alexandra Theatre.

He stood in the wings while his nerves did their best to share their discomfort with the rest of his body. Keeping to the shadows, he waited for the tenor ('Lloyd Evans, the Welsh Wonder') to finish a heartrending – and stomach-turning – rendition of 'Nellie Dean'. Kingsley understood that nervousness was natural prior to a professional debut. Of course, it was made worse by the possibility of his wild self breaking loose in the middle of the performance.

Which would certainly emphasise the 'variety' component of this variety show, Kingsley decided.

His left knee gave a tentative tremor.

The Alexandra Theatre in Aldershot wasn't his first choice of venue, but he was prepared to accept that seventeen-year-old novice performers were very much like beggars – choosiness shouldn't be part of their professional entitlements.

He took a deep breath and held out his hands. Steady enough, and his knee had decided it was up for the job, too. He brushed the lapels of his tailcoat and straightened his starched collar for possibly the three thousandth time.

Kingsley was pleased that, so far, the audience had been good-humoured. They had particularly enjoyed the performing dog troupe ('Taine's Tip-Top Terriers!'). Mr Bernadetti, the stage manager, had admitted in a moment of weakness that the week-long booking looked like being a solid earner.

Kingsley had found Mr Bernadetti to be the most relentlessly gloomy person he'd ever encountered. 'Not a disaster' was the highest praise Kingsley had ever heard pass the man's lips. 'Appalling', 'dreadful' and 'sod-awful' were the standard descriptions of the acts Bernadetti shepherded around a country that would never appreciate his genius. This genius, from Kingsley's observation, was composed of an ability to browbeat theatre owners, a propensity to organise extremely frugal travel arrangements, and a resistance to suggestion so awesome that, if properly harnessed, it could armour battleships.

The tenor reached for a high note, quickly revised his estimation of his own ability and settled for something on an altogether more achievable shelf, sliding about a little before he nailed it down. Kingsley guessed that the cheeky grin was meant to suggest that the effect was deliberate.

Kingsley took another deep breath and momentarily wondered why he was subjecting himself to this ordeal. Money wasn't a spur. His foster father wouldn't actually allow him to starve, even if he disapproved of Kingsley's abandoning his studies. The lure of fame wasn't strong, either, as Kingsley could quite comfortably live without being recognised on the street.

Was it simply the fulfilment of years of practice? Since his introduction to the world of magic, Kingsley had devoted much of his time to developing his skills. He was prepared to admit that he'd gone about it in a way that even he would have called obsessive in someone else.

Kingsley's fingers twitched. Flourish, cut, drop, produce. Fan, waterfall, palm, display. Repeat. Repeat again.

He recalled how, once he'd discovered the marvels of the craft, he'd worked the cards until his fingers bled. Then he'd moved from sleight of hand to other aspects of magic, pursuing something that beckoned to him without ever making itself clear. At one stage he'd even perfected what he'd thought was the acme of his craft: pulling a rabbit from a hat. He'd soon given this up. He was sorry for the indignities suffered by Oscar, his rabbit, who went on to live a happy and indulged life as Kingsley's least critical audience.

Despite his edginess, Kingsley smiled when he recalled Oscar. With twin motives, he'd begged his foster father for a pet rabbit. It was to be part of his magical act, but it was also a test. Small furry animals tended to rouse certain animal impulses that sometimes came upon him unexpectedly. He wanted a rabbit so that he would become accustomed to their presence and react to them in a civilised manner.

At the time, he'd never thought he'd become so attached to the bright-eyed, affectionate creature.

Two stagehands hurried past, waist-coated, sleeves rolled up, off to indulge in the mysteries of stagecraft to which they'd been initiated and Kingsley was still an outsider: possibly shifting sandbags, possibly sweeping, or possibly conducting arcane rituals in the fly tower overhead. Kingsley had no idea. In his short time as part of a professional troupe, he had come to realise that it was a different world, one replete with its own mysteries.

'Nellie Dean' dragged on, Lloyd Evans wringing every bit of sentiment from the song, much in the same way a washerwoman would wring water from sheets – but without as much finesse. The tenor stood right out on the apron, as close as he could get to the audience, and reached towards them, arms extended, a picture of heartfelt longing. Kingsley admired the way he was enjoying himself – even if the audience wasn't as convinced as he was.

· Certainty. Lloyd Evans had it, Kingsley realised. Call it confidence, or poise, or self-possession, Lloyd Evans *believed* in who he was. He believed so much that it went a great way to convincing the audience to go along with his performance.

Kingsley was convinced. Some performers simply owned the stage. Showing no doubt, they gave themselves to the audience wholly and completely.

While Lloyd Evans strolled into his last verse, Kingsley

touched his scarlet turban, making sure it was straight. He'd thought the turban a fine idea initially, as it covered his curly, fair hair as well as adding what he hoped was a much-needed air of mystery, but the dashed thing had a habit of slipping. A freckled stagehand crouched at the base of the fly tower was enjoying Kingsley's nerves and knuckled the peak of his cap with mock respect.

Kingsley bridled for an instant. A growl rose at the back of his throat before he clamped down on it by biting so hard his teeth hurt. To make sure, he brought his hands together and squeezed them until his knuckles creaked.

To distract himself, he launched into another check of his stage necessities, patting his jacket to make sure his sleight of hand materials were in place before going on to check his chains, manacles and the all-important metal trunk. As a seventeen-year-old tyro magician, Kingsley didn't have the luxury of an *ingenieur*, the craftsman who could construct equipment for him. However, he'd always been a solitary lad so he didn't really feel the lack. Never lonely, he told himself, just independent.

Even without the assistance of an *ingenieur*, escapology was Kingsley's real passion. Dexterity meeting strength meeting showmanship. It was performance of an altogether more elevated sort. He could, if he chose, see escapology as a metaphor for his life, breaking free of restraints and that sort of thing, but he preferred to think of it as the perfect expression of his desire never to give in. Once he had his teeth into something, he hung on until he was finished.

In the wings opposite, the stage manager rolled his eyes when he saw Kingsley looking about, and pointed at the straitjacket, the ropes and the handcuffs that he had ready on the props table. Kingsley settled, as much as he was able. He'd had enough dreams about being left, embarrassed, alone on the stage with no props and no equipment – sometimes with no clothes on, dreams being what they were.

His heart began to pick up pace as he recognised the final bars of the ballad. Lloyd Evans, down on one knee, fists clenched over his heart, assured Nellie Dean that she was his heart's desire – just in case there was any doubt left. The orchestra ambled to a finish, the individual members deciding that enough was enough.

The stalls were full, even though it was a Thursday. The balcony and circle were empty, however, apart from one lucky spectator on the far right of the house, leaning over so far that his chin was on the rail. Kingsley could just make out the lights glinting on his round spectacles.

Lloyd Evans doffed his bowler to the audience, bowed and exited the stage. The assistant stage manager replaced the number 5 with a 6 on the display board. A sweeping rustle indicated that the audience members were consulting their programs and wondering whether to stay for 'Item 6: Lorenzo the Great' or nip out for a choc ice.

Deep breath, Kingsley told himself. *Flex those fingers.*

Ignoring the glare from Mr Bernadetti, he took a moment and pressed both hands together in front of him. He closed his eyes and dropped his head. When he straightened, he was no longer Kingsley Ward, novice conjurer, but Lorenzo the Great, the Master of a Thousand Mysteries.

He caught the eye of the orchestra leader. Immediately, the carefully chosen snippet of the overture from

Scheherazade wafted over the auditorium. Two stagehands scuttled onto the apron in front of the garishly painted backdrop, carrying the small table that was essential for the first half of his eight minutes.

Eight minutes. Much could be achieved in eight minutes.

He strode from the wings with the last notes of his introduction still alive. He raised a hand, forefinger extended, and was caught in the flare of a spot. Without speaking, he regarded the audience, his face aloof and commanding, a performer not afraid of silence. As the darkened auditorium gazed back, another part of him roused. This part was more base, more animal – his wild self was alert. It was aware of the audience, curious and waiting, a many-headed beast in the darkness. It could smell them. A thousand different odours announced their presence to his lupine senses as clearly as if he could see them. In their anticipation, audience members made small noises in the hush – shifting in seats, shuffling feet, a cough or two. Above, slight noises came from the fly tower, stagehands ready to move and watching the newcomer below with professional interest. On either side, in the wings, other performers waited for their cue, or lingered to see what the new boy was up to.

His wild self built a picture of his surroundings in an instant, aware for threats, ready to fight or flee.

Kingsley stiffened. This wouldn't do. He needed to be an urbane, commanding conjurer, not a wolf backed into a corner. He pushed his wild self aside and launched into his patter.

This was a vital step in the whole performance. The audience was already primed, full of expectations from hearing the lush musical introduction and from taking in his appearance. They were ready to see magic, but he had to give them permission to *believe*. After all, the program announced that Lorenzo the Great was about to present illusions. His carefully crafted routines would simulate the extraordinary, but if the audience wasn't on his side, they would simply remain tricks. He had to invite them to *be* part of the illusion, to hand over doubt and to collaborate in creating something wonderful. If he commanded with the right touch of authority, they would surrender to him and share in the astonishing.

Kingsley had seen this happen again and again while he studied the performances of the greats, going to their shows and noting every gesture, every portentous announcement, every action dominating the stage and drawing the eye of each audience member. Chung Ling Soo, Adelaide Herrmann, Devant and Maskelyne at St George's Hall. Each of them had their method for inveigling the audience and making them co-conspirators for the duration of the show.

Kingsley's introduction was designed to claim the audience by invoking the mysteries of the East. Hint and allusion, nothing that could be contradicted outright, his beginning was a miracle of concision and misdirection, revised and honed again and again, usually late at night after Kingsley had finished studying. His Indian background helped, what he could remember of the time before his foster father brought him to England. Steamy, heady exoticism with the wilderness calling, while underneath darkness lurked and life was valued in ways that were both extraordinary and unknowable.

It was verbal sleight of hand. By the end of his delivery,

he knew he had them. The quality of the silence told him that the audience was his. He paused and held the silence again, unafraid. It was his, after all, something he'd created.

At that critical moment, a mighty crash resounded from off stage left. Laughter erupted from the audience, nervous and sudden, rippling and then growing, running along the rows of stalls like mice through wheat. The precious mood of complicity was shattered.

The laughter grew. Kingsley winced, which only provoked more hilarity. He glanced into the wings to see the freckled stagehand sweeping up the remains of a large glass jug and shrugging. His mates around him mirrored his grin.

Kingsley had heard about the traditional testing of new performers. In the weeks of rehearsal he'd endured some chaffing backstage, but he hadn't thought it would continue into his actual performance.

Anger flared at the back of his throat. He clenched his teeth. His hands, so carefully arranged in a languid pose at chest level, fell to his sides and curled into fists.

The freckled stagehand stopped sweeping and, in defiance of all backstage practice, brayed a laugh.

Fury descended on Kingsley, blotting out all his rationality. His wild self roared free. His shoulders hunched, then his chin lowered to his chest. He dropped to all fours. Snarling, he focused on the stagehand who pointed, guffawing, all propriety forgotten.

For Kingsley, the world went away. All he could see was his tormentor, freckled, reeking of stupidity and coarseness, head back and laughing, exposing his throat in a way that made Kingsley's blood sing.

He growled, rasping his throat, a death challenge. Then he twisted, snapping. *Stupid* collar! He clawed it off, flung it away. It was wrong, *everything* was wrong. Clothes were nasty, constricting, feet wrapped in dead cow. He wanted the earth between his toes, to be free!

The wild was upon him.

Hackles rising, he advanced on all fours, ready to hurl himself at his prey. Then he propped and threw back his head to howl a challenge.

The sky fell on him.

TWO

In the darkness, Kingsley hammered a fist on the floor-boards upon which he found himself. Despite his efforts, his wolfishness had emerged again. Every time he thought he had established control, it came and stripped civilisation away from him.

Fortunately, the shock of the stage curtain landing on top of him had dispelled his wild self. Dispelling his mortification was going to be more difficult. Formulating explanations and discarding them one by one, Kingsley wrestled with the heavy velvet while pandemonium reigned outside his small, dusty world: cries of outrage from the audience, catcalls, loud crashes, shouting and running, as if the theatre had suddenly become the site of a battle between a brass band and a herd of elephants.

A loud bang a few feet away made Kingsley jump, but he guessed it was only the steel safety curtain dropping into place. Uneasily, he sniffed for smoke and immediately regretted it. The years of accumulated dust trapped in the curtain shot up his nose. He grabbed at it but, before he could sneeze, he had to tuck his head in and protect it as he was pelted by objects from above: rope, wire, a few sandbag counterweights thumping down far too close and what felt like a large — but fortunately not very heavy — scenery flat slowly collapsing on top of him.

When this avalanche ceased, Kingsley let go of his nose and began to feel at ease. Being in the dark, wrapped up and contorted with both legs bent at awkward angles and one arm extended over his head, meant that he was actually in familiar territory — for an escapologist.

He flexed his shoulders. Some impressively colourful language was nearly drowned out by a chorus of joyous barking. Taine's Terriers, he hoped, were taking advantage of the chaos and heading for freedom. Kingsley cheered them on. *Run your hardest, cousins*, he thought, then grunted while he changed his position. *Freedom is worth it.*

He took stock of his situation — one of his Basic Principles of Escapology. To an exponent of anti-incarceration, a trap is not a trap: it is a challenge. Breaking free of restraint gave him a feeling of exultation like no other, an almost dizzying sense of his own capabilities. To this end, he'd studied locks, he'd exercised, he'd sought insights from tradesmen and showmen. He'd practised, alone in the basement of the family Bayswater home, until he could open handcuffs in the dark, free himself from ropes and slip out of manacles and shackles, even — with the assistance of his foster father's valet — when shut in trunks or sewn into mail bags or underwater. Such escapes often left him shaking, bruised and breathless, but with a soaring spirit.

A heavy velvet curtain, tangled rope, wire and sundry theatre apparatus was, therefore, hardly a trap – it was a momentary inconvenience.

The din about him receded as he concentrated. No handcuffs this time, no weighty chains. It was simply a matter of orientating himself just *so*, rotating his shoulders like *that*, arching his back *thus*, twisting a little *this way* then *that*, and he could see the line of light that announced where the edge of the curtain met the stage. A slow, shuffling crawl and, quite aware that he was bound to look like an exceptionally well-appointed turtle, he poked out his head, ready to apologise for the disaster.

A slim white hand thrust at him. 'Here. It's best that we leave.'

It was the juggler. The young female juggler. The young female juggler with the white hair, white skin and pink eyes. The startlingly beautiful young female juggler with her long white hair, white skin and pink eyes behind the spectacles she was looking at him over.

All week, during run-throughs and rehearsals, he'd been careful not to stare at her, even when she was dressed in her stage costume, which was made of spangles and not much else. Crawling out from under a collapsed stage curtain, however, had discomposed him enough that he forgot his manners, even though she was wearing a demure ankle-length, midnight blue coat buttoned to her throat, and a smart Langtry toque on her head.

This time, he stared.

'Yes.' She glanced to either side. 'I'm different from anyone you've ever met before and you don't really know how to treat me. Let's take that for granted, shall we? If we slip off right now and let everyone settle down, we might get away with it.'

She had a surprisingly strong grip. He climbed to his feet as a wire-haired terrier scampered past, barking in the sheer berserk joy of liberation. 'Get away with what?'

'Your bizarre performance and my dropping the curtain on you and ...' She waved a hand. Kingsley looked around to see that the safety curtain had indeed cut off the auditorium from the stage. In addition, most of the backdrops, sandbag counterweights and gaudy flats had fallen. Performers and stagehands were running around shouting and flinging their arms about, giving the impression of a bizarre folk dance. 'Sundry other distractions.'

'Distractions.' Kingsley's jacket and trousers were a mess. His turban had collapsed and he unwound it slowly, pocketing the brass medallion with which it had been pinned. '*You* dropped the curtain? Why?'

'To save you.'

'And why would you do that? Even if I needed saving, which I deny utterly.'

'You're my project.'

'I beg your pardon?'

She took his hand. 'We really should go. If Billy finds us while he's still in a state, we're doomed. But if we let him seethe a little, I'm sure I can talk him around.'

'Billy? Mr Bernadetti? The stage manager?'

She gripped his elbow. 'Billy owes me more than a few favours, but he's liable to forget them if he's in a temper.'

Kingsley was teetering. He saw his entire stage career vanishing before his eyes. Should he stay and see if he

14

could talk his way out of the situation? Or should he throw in his lot with this extraordinary young woman?

'Are you sure you can make him overlook this?'

'I have my ways,' she said darkly. 'Trust me.'

He did, immediately and instinctively, at a level he suspected had something to do with his wild self. 'Thank you, Miss . . .?'

She cocked her head. 'You are a piece, aren't you? I'll wager you don't know the names of any of the other performers.'

'Not the ones after me on the program.'

'Stephens. Evadne Stephens. Now, look sharp and we'll exit, stage right. Or what remains of stage right, anyway.'

Kingsley and Evadne joined a stream of performers and crew barging towards the stage door, laughing and chattering at the unexpected turn of events. Evadne took his arm and Kingsley hunched, trying to keep his imposing stature as discreet as possible. He was grateful for the towering headdress of Madame Olivansky ('the Bird Whistler'), just in front of him.

'Mr Ward! Mr Ward!'

Kingsley quailed, but it was only Todd, the ancient and perennially doleful Stage Door Manager, gamely struggling towards him through the crowd with one hand thrusting an envelope above his head.

Todd reached Kingsley. He clung to him very much like a drowning man finding a life preserver, while Doran and Bedlow ('the Merry Jokers') pushed past, arguing about punchlines. 'Mr Ward,' Todd panted. 'A letter for you.'

Evadne plucked at the old man's sleeve, and raised an eyebrow when the ancient cloth parted under her fingers. 'Todd,' she said, after a momentary pause, 'have you seen Mr Bernadetti?'

Todd's face grew even more doleful. 'He's in the foyer, miss, shouting.'

'At anyone in particular? Or is he just practising?'

'He's with the theatre owners, miss. They're not happy about the way the performance has gone.'

'Oh.'

Kingsley hardly heard this exchange. He was re-reading the letter Todd had given him, slowly. 'I have to go to London.'

Evadne shook her head. 'You'll do no such thing. I'll need you around when Billy has calmed down and I can go to work on him, which may be–' Evadne stopped herself and scrutinised Kingsley. 'What is it?'

'It's from my foster father's valet.' Kingsley was already planning. What time did the last train leave? He sighed. This *wasn't* a good time for such a thing. 'My foster father's gone missing. He hasn't been seen for weeks.'

'Todd,' Evadne snapped. 'Tell Mr Bernadetti that I want to speak to him later.'

'Yes, miss.'

Kingsley pushed towards the door, easing past a knot of stagehands, and was startled to find Evadne keeping pace with him. 'What are you doing?' he said, as they emerged into a narrow lane that smelled of cats, and were swept towards the lights of Alexandra Road ahead.

'Coming with you. You're my project, after all.'

'What?'

'You interest me, Kingsley Ward. Strange behaviour always does.'

A man who had been leaning against the brick wall of the theatre straightened and waved. 'Mr Ward! I have to speak to you!'

The man was small – five feet five or six – and well dressed, with distinctive oval wire-rimmed spectacles. He had a thick moustache and Kingsley recognised him as the man in the balcony, the one who had been watching so attentively.

'Sorry, sir,' Evadne called, hustling Kingsley along, 'we're on a mission.'

'A mission?' Kingsley asked. He looked back, but the little man had disappeared, swallowed up in the tide of performers. 'Where?'

'The station first.' She pushed her spectacles up on her nose. They were small and rectangular and slightly tinged blue, which Kingsley found odd. Hadn't they been clear when she found him under the stage curtain? 'Then we're off to London.'

'What?'

'I'm coming with you. It'll give Mr Bernadetti a chance to calm down. Then I can have a nice chat with him and get your career back on track.'

'Because I'm your project.'

'That's part of it.'

'You're sure he'll overlook this fiasco?'

'Sure?' Evadne donned a pair of blue gloves she took from the pocket of her coat, then put a finger to her very pale lips. Not as pale as her skin, Kingsley noted, but with only a ghost of rosiness, the merest blush of colour. 'I wouldn't say that. Certainty is the refuge of the small minded.'

'Really?' Kingsley rallied. This breathtaking young woman needed to know that he wasn't entirely a dunder-head. 'Are you sure it isn't the capital of Siam?'

She eyed him. 'A nice attempt at levity, in a non sequitur kind of way, and a sign you're recovering from whatever overcame you.' She held up a hand, interrupting him. 'No explanations, not yet. Let me talk Billy Berna-detti around. He won't want his dirty laundry aired and I happen to know where he keeps stuff that should never see the light of day.'

Kingsley glanced back down the lane. Artistes were still plunging out of the stage door, most of them in costume – plenty of feathers, tassels, that sort of thing. His fears were assuaged somewhat by the carnival atmosphere.

He frowned.

'What is it?' Evadne asked.

'That man. The one with the spectacles. Have you seen him before?'

'Him?' Evadne made a face. 'He's been here all week, sniffing about. I thought he might be one of Maisie's beaus.'

'Don't you like Maisie?'

Maisie was the most famous performer on the bill, a sweet-voiced and pretty singer who had done well in West End theatres until, Kingsley had been told by one of the more gossipy mime artists, a mysterious falling out with a certain music hall owner.

'It's not her. It's her monkey.'

'It's a harmless pet,' he said, and remembered how on his first rehearsal he'd barely avoided being sconed by an orange it had accidentally dropped from the fly tower. Or had it been accidental?

'I can't abide monkeys. They disquiet me.'

'Monkeys? Give them a banana and they're your friend for life.'

'They're too human, to my way of thinking. Made pets of or caged up, scheming and thinking vengeful thoughts.'

'Vengeful thoughts? Really?'

'Really.'

Kingsley looked back. The little man had gone. To see a singer about a monkey?

'Did he look familiar to you?'

Evadne looked thoughtful. 'Perhaps.' She shrugged. 'Maisie's beaus tend to be prominent men. He's probably a politician or a lord or someone else with a lot of time on their hands. Still . . .' She tapped her chin with a finger, then, quite obviously, put her cogitation aside. 'The station's this way.'

'You know Aldershot well, do you?'

She pointed at a sign on the other side of the street. It was a small sign, shrouded in the shadows thrown by a large plane tree.

He shrugged. 'I'll trust you.'

'And that, I'll say, is an excellent beginning.'

~ THREE ~

In the carriage, Kingsley sat opposite Evadne. She studied him solemnly while her gloved hands tossed an indeterminate number of silver sixpences backward and forward.

'You'll do,' she said finally, pocketing her coins.

Her announcement jerked Kingsley from brooding about his foster father. Dr Ward often left home abruptly, pursuing one of his many academic investigations, but he always left instructions. *Always.* He was a man who loved a list of things to do, preferably for other people. 'I'm glad.' Kingsley caught himself. 'I'll do for what?'

'My project, remember?' The sixpences reappeared in her hand and she absently rolled them between her fingers. 'When you started your act I thought I'd made a poor decision, but things became far more interesting after that.'

Kingsley frowned. Perhaps this was some sort of music hall argot he was unfamiliar with. 'Go on,' he said, carefully.

'That's the way.' She reached out and patted his hand. 'Each season, I make it my job to take up with one of the less experienced members of the cast and befriend them. I was about to say "show them the ropes" but I hardly think that's what's needed in your case, is it?'

'I know my ropes,' he said faintly. 'It sounds as if you've apprenticed me.'

She smiled. It was a cheeky smile and Kingsley could imagine himself growing to like it. 'I've seen your details,' she said, 'and I know that I'm older than you are. From my lofty advantage of two extra months on the planet, I'm making it my responsibility to help you along.'

'You make it sound as if you're adopting a puppy.'

'And what's wrong with that? Don't you like puppies? Clarence has a wolf-hound, you know, that he raised from a puppy. It can fetch, when it wants to.'

'No, I do, it's not that.' He stopped, reviewed what Evadne had just said, and blinked. 'Clarence?'

Evadne stopped juggling. Kingsley wasn't sure how, but the sixpences disappeared. Then she produced a locket on the end of a silver chain that, apparently, hung from her neck. She flipped it open. 'This is Clarence. He's my intended.'

Kingsley had never actually heard anyone called an 'intended' before. 'Congratulations. A respectable fellow, from the looks of him.'

She raised a very precise eyebrow. 'Clarence is more than respectable. He's well-to-do. You'd be startled if I told you his family name.'

'I'm sure I would be.'

'He's studying. Brilliantly. Kings College.'

'I see.' Kingsley peered at the locket. 'It looks as if you've torn his picture from a magazine.'

Evadne sniffed. Kingsley had never seen anyone sniff elegantly before, but Evadne achieved this difficult feat. She snapped the locket closed. 'Clarence has featured in any number of journals of the better kind.'

'Not as the defendant in one of the more sensational court cases, I hope.'

She ignored this. 'I'm telling you about him so we won't misunderstand each other. When I say that you interest me, I want it clear that it's not like that.'

'That?'

'That.'

'Oh, *that*!'

'Exactly. Which doesn't mean I'm being unfriendly. You're not without a rough and ready charm, after all.'

Rough and ready? Charm? Kingsley was wary of Evadne's quicksilveriness, and not quite certain how to approach her. He sensed that half her jibes were challenges, and that he'd lose her respect if he couldn't rise to them – but the other half?

She opened her locket and peeked at it again. 'A magazine, you say?'

'Trim the edges a little neater next time.'

Evadne pursed her lips and snapped the locket shut with a flourish. It disappeared down her neckline, something that Kingsley hardly noticed at all.

'Now,' she said. 'If I'm to make you my project, we need to have a few things clear.'

'I, for one, would appreciate having a single thing clear.'

She flashed him a smile. 'You're game, at least, I'll grant

you that.' She composed herself. 'Do remember, at all times, that the polite term is "albino". Not "snowdrop", "chalky" or "ghosty pants". The condition can be termed achromia, if you're feeling pedantic.'

'I rarely feel pedantic. I occasionally feel Atlantic, but only when I'm at sea.'

She awarded an instant's scorn to this sally, which Kingsley took as a victory, then went on. 'How much do you know about albinism?'

'With some trepidation that I'm presenting myself for rightful ridicule, I'll say: "as much as the next man".'

'Next to nothing, then.'

'Correct,' Kingsley said, with the impression he'd escaped lightly. Already, he appreciated that he needed to be on his toes when talking to Evadne Stephens.

'Then I won't attempt to transform you into an expert straight away.' She drummed her fingers on her knee in an interesting syncopated beat. 'Let it be said that on top of the obvious skin and hair characteristics, achromatic people also tend to have vision problems – short-sightedness, astigmatism, things like that.'

'Let me see if I understand this properly. You have vision problems and yet you were able to read that sign pointing to the station from yards away, at night.'

Evadne stood. She turned off the gaslights in the carriage, and her whiteness was even more ghostly in the shadows. She took off her spectacles and held them out to him. 'Put these on.'

He gasped. It was as if the carriage were bathed in gentle sunlight. Everything was dizzyingly blurry, swooping and swelling as he moved his head, but it was a well-lit blurriness.

Evadne plucked the spectacles from his face and adjusted up the lights. She inspected the spectacles before slipping them back on.

'That's remarkable,' he managed.

'I have a number of pairs of corrective spectacles. Some are for special purposes. Others can be adjusted for varying circumstances.' Evadne sat and patted her coat. 'I can't go out in the daylight without something strongly tinted. At night, though, some light enhancement is useful.'

'Where did you get them?'

'I made them.'

'I beg your pardon?'

'You say that as if juggling and practical optometry were an odd combination.'

'Well, not so much odd as unexpected.'

She waved that away. 'Now, is there anything else you wanted to know?'

'There is indeed something else I wanted to know.' He crossed his arms and settled them on his chest. 'Where did you learn to juggle?'

Evadne put a hand over her mouth, then burst out laughing. 'Oh, well played, sir,' she said, 'well played.'

'Thank you.' Kingsley felt as if he'd passed another test. 'But I'm genuinely interested in an answer.'

Evadne touched the chain at her neck. 'You can imagine that I've grown accustomed to being an object of attention.'

'For your juggling.'

She peered over the top of her spectacles. 'Now you're almost being tiresome.'

'Sorry.'

'You need to understand that I've been called a freak,'

she said, 'and worse, so I've developed a number of ways of coping with people. Anticipating their reactions is one of them.'

'And I confounded you when I asked about your juggling instead of your albinism? I apologise.'

'Don't. I enjoy being confounded. It happens so seldom, after all.' She grinned. It was a totally unaffected expression of impish delight. She had excellent teeth, Kingsley noted. 'I learned juggling from my uncle Frederick, who must never be mentioned.'

'Anywhere, or just in your family home?'

'You've heard of families having black sheep? Uncle Frederick is the sort of black sheep that black sheep shun.'

'He sounds like a useful uncle to have.'

'He is. Once he taught me juggling, to my parents' horror, he went to sea and I didn't see him for years so I had to find help wherever I could.'

'It was the same with my magic.'

'My uncle Frederick taught you magic? I knew he'd been around, but I never . . .' She took out a pocket watch, a handsome gold repeater. A man's watch, if Kingsley was any judge, but he'd already come to understand that Evadne Stephens was anything but conventional.

He sat back, easing into the rhythm of the train as it clicketty-clacked towards London, and he tried not to worry about his foster father. Kingsley had always feared for his foster father's safety, despite his reassurances that the scrapes he'd encountered and the disreputable characters he dealt with presented no real danger. The letter from his foster father's valet had echoed Kingsley's misgivings, and thus amplified them.

What had the old man found himself in this time?

⇜ FOUR ⇝

Jabez Soames was not a bad man. He told himself so every morning when he rose from his bed and slipped the nightcap from a head that was far more balding than he wished. It was simply a fact of existence that unpleasant things needed to be done, at times. Since unpleasant things needed to be done, Jabez Soames was dedicated to doing them as efficiently as possible.

It was irrelevant that Jabez Soames enjoyed his work and had for all forty years of his working life. He especially enjoyed it when it offered him the prospect of riches. It added a certain piquancy to whatever needed doing.

These were profitable days for Soames. The Franco-British Exhibition had brought many foreigners to London and the Olympic Games promised more. Soames loved foreigners of all sorts. So unfamiliar with British ways, so far from home ...

On the way to his office, he made a mental note to see about outlaying some money on the Marathon race the papers were full of. He was sure he could make arrangements to have the event favour his wager. Perhaps administering something to the favoured runner?

Jabez, Jabez, Jabez, he thought, *you are a veritable ferment of ideas!*

He smiled to himself.

Even this late at night Soames was warm in his overcoat, as the weather had improved considerably since the rain of the previous few days. Being of a practical mind, however, he still had his umbrella. He glanced at the lift operator. 'Have you killed anyone lately, Higgs?'

The night operator, one hand on the brass control lever, was dapper in his red and blue uniform. He had the knack of moving his eyes while the rest of his face stayed impassive. 'Depends on what you mean by "lately", Mr Soames, sir.'

'What about in the last week?'

'No, sir.' Higgs was a small man who always reminded Soames of one of the *mustelidae* family. A ferret, or something less domesticated? 'Definitely no-one in the last seven days. Not much call for it at the moment, what with the grippe and all laying 'em low.'

'You have my commiserations. What's the world coming to when a lift operator can't supplement his income with a little pre-emptive body snatching?'

'Wouldn't know, sir, and here's your floor.'

'Wonderful.'

The lift operator dragged back the gate. Once again, Soames stepped onto the floor that existed between the fourth and nominal fifth of the unobtrusive office building in Lambeth. Soames was cheered by setting foot on its utilitarian linoleum and he was heartened by the single corridor, dark and windowless, with a dozen or so doors opening onto it, because as soon as he did he was entering the Demimonde.

Striding towards his office, Soames whispered the word to himself, savouring its outlandishness and marvelling how it described, so perfectly, the place in which he spent much of his life.

The Demimonde, the half-world, the realm on the edges of civilised society. The world of the dispossessed and the fugitive, of outlaws, thieves and cutthroats, of the lost and abandoned, of the strange and uncanny. It was the world of forgotten heroes, of neglected villains, of conspiracies, calamities and chimaeras. Lost legends stalked the Demimonde, fortunes were made in the Demimonde and people lost their souls in the Demimonde – sometimes more than once.

The Demimonde was an irresistible source of opportunity, provided one had very few scruples. Soames had a joke – just the one – about how he once had scruples, but he'd sold them a long time ago. He repeated it whenever he could, but those hearing it were rarely in a position to enjoy the humour, more's the pity.

Soames barely registered the signs on the doors of the other offices. Some were familiar, having been there ever since he'd become a tenant – the 'Red-Headed League' and the 'Eldorado Exploring Expedition', for instance – but others came and went. As he slipped the key into his door, his gaze lit on the office next to his that had been, until recently, 'Capt. Benjamin Briggs' but now read

'Tunguska Enterprises'. He made another mental note to make some enquiries about the firm.

Soames paused for a moment on the threshold of his office. He was at home here in the Demimonde. Some people confused it with the underworld, the domain of criminals, but this would never do. The underworld intersected with the Demimonde and some rogues were definitely part of it, but the Demimonde was altogether larger, richer, both more wonderful and more sordid, than merely being the haunt of those outside the law.

Of course, the laws of the mundane world did not apply in the Demimonde, which suited Jabez Soames perfectly.

He was almost tempted to whistle as he stepped into his office and closed the door behind him. The floor on which his office was situated was, in reality, the fifth floor but special arrangements had been made decades ago to make it part of the Demimonde, as many other places through-out the city had been: lanes, whole buildings, underground tunnels and byways, those places less frequented by the ordinary folk. Theatres had a special status. Theatre people were almost always welcome in the Demimonde; they respected its nature and understood the way that appear-ances were not always a true representation of what lay beneath. Two years ago, Soames had enjoyed an extremely lucrative venture with a theatre troupe who had marched into a village in Surrey, claiming to be government health inspectors. Soames had heard hints that some of the actors were still about, in far-off lands, having left the world of the theatre to enjoy the fruits of their labour.

That reminded him. Devant's new show was opening at the Egyptian Hall soon. He would need to get tickets.

The thought of missing the famous magician's new illusions made him quite ill.

After hanging his hat and coat on the rack by the door – and making sure they were neatly arranged – Soames went to the window. His office had a fine view towards the river and the lights of Westminster. Soames had plans in that direction and he enjoyed taking a moment to contemplate them. Oh, the world would be a different place when Jabez Soames had his way!

Jabez, he thought, *there would be no better man for the job!*

A rambling bank of pigeonholes took up an entire wall of Soames's office and it was to this he now addressed himself. Slips of paper poked out of most of them, paper of the most confounding variety of hues and textures. Some appeared have been torn from books, others could have come from the stationery belonging to an earl. Soames kept a network of informants throughout the city, both the mundane world and the Demimonde. His day clerk had taken delivery of all of these snippets and deposited them in the correct slots, ready for Soames to peruse.

One of them alerted him to activity among the Neanderthals. He went to his desk and found the ledger he devoted to his dealings with what he'd once considered sub-humans, but had quickly been convinced were just as intelligent as regular humanity. Their particular aptitude lay with mechanical devices, which led to a need for certain materials that Jabez Soames was only too happy to supply. At a price, of course.

After his first contact with them, so many years ago, he'd been startled to learn that they'd carved out a sanctuary deep beneath the city, a retreat that was difficult to find and impossible to enter, if you weren't one of them. The sophistication of their building hadn't jibed with his conception of the creatures at all, so he'd undertaken some research and found that the current thinking was that the brutes were cousins of modern humans, supposedly long extinct, and fine tool-users, to judge from artefacts recently unearthed. Extinct everywhere but the Demimonde, Soames now knew.

How they hated him! He saw it in their eyes every time they dealt with him, shipping in foodstuffs and other necessities. He didn't take it personally, though. They hated all regular humans. Invaders, they called them, the people who had come and taken their lands, hunted their game, driven them to the margins of the world.

He ran his eye down the columns of figures. The Neanderthals had been excellent customers for years, and if they were becoming even more industrious, it was a marvellous thing. Jabez Soames could forgive them their brutishness and coarseness, because they paid their debts promptly. Not the world's greatest conversationalists, which was a shame for Jabez Soames enjoyed a chat. They spoke English well enough, that wasn't the problem, but the Neanderthals preferred actions to words, he gathered. He also had a feeling that they hated using the language of their dominant cousins and regretted adopting it centuries ago. Idly, he'd wondered what had happened to their own language. Gone, as the snows of yesterday?

The thought made him smile. Progress was inevitable. Away with the old, bring on the new.

Soames gathered the notes into an irregular bundle, pursing his lips at some, chuckling at others, drawing his mouth into a tight line at a few. He was about to take his place at his desk when his gaze fell on the envelope on his blotter.

Everything about it was wrong in a horribly familiar way. If pressed, however, Soames would have had difficulty pointing out exactly why it was so unsettling. Was it because it was almost, but not quite, rectangular, with the corners subtly not meeting at right angles? Was it that the paper was a shade that spoke of pallid, slinking creatures that never saw the light of day? He knew, even without touching it, that the paper had a slightly greasy feel. Soames, no stranger to handling distasteful objects, wanted to don gloves before handling it.

He cursed when the only gloves he could find were the ones he'd worn in to the office, a brand new pair that he'd just purchased from Turnbull & Asser. He'd have to discard them once he touched the letter. This irked him decidedly.

Settle, Jabez, he told himself. *Bring your renowned sang-froid to the fore! Opportunity, opportunity, opportunity!*

He read the letter and it was as he feared: the Immortals were back from India, and they wanted to see him.

⇜ FIVE ⇝

Light flared at the back of the control compartment. Damona tore away the steel cover plate too late.

The machine exploded.

Later. Damona on her back, looking up. Pain. She choked on the smoke. She rolled, stood, coughed, winced at the pain in her hip. Her hair had come undone. It hung over her face. She heard shouting.

A draught. The smoke began to move. Damona grunted. Someone had opened the steel doors at either end of the workshop. Good thinking.

The smoke cleared. She squinted, batted it away. She peered up past the gantry crane and its rails to the ventilator shaft. She swore. The screw turbine had shattered. No more air from above until it was fixed. She shuddered. Metal shards must have sprayed through the whole workshop. She'd been lucky.

She grunted again. Death wasn't for her. Not yet.

The smoke had gone. She screwed up her nose at the smell of charred insulation. She laced both hands in the middle of her lower back. The old hip injury was flaring, too. She felt every one of her two hundred years. She growled and studied the remains of the machine she'd been working on.

It was a wreck.

She plucked a screwdriver from the bench as she passed. Then: careful stalking towards the wreck. Big steps over casing panels that had been blown aside.

She prodded at the steel and brass machine. What had she been doing just before the explosion? After months of work, what had gone wrong? The principles were right. She knew it. Implementation was at fault.

Was she becoming less dextrous? Age catching up with her?

She stood back, hands flexing, taking stock. The original lines of the extractor were still there. She'd avoided straight lines and corners. The flanks of the wagon-sized machine curved like wave-worn rock. Both sides rolled around to grip the control panel at the end. She shook her head. The control panel that was now a mess of melted glass and metal. The top third of the extractor had been sheared off by the explosion. The contours she'd been so satisfied with were no more.

She stood on tiptoe and nearly cried. Inside, the machine was ruined. She tried to remember where she'd left the plans, her notes, her grand scheme.

'Hurt?'

Damona didn't look around. Could she salvage that thermal bridge? 'No, Gustave.'

34

'What happened?'

'Phlogiston uptake error.'

'Dangerous, that.'

Damona almost laughed. Phlogiston was more than dangerous. It was treacherous. But without it, their existence would be even more precarious than it was. 'Sometimes dangers are necessary.'

'Put dangers aside. Be at ease. Stop your work.'

She turned, then. Gustave was stocky, even for a True Person. A youngster, broad in the shoulders, thick of limb. He had heavy khaki overalls and steel-tipped boots of his own design. He wore his coarse red hair and beard long.

Damona sighed. She'd have to wait for the remains to cool down before she'd be able to investigate properly. 'How can I save the True People if I stop working?'

'An honourable goal, eldest.' Gustave coughed. He shifted, uneasily.

'What is it?'

He didn't look at her. 'An Assembly has been called. You have been summoned.'

Damona sat on the dais at the front of the assembly chamber. She rested her chin in her hand, waited for the rest of the True People to file in. They were old. So few younglings.

She knuckled her brow. *Even fewer after Signe died.*

It had been a year since her only great-granddaughter had passed. She still mourned.

The Assembly was a shock. She hadn't heard a thing.

No-one had dropped a hint. No-one had muttered a warning in her ear.

I'm getting old, too. She ran her gaze over the crowd. The chamber was filling up, past the fourth set of pillars. *Or distracted. Or both.*

A distant rumbling. She cocked her head. She took out her pocket watch. It was a sturdy steel model she'd made years ago. She nodded. The noise above was the Circle line train on its way to Cannon Street Station. Right on time.

The assembly chamber was four hundred years old. It was the first large space carved by the True People when they'd congregated under London. It was now at the heart of a complex that had grown into a maze. Families had added chambers, corridors and extensions wherever they were needed. When the Invaders had been digging tunnels for their underground railway it had been a worrying time, but the spaces the True People had opened out were deep. Far deeper than the puny delvings of the Invaders. Their efforts were scratchings and finished far overhead. Noise of the trains reminded the True People that their enemy was close. Damona thought this was a good thing. She didn't mind the closeness of the Invaders. It meant that none of the True People would forget what they had done.

She climbed to her feet, ignored the twinge from her back. The three hundred True People, the last Neander-thals in the world, hushed.

'I am Damona,' she said. Ritual demanded no less. 'As Eldest, I am your leader. An Assembly has been called. Speak, those who will.'

It was Gustave who stood. Nervous, he was pushed forward by others. He would not meet Damona's eyes.

'Eldest,' he said. Damona saw sweat on his brow. 'Each of the True People has the right to pursue a life undisturbed by the others.'

'That is our way. As it has always been.'

'Except if their life harms another.'

'Go on.'

'Your work, Eldest, is dangerous. You have been purchasing materials. You have been contacting the outside world. You jeopardise our security. You cannot continue this without the agreement of the Assembly.'

Murmurs of approval ran through the rows of True People. No animosity, Damona thought, just concern. Gustave stroked his beard, sat down.

Damona let out a long, tired breath. She had led the True People for more than five decades. A hard labour. Individuals never liked being told what to do.

The history of the True People had ever been thus. They united only in extremity. An outside foe, a natural disaster, a threat. Large projects were almost unheard of. Standards meant nothing. It was one of the few things that Damona admired about the Invaders. In their world nails were nails and bricks were bricks, no matter where they were made. For the True People, bricks by different makers were different. Sizes, shapes unlikely to sit together at all.

She had always thought to bring her grand plan to the Assembly. Was it now the time?

She flexed her shoulders. Her right arm hurt after the explosion.

'Speak!' someone cried from the back of the chamber. 'Explain yourself!'

Damona stood. She began by breaking a taboo. 'The

True People are dying,' she said. Everyone assembled in front of her gasped.

The plight of the True People was never spoken aloud. Everyone knew the truth, but to speak it was forbidden. As if ignoring it would make it go away.

Damona was only stating the obvious. Their numbers had dwindled generation after generation. First they were shunned by the Invaders. Then they were hunted by them. Communities of True People scattered, lost track of each other, falling silent, falling away.

Heads bowed at Damona's words. Others shrugged and Damona was angered. Apathy was bad. Resignation would only speed their end.

'Long ago, our ancestors fought the Invaders.' Her anger rose and she swallowed it. 'Look at us now. Once we were fierce. We were warriors. Now we go to our doom. Meek. Quiet. Sheep.'

Heads lifted at this. A few angry shouts. Damona was pleased. She would speak truths, here and now, while she still could.

'Look around you. Has our hiding helped us? Is this the world we deserve, deep underground, huddled like animals?'

A shout came from the rear of the chamber: 'No!' Others followed. Support. Damona smiled. She settled. She unclenched fists that had curled tight of their own accord. 'I have begun a grand enterprise. It is one that will require us all to work together.'

Laughter. Work together? True People? True People worked for themselves, their family!

'To what end?' Gustave called out.

'To save the True People from extinction.' Damona

paused. A great silence filled the chamber. She had them. 'If we unite, if we dedicate ourselves to my project, we can wipe out the Invaders. We can reclaim the world as our own.'

A low mutter. Growling. Nods. They were with her. Good.

'We are the supreme artificers,' she said. 'We build. We create. We master. We will use our skills to rebuild our world.'

The question came just when Damona wanted it. 'How?' Gustave cried.

'First: we build a better phlogiston extractor. Second: we build a time machine.'

Bewilderment. She went on. 'We will build a time machine. We will send warriors back to wipe out the ancestors of the Invaders while they are few. They will never grow. Never spread. Never dominate the world. The True People will triumph.'

Damona exulted in the uproar. She hoped her prisoner would hear it. He might tell her what she needed to know.

SIX

Midnight was approaching and Kingsley was yawning when the train rolled into Waterloo Station. With some difficulty because of the crowds of international visitors milling about the station looking for their Olympic billets, they caught a cab. The traffic was light as they crossed Westminster Bridge and rounded the Palace, where a few lonely windows were lit. Hyde Park, past Marble Arch and then into Bayswater Road.

Kingsley was trapped in his thoughts and started when Evadne touched his hand. 'I think someone's following us.' She tapped her spectacles. In the light of a streetlamp Kingsley saw that they were tinted yellow. 'That hansom back there has had the same passenger since the station.'

'Are you normally this suspicious?'

'I'd call it alert rather than suspicious.'

Kingsley directed the cab into Porchester Terrace. The

houses on either side – three- and four-storey stuccoed villas, for the most part – made the street darker than the relative openness of Bayswater Road. The streetlamps were lonely splashes of light stretching away from them, illuminated stepping stones in a river of blackness.

Kingsley flung some money at the driver and bounded from the cab. As soon as Evadne alighted, the cab hurried off.

A light shone through the fan window over the front door. 'Brown said he'd wait up for me, with Mrs Walters,' Kingsley said. 'The housekeeper,' he explained.

'There should be more lights on, then,' Evadne said.

'That's what I thought.' Kingsley glanced up and down the street. 'Wait here.'

'I think not.' Evadne reached into the pocket of her coat. Light glinted on metal.

Kingsley had to look twice at the brass and wood device she held. 'It that a pistol?'

'It's a distant relative.'

'Where did you get it?'

'I made it.'

Kingsley had trouble imagining Evadne Stephens as a weapon maker and optometrist, but the alternative was to imagine her as a bald-faced liar – and he had more pressing concerns. 'Follow me, then.'

It had been nearly six months since Kingsley had left home. With some reluctance, he'd decided that if he had no real past – for his foster father was loath to talk about how he came to be responsible for the foundling Kingsley – he'd at least make a real future for himself on the stage.

Once inside, Kingsley loosened his tie and left his

jacket on the newel post at the bottom of the stairs. He avoided the fourth stair from the top, knowing its penchant for creaking, and paused on the landing, signalling so Evadne would avoid the noisy stair. The landscape on the wall was even more depressing than usual. The storm threatening the lusty farm workers looked actively malign.

'My goodness,' Evadne whispered, 'you can move quietly.'

Kingsley didn't reply. He glanced through the window at the landing, the one overlooking the street. Gaslight filtered through the plane trees. Kingsley put a hand against the panelling and listened, hard, then he sniffed. His hackles rose at what he smelled, and it was only by clenching his jaw that he prevented a low growl escaping from his throat.

'I can see a light up there,' Evadne whispered.

'It's coming from the study.' Kingsley sniffed again.

'What can you smell? Gas?'

'No, but it's coming from the study, too.' Kingsley glanced over his shoulder, then crouched, hissing.

Evadne flattened herself against the wall. 'What?'

'That man. The one we saw at the theatre. He's out there.'

Evadne inched to the window. 'He's not being very secretive about it, standing in the middle of the road like that.'

Kingsley licked his lips. His wolfishness was on the rise – he could feel it in his shoulders, the long muscles of his legs. Threats, real or imagined, tended to do that. Grimly, he imagined helping someone write a pithy monograph titled 'The Wolf at Bay: Some Personal Insights'.

He was torn. The man out there or the study? He shifted from one foot to the other in mute demonstration of his indecision until Evadne rolled her eyes. 'You go on. I'll see what our theatre-lover wants.'

She left, silently, and Kingsley recommenced his ascent. He stood at the head of the stairs for a moment and, in the shadows, he had the unsettling impression that everything he'd grown up with had been taken away and replaced by duplicates. The carpet, the slightly worn spots outside each door, the side table with the nick in one leg from where he'd swung a golf club a little too carelessly, it was all there but with a layer of unfamiliarity that made his soul ache.

He closed his eyes, willing the awful sensation to go away, and when he opened them his surroundings were once again familiar – but he could still hear noises coming from the study. They were the furtive, muffled sounds of someone who didn't want to be heard.

Kingsley paused outside the door to the study. It was open a crack. Light spilled from it. 'Mrs Walters?'

Nothing.

Kingsley swallowed. He pushed the door back.

Afterwards, he was never sure how long he stood on the threshold, unwilling to enter, assaulted by the sight, the smell, the disarray. Books had been dragged down from the shelves and strewn about. Chairs had been over-turned. The two prints of farm scenes had been ripped from the walls.

Torn apart by wild beasts. The phrase repeated itself in Kingsley's head again and again as he gazed at Mrs Walters' remains. She'd been good to him, indulgent even, tolerating the mess he'd made when his magical practice went wrong. *Torn apart by wild beasts.*

All the blood, pooled and spattered, was the source of the awful smell he'd been aware of ever since he'd stepped inside. It caught and held him so much that he barely saw the two hulking figures with their backs to him, pawing at his foster father's bookshelves.

One of the brutes looked back over his shoulder. He grunted, slapped his partner on the back, and confronted Kingsley, who was grimly aware that he'd let out a sob.

The intruder was even larger than Kingsley had thought, a nightmarish, troll-like creature with a flat face and heavy brows. Not tall, but he had the build of two wrestlers pressed into one body. His arms bulged with muscle under his leather jacket. Wild red hair stuck out from his head, complemented by a bushy red beard that surrounded a face that was broad and hard. He chuckled and it sounded like a bag full of stones. He reached for Kingsley with a meaty hand.

Kingsley slapped it away.

The intruder's eyes narrowed. He grunted at his partner, who was piling books into a wooden crate, then he advanced on Kingsley again.

Overwhelmed – the blood, the loss, the chaos of the night – Kingsley couldn't control himself. His wild self burst free, snarled, lashed out and kicked the intruder in his vast stomach.

The intruder staggered back a step or two, then laughed, which only added to Kingsley's rage. His wild self was truly roused. It knew what to do with an outsider who had brought death to the pack. It had to be taken down and dealt with.

Kingsley's hands curled into claws. His chest heaved. He wanted to cast himself on the brute and take his throat, to throw him to the ground, to make him cry for mercy that wouldn't come.

He bared his teeth.

The intruder paused. For a moment, they were both still. Kingsley was looking for an opening – did the brute favour his left side? – and then the intruder backed away.

Kingsley was astonished, but then he saw the intruder's partner was almost out of the window, a crate of books under one arm. Kingsley lunged, but the first brute smashed him with a fist, a mighty buffet that caught his arm and spun him aside. He slipped on the blood, fell against the firescreen, and rolled to collide with the body of poor Mrs Walters.

The intruder bounded for the window and followed his partner. Horrified and bloody, Kingsley was up, but he knew from experience and the heavy sound of feet that the intruders had landed on the roof of the old stable that led to the lane at the back of the property.

Kingsley bolted out of the room and down the stairs. He flung himself out of the front door and immediately cannoned into two police officers.

Kingsley tumbled into the garden bed amid the anemones and foxgloves. Growling with frustration and rage, he picked himself up to see one of the young police officers stretched out, unconscious, his head against the stairs leading to the gate. The second constable was backing away, eyes wide as he groped for his whistle. 'Don't move!' His voice was shrill with fear. 'Just stay where you are!'

Dimly, Kingsley realised what the police officer was seeing – a bloody young man, clothing askew, wild-faced and growling, a tabloid newspaper image of a murderer.

The knowledge cut through his wildness, sobering him immediately. Kingsley was suddenly calm as his wild self fled, but before he could explain, the constable found his whistle. He blew it long and hard, and was rewarded by a similar blast not far away.

Evadne ghosted to Kingsley's side.

'Be careful, miss!' the constable cried. 'He's a dangerous one, just look at him!'

'I don't think so,' Evadne said. With no fuss, she raised her pistol and shot the constable.

Kingsley gaped. The police officer crumpled and joined his comrade on the stairs. 'What did you do that for?'

'Don't worry. I've rendered him unconscious, that's all.' She held up her pistol. 'Sleep-inducing darts.'

'I —' Kingsley swallowed. 'Up there. Monsters. Mrs Walters. Dead.'

Evadne grimaced. 'The Neanderthals killed someone?'

'Neanderthals?'

'I saw them escaping over the rooftops.'

'But . . . I . . .' Kingsley sagged. He wanted to sit, or lie down, or for this horrible nightmare to go away. *Cavemen? In Bayswater?*

'Yes, Neanderthals. Most people think they died out a few hundred thousand years ago, but a few survived, hidden away and keeping to themselves.' Evadne pocketed her pistol. 'Look at you. I think it best to let things calm down before we see the police again. You might like to choose the occasion that happens, preferably when you're presentable and flanked by a pet barrister. I'd recommend a QC.' She cocked her head at him. 'Your family has a trusty law firm on the books?'

'Leaving is a capital idea.' At the gate, a figure stepped into the pool of light cast by the nearest gas lamp. His round spectacles glinted and he touched the brim of his hat. 'I have a motor car nearby.'

It was the man from the theatre – short, slight, with rounded shoulders, a tiny moustache and an air of precise watchfulness. Evadne's eyes widened and she lowered the pistol she'd raised at the stranger's approach. 'I know you,' she said to him. 'You're that writer, Kipling, aren't you?

The man gave a hasty smile. 'I am indeed Rudyard Kipling, and I hope to be at your service immediately.'

SEVEN

Damona was in the middle of a revolution.

The younger ones had responded to the call for cooperation. They were keen, afire. Damona loved their enthusiasm. It swamped the naysaying of the oldsters.

A dozen youngsters were in her workshop. Busy. Excited. Some crawled over her failed extractor, probing, arguing. More were at the wall that separated her workshop from next door. It would come down soon and that was good.

Years ago the workshop next door had belonged to her distant cousin Freya. She had spent decades working on a combustion engine. In silence. Not once did she talk to Damona about it.

Damona had heard that a pair of youngsters had stolen an engine from the overworld to show Freya. She was crushed at being beaten by the Invaders. She disappeared not long after that.

Damona watched the activity in the workshop. She pondered unfulfilled dreams and broken hearts.

Gustave came to her. He slapped a spanner in his hand, bounced up and down on his toes. 'We will achieve more this way.'

'I'm glad.' One of the youngsters wrenched at the beautiful cowling of Damona's failed phlogiston extractor in order to get at the workings. She winced.

Four or five others pored over her schematic diagrams for the time machine. Damona smiled at their astonishment. Her methods were sound.

Perhaps my years weren't wasted, Damona thought. But they were years working alone. Could she have brought the plan to the Assembly earlier?

She screwed up the thought. Discarded it. This was not the time for regret.

Two more youngsters hesitated at the door of the workshop. They stared at the group enterprise. Astounded. Relieved when they saw Damona.

Damona waved to them. 'I may have something useful,' she said to Gustave.

'From the overworld or from the Demimonde?'

'Both.'

She squeezed past some youngsters who were arguing over her wiring. She found the newcomers at the door. 'Come with me.'

Many parts of the underground sanctuary were vacant these days. Too few People. Damona had marked out a few rooms near her workshop for her private use. She led the way, limping slightly, under the string of globes that lit the corridor. This stretch was curved. No right angles. A sinewy conduit through the rock. Damona liked this

49

part of the complex. The walls rippled, bulged. Carvings turned them into jungles, coral reefs, gardens of paradise.

The door was heavy steel, the lock of her own making. First, she inserted a small, secret key into the hidden slot near the hasp. Second, she used the large key on her belt. She closed the door behind the two youngsters. It thudded. The rubbers seals worked well.

She sat on a wooden bench she'd carved far too long ago. 'Tell me what went wrong.'

They were distant cousins. She wished they weren't. Their stupidity was deeply shaming. Rolf was the older, a stripling of forty years or so. He had a black beard and wild eyebrows. Magnus was a few years younger. He had hands that looked much too large for him.

'We found the books you wanted.' Rolf shrugged. 'All is good.'

'You should have brought them the first time. When you took the man.' She sniffed. 'I can smell the blood on you.'

'What blood?' Magnus said. 'I washed it all off!'

His brother rolled his eyes. 'An old woman.' Rolf shrugged. 'She screamed and Magnus stopped her.'

Magnus looked at his feet. 'I didn't know that the Invaders were so puny.'

'The boy wasn't,' Rolf said. 'He had muscle.'

'Boy?' Damona massaged her knee. 'What boy?'

'We were collecting the books,' Magnus said. 'He came. He was different.'

'How so?'

'He was afraid, at first,' Rolf said slowly. 'Then he changed. He wanted my throat.'

'Ah.' Damona knuckled the side of her head, thinking.

A witness could be dangerous but the boy could be useful. If he was who she thought he was.

She rubbed her cheeks with both hands. She was weary of it all. 'The books?'

'We brought them, all the ones you asked for,' Rolf said. 'We left them near the prisoner's cell.'

'I have news for you, Eldest,' Magnus said, eager to please to make up for his blunder. 'News from the Demimonde.'

Damona could never resist such an offer. Information was power. 'What have you heard?'

'The Spawn are about.'

Damona chewed on this and tried not to show fear. 'It's long since they've been abroad. Spread the word. Look out for them.' She clapped her hands. 'And send scouts to look for this boy, the one you saw.'

Damona waited for them to leave. She climbed to her feet. Every joint in her body ached. She had no choice, though. She had to go out into the Demimonde. Her plans required many materials, much purchasing. Some copper, to start with. Then, a great deal of rubber. And she'd send a message to the Soames creature. He may know something about this boy.

She paused. Smiled. First, however, she'd go and talk to the prisoner again. The boy's father, Dr Malcolm Ward, the Invader who could help her wipe out the Invaders.

❧ EIGHT ❧

The Immortals had been among Soames's customers for a dozen years, but always at a comfortable distance. Their letters arrived from India, demanding one hard-to-find item or another, and Soames arranged procurement and delivery. Books, quite often, unusual and ghastly inside. A few owners had cause to regret their reluctance to part with them. Soames had also supplied materials that some people would call unholy, if they ever had the chance to confront them.

A fine and profitable enterprise.

On the one hand, Soames never had any difficulty with extracting payment from the Immortals, unlike many of his other clients. On the other hand, they terrified him like few other Demimonders did. Having them back in England wasn't Soames's notion of an improved working arrangement. No, he was quite happy with the Immortals being on the other side of the globe.

Fear wasn't one of Soames's more common emotions. He'd long ago become inured to most of that which would send ordinary people insane. He attributed it to a disciplined mind, even though a small, secret voice suggested that greed allowed him to overcome just about every remnant of finer emotion. Gold was a great balm to Jabez Soames.

Uncharacteristically, Soames dithered after he read the summons from the Immortals. According to the information he'd gathered about them – a standard procedure that Soames undertook with all his clients – the Immortals had little patience and their displeasure was meted out in spectacular, if dispassionate, ways. Yet he shuffled about his office, assembling his thoughts and sifting through options, until it was early morning, just as the city was rousing from its rest.

Jabez, he thought, with an unaccustomed tremor, *perhaps they've found out.*

It was impossible, but what if the Immortals had divined his plan to usurp them?

Of all his clients, the Immortals were the richest and, if his clandestine research was accurate, by far the most powerful. While dealing with them was lucrative, lately Soames had found his mind turning to something altogether more ambitious. It may have simply been a function of growing older, but he had begun to ask why he should settle for mundane and earthly riches if he could supplant the undying sorcerers. One life, after all, couldn't be enough for Jabez Soames. Not when he could inveigle his way into the Immortals' good graces, learn their secrets, betray and replace them. A simple plan, well suited to Soames's innumerable talents for duplicity, mendacity and treachery.

In a drawer of his desk — second from the bottom — he found his trusty British Bulldog and slipped it into his jacket pocket, adjusting it so the lines of the jacket weren't spoiled. The little snub-nosed pistol had served him well for years and the thought of using it again made him quite nostalgic.

Fortified, he took his bowler from the hatstand and spent a moment or two settling the brim before he acknowledged to himself that he was procrastinating.

The long mirror beside the door wasn't for procrastinating. It gave Soames a last chance to check an appearance that was important to him. Neat, straight and organised, he stepped through the door to find someone waiting for him in the corridor.

Even though Soames would never permit himself to feel frightened by an underling, the unexpectedness of the appearance of the Spawn took him aback so much that he collided quite painfully with the door frame. 'I say,' he exclaimed, rubbing his elbow. 'Why don't you creatures announce yourself like a decent fellow would?'

The Immortals, eternally suspicious as they were, had difficulty trusting underlings unless they were totally under their thrall — like the Thuggees in India, if Soames's intelligence was accurate. This would have made their lot impossible if it weren't for the Spawn, their constant, ever-biddable minions. The Immortals kept a few in London while they were in India, attending to the upkeep of their lair and other sundry — and unpleasant — tasks. This one had the appearance of a City banker, right down to the bowler hat, striped trousers and umbrella, but anyone looking closely would soon see that the creature lacked even that animation granted to financial workers.

People loathed Spawn almost instinctively, Soames knew, which made them extremely useful as agents of fear. He'd studied them as much as he was able. The horror they inspired came from the innumerable ways they were like humans, but lacking. Despite coming in a range of shapes and sizes, whenever they aped humanity, they betrayed their origins in a number of ways. The eyes, for instance, were consistently flat and without lustre; the eyes of the dead. They never blinked and the Spawn had a disconcerting habit of moving their heads to look about them instead of moving their eyes.

Unless they were concentrating, they often forgot to move their arms while they walked. They smelled of something that, if it wasn't corruption, Soames didn't want to know what it was.

What set Soames's teeth most on edge, however, was their skin. It, too, lacked vitality. It was dull and lifeless. Grey underneath the nominal pinkness.

'Come with me,' the Spawn said in a tone as dead as the air in a mausoleum.

'I was already on my way.' Soames fumbled with his keys to hide his discomfiture and only faced the Spawn when he'd locked the door. 'I don't see why I need a custodian.'

'Come with me,' it repeated. Soames didn't want to give it a chance to speak again in that dusty voice. He set off down the corridor.

Soames endured the journey to Greenwich with as much stoicism as he could summon. People on the

Underground looked at him with unseemly directness. They were unwilling to look at his travelling companion, who sat far too close, and far too still, so he bore the brunt of their unease. At the pier, the steamer captain cast off as soon as they were aboard, flinching at the sight of the Spawn and shouting at his crew in compensation for his fright.

Soames had often wondered, with the curiosity that was deeply embedded in the perpetually greedy, about the Immortals' choice in locating their lair. Several hundred feet beneath the Royal Observatory didn't strike him as the most desirable address. With their riches – which Soames knew to be immense – they could afford a mansion in Mayfair, or a whole hotel in Kensington, so he assumed that their subterranean Greenwich location must have some other allure. Perhaps it had something to do with it being directly beneath the Prime Meridian, zero degrees longitude, the place from which all locations across the earth were measured, but he'd heard stories that the Immortals had been there before the building of the Royal Observatory and well before the fixing of the meridian.

When they reached Greenwich, the Spawn led the way. Its mere presence in the park made the few people about on the wet Friday morning scurry off and find something more interesting to look at. Much to Soames's irritation, the Spawn abandoned the path. Soames's shoes were soon soaking from the wet grass as they approached the dumpy brick Conduit House. Not one of Hawksmoor's more inspired creations, Soames thought, but then again, perhaps the architect's heart hadn't been in it. Designing a building just to hide the pipes and outlets leading into an underground reservoir? He probably gave the task to an apprentice as punishment.

Behind the Conduit House, the Spawn stood still, facing up the hill. Soames waited patiently. Even if it didn't appear to be taking in its surroundings, the Spawn was either waiting for a signal conveyed in some arcane manner, or simply waiting until it was sure they were unobserved. When it moved, without warning, Soames was ready. The lock on the Conduit House was easily bypassed and they were inside within seconds. The Spawn then found the iron manhole cover and lifted it with immensely strong fingers.

Soames went first, climbing down the ladder and flinching at the boom as the Spawn reseated the manhole cover and then came down after him. It was only a few yards to the underground reservoir and the Spawn stopped there for its lantern. The match it struck revealed the two-hundred-year-old space to be in reasonable shape. The brickwork had allowed some stubborn roots to gain access, but, with its gently arched roof and supporting columns, it was still remarkable.

The Spawn slogged through a slurry of mud and water in the bottom of the reservoir, but Soames kept to the relatively dry edges. In the fifth of the eight chambers, each separated by a decorative brick arch, the Spawn dragged itself out of the muck and stood in front of a blank wall. Then it reached up and hammered on a brick well above the height Soames could reach.

A rectangular section of the wall swung in and they were on their way to the Hall of the Immortals.

Don't slouch, Jabez, he told himself, *hold your head up high and look them in the eye. After all, they're lucky to have you.*

Soames couldn't help but be impressed. He knew that part of the purpose of the immense chamber was just that, but he was helpless not to feel daunted when he stepped alone through the final doorway.

Pentagons. Pentagons everywhere. Dazed, Soames decided that the Immortals must have had a liking for the five-sided figure, for the whole colossal space was composed of them. The floor was a vast pentagon made of dull black stone. Marble? Granite? The ceiling was the same. Five pentagons leaned away from the floor and were joined by five more slanting down from the ceiling.

The ceiling must have been three hundred feet above the floor.

It was the most extraordinary construction Soames had ever seen. In the Demimonde, he had seen some outlandish structures and encountered much uncanny magic, but this colossal, arrogant building was the clearest display of cosmic sorcery he knew. He looked down at the floor. The polished surface threw soft and distorted reflections that Soames didn't like to study too closely.

Jabez, remember your mathematics. A dodecahedron, isn't it?

He nodded, satisfied. Giving a name to the unlikely space went some way to making it less disturbing.

A large pentagonal alcove was carved into each of the lower walls. Three were empty. Two contained objects that rotated slowly in midair – a triangular pyramid and a cube, each three or four feet in diameter.

The Spawn at his side directed Soames towards the centre of the chamber. As he neared, he saw he was approaching a long golden bench with a high back. It had three separate seats, complete with armrests, and the entire piece was covered with carvings, most of which were obscured by brightly coloured cushions. It quivered a little, like a barely restrained guard dog. It shone with the sort of lustre that spoke of regular attention – and also defined the difference between gilt and gold.

He walked the entire way with his hat in hand, not happy about being placed in the position of a beggar. He was a businessman, damn it, not some terrified ruffian!

The Immortals sat on the throne. They looked like three six-year-old children playing at grown-ups. Three chubby faces glared at Soames, two male, one female. Their clothes were rich and archaic. Their eyes were flat, but their expressions could never be mistaken for those of children. No child could produce such looks of disdain, boredom and hunger. These could only come about after years of experience, as long as the experiences were full of depravity and venality.

Their feet didn't touch the ground.

'You are Soames?' the female asked. Her voice was squeaky, but as far from comic as it was possible to be. She was clad in a long scarlet robe, silk, with wide sleeves and lapels. One of her companions wore a robe as well, but it was in the Roman style, dyed the purple of kings. The other was the odd one out. He had furs strapped onto his body with leather belts. He wore leather boots on his dangling feet instead of expensive-looking slippers. He pouted.

'I am.'

'I am Jia,' the female said. 'This is Augustus.' The Roman. 'And Forkbeard.' Fur.

Soames essayed a polite, interested expression, his normal approach to a new and possibly lucrative engagement. Briefly, he wondered why the creature had adopted the name 'Augustus'. Then he had a moment of unaccustomed unease when he considered the alternative – that the name belonged to him. 'I'm pleased to finally meet you.'

'You're not,' Augustus said. His voice, too, was squeaky, but Soames could hear a hundred lifetimes' experience in giving orders. 'No-one is pleased to see us.'

'With reason,' Forkbeard said. He shifted in his seat and looked away, over his shoulder. 'Finish with him quickly. I'm hungry.'

Soames's gaze went to the extremities of the Immortals. Forkbeard's hands were wrapped in bandages, gauze-swathed mittens on the end of his arms.

Years ago, when he had first been contacted by the Immortals to arrange shipping of various exotic items to them in India, Soames had made discreet enquiries in the Demimonde, as was his habit. The more he knew about his clients, the better off he was. The most reliable rumour suggested that the Immortals used their magic to create the Spawn from lopped-off pieces of their own bodies. The notion was a novel one, with a significant disadvantage that Soames was quick to realise. If one wanted a minion horde, one would soon run out of body parts. Soames had uncovered a blind, half-mad collector of magical documents who revealed, after some persuasion, the secret to the Immortals' immortality and why the loss of body parts was only a minor nuisance.

The Immortals had perfected the transference of souls. After hundreds of years – perhaps thousands – they no longer occupied the bodies into which they had been born. They had passed through a succession. As each body wore out, sickened or weakened in any way, the Immortals migrated their essence to a new one. Unfortunately for the owner of the new body, their essence was extinguished in the process ...

Over time, however, the essence of each of the Immortals had become rich with accumulated decadence, steeped in the horror of their existence. This putrid essence tended to corrupt each new body, wearing it out all the faster. Much as acid would eat away at an iron vessel until it gave way, the soul of an Immortal was too much for an ordinary human body to bear for long.

The younger the body, however, the more resilient it was. Perhaps it was due to the freshness, or to the innocence, or to some other factor about humanity, but the Immortals had worked their way through host bodies, younger and younger, until they now occupied the bodies of children.

Foul, ancient beings dwelling inside the bodies of children gave Soames pause, but mostly to consider that if the Immortals were back in London, they would be needing a supply of hosts.

Jabez, he thought, *the Immortals are lucky, lucky clients with you to attend to their needs!*

Jia hissed between her teeth and threw a glare Forkbeard's way. Then she speared Soames with a look. 'Shipping,' she squeaked. 'You can make arrangements?'

'As I have in the past. Efficiently, discreetly and inexpensively.'

A look of puzzlement so brief that Soames doubted that he'd actually seen it crossed Jia's face. Augustus glanced at her and cleared his throat. 'Of course you have.

This time we need you to bring something from India, rather than ship it the other way.'

'Something you've left behind?'

Forkbeard jerked his head around. 'Do not ask questions unless you value your hide at naught!'

Soames rocked back on his heels at the force of the creature's fury, but as soon as Forkbeard had spoken, he looked away again, muttering, Soames forgotten.

Augustus went on as if Forkbeard hadn't said a word. 'The Spawn will give you details.'

Soames was still taken aback by Forkbeard's abrupt anger, but he couldn't help wondering why the Immortals had asked to see him if the Spawn could have communicated such. Taking his courage in his hands, he asked: 'Is there anything else?'

Jia barked a laugh. 'Of course! You are ours, now, Soames! Once you work for the Immortals, you are bound to us!'

'I am bound to all my clients,' Soames said carefully. He felt as if he were negotiating with a keg of nitroglycerine.

'Good. Remember it,' Jia said.

'This other matter?'

'You know this writer, Kipling.' It was a statement rather than a question. 'Find him.'

Soames was taken aback. Of all the things he could have been asked ... 'I shall bring him here immediately,' he said.

Augustus raised his hand. Soames had seen many dangerous people and many dangerous creatures in his time in the Demimonde, but he had never seen any as familiar with death as the Immortals who addressed him.

Tolerance, patience and understanding were alien to such beings. 'Do not disappoint us,' Augustus piped in his horrible child's voice. 'We do not want Kipling. We want the boy.'

'Kipling has been searching for a boy,' Jia said. 'A special boy. We have reports of them in the vicinity of your Hyde Park. Find Kipling and you will find the boy. Bring him to us.'

'May I use some of your assistants? I may need to penetrate their police service, other officials ...'

'Spawn?' Augustus glanced at Forkbeard, who was scowling. 'By all means.'

Soames bowed, but his thoughts were circling. If he could find out what was so interesting about Kipling's target, he might be able to use it as a first step in ousting the Immortals and assuming their place.

Jabez, he thought, *only you could identify such a fleeting opportunity!*

'I will set to work with alacrity.'

Forkbeard jerked his head around. His baby face was a dreadful blend of madness and hunger. 'And you will bring us children.'

'I beg your pardon?'

'We need children. Young children. Many of them. Soon.'

Soames stared at Jia and Augustus. 'You will be well paid,' Augustus said.

'Phlogiston?'

'No. We need it to power our manipulating machines. Gold will do.'

'But of course,' Soames said. He was already riffling through the long list of felons and cut-throats he employed, choosing the worst of them. 'I will supply your needs immediately.'

Jia pointed at him. 'And then you will do something for us at the site of the great gathering in your city. Most secret, most careful.'

'Great gathering?'

'We have not left India on a whim,' Augustus said with relish. The other two Immortals smiled. 'These Olympic Games are an auspicious moment that we simply could not ignore.'

~ NINE ~

The motor car raced along Bayswater Road as if fired from a gun. Kipling peered through the side window, hissed, then tapped his driver on the shoulder. 'Faster, Trubshawe, if you please.'

Next to Evadne, Kingsley was pressed into the rear seat as the automobile accelerated. He was numb.

'It's more serious than I thought,' Kipling said after he turned around to face them.

'*More* serious?' Kingsley said.

'They're following us.' Kipling pointed.

Kingsley and Evadne leaned towards the window. After a moment's embarrassed rearranging, they both found a position to view Hyde Park as it flew past – and Kingsley felt Evadne stiffen.

He pressed his face close to the glass. He didn't see police constables or the brutish figures of the intruders who had been in his foster father's study. Instead, four or five shadowy forms were loping through the shadows on the far side of the fence. Behind the pickets as they were, it was difficult to discern details, but Kingsley shuddered at the sight. The creatures were unnaturally thin and long-armed, almost pawing at the ground as they ran. He was glad when the swiftness of the automobile left them behind.

'What are they?' he breathed, and he became aware that his heart was pounding.

Kipling's face was grim. 'They're a sign that we are in great strife indeed.'

'I'd prefer to entertain you at home,' Kipling said as he poured the tea for Evadne and Kingsley. Thin, early morning light came through the lace curtains of the hotel room. Traffic was beginning to cast its noise about, but the sounds coming from the street were still muted – horses' hooves, a motor car or two. 'But home is in the country, and here we are.'

Kingsley took the cup Kipling offered him. He knew he should be tired, but the events of the night had pushed him past exhaustion into that stretched state where exhaustion was strangely irrelevant.

Kipling wasn't exactly unknown to Kingsley. His foster father had copies of all of the writer's work in neat, identical leather volumes, each containing a thorough Kipling bibliography, but discouraged Kingsley from reading them – so naturally he'd done so in secret. He'd read them all, particularly enjoying *Barrack-Room Ballads*, but he'd never been able to find either of the *Jungle Books*, which were missing from the shelves of Dr Ward's study.

At the theatre Kipling had appeared to be a small man, but now Kingsley could see that even though he was short, he wasn't small – his shoulders were broad and he was well built. His posture was upright and he moved about the hotel room with ease, never fumbling or uncertain in his movements. His thick spectacles naturally made him look studious, and already Kingsley had noticed how the writer listened intently, with all his being, whenever Evadne or he were speaking. He moved his top lip under the thick moustache while he listened, as if chewing on every word. He also showed a writer's curiosity about Evadne's exotic looks. He was frankly fascinated, but not rude.

'We're grateful, Mr Kipling.' Evadne stirred her tea with a silver spoon. 'But why on earth would a respected writer help two fugitives escape the police?'

Kipling looked startled, then took another of the large armchairs that Kingsley and Evadne were occupying. He pressed his hands together. 'I thought my assistance could be valuable.'

'That it was, Mr Kipling,' Kingsley said. 'Most timely. Puzzling, but most timely.'

'I could say it's because I'm an admirer of Miss Stephens's skill,' Kipling said. 'I saw you at the Bedford, last year,' he said in response to her sceptical look. 'Your juggling is sublime.'

'But that's not the reason for your rescue,' Kingsley said. 'Nor for your watching us in Aldershot, is it?'

'Ah. You noticed me.' Kipling looked disappointed. 'I hoped I was doing a good job of being clandestine.'

'There's been altogether too much that's clandestine for my liking,' Kingsley said. 'That's why I'm asking you to throw some light on things.'

'With apologies to Miss Stephens, it's you I'm interested in, Mr Ward.' Kipling paused. 'Perhaps interested is too mild a word. Fascinated would be better. You were born in India, weren't you?'

'You're fascinated in me because I was born in India? That's hardly unusual, is it?'

'I was born in Bombay myself, so I'd agree with you there.'

'Then what is it?' Kingsley was beginning to feel nettled. Granted, Kipling had whisked them away from a sticky situation, but Kingsley's gratitude was wearing thin.

'I'm after details, you see, details that could confirm my theory.'

'What theory?'

'That you're Mowgli.'

While Kingsley battled stupefaction, Evadne tapped her teacup with a fingernail. 'Now, there's a thought.'

Even though Kingsley hadn't read *The Jungle Book*, he'd heard of Kipling's wild boy hero, mostly in taunts from lads at school who were unaware of just how apposite the epithet was. 'What on earth do you mean?'

'It might explain a few things, Mr Kipling, and he *does* look a little Mowglish.'

'Mowglish?' Kingsley said. 'Really, Evadne, you've lost me now.'

'It's not his looks, Miss Stephens,' Kipling said, 'it's his background. I have reason to believe that our young Mr Ward might once have been the child who was found by the Indian Forestry Service after being raised by wolves. The newspaper story about this child was the inspiration for my *Jungle Book* tales.'

With an uncertain hand, Kingsley placed his cup of tea on the side table. 'Wolves?'

Kipling leaned forward, his eyes bright behind his spectacles. 'I didn't believe it when I first read the story, so I travelled to the Central Provinces and spoke to the forestry officers myself. Decent chaps, they convinced me that they had indeed found a child whose nurture had been solely undertaken by wolves.'

'That sort of a start to life would tend to stay with one.' Evadne looked pointedly at Kingsley.

'What happened to the child's parents?' Kingsley managed to ask, while memories of his schooldays clamoured for attention – the yearning for freedom, the realisation that others did not have the same sort of wild side that he did, the understanding that he was different. With a start, he realised that for a long time he had shied away from his Indian past in an effort to be as the others around him.

'The parents?' Kipling looked away. 'The forestry officers had no idea. There was no sign of them when they rescued the boy.'

'Rescued.' Kingsley's memories of his earliest days were crowded and confused, but the notion of rescue didn't jibe with them. He recalled terror and separation, but not rescue. Any memories of the wild came with feelings of exhilaration, four-footed security and the smells of familiar beasts surrounding him. He had comfort amid the pack, and the two-legged intruders had taken him away from it.

He almost cried out as the loss he'd felt all those years ago reached out and plucked at his heart.

'And what makes you think that Kingsley here is your Mowgli, apart from his being born in India?' Evadne asked.

'A month ago, your foster father delivered a lecture that I attended. It alerted me to several intriguing features of your background, Mr Ward. How your foster father brought you back from India, for a start, and of his business travelling about that country and the possibility he was in or around the town of Seoni at the time of your discovery.'

'Discovery?' Kingsley echoed, and his voice sounded thick in his own ears. His back ached, and he realised he was holding himself poised, tense, until his muscles were screaming. 'You make me sound like an uncharted island.'

The pain caused by the memories that had launched themselves upon him unbidden was redoubled by Kipling's revelation. Even though Kingsley knew it was in his foster father's nature to be forthcoming where science was concerned, he was still hurt to think his peculiar past had been shared with strangers.

Kipling looked pained. 'I apologise, Mr Ward, I truly do. It's at times like this that my enthusiasm gets the better of me. I have a horror of those who intrude on my own privacy, and yet here I am doing the same to you.'

Try as he might, Kingsley couldn't dislike Kipling. The man's enthusiasm was appealing, as was his careful formality. 'You heard my father speak?'

'At the Royal Society about the recent discovery of *Homo heidelbergensis* remains. He did tend to wander from the topic when he became excited.'

'That is a weakness of his.' Kingsley was spent, stretched thin by exhaustion and the events of the last half-day. His foster father was missing, his housekeeper had been murdered in the most horrible fashion and now, on top of all this, a writer was hinting at the origins that Kingsley had thought long forgotten. His hands trembled and it wasn't solely due to lack of sleep.

'Aldershot,' Evadne said to Kipling. 'How did you end up there?'

'I have a great many acquaintances of all kinds.' Kipling flipped the pages of his notebook. 'Once it was clear that you had embarked on a career in the theatre, Mr Ward, I was able to make enquiries. Eventually, it was suggested that I visit the Alexandra Theatre and "I might see something to my advantage", I believe is how my informant put it.'

'You were in the balcony,' Kingsley said.

'For an unexpectedly captivating show,' Kipling said, 'ending in pandemonium.'

Kingsley had almost forgotten. His stage career could be at an end before it even started. His life was in ruins. 'Mr Kipling, I'm glad, and a little unsettled, to find that I'm your literary inspiration . . .'

'A part of it,' the small man said.

'A part of it, then, but I'm not sure why you're so excited.'

'You don't understand what it means to a writer to see a character he has written come to life and stand in front of him and . . . well.' Kipling took off his spectacles and polished them sturdily. 'But it is more than that. Since I first heard of your origins and first began planning the story that would become *The Jungle Book*, I have learned much. I do not exaggerate when I say that your fate and the fate of our species may be intertwined.'

'I say.' Kingsley rocked back in his chair as if he'd taken a blow on the chin. 'One likes to think one is important, but don't you think you're overstating things a little here?'

'I love India, my boy. When I was there, however, I saw things.' Kipling paused, and for an instant Kingsley saw fear in the man's eyes. 'Things that here, in civilised England, I have difficulty believing weren't a dream. Wonders and nightmares. Splendour and terror. Miracles and horrors.'

Evadne chanted, in a whisper: '*Hard her service, poor her payment – she in ancient, tattered raiment – India, she the grim Stepmother of our kind.*'

Kipling smiled. 'You know my work?'

'Of course.'

'Then you will understand that it – that everything – is a matter of the struggle between civilisation and the wild. Both impulses are in us, both tendencies have their strengths. You, my boy, because of your origins and your upbringing, have managed to unite both within you. If you are as I hope, you show that the wild can be controlled. Civilisation can subdue and benefit from the wildness within. You are unique.'

'He doesn't look unique,' Evadne said. 'He looks nonplussed.'

'I'm tired,' Kingsley said. 'And worried. And suspected of a murder. The combination is often mistaken for nonplussment.'

'That's better,' Evadne said. 'Meet adversity with a quip. It mightn't help, but it will give your obituary readers a smile.'

'None of us will have obituary readers,' Kipling said. 'Nor obituary writers. Not unless we manage to do something about the horror that is unfolding.'

'We've seen horror tonight,' Kingsley said.

'I gathered as much.' Kipling consulted his notebook, turned a page, and looked up, pencil poised. 'Our motor car escape was a little too fraught for you to inform me about what you found at your home. Would you mind?'

Kingsley began to explain, but stumbled badly when it came to the scene in the study. It took him a few false starts before he completed his story, and Kingsley was grateful for Evadne's lack of mockery while she listened.

Kipling blanched as the story unfolded but he gamely maintained his jotting. 'Brutish burglars? I was more worried about those things in the park.'

'Who were they?' Kingsley asked.

'They are minions of some depraved individuals I encountered in India, barely escaping with my life.' Kipling eyed them carefully. 'Sorcerers.'

Kingsley went to scoff at this, but he caught Evadne's expression. She was intently listening to Kipling, tight-lipped and angry. 'Go on,' she said.

'I guessed that you were prepared for this, Miss Stephens. Theatre folk often are.'

'You may have seen things, Mr Kipling, but so have I.'

'The Demimonde?'

'Indeed.'

'The Demimonde,' Kingsley repeated. 'We're not talking about courtesans and wastrels and people like that, are we?'

Evadne and Kipling exchanged glances. 'Not exactly.' She touched her lips with her forefinger, then appeared to come to a decision. 'I'm not sure that you're ready for this, but it seems as if we have little choice.' She took a deep breath. 'Pay attention. This is a rather abrupt introduction to the Demimonde. Usually we'd watch over you for a year or so before introducing it to you, if we thought you were ready, but sometimes, as all theatre people know, you have to ad lib.'

'Wait,' Kingsley said. 'The Demimonde? The half-world?'

'I knew you had an education behind you.' Evadne pushed up her spectacles. She'd changed them; these were tinted slightly green. 'Your courtesans and wastrels, as you so coyly describe them, are part of a realm that had been around long before absinthe had been invented.' Evadne put her hands together for a moment, nodding. 'It's like this. Just as the curtain divides the world of the groundlings from the magic world that is the theatre, so there exists a curtain that divides the rest of the mundane world from the Demimonde.'

'Ah,' Kingsley said, not in comprehension but more because some sort of response seemed to be expected. *Curtains?*

'It's more a curtain of perception and tradition than a curtain of true magic, but it's powerful nevertheless.'

'Magic.'

For a moment, she ran an upright finger left and right over her lips. 'I shouldn't have used that word yet. It only confuses things.' She brightened. 'What about an example? Everything works better with an example.'

'Please.'

'Try this. Sometimes when you see a banker walk straight past a beggar, it isn't because he is making a point. The beggar is truly invisible to him, even though he is only inches away.'

74

Kingsley frowned. 'The beggar isn't there?'

'No. I'm talking about the two worlds, the world of the banker and the world of the beggar. Sometimes they intersect and the banker can see the beggar, but at other times the beggar is truly invisible.'

'The beggar belongs to the Demimonde.'

'That's it. Beggars always do. Anyone who slips to the edge of the mundane world has a chance of accidentally wandering into the Demimonde. Others seek it out, while some are naturally part of it. The Demimonde exists side by side with the mundane world, but is mostly invisible to it. Places ordinary people don't go, or don't want to go, or couldn't find even if they wanted to go.'

Kingsley wasn't exactly predisposed to accept this. He prided himself on being a rationalist. Like Maskelyne – one of his magical heroes – he had no time for spiritualists and their seances, and even less for the calculating frauds who preyed on the weak and vulnerable using tricks derived from stage magic. This side of him was at war, however, with dim memories from India, memories that made him tremble, memories of people who came out of the darkness, changing shape as they went, disappearing again in a state that was half-human, half-animal. If what Evadne was saying were true, in India the curtain between the real world and the Demimonde might be a slim one indeed.

Nevertheless, he reserved judgement. While he tasted the allure of such a world as Evadne described – especially if it went hand in hand with the world of the theatre – it sounded unseemly, perhaps dangerous. 'Let's just say that I'm unconvinced.'

'Of course. It's a great deal to take in at once.' She

put her head on one side. Then, with a quick movement, she bridged the gap between the chairs and leaned close, looking into his eyes. 'Well,' she declared after a moment that Kingsley found intensely uncomfortable, despite enjoying her scent. He could tell that it was gardenia, with an underlying bed of sandalwood. 'That's interesting.'

'My eyes are interesting?'

She uncoiled back to her chair and addressed Kipling, who had been watching this exchange closely. 'I do believe he would have found his way into the Demi-monde, come what may. There's something about him.'

'There's something about everyone,' Kingsley said briskly, doing his best to disengage from the intensity of her interest.

'And you in particular,' Kipling said. 'This only confirms my opinion that you are special.'

'I'm glad to hear it.'

'Which is why these sorcerers want you.'

'Ah. That sort of special.'

'You've heard of the Thuggee cult?'

'Indian villains and murderers,' Kingsley said. 'Everyone knows that.'

'And everyone knows very little,' Kipling said. 'The truth is darker and more ghastly than even the most sensational English newspapers reported.'

'Death worshippers,' Evadne breathed. 'Kali-Durga.'

'In her aspect of Bhowanee,' Kipling added.

A chill reached from the past and stroked Kingsley's neck. He'd have sworn he'd never heard those names before, but he was gripped by them. 'You're saying that these sorcerers of yours are mixed up with the Thuggees?'

'With the worst of them, a sort of inner circle. The Three Immortals controlled them and sent them on their way, wreaking havoc among the British and among the Indians, slaughtering indiscriminately.'

'What for?'

Kipling grimaced. 'I don't know. All my sources, all my investigations cannot divine the reason for the reign of terror they created, nor what the worst of the worst they cultivated were actually doing.'

'But the Thuggees were wiped out,' Kingsley said. 'The authorities made sure of it.'

'India can hide much,' Kipling said, 'but that's not the point. I have friends still out there, still alert. They've recently written to me to let me know that the Three have left India.'

'The Three?'

'Three immortal sorcerers dedicated to establishing dominion over humanity. I fear that they are here and looking for you, Mr Ward.'

TEN

It was mid-morning when Kipling shepherded them through the door of the Hyde Park police station, the writer having insisted that Kingsley and Evadne catch a few hours' sleep and eat a proper breakfast before approaching the authorities.

The rain meant that the front desk was lonely apart from a sergeant. As soon as they entered, he goggled at Evadne and put his mug on the bench in front of him. 'And what can I do for you, young lady?' he asked as he brushed at the front of his blue serge. Then he noticed Kipling and Kingsley, who was still dressed in his black tie stage costume. 'And you, sirs?' he asked in a tone that Kingsley suspected was very useful in interrogations.

'Is Superintendent Norris in yet?' Kipling gave the sergeant his card. 'I'd like a word with him.'

The sergeant glanced at the card, then studied it again. 'He should be here, Mr Kipling. I'll find him for you.'

'Norris is an old acquaintance of mine. He's sure to be able to straighten out the mess you've found yourself in, Kingsley,' Kipling said after the sergeant disappeared past the charge station, where an officer was organising a lumpish fellow who didn't look at all unhappy at the prospect of being thrown into a cell. 'When I came back to London, being an old newspaperman I couldn't help but renew our acquaintance. I always feel better if I know a few of our law enforcement officials.'

'Professional curiosity,' Evadne said.

'I beg your pardon?'

'Professional curiosity. I see it in many occupations, and writing is one of them.'

Kipling's moustache twitched. 'A neat way of putting it, my dear. I am, indeed, inquisitive, and I've found that our police officers are often the first to know about anything. Fine storytellers, too, many of them.'

'They'd have a few stories to tell,' Kingsley said. He rocked back and forth on his heels impatiently. He hoped that Norris was as understanding as Kipling suggested. The horrible demise of Mrs Walters and the intruders Kingsley had disturbed had certainly made the matter of his foster father's disappearance even more worrying.

The sergeant returned, looking puzzled. 'I can't find the super, sir, but someone from the Yard is here. A Commander Harvey, said he wanted to see you.'

'Ah.' Kipling shared a significant look with Kingsley and Evadne. 'I think we might know what that's about, but I'd rather wait and see my friend the superintendent.'

'The commander was insistent, sir, when I told him you were here.'

Kipling protested, but the sergeant showed them to an office towards the rear of the station. A tall, uniformed man stood behind the desk. 'The boy,' he said. 'I want to see the boy.'

Kipling wasn't happy. 'I thought we could work things out, the superintendent and I, but now I'm not sure that we shouldn't have some legal representation.'

'They can wait,' the commander said. Kingsley shifted uncomfortably. The man's gaze hadn't moved from him. 'The girl and the man. They can wait.'

'I say,' Kipling burst out as the sergeant hustled Evadne and him away. 'This isn't what I expected.'

'Close the door,' the commander said. Kingsley swallowed. He didn't like the man's voice. It had all the warmth of an icicle wrapped in a snow blanket.

'Sit.'

The commander's eyes were as flat as his voice. He was gaunt, his cheeks hollow, and his skin had a peculiar greyish quality.

Kingsley shifted on the hard wooden chair as the commander studied him silently, conscious that his animal self was becoming increasingly unhappy. The commander disturbed him – all sides of him. Every detail about the man was deeply unsettling. The way he stood was slightly awkward, the way he held his head wasn't right, the whole line of his balance was askew.

When Kingsley became aware that the man also smelled wrong, his lips began to curl and the skin at the back of his neck tighten. *Flee!* his wildness screamed. *Leave this place! Get away from him!*

Kingsley was half out of his chair when two peculiarly grey-faced constables burst in. One swung a baton and darkness carried him away.

When Kingsley woke, he instantly knew where he was: he was in a lightless confined space that smelled of motor exhaust. Since it jolted and rocked, and since the sound of an engine hammered at him, it didn't take him long to conclude that he was in the back of a lorry. The question of how he'd made the transition from being in a police station to this predicament eluded him, thanks to the waves of nausea that kept him doubled up on the floor of the van. But after the events of the night before, had had to assume he'd been taken by Kipling's immortal sorcerers. The implications were chilling. If they'd been able to cast a net like this so quickly, their reach was fearsome.

Grimacing with every bump and every lurch, Kingsley crawled to the doors. Panting heavily, with pain swirling inside his skull, he found the lock with a hand. Even in his distress, he managed a chuckle. The locksmith who made this was taking money under false pretences.

At that moment, however, the van conspired to test Kingsley's skill. It both jolted *and* lurched, so much so that his forehead hit the lock sharply enough for his teeth to snap together – right onto the tip of his tongue, which he customarily stuck out while working. He reeled back in time for a second violent lurch to hurl him against the door again. He managed to protect his hands by the novel method of taking the entire force on his nose, thus making his head a veritable explosion of pain.

He lost control. His wolfish state came roaring out to possess him.

Immediately, he howled and backed away from the door. The noise, the smell and his physical distress frightened him. Scrabbling at the metal floor, he levered himself up and threw himself from side to side, furious and afraid of the confines of the moving prison. He growled until his throat was sore and then, finally, he cowered in a corner, shivering. Finally, he took the last refuge of the beast: he slept.

When he awoke, the vestiges of nausea were still with him, enough to make him wince when the doors of the van were dragged open. He put a hand up to shield his eyes. Two uniformed figures were reaching for him and he was reasonably sure they weren't matadors. As one, they leaped into the back of the van and dragged him out. Kingsley protested, and lashed out with a few aimless punches, but he was weak – both from the energy uselessly expended when his wolfish self was in charge and from the effects of whatever had rendered him unconscious.

He was carried through a lane that smelled of rotting onions. Face down, he could make out shouting nearby and the sounds of traffic, generic enough noises to make them almost useless in identifying his surroundings. He smelled steam and thought he was near a station, but then a wave of fishiness and the sight of water told him that he'd been brought to the Thames. The glimpse was short, for he was hustled into the stony darkness of a warehouse and thrown against a wall.

✥ ELEVEN ✥

Billingsgate fish market. Damona wore a wide-brimmed hat and overcoat. Protection, disguise. Rain clearing, she leaned against a lamp post, gazing at the swarming Invaders. She was contemptuous and pitying. Pale, soft creatures. How did they ever become so dominant? Looking harder, she saw their activity, their energy, their enterprise. A hint?

She grunted. Where were the Spalnitz brothers? She'd bought copper from them in the past, needed plenty now. Slippery, like most Invaders, but the Spalnitzes were greedy enough to sell to the True People. Damona could work with that.

Olaf sidled up to her. Large hat, tattered velvet coat. A good scout, Olaf was often abroad in the overworld. He was shorter than most of the True People, smaller. Wrapped in his rags he caused no comment. A beggar, one of many.

Damona admired his fortitude.

Olaf squatted next to her. 'The boy you're after. The Spawn have him. Here.'

Damona bared her teeth. Finding the boy was good. She could use him to put pressure on Dr Ward. But the Spawn? She spat on the cobbles. They were a problem.

Damona hated the Spawn even more than she hated their Immortal masters. Spawn turned her stomach. She gave Olaf a coin. In case anyone was wondering why she was talking to a beggar. 'Where?'

He pointed, a barest twitch of a finger. She tossed him another coin, set off in the direction he indicated. Around her the business of the fish market swirled and roared. She ignored it.

The Invaders had a Golden Rule. Damona had heard of it. Treat others as one would wish to be treated. Stupid. Unworkable.

The True People had a Golden Rule: always repay. Good or bad, always repay. Debts were honoured. Revenge was taken. It was natural.

She was sure that the Golden Rule of the True People was observed more wholly than the Golden Rule of the Invaders. Theirs was too complicated. An Invader had to imagine himself as someone else, for a start. Much too hard for most Invaders, from what she'd seen.

The code of the True People was simpler. It took a natural impulse, made it part of their culture. In the past, when the Invaders burned a village of the True People, the survivors sought revenge. Every time.

It was simple. It was clear. It was inborn. It was satisfying.

Damona had had a long life to consider such things. In her heart, she knew that this custom had helped destroy her people. True People sought revenge even when badly placed, outnumbered, hurt, lost. Each defeat had diminished her people. Hot-blooded revenge could be a disaster. Cold, thoughtful revenge, though. That was different. The Immortals were a different case from the Invaders. More dangerous, less predictable. Damona didn't care what their motives were. She just knew that the self-proclaimed sorcerers were enemies.

It happened many, many years ago, when she was young. A small clan of True People wanted to start their own stronghold. The plan had caused much heartache, families divided, arguing, friend against friend. In the end the self-determination of the True People prevailed.

A year passed with no news. Then a sole survivor of the clan dragged herself back to London. She brought news that the clan had been abducted by the Immortals, and died.

The outrage created anger that had not been seen for an age. Damona was in the troop that went to rescue the missing clan. They found only bones, so their mission became one of revenge. They destroyed scores of the Spawn but weren't able to find the Immortals themselves.

The Immortals disappeared soon after this disaster. Vanished. No word of them in the Demimonde.

Then news came of them from India. They were ensconced in the shadow world there, breeding horrors.

Damona had spent time learning about the Immortals. Many whispers, few facts. Everyone she spoke to agreed that they were magicians. This meant little to Damona. The Demimonde was full of those who called themselves heirs to Pharaohs, Speakers to the Dead and travellers from other worlds. Claims were easy to make in the Demimonde and hard to disprove.

The Immortals were like a squeaky gear to Damona. Hard to ignore, but not that important. They were in India, the True People were under London.

A smile spread on her broad face. Taking the boy would be of benefit to the True People. It would also upset the Immortals. Two good outcomes, one action. Efficient and pleasing.

Damona went to the rear of the warehouse. Crates stacked high, smelling of fish. She pushed her way through them. Cats scattered, glared at her.

An iron ladder led to the roof. Skylight, easy entrance. A catwalk and she was in a loft with a fine view below.

She peered down. Smiled.

Cobwebs, dust, broken crates. Two Spawn were dressed as police constables. Damona sniffed. No mistaking their smell. Not alive, not dead. Stronger than they looked, she knew.

They were tying the hands of their victim. The boy was tall, well built, curly haired, unhappy. He kicked, struggled. Uselessly. The Spawn had already thrown back a steel hatch in the floor. A Demimonde entrance.

Damona could move quietly when she chose, like all True People. Her bulk was deceptive. She ignored the ache in her hip. Crept along the catwalk to the other end of the warehouse. She found a ladder. It creaked under her weight. Her heart caught a beat until it steadied. Then she was on the cobbled floor.

Damona smiled again. A few steps, a slide around a pillar, and she'd be on them.

She paused for a moment. Hesitated. Was she too old for such nonsense?

Of course I am. But it's not going to stop me.

She roared and charged straight at them. Stiff-armed the Spawn on the right. He flew backward, squawking. The one on the left stopped blindfolding the lad. Damona swung a fist. He didn't have time to move. His head snapped back. His police helmet flew off. He toppled, senseless.

Damona pushed the Invader lad aside. She crouched to meet the first Spawn. He hissed, launched himself at her, eyes mad.

She drew her head in to protect her throat. She clasped both hands together, brought them up with all her True People strength. She caught him right under his chin. His jaw crunched. His eyes rolled up. He collapsed at her feet.

Damona bent. She grasped her knees and panted. She *definitely* wasn't as young as she once was.

The boy. She lifted her head, found him on the floor, bound and angry.

He growled at her from behind his gag.

She almost laughed, then she saw his eyes. Wild eyes. The eyes of a hunter. She backed away a step or two. The boy had no restraint left in him. He was about to attack.

'Don't,' she said. She kept her voice calm, her movements slow. She reached across the body of the Spawn, grasped a steel rung. She grunted, wrenched it from its mountings. She swung it in front of her. Two feet of solid metal whistled, slicing through the air. 'I'll hurt you,' she said to the wild boy.

He swarmed up and out of the ropes. She gaped. *How did he do that?* He leaned one way, then the other, looking for the range of the metal bar. He didn't back away.

Damona kept up a soft chant: 'Easy now. Easy now.'

He stripped off his gag. Bared his teeth. Growled a challenge from deep in his chest. His eyes darted to the dark hole in the floor. Before Damona could move he took a few steps and dived down it.

Damona sat back on her haunches. She took a deep breath, thinking. She tossed the metal bar away. It rang on the concrete like a bell.

She glanced at the bodies of the Spawn. 'What were you two doing with him?' She shuffled over and sifted their pockets, found nothing.

Why would they want a wild boy?

She sighed, climbed to her feet. 'They can't have him. I want him.'

~ TWELVE ~

Kingsley ran with the single-mindedness of the jungle animals among which he'd been raised. His one impulse was to put distance between him and that creature, the one like the trolls who'd murdered Mrs Walters.

At the bottom of the ladder, he was faced with a red-brick tunnel, large enough that he only had to stoop slightly. One way – to judge from the smell – led to the river. Hardly thinking, acting instinctively, he set off along the other. Twenty yards of scrambling and he came to a hole in a brick wall. He tumbled down a fall of loose masonry and timber. Unnerved by the closeness in which he'd found himself – the opposite of the freedom he'd been seeking – he jogged through another brick arched tunnel, darker than the first, panting heavily until he came to a spiral staircase leading down.

He paused, one hand on the iron railing, his heart battering his ribs, then looked back along the tunnel.

Echoes. Footsteps, slow but dogged.

It was enough. He took to the stairs and, despite an animalistic recoiling from the prospect of close confines, hammered downward into the darkness, eager to flee.

The time that passed was not measured in minutes and seconds, those arbitrary markers made by humanity. A distant, civilised part of Kingsley grasped for them but they slipped by, caught up as he was in the need to escape. *Run, run!* was a drumbeat behind his forehead as he took turns quickly, chose options after a quick sniff and listen, scrambled down shafts as they presented themselves.

Run, make distance, then hide. Run, make distance, then hide.

A long time later, Kingsley came to himself again. He was backed into a gap in a stone wall, a ragged hole that smelled of damp. It was large enough for him and no-one else.

It was a bolthole.

Through dim, strained light – grates? Drain holes? – he was looking out over a stretch of water that was undecided about which way it was moving. A shore of stones separated him from the ill-favoured water by a few yards, and on the other side another few yards of shingle ran up to the stone wall that curved up and over the water. He heard rumbling, the omnipresent noise of the city, but it didn't sound as if were coming from his left or his right. Overhead?

Kingsley shivered. He dropped his chin and realised, glumly, that he was a horrid mess. His trousers were spattered with mud. He'd lost his shoes. His jacket and tie were gone. One sleeve of his shirt flapped uselessly, his cuff link having torn away. He rolled it up over his elbow while he wondered what to do. He'd walked away from his job, his foster father was missing – possibly abducted – his housekeeper had been murdered and he was a fugitive.

In some ways, he'd accomplished a great deal. The sad fact was that little of it was good.

The scene in front of him was tranquil, but hardly welcoming. Drops fell into the water erratically, as if reluctant to join what he now knew – from the evidence of his sense of smell – to be little more than a drain.

He was hungry.

A rat the size of a small terrier poked its head into the hole. Kingsley reared back in alarm. He cried out not just at its size, but because of its three eyes. Two black and blinking eyes and one round, in the middle of its head above the other two.

The rat wasn't upset by his performance. It merely rocked its head to one side and scurried off.

Kingsley passed a hand over his face. His trembling definitely wasn't because of lack of food or cold. Strangeness was assaulting him on every side and it was testing his mettle.

He clenched his teeth, hard. He clenched his hands into fists until his fingers hurt, then he relaxed. He took a deep breath, then another, until the trembling stopped, putting himself in the calm frame of mind he would if he were about to perform a dangerous escape.

It helped.

Kingsley had been sitting with his knees drawn up and his arms around them. He let go and swivelled his neck, stretching. He gazed out of his hole. He'd been in worse situations. The time when his foster father's valet had reluctantly thrown the chained trunk into the canal, for instance, had been sheer terror where seconds stretched out in the rubbery way that crisis time had. Seconds moved like monoliths when one's life was in the balance.

Now, *that* had been a difficult situation. No matter how he'd practised, no matter how well he knew the theory, working on the chains and locks in the dark, while the water sluiced in through the cracks – cold and smelling of refuse – was a test of his skill and his bravery. Panic would have been the worst thing, for trembling and doubt would have been fatal.

That time, he'd emerged, draped in slime, much to Brown's relief. He'd proved to himself that he could escape from death's clutches.

He shook his head. He mightn't be in death's clutches right now, but he had no idea where he was. He was still shivering and uncertain, lost and hunted. He had enemies all around. He was being chased by a troll and by loathsome creatures impersonating policemen. He was suspected of murder. He was in danger and he was further away from finding his foster father than ever.

He ran a hand over his face and shivered. Go and confront those creatures to see what connection they had with his foster father's disappearance? Find a genuine law enforcement official? He shook his head. Who could he trust?

Kingsley froze. *That* noise wasn't natural. He groped

for a weapon. He had lock picks still in his collar, and a thin length of metal sewn into the back of his shirt could be used as a slashing tool if he had the chance to retrieve it, but he scrabbled for a hand-sized rock as a better, more solid alternative. If he could get in a good blow, he might have a chance to scuttle out of his bolthole and escape.

A face appeared just as Kingsley's fingers found a rock. He restrained himself.

'Found you.' Evadne Stephens was wearing a brass headpiece with telescopic arrangements and goggles that made her visage insect-like. 'And none too soon, from the looks of you.' She tapped her chin. 'As a project, you're more complicated than I thought you'd be.'

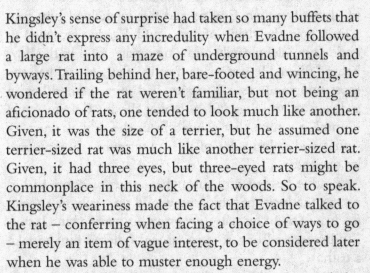

Kingsley's sense of surprise had taken so many buffets that he didn't express any incredulity when Evadne followed a large rat into a maze of underground tunnels and byways. Trailing behind her, bare-footed and wincing, he wondered if the rat weren't familiar, but not being an aficionado of rats, one tended to look much like another. Given, it was the size of a terrier, but he assumed one terrier-sized rat was much like another terrier-sized rat. Given, it had three eyes, but three-eyed rats might be commonplace in this neck of the woods. So to speak. Kingsley's weariness made the fact that Evadne talked to the rat – conferring when facing a choice of ways to go – merely an item of vague interest, to be considered later when he was able to muster enough energy.

As they went, Evadne produced a slim electric light, the size and shape of a pencil. She chatted mildly about how she and Kipling had separated after the uproar at the police station and how difficult it had been to find Kingsley and how curious she was about his ending up in the Demimonde. She told him about how he'd ended up in one of the older sections of the Fleet River, one of London's mostly forgotten subterranean waterways.

Kingsley shrugged at this, too weary and too overwhelmed to be amazed. He tried to offer responses that made sense, but her questions grew fewer and her glances at him more concerned until she patted him on the arm and told him not to worry.

Which was useful advice, for Kingsley took the opportunity to fall asleep while he walked. He lapsed into one of those wonderful dreams where one knows one is dreaming, but is able simply to enjoy the experience. At least, that was the only explanation he could think of, drowsily, when Evadne and her rat helped him into a little boat the shape of a pea pod. Evadne crowded in beside him, delightfully, and a tiny man stood in the bow behind them. He was made mostly of angles and had the most enormous eyes Kingsley had ever seen, either in a dream or waking, and he poled the boat along while humming a tune that echoed from the corbels, cornerstones and colonnades of the subterranean watercourse he navigated.

Evadne herded him through a series of doors to her refuge, the locks of which he would normally have been fascinated by. In his state, however, they were a blur. Inside, Evadne steered him to a room and ordered him to take a bath.

Some time later, and somewhere closer to human, Kingsley relaxed and let the water come up to his chin.

The bathroom in Evadne's retreat was white-tiled from floor to ceiling. At the moment it was totally filled with steam and Kingsley's gratitude.

He tried to remember the last time he'd had a bath and, with a start, realised it was only a day ago, the morning of his disastrous debut. Idly, while he sought for the soap that was somewhere in the water, he wondered what Mr Bernadetti was doing. Hiring some more dog acts, most likely, to fill the gaps that Evadne and Kingsley had left.

A stab of guilt took him. How could he be worrying about his stage career with all that had happened? His foster father's abduction, in particular, and Mr Kipling's hints about shadowy events and nearing doom. The world had become altogether darker and more complicated than it had been a day ago.

The nature of his abductors, too, had shaken Kingsley. He flinched when he recalled their touch. Their skin was doughy, but their grip was steely. On top of that, the shock of what happened to them, the way they'd been dispatched by the brutish woman who had then advanced on him, had been enough to shake his wild self free.

He was angry with himself. Twice in a single day his control had slipped and his wild side had run amok. In doing so, he'd forgotten all about his missing foster father and was no doubt still sought for the murder of poor Mrs Walters.

Kingsley found the soap. He grimaced at its lavender fragrance, but stoically lathered up a wash cloth. He set to work on the sweat and grime of the most outrageous twenty-four hours in his life.

THIRTEEN

Kingsley woke to the sound of a bell ringing. Not a church bell; it was far more insistent. It took his sleep-befuddled brain a moment to realise it was more like a fire bell and then he bolted out of the supremely soft bed Evadne had shepherded him to after his bath the previous day.

For a moment, he was unsure exactly where he was and that disconcerted him. Bath, bed, he remembered, but his whereabouts beyond that eluded him. He *liked* knowing where he was. Their arrival was only a fuzzy memory, exhausted and mind-battered as he had been, and confused by his ridiculous dream of a boat voyage. He had vague recollections of heavy rain, crowds of people underneath a field of umbrellas, and another stair-enabled descent, but everything else was a jumble.

He was still fumbling with his tie – clean and pressed like the rest of his clothes – when he found Evadne in a round room, twice as tall as it was wide. She was peering at one of a dozen or so oval windows that were set into the wall like a double row of plaques. Underneath them ran a long shelf with an array of switches, knobs and levers. She was wearing a long green leather coat over a dark blue dress that was piped with cream. She had a small hat, quite the opposite of the fashion, something like a top hat much reduced and much less masculine, probably due to the light blue feather stuck in the band.

When he entered, she glanced at him. 'Stay there!' she ordered. 'Don't move!'

She left the bank of glasses, disappeared through a door and emerged a moment later hefting a rifle that was a cousin of the pistol she'd used on the hapless police constable: black, sleek and deadly.

'What is it?'

She ignored him and ran past, disappearing through the door he'd entered by.

A door banged, the bells continued to ring, and all Kingsley was left with was the scent of gardenia in the air.

He went to the door opposite and peered inside. He was confronted by a workshop that looked like a university physics laboratory that had surrounded and taken over a foundry, with power cables strung willy-nilly from roof beams, a brace of workbenches heavily laden with impressive glassware and a row of metal cabinets that looked as if they could take a direct hit from an artillery shell without flinching. For a moment, he hesitated, but the urgency of the bells made him move. He grabbed a bullseye lantern and a shiny metal bar, then set off after Evadne.

Kinsley counted five doors. All of them were open, the last still swinging. He hesitated, reluctant to leave the refuge unprotected, but angry cries echoed down the tunnel in front of him and set him running in that direction.

A stutter of sharp, hard reports came to him, loud enough to hurt his ears. He lurched against the bricks of the tunnel, shivering as the noise of conflict set his wild side on edge. Should he ready to fight, or should he turn tail and run?

Another hammering of gunfire and a chorus of unearthly wails made him bite down on his animal self. His head pounding with the effort, he staggered on, using the metal bar for support and bent over to avoid hitting his head on the roof of the tunnel. He held up the lantern just in time to avoid plunging over the edge where the tunnel gave out onto a shallow, precarious ledge.

Light flashed and a rifle cracked. Echoes swallowed it, tumbled it up with shouts and screeching, a wicked brew of pain and anger. Kingsley swept the lantern and found he'd come to an open space with four or five drains emptying into it – one of which was choked with the rangy figures of those who'd abducted him from the police station.

For an instant, Kingsley pulled back, recoiling from the horrible creatures. Then he crept forward, keeping himself concealed, unwilling to let them daunt him.

The creatures were trapped in the tunnel mouth, pinned by Evadne's rifle fire, but they weren't defeated. They howled and shrieked and threw themselves out, tumbling one over another in a battle frenzy, plunging into the pool and floundering forward before Evadne struck them down.

She stood on a small promontory that jutted into the pool, balanced on a pile of broken masonry, a silver-maned Fury. She fired again. The sound of ricochets added to the cacophony, but she didn't stop. No doubt aided by her light-enhancing spectacles, she fired again, and again with accuracy that bordered on the phenomenal.

She was crying.

The light was poor, but Kingsley could just make out that she was sobbing as she worked the bolt of the rifle, gasping for breath in between tracking the Spawn as they sought her. She dashed tears away with the back of her hand but she held the rifle steady.

Two Spawn threw themselves into the pool, rose roaring and were thrown backward by Evadne's accurate fire.

Kingsley rose from his crouch, squinting, trying to make out figures moving in the shifting shadows. There, on the other side of the pool – where Evadne had no hope of seeing them from her position out on the promontory of rubble.

He abandoned the lamp. He leaped from the ledge and landed on a narrow, noisome shore. He ran, metal bar in one hand, skirting the pool, aware that if Evadne caught sight of him she could mistake him for one of the Spawn, but not hesitating for an instant – for he'd seen that the two vile creatures had emerged and were creeping up on her, well behind her field of vision.

Kingsley hurdled over a broken wooden crate in time to see the first of these stealthy Spawn rear up behind her. She didn't have a chance to move – it clawed her from her position. She fell and her spectacles flew from her head, glinting in the sparse light of Kingsley's lonely lantern on the other side of the pool.

Instantly, Kingsley was there. He swung the metal bar and the Spawn howled as it was driven back. Its companion wheeled on Kingsley in time to meet the bar coming the other way. It folded when the bar caught it across the midriff. Kingsley kicked and it toppled into the pool.

The first Spawn staggered to its feet. This time Kingsley jabbed at it and took it in the throat. It gurgled and joined its partner in the mucky water.

Kingsley reached Evadne. She was dazed and her head lolled from the Spawn's blow. Panting, muscles burning, he scooped her up, threw her over his shoulder, tucked her rifle under his arm. 'This is so undignified,' she mumbled.

'I apologise,' he said. More Spawn were assembling at the tunnel mouth. He set off in the other direction, back towards Evadne's refuge. 'It seems practical.'

Evadne didn't reply. Kingsley cast around for her spectacles, couldn't see them, then set his teeth and began to jog as fast as he could.

He carried Evadne inside the refuge, following her ragged instructions for bolting each of the doors as they went, holding her in his arms so she could see. 'The viewing room,' she gasped over the relentless alarm bells. Her face was streaked with grime and looked different without the spectacles. Kingsley wouldn't have dared say more vulnerable, but he was willing to wager someone else might have.

'Push that switch up!' she shouted over the bells.

A dozen switches confronted him on the wall near

the door. All of them were large and brass with rubber handles. 'Which one?' he shouted back.

'The green one!'

Kingsley had to use a knee, but he managed to slam the lever home. Instantly, the ringing cut off. She looked him in the eye. 'You can put me down now.'

She was hardly a burden. 'Are you sure?'

'Not really. If you're willing to carry me around everywhere, I'll feign a weakness I don't feel, just for the luxury.'

'I've always aspired to be a human palanquin.' Kingsley carefully deposited her on her feet in front of the bank of glasses. He was attentive for any sign of injury, but she was steady enough, if a little grimy from the underground skirmish.

Evadne slipped off to the workshop and came back bespectacled. She stood in front of the wall of glasses, scanning them intently.

'What on earth is going on?' he asked.

'It looks as if the Immortals have tracked you here.' She pointed at the glass. Kingsley came closer and stood next to her. It wasn't a window at all, not unless they were looking down on a tunnel from a very lofty vantage point. With growing wonder, he realised that each of the glasses showed a different view. In the one Evadne was gesturing at, a dozen figures were crawling through a tunnel on their hands and knees. It was more like a film in a cinematograph theatre than a window, all greys and blacks, but it was clear enough for Kingsley to recognise the spindly forms.

'They're like the ones who abducted me at the police station,' he said.

'They're Spawn, the servants of the Immortals.'

'Kipling's evil sorcerers.'

'He knows what he's talking about,' Evadne said through gritted teeth. 'I'd wipe them out in a second if I could find them.'

The intensity of her loathing concerned Kingsley. Where was the insouciant juggler who had befriended him? He'd assumed that she went through life with an attitude of tolerant amusement – the same sort of attitude that had brought her to nominate him as her project. 'You have a grudge against them?'

'The Immortals? I've never met them.'

'And yet you want to destroy them.'

'I've heard of them.' She glanced at him, but quickly turned her attention back to the glasses. 'And what I heard put them at the top of my list.' Her voice was both brittle and uncompromising. She touched a brass knob and the view in the glass brightened a little. 'Leave it at that, Kingsley, I beg of you.'

With difficulty, Kingsley swallowed the multitude of questions that Evadne's confession – and behaviour – had prompted. 'What are you going to do?'

'What I should have done in the first place.' Evadne reached for another lever and pushed it to the left. Her lips moved silently for a moment, her expression distant, then she nodded when the glass showed the Spawn recoiling, spinning on their heels and scrambling back the way they'd come. They were followed by a surge of water that rapidly filled the tunnel. 'That should take care of them.'

'You did that?'

'A tiny explosive charge in a spot I'd marked earlier, a tunnel about half a mile away, somewhere under

Holland Park. They won't be using that way again.' She touched her lips with a finger. 'I do love explosives. I just don't get the opportunity to use them as much as I'd like to.'

Kingsley wanted to wave a white flag over his head. 'I need a cup of tea.'

FOURTEEN

'Firstly, Kingsley, I need to apologise.'

Evadne didn't look at him. In a small kitchen that wouldn't have been out of place in Surbiton, she busied herself with the breakfast making, taking an inordinate amount of care measuring out the tea while he sat on a stylish wooden chair.

'Apologise? For saving me and bringing me here?' He stuck out his feet. 'For providing me with a pair of distinctly smart Oxfords in my size?'

'For my display earlier.'

'Ah. Where you ran out as if you were possessed and single-handedly tried to wipe out a troop of those creatures.'

'Yes, that's the one. It was quite unlike me.' She paused, kettle in hand. 'Well, that may not be entirely accurate. I do have an outrageous temper but it's rarely provoked.'

While making a note to himself never to provoke her, Kingsley asked: 'And these Spawn set you off, so to speak?'

'They're soulless creatures, underlings, but I'll strike at them until I can get at their masters.'

'The ones on your list.' Understanding that he might need his caution some time in the future, instead of throwing it to the winds, he tucked it into a pocket for later use before he asked: 'What list?'

Evadne paused, then studied the kettle for some time, as if it were the most interesting thing in the world. She cleared her throat, put the kettle down and faced him, leaning against the sink and absently twisting the silver ring on her finger. 'I have a list of those who hurt children.'

'Oh.' *Inadequacy, thy name is Kingsley.*

She didn't look at him. 'The Demimonde can be a dreadful place.'

'So I've gathered. Then again, so can the ordinary world.'

A small, sweet smile made its way to him, quite unlike the boldness he'd thought her way. 'That's true. I can't abide those who hurt children in the ordinary world, either.'

'You sound as if you have a cause.'

'Like those who go about saving fallen women? Or helping old sailors? Perhaps. I like to think that I'm more ... vigorous than that.'

'A crusade rather than a cause?'

'*That* makes it sound rather spiritual.' Kingsley was pleased to hear a more acerbic tone in her voice. 'I'm rather more down to earth than a crusader. I see myself as a scourge.'

105

'A scourge.'

'I can't abide those who exploit and hurt children. I'm down on them and I'll do what I can to confound them.' She shook her head and her white hair flew. 'The Immortals are among the worst of them. They've hurt hundreds of children, thousands perhaps, if the stories are correct.'

'And they've just come back from India.'

'So it would seem. Wicked creatures.' Evadne fussed about in a cupboard, looking for teacups. Kingsley deliberately didn't notice her dashing a tear from her cheek with her forearm. 'Immortal and wicked. It's a terrible combination.'

'How do you know so much about them?'

'By and large, the denizens of the Demimonde all know about the Immortals, and are appalled by them. They dwell outside even the loose notions of morality that exist here. Over the centuries various groups have arisen to exterminate them, but they've had a singular lack of success.'

'They're powerful.'

'Extremely.'

'And you want to destroy them.'

'They deserve it.'

This was a new Evadne, one that Kingsley hadn't seen before. Her passion was clear, but Kingsley saw more than that. Was it sorrow behind the anger? It was clearly a tender area, and he didn't feel he had the right to press. They'd only known each other a few days, after all. A harum-scarum few days, but propriety demanded that he respect her pain.

'This refuge is part of the Demimonde?'

'I hope you like it,' she said with a gallant effort. 'It's comfortable and secure, what more could you ask?'

'A view?'

'If you want a view I'll find a painting for you.' She pushed her spectacles up on her nose. 'Since I move between the ordinary world and the Demimonde, I make sure that I have safe places in both. This is my Demimonde refuge. Living quarters, facilities, viewing room, workshop over there.'

Kingsley took a closer look at the chaotic space he'd barely glanced at earlier. Between the power cables, he could now make out beaten, coppery figures that looked like giant insects hung from hooks near the ceiling and a rack displaying dozens of goggles where glass, leather, rubber, brass and silver were flung together in a variety of combinations. The workshop was an Aladdin's Cave with strange and exotic treasures everywhere he looked.

'Impressive, but where exactly are we?' he asked over his shoulder and, with embarrassment, he heard the plaintiveness in his voice.

'That's not always a meaningful question in the Demimonde,' Evadne replied, 'but in this case, it is. We're right underneath the main stadium at the White City. The Olympic Games are going on right over our heads.'

'Construction in London is a blessing for the Demimonde,' Evadne explained while Kingsley grappled with bewilderment that had assumed the proportions of an airship. 'When Wren and Hooke were rebuilding London after the Great Fire, many a lair or warren was worked into the developments, above and below ground. Forgotten parts of the city – parts that were supposed to be demolished – were just appropriated and now have thriving communities away from the overworlders. The Olympics has meant a further frenzy of furtive fabrication.' She clapped her hands together and beamed. 'Oh, I like that!'

'It's a gem,' Kingsley said, even though he felt as if his world had previously been confined to a narrow stretch of beach – and now the tide had gone out, making it bigger, wider and more mysterious than he'd ever believed.

Evadne held up the teapot. 'Another cup?'

'Please.'

'Oh. I forgot to ask if you take milk. You don't, do you?'

'What would you say if I did?'

'I'd have to send one of my myrmidons to find some.'

'Myrmidons? Some sort of softly spoken professor?'

Evadne pointed the strainer at him. 'What on earth are you talking about?'

'Myrmidons. Murmur. Don.'

'Please,' she said, 'don't do that again.'

'I shan't. Unless the appropriate occasion presents itself.'

'Hmm.' She sipped her tea before returning to her explanation. 'Do you remember the rat that found your hiding place near the Fleet?'

'Let me see. It didn't have three eyes, perchance?'

'That three-eyed rat wasn't a rat at all. It was one of my myrmidons.'

'Thank you. That makes it all so much clearer.'

'Kingsley, you're a nice chap but you're going to have to be quicker than that.' She lifted the teapot and poured him a fresh cup.

'The Myrmidons were ancient Greeks,' he said. He held his teacup in both hands and felt its warmth. 'Immensely loyal to their king. Or so Homer said.'

'That's better.' Evadne's approval did something to Kingsley. Something awkward and unsettling but not altogether unwelcome. 'Since Homer, the term "myrmidon" has been used to describe steadfast and devoted followers.'

'And your rat is one of those.'

'My rat is a machine I made. More or less. They're my scouts, my messengers, my general runabouts. Bring your tea and I'll show you.'

Evadne took him back to the viewing room. The banks of glasses were alive. She pointed at the last two. 'These are my myrmidon sentinels. What their third eye sees is relayed here. I've sent them scouting and it looks as if the Spawn have all retreated.' She tapped her chin with a finger. 'I think I managed to intercept them far enough away for this refuge still to be secret.'

Kingsley didn't think that any who'd come close enough to Evadne's refuge survived to tell the tale either. She'd been very efficient in dealing with them. 'I imagine you've blended cinematograph cameras with wireless Marconi technology?'

'That, Kingsley, was a very educated guess.'

He bowed. 'Thank you.'

'Completely wrong, but very educated. I'll let it rest at that.'

For a moment, Kingsley was prepared to gnaw at this

bone, but he was happy to leave the matter lie. Once, he would have said his grasp of science and engineering was solid enough, but Evadne was at home in a realm far from his ken. Besides, he had a task he'd left undone. 'I've been remiss. I haven't thanked you for rescuing me.'

'I couldn't simply let you disappear like that. Mr Kipling was most upset until I assured him that I'd find you. He went to consult some friends, he told me.'

'I hope he's safe.'

'I think Mr Kipling has considerable resources. More than meets the eye.'

'He's not the only one.'

~ FIFTEEN ~

Jabez Soames sat at his desk, shredded one corner of his blotter and wondered how to detach the stink of failure. Higgs, the lift operator, had been positively surly. Such an attitude could be contagious, especially in the Demimonde. If he gained a reputation for ineptness, the taint could linger forever.

He hadn't been able to find the boy for the Immortals.

Shredding slightly faster, and creating a veritable snowstorm, he decided that immediate action was called for. A demonstration of his worth, something showy – something that would make the Immortals sit up and take notice instead of ordering that he be snuffed out. His efforts in arranging a troop of hirelings to find the children for the Immortals, and to secrete a collection of devices about the new Olympic Games stadium simply wouldn't be good enough. The Immortals, he knew, weren't in the habit of overlooking deficiencies.

Jabez, it's time for one of your remarkable plans.

His fingers shredded at a blur as he stared at the window, hardly seeing the grey clouds scudding across the sky. Rain was about, but hadn't fallen seriously since the night before.

In the tide of affairs in which any middleman found himself, sometimes there came an opportunity so unlikely that it took a special mind to apprehend it. Soames liked to think that he possessed that kind of mind. To do otherwise would be to assume the sort of false modesty that he found puzzling.

What if instead of being on the verge of disaster, this was the time for him to advance his plans to usurp the Immortals? They would hardly think that he would be plotting such a thing, since he was so incompetent as to fail to present them with the boy Kipling was interested in. After going to all the trouble of locating this scamp and using some seconded Spawn to abduct him; losing him didn't just smack of incompetence, it was the sort of thing to make the notoriously touchy Immortals extremely irritated.

Especially if they heard – as he had – that the leader of the Neanderthals was after the boy as well.

Absently, Soames made a pile of blotting paper shreds and he stroked through it, arranging and re-arranging as he sifted through possible courses of action.

Soames was aware of the movements and alliances in the world of the Demimonde. He made it his job. With such knowledge, he could do something about inconveniencing the Immortals, at the very least. It would divert any attention from him, for a start. Of course, this could be a very dangerous game. He shuddered as he contemplated what would happen if the Immortals found out, or the Neanderthals found out. Or both.

An idea struck him. Soames swept his arm across the desk and sent paper shreds whirling. He rushed to his pigeon holes. He remembered something, a recent report, something one of his informants had noted about increased activity among the Neanderthals ...

He whipped slips of paper from pigeonholes, glanced at them, and rammed them home again until, finally, he found what he was looking for. He gave a crow of triumph and, certain no-one could see him, performed a little jig, his patent leather shoes winking in the morning light that spilled through the window.

Jabez, no-one senses an opportunity like you!

Feverishly, he returned to the desk, found a pencil and a sheaf of foolscap in the top drawer and began to make a list.

Soames sat on a chair that was meant for hips much broader than his, and legs slightly shorter, but he hid his discomfort in the way that business people and diplomats had done forever, willing to sit in uncomfortable chairs until the end of time if it helped them advance their position.

The location he'd been directed to, after requesting the meeting by convoluted methods, was in a room deep underneath the Abbey Mills pumping station. The rumbling of the giant steam engines made the green tiles vibrate on the floor, and the tiny room seemed even smaller. The room smelled of mildew, and Soames pursed his lips at the rankness. And was that a rat peering down at them from the cobwebbed rafters? He shuddered.

The sooner he'd finished his business with the Neanderthal woman, the better.

'You know that I have been of service in the past,' he said to her. She showed no sign of discomfort, but the chairs were meant for such as she. 'And that I have dealt fairly with you.'

The Neanderthal woman had her elbows on her knees. She wore peculiar canvas overalls that had pockets and loops right down each leg. She grunted. 'Means nothing. If you deal false with us ...'

She bared her teeth at him. When she snapped them together, twice, hard, Soames swallowed at the narrow joy in her eyes, as if she couldn't wait to lunch upon him if he crossed her.

'Perish the thought.' He spread his hands quickly. 'Trust, that's the ticket. I'm glad we understand each other, Damona. You desire certain items. I procure them for you.'

'At a price.'

'Of course.' Soames coughed into a fist. 'This time, I have some information, something that might be of interest to you.'

Damona grunted again, but the way she looked at him made Soames uneasy. He eyed the distance between them and cursed himself for having been manoeuvred so the Neanderthal woman was sitting between him and the door. He had his trusty Bulldog, but he had doubts about how effective it would be on the massive woman.

He'd seen Neanderthals shot before. A single bullet often made them angry, and it took a number of rounds from a significantly larger calibre firearm than the Bulldog to inconvenience them.

Soames wanted to pat his forehead dry but knew it was a poor move in a negotiation. 'With respect – and please do not become agitated – I understand that you have some antipathy for the group known as the Immortals.'

Damona stiffened. Her eyes narrowed. 'You heard this? Where?'

'You know what they say about the Demimonde, madam. No-one has any secrets.'

'Go on.'

'I understand how independent your people are,' Soames paused, then rolled out the lie he'd prepared, 'but what if you knew that the Immortals were interested in moving on you?'

'What?'

'Information has come into my possession to indicate that the Immortals are keen to possess some of your machines.'

Damona put her fists together, one on top of the other. Massive fists. Soames wasn't heartened to see the scabs on the knuckles. 'Of course,' she said softly.

Soames was relieved. Paranoia was useful in others, especially when it could be manipulated. The Immortals had indicated no such thing, but the Neanderthal was more than willing to believe it. 'Quite interested in machines, the Immortals are. They've brought a number of interesting devices back from India. Manipulators, they call them, blending magic and mechanics.' He chuckled. 'They say they can change matter, move things about without any visible means, even propel people through time.'

'Hah?' Damona put a hand to her mouth and rubbed it while frowning furiously. 'Time?'

Jabez, you are a master! He'd planted multiple hooks, and now it was time to reel in his prize. 'As a trusted customer,' he said, 'I didn't like to consider your people being wiped out.'

'Wiped out?'

'This is what the Immortals are planning, in order to put their hands on your machines. Or so I understand.'

Damona stood. For a heartbeat, Soames thought she was going to advance on him and his hand went to his pocket. His Bulldog might be useless, but he was prepared to give it a chance to bite.

The Neanderthal, however, stalked to the door before turning. 'Where are they?'

'The Immortals? Currently?' The lie came easily to his lips. 'I don't know.'

'You can find out?'

'I can.'

'Price?'

This was the nub of the nub of the negotiation. 'I'd like to suggest an arrangement. If I can facilitate your – how shall we put it? – *access* to the Immortals, I want to take possession of the real estate where we find them.'

'You have it.'

She slammed the door behind her.

Soames mopped his brow with a handkerchief, allowed himself a small level of satisfaction as he ticked one item from his list, and grinned up at the rat in the rafters.

116

∽ SIXTEEN ∽

Anger mounted inside Damona like steam in a boiler. She seethed. She climbed the shaft that connected the pumping station to a disused railway spur. The Immortals wanted the creations of the True People! She cursed. It echoed from the bricks.

She should have asked Soames for more details. What exactly were the Immortals after? Was it the phlogiston extractor? Or was it the air interchange mechanism?

She punched the wall of the shaft. She was so angry she could hardly walk straight.

She stopped. Her jaw sagged. Could they be after the time machine?

No! Her fury redoubled. She had trouble breathing. She steadied herself against the side of the tunnel. It was cool under her cheek. Soothing.

Soames. Loathsome, cunning but necessary Soames.

She would rather tear him to pieces but he had his uses. Perhaps in the future his usefulness would diminish. Then she would see how he'd taste.

Rolf and Magnus were waiting for her. They stood at a collapsed archway. 'Your armoury is well stocked?' she asked.

Magnus beamed. 'It's in prime shape, Eldest.'

'How many of your kin can you assemble for a raid?'

'A raid?' Rolf gaped. 'We haven't raided for years!'

'Two dozen, immediately.' Magnus nudged his brother in the ribs. 'Twice that by the end of the day.'

'Bring them all to my workshop. And any others you can find.'

'We shall, Eldest.' Magnus paused. 'Who are we raiding?'

'Leave that to me.' Damona swung around. 'Go.'

Magnus lit two lanterns. He handed one to Damona. Then Rolf and he hurried off. They leaped over rubble from the ceiling of the tunnel, joy in every bound.

Damona trudged after them.

True People had once been great raiders. Raids were now few. With their dwindling numbers, the Assembly had voted that raiding was dangerous and needless. Damona had agreed but it hurt. Even when they were so few, what of the warrior spirit? What of their martial skills?

Battle was one of the few times the True People worked well together. A raid might let them know the value of such cooperation. It could help in the project to come.

Damona spat on the floor of the tunnel. The True People today were passive. Lost. Drowning in gloom. She would right this. She would restore their spirit.

Damona climbed a rough stairway. Ruins of an ancient Roman temple. Damona liked the idea of the Romans. She liked their engineering, their building. She also liked Invaders invading Invaders. Any harm they could do to each other was good.

Her grand plan needed warriors. A raid now would help her select a team. Many young people were engineering in the workshop, but not all. Raiding would occupy the others.

Her plan would work. A time machine could be built. Her people were capable. The only uncertainty was the timing. How far back should they go? When did the True People and the Invaders diverge from the common ancestor? A mistake could wipe out the True People as well as their hated foe. Determine the right time. When the numbers of Invaders would be small. Crushing them would be easy. The True People would dominate.

Damona was close to finding the answer. Dr Malcolm Ward was stubborn but he would crack. She would have it.

Damona laughed. It was wheezy, creaky. She put a hand to her chest. If she could find Ward's son she would have the answer sooner. Much sooner.

Damona slogged through knee-deep water. Cold in the tunnel. Dark. Old. Then she lifted herself up by a rope through a hole in the ruin. Awkward. She lost some skin from an elbow. Finally she wrenched herself into a short tunnel.

It led to the workshops.

Drilling. Clamour. Smoke. Activity. True People crowded into one large space together. A sight unseen for decades. Damona was impressed. She clapped but couldn't hear it over the din.

Gustave straightened from tightening a bolt. He wiped his face with the back of his hand. He waved to her. He had grease on one sleeve of his green overalls.

The east wall was gone. The space was three times what it had been. No signs of hastiness in the work. The pillars that supported the ceiling were solid, patterned, as if they'd been there forever.

Three separate work areas. The gantry crane had been extended, covering all of them. Cables snaked in and around the girders. Large machines were taking shape in each of the work bays. Each had a dozen or more True People swarming over them. Sparks. Haze. Steam.

Damona wandered about the giant workshop. Inspecting. She was heartened by what she saw.

The pace of construction was remarkable. A single one of her kind could build faster than three Invaders. A team of True People was an elemental force. Machines grew while she watched. Brass, steel, glass. Shaped, welded, moulded.

What made Damona even more satisfied was the demeanour of the workers. Gone was the listlessness, the gloom, the resignation. Faces beamed. Backs were slapped. Good-natured chaffing while two young women heaved at a bar of steel large enough to anchor an Invader battle-ship. Arguments, of course, over designs, functions, but not harsh, not violent.

And laughter. She hadn't heard so much laughter for years. Good spirits as the True People dedicated them-selves to reclaiming their future.

Damona passed a hand over her eyes. She wasn't going to cry. Not yet. Not until the job was done.

The remains of her unfortunate phlogiston extractor had disappeared. Damona squeezed between a half-constructed sheet metal mill and an electrical transformer. She wrinkled her nose at the smell of ozone, shook her head at the two youngsters who flailed away at the transformers with hammers.

'Eldest?'

Gustave approached, wiped his forehead. His beard dripped with sweat.

'The phlogiston supply?' she asked immediately.

'We have a new machine already. Over there.' He pointed at the far wall. 'Prospects are much better than the old ways, already. Your plans were good.'

Damona nodded. Her grand plan. First, build a better phlogiston extractor. The True People had four of them. Old, slow, inefficient. They produced barely enough to power their subterranean life. A time machine would need much more phlogiston than they could process.

'The time machine?'

'Much work done already. Great progress.' Gustave looked at his hands. He rubbed them together. 'Hilda has taken your plans. She's improving them.'

'Improving?'

Gustave shrugged. 'She's very good. Looks at things differently.'

Damona was pleased. She'd always thought Hilda the brightest of the youngest True People. Hilda saw things others didn't.

'She is also moving the phlogiston stockpile. The time machine will need it most.'

It made good sense, but Damona was nervous. The stockpile was the work of years. 'If she thinks it best.'

She looked around the giant workshop. Her throat tightened with emotion. Her dying people weren't going to slip quietly into the darkness.

Good, she thought. *Fight. Struggle. Refuse to surrender.*

A huge burst of steam billowed across the workshop. Hoots and catcalls. Someone rang a bell that was decidedly derisory. Every single one of the workers cheered. A white-coated figure threw his hands up and then bowed. *I take responsibility for this embarrassing error*, his bow said, *and I revel in it in front of you all!*

Damona was grateful for the cloak of steam. It gave her time to compose herself.

SEVENTEEN

The next day, Kingsley was grateful, and amazed, when Evadne presented him with a new suit before they left her refuge. His stage outfit had become a sad ruin but he wondered where she had obtained his measurements. He gave up wondering when his conclusions made him blush, and instead he admired the deep charcoal wool of the suit and how it went with the lighter grey of the waistcoat and the straw boater.

'You're presentable,' she announced after standing back and subjecting him to the sort of scrutiny he imagined stock agents gave to potential steeplechasers.

'I'm glad.'

'And you remember your instructions?'

'I go to the Imperial Sports Club, ask to be seated at Mr Kipling's table, and wait for you to bring him along.'

'Excellent.'

'And remind me again why going out in public is a sensible idea for someone who is no doubt being pursued by the police for the murder of his housekeeper and the disappearance of his foster father?'

'Ah. That person, if you remember, was only glimpsed by a somewhat terrified young constable, and looked rather more fiendish than your current debonair self.'

'What about the desk sergeant at the Hyde Park police station?'

'You were only there as a young man accompanying Rudyard Kipling, the famous writer.' She brushed his shoulder with the tips of her fingers. 'Regardless, you can't stay in the Demimonde forever, not if you want to resume your stage career.'

'Finding my foster father comes first.'

'Of course, and limiting yourself to a Demimonde existence would make that more difficult.'

'True.'

'And Mr Kipling has asked to meet there.'

'Why didn't you mention that first? And how do you know?'

'I was working up to it. Myrmidon.'

'You've lost me.'

'Two answers to two questions. Mr Kipling asked to meet us at the Imperial Sports Club, and I received this message via myrmidon, which confirms that Mr Kipling knows his way around the Demimonde. He found someone who – for a goodly price, no doubt – passed his message on to Lady Aglaia, an old and very strange friend of mine, who found one of my messengers.'

'But Kipling? The Demimonde? He's so ...'

'Respectable?'

'Something like that.'

'Many respectable people move in and out of the Demimonde. It's important to them.'

'I imagine a writer might be interested in what he could find there.'

'Many a tale has begun in the Demimonde.'

'I hope he has news about my foster father.'

'I'll fetch him and we shall find out.'

'You'll fetch him? *He* requested the meeting; can't he find his own way to the club?'

'Almost certainly, but I want to observe him a little before we meet, just in case.'

'Oh. Can we trust him, you mean?'

'Precisely.'

Kingsley decided that the Olympic Committee knew what it was doing when it built the Imperial Sports Club. The club was near the elaborate confection that was the Palace of Fine Arts, an elegant domed edifice with a covered loggia on the western side of the Great White City – home to the vast Franco-British Exhibition. More importantly, the Imperial Sports Club was close to the stadium for the Olympic Games and provided a venue for the upper crust of society unused to the environs of Shepherd's Bush, so far from what they no doubt thought of as the comforts of the city.

It was a measure of the writer's influence that the porter's disdain for Kingsley's youth didn't prevent him from showing Kingsley to a seat in a drawing room. Kingsley sat and waited while the crowd in the stadium nearby cheered lustily at whatever running, jumping or throwing was happening at the moment, while those in the club continued their business in blithe unconcern.

Kingsley envied all of them for living simple lives, untroubled by bloody murder and missing foster fathers.

He put such thoughts to one side and gazed about with what he hoped was the requisite degree of surreptitiousness.

The Olympic Committee had spared nothing in order to make comfortable those whom they deemed necessary for the success of the sporting competition. The upshot was a building jammed full of drawing rooms, smoking rooms and dining rooms, all stuffed with furniture so heavy it had probably needed a team of elephants to drag it into place. The overwhelming decor was dark wood, and it had been applied with lavishness on panels, doors, fireplaces and trout stretchers. This was only leavened by a splash of marble and silver here and there, to remind one that there were things in life other than cutting down forests.

The club was designed to be a place where a chap could read a newspaper and tuck into a lamb chop or two before ambling over to watch our boys give the foreigners a thrashing.

Kingsley had come to this conclusion because he was surrounded by those doing exactly that. Men – or some strange hybrid of man and walrus – stalked about in tweeds and expensive sporting suits, muttering knowledgeably about the deficiencies of the cinder track, or the practicalities of having the racing pool in the middle of the arena. All of them, in the time he'd been sitting in a corner, had glanced at him and wondered from what far-off country he'd come, to be so unwhiskered.

This is civilisation, Kingsley thought as he tried to be inconspicuous in his corner. *A great and shining expression of it*. The suspicion between nations, the jealousies and rivalries, had been mostly put aside for this manifestation of civilisation. Kingsley decided that if this was what civilisation could do, he was in favour of it.

He also wondered if Kipling were making a point by choosing this place to meet.

A huge clock in the corner opposite, near a piano that looked as if had never been played, told him that just over an hour had passed, which meant that Evadne was half an hour late. Which obviously indicated that Evadne had abandoned him, or forgotten him, or denounced him to the police, who were no doubt surrounding the club at this very moment.

Or had she observed something dangerous about Kipling?

A crackling of newspapers swept through the room as, one by one, the walrus gentlemen lowered their reading matter in profound astonishment. A female had entered their domain! And not just a female, but a young female with snowy white skin and pink eyes!

Relieved, Kingsley stood as Evadne and Kipling approached. 'I hope they have good medical staff on the premises,' he said to Evadne, whose lips were twitching with amusement. She was wearing a pale yellow coat over a lavender dress, topped with a sharp vermilion hat that Kingsley imagined deserved the description 'dashing'. She carried something larger than a parasol and smaller than an umbrella. A parabella? An umbersol? 'You've probably inspired a few heart attacks already.'

'That, Kingsley, was most gallant.'

'I'm glad. I've always aspired to gallantry,' Kingsley said. 'Hello, Mr Kipling.'

'I'm glad you're safe.' The writer shook Kingsley's hand and studied his face intently before taking them to a trio of unoccupied chairs near a window that looked towards the stadium. 'After that business at the police station I was distressed. If it weren't for Miss Stephens's advising that we should retreat, I fear what might have happened.'

'Safe is a relative matter, sir,' Kingsley replied, 'as I'm starting to understand.'

Kipling gestured with his head. 'You should be well enough in this place. At least, for the time being.'

'That, Mr Kipling,' Evadne said, 'sounds ominous.'

'I should hope so. We've landed ourselves in some deep stuff indeed.' He looked about, casually, but Kingsley could see the observer's eye in the way the writer took in the surroundings. 'While I'm happy with ominous, I don't want to stray into the melodramatic, but I need to say that dark forces are afoot.'

'We've already encountered some,' Kingsley muttered. He told Kipling about the attack of the Spawn on Evadne's refuge.

'You have an underground retreat, my dear?' The writer reached inside his jacket pocket and began to pull out a notebook. With an effort, he pushed it back. He smiled ruefully. 'I imagine you'd prefer such a thing remain private.'

'And undiscovered by creatures belonging to the Immortals,' Evadne said. 'Which is why they were dealt with.'

Somewhat of an understatement, Kingsley thought, but he didn't draw attention to the matter. 'You have news, Mr Kipling?'

'Ah, yes, and it's about these very same Immortals.'

Kingsley saw Evadne tense. It was infinitesimal – mostly in the way she held her shoulders – but it was there. 'You wouldn't have found where they are hiding, would you?' she asked the writer.

'No, nothing as concrete as that. All I have are rumours, some stories, some theories.'

'And where do these come from?' Kingsley asked.

The writer smiled a little. 'I have my sources.'

Evadne snagged a passing steward and ordered a lemon squash. Kipling asked for one as well, while Kingsley opted for water. While they waited, their conversation drifted to the Olympic Games and the spirited nature of the competition. Civilised though it may be, Kipling chuckled at some of the friction that was becoming apparent between British and American officials.

A waitress appeared and distributed the refreshments. Kingsley glanced outside. Rain had begun to fall again.

'You understand that I met your father, years ago.'

Kingsley whipped his head around. He stared at the writer, then he hesitated. 'Dr Ward?'

'He was in India while I was there. An extraordinary man. He spent months at a time travelling about on his own, you know, not speaking to a European all that time.'

Kingsley sagged. For a moment, he'd thought Kipling was about to tell him of his real father, the man he'd never known. Dr Ward had been good to him, but Kingsley had always wondered about his real parents. Who were they? What had happened to them for him to end up nurtured by wolves?

'Do you have any news of him?' Evadne said after glancing at Kingsley.

'I'm afraid not, but the news I do have is more important.'

Kingsley straightened. 'More important than finding my foster father?'

'I understand your desire to find him,' Kipling said. 'He's a good man and an outstanding thinker, but he is only one man.'

Evadne put a hand on Kingsley's forearm and interrupted the retort that was rising to his tongue. 'Your meaning?' she asked the writer.

'In coming back to London, the Immortals have taken the first step in their age-long plan to dominate all humanity.'

Kingsley started, then settled, aided by the firm pressure of Evadne's hand on his forearm. Juggler's muscles, he supposed.

Kipling explained. 'I've been talking to some old friends who'd been in India while I was there. We combined notes and concluded that the Immortals' presence in India, appalling though their deeds were, was just a precursor, a step towards their real goal, the domination of humankind.' He smiled grimly. 'When a two-hundred-year reign of terror and the assembling of vast riches is just a small step, then we are dealing with creatures who are evil beyond reckoning.'

'Oh, yes,' Evadne breathed. 'That we are.'

'The best guess is that they have come back to England for two reasons. Firstly, they have become obsessed with the notion of mass animus.'

'Animus?' Kingsley frowned. 'Spirit?'

'It's not the soul, or anything like that. It's more an insubstantial expression of the attitudes of a person, their morals and beliefs. Massed animus is the collective expression of a group of people gathered for a purpose, be it worship, play or something more sinister.'

Kingsley thought of the way applause seemed to float above an audience, a shared manifestation of goodwill and appreciation. Was this what Kipling was talking about?

'And what do they do with this massed animus?' Evadne asked.

'They harvest it.'

'Harvest?' Kingsley grimaced. This sounded more than a little sordid.

'They collect it. How and why, though, no-one knows. The reports I have from India talk of terrible underground rituals performed by the Immortals to draw out and harvest evil animus.'

Kingsley had a moment where he smelled Kipling's trail and bounded ahead to its conclusion. 'The Olympic Games,' he said. 'That's why they're here.'

'Very good, Mr Ward,' Kipling said. 'You have it. Right here, you have 90,000 people in one place. It promises a fine harvest indeed.'

'Of what?' Evadne said. 'Of patriotism? Of enjoyment? The Games are hardly likely to produce vast amounts of evil animus, are they?'

'And to what end?' Kingsley asked, his mind sifting through possibilities that were so hideous to contemplate that he was sickened.

'As I said, here is where we draw a blank. But I'll hazard a guess that it may have a connection with the second reason these horrors have come back to London.' He turned. 'It's you, Mr Ward,' Kipling said.

'Because of my upbringing.'

'It's not only that. The Immortals believe that you can control the wild within because you are different, that you have something special about you.' Kipling paused. 'Forgive me if I'm graphic here, but before they left India, the Immortals were called the Brain Eaters.'

'Charming,' Kingsley said. Evadne said nothing.

'Their Thuggee devotees would bring offerings to the Immortals. The authorities found dozens, hundreds over the years, all with one thing in common.'

'Apart from being dead?' Evadne asked.

'Quite. Apart from being dead, all of those taken to the Immortals had had their brains removed.'

'They want my brain,' Kingsley said slowly.

'I'm afraid it's more than that. The Indian brain removal was preliminary. They were searching for something that they believe your brain has – a special region, or gland, that has given you control over the wild within. They want that gland, and they'll remove your brain to get it.'

Kingsley couldn't help it. He put a hand to the back of his head. 'I'm afraid I'm using it at the moment.'

'That won't stop them.'

'I'm unconvinced,' Evadne said. 'Kingsley has a special gland in his brain? Who'd have thought?'

Kingsley didn't know whether to be relieved or insulted. 'I suppose it doesn't matter whether I do or not, as long as the Immortals believe I do.'

'That's it in a nutshell,' Kipling said. 'It will be rather too late for you once the Immortals discover their mistake.'

'Mr Kipling,' Evadne said abruptly, 'did your inform-ants mention anything about missing children in India? While the Immortals were there?'

'Children go astray in India all the time, my dear,'

Kipling said, 'but I'm assuming you're hinting at the Immortals' horrible needs. Police records do, indeed, indicate pockets of child disappearances in the areas where the Immortals were rumoured to dwell.'

Evadne's face was cold and set. It was Kingsley's turn to steady her, and he placed his other hand on hers. She didn't respond.

'So the Olympic Games are being jeopardised by a band of evil sorcerers who want my brain,' Kingsley said, 'while I try to find my foster father who may have been abducted by creatures from the dawn of time.'

Evadne had withdrawn her hand from Kingsley's and was now twisting the silver ring on her finger. 'Have you discovered anything else, Mr Kipling?'

'One last item: I think I know where the Immortals have hidden themselves.'

Evadne stiffened, all movement ceasing. 'Oh?'

'They appear to have re-occupied one of their old haunts,' Kipling said. 'This one is under Greenwich.'

Evadne nodded sharply, once. She turned the ring on her finger completely around, then nodded again to herself. Kingsley could see that she had make up her mind. About what, though, he wasn't sure.

'You must have connections, Mr Kipling. Can you help?' she said finally.

The writer blinked. 'I hoped that I had been, Miss Stephens, but what were you thinking of?'

'You have a position in the mundane world. You could speak to the authorities about Kingsley's situation. Let them know that Kingsley couldn't have done anything to his housekeeper since he was on stage in Aldershot at the time, that sort of thing.'

'Of course. I have a few friends at Scotland Yard. I'm sure I can count on them.'

'Would you be able to take up my foster father's case with them?' Kingsley added. 'Just in case his disappearance is more ... mundane than it appears.'

'I can do all that.' Kipling scribbled a few notes in his notebook. He signed to the waiter, who appeared with Kipling's homburg and umbrella. Kipling stood, took his homburg in one hand and his umbrella in the other. He carried it by the tip instead of the handle, as if he had unusual uses in mind for it. He bowed slightly. 'Miss Stephens. Mr Ward.' He went to go, but paused and addressed Kingsley. 'Mr Ward. My boy. When I last saw you I said how amazed I was to encounter someone who stepped directly from a story of mine. I realise now that this was most presumptuous of me. You are your own person, not someone dreamed up by a fellow whose primary talent lies in imagining.'

Kingsley stood. 'Please, Mr Kipling –'

'No, my boy, let me finish.' The writer took a deep breath. 'When imagining, a fellow can become carried away, immersed in what he has created. When I saw you, and once I became convinced of your origin, I'm afraid I went that way, oblivious to your pain.' He looked about and essayed a smile. 'Now, instead of your stepping out of one of my stories, I feel as if I've stepped *into* one. It serves me right.' He brightened. 'Let me help you, Mr Ward, not because I'm fascinated by my own creation coming to life, but because it's the right thing to do.'

Kingsley reached out and took the writer's hand. They shook. Kipling left, briskly, and disappeared through the glass doors.

'I think we can trust him,' Evadne said before Kingsley could say anything. 'Lady Aglaia says he has a reputation in the Demimonde as a good man.'

'Lady Aglaia?'

'My friend, who gave Kipling's note to my myrmidon. She added a letter of her own. Chatty, it was, but she did include her opinion of Kipling.'

'I'm glad,' Kingsley said. 'And what do we do while we're waiting for him?'

'We don't wait.' Evadne took off her spectacles. Kingsley had imagined that without them she would peer about, blinking, like a night creature in strong light, but her unearthly eyes were steady as she cleaned her spectacles on a cloth she extracted from her belt. 'We do something.'

EIGHTEEN

After leaving the Imperial Sports Club, Evadne took Kingsley's arm and steered them through the crowds with the determination of a naval destroyer. She swept them through the Central Circle and along the Algerian Avenue, emerging through the Wood Lane entrance. Queues of people waiting to get into the Exhibition, in orderly British fashion, stretched up the road. The stands of the stadium loomed not far to the south and cheers cascaded over the lip. Flags flew gaily, reminding everyone that this part of the site was truly international.

They passed the stadium and Evadne took them to a lamp post where a young girl was standing, absorbed in a toffee apple. 'Look up at the stadium,' Evadne told Kingsley. She mimicked him, shading her eyes, but spoke to the girl on the other side of the lamp post. 'All's well, Meg?'

Meg wore a white sundress and a straw hat. Her black hair hung in a neat braid. She didn't look at Evadne, but answered in a murmur around her toffee apple. 'Just that man, ma'am.' She inclined her head the merest fraction of an inch, but left no doubt who she was indicating.

A small man stood a stone's throw away. He too, was looking up at the stadium and the flags flying against the scudding clouds.

'He's been there all morning,' Meg murmured.

'Demimonder?'

Meg tilted her head in assent, another fractional gesture.

Kingsley coughed, and used this to cover a furtive study of the man in question. He was nondescript. As medium a height as medium could be. Clean, unremarkable coat and hat. A face that held not a single noteworthy feature. Kingsley looked away and immediately had trouble remembering what the man looked like.

'He hasn't done anything?' Evadne asked, looking sidelong at this phenomenon.

'Just waiting, he is.'

Evadne shook her head. 'I don't like this.'

'Do you want me to accost him?' Kingsley offered. Never having accosted anyone before, he wasn't entirely sure how accosting was done, but he was sure he could give it a decent shot.

'No. Meg, do you think you could make a scene right next to him?'

Meg gave a twitch of a smile. Kingsley decided she could grow up to be a very fine cards player. 'Easy, ma'am.'

Evadne spun a half sovereign in her hand, then slipped

it to the young girl. Meg didn't acknowledge this. She simply closed her fist on the coin and skipped away.

Kingsley watched her go, and saw the wistfulness with which Evadne followed the child's bobbing straw hat. 'Who was that?'

'Meg's someone I look out for.'

'Another project?'

'Meg is ten years old, and has been an orphan for five of them. She lives at Mrs Oldham's Home for Girls, which I sponsor. She, and a few others, do odd jobs for me.' Evadne touched her cheek, briefly, then pushed back her hair. 'She's a good girl. Now, be ready.'

Kingsley was abashed. 'What for?'

'Watch.'

Just in front of the extraordinarily unexceptional man, Meg tripped. She tumbled and when she came up holding her knee, right in front of him, she shrieked as if she'd been shot several times with an elephant gun.

Within seconds, the girl and the startled man were enveloped by a knot of onlookers, well-meaners and self-appointed experts. This attracted more attention and the entire flow of Wood Lane turned in the direction of the hullabaloo.

'Right,' Evadne said. 'Now hurry.'

Evadne dragged Kingsley to the other side of the road. She leaned against the fence and put a hand to her brow. 'Look at me as if you're concerned, as if I'm having a spell or something.'

'How's this?' Kingsley drew close. He screwed up his brow and peered into her face, doing his best not to become befuddled by gardenia.

'Laughable, but it will have to do.'

Evadne reached into her pocket and, still leaning against the fence, fiddled away behind her back. 'Now, look up and down the road, as if you're after help.'

He did, putting his heart into the thespian efforts, but was taken by surprise when he was tugged backward. He whipped around, but couldn't stop himself falling into Evadne's arms.

She kicked the door closed from the other side. The fence was whole again and she held him at arm's length. 'Comfortable?'

'Sublimely.'

'Don't be.'

Evadne released her grip, but Kingsley was ready this time and managed to catch himself before he went sprawling.

Around them and over their heads, the struts and girders supporting the stands sliced the dim light into criss-cross pieces. Evadne confidently picked her way through the metal jungle, moving east until she found a small windowless shed made of corrugated iron. It sported a strident warning sign, promising certain death due to the untold voltages unleashed within. Naturally, Evadne ignored this and after a moment's work had the door open. A bolted steel door set into the concrete floor led to a short, dark tunnel that took them to a heavy grate, after which a short crawl brought them to a rubble-filled dead end.

Evadne produced another of the pen-like electric lights and studied the rubble. 'No-one has made it this far. Good.'

'How can you tell?'

'Myrmidon.' She pointed. Up in the shadows was

a ratty shape that made Kingsley jump. 'It wouldn't be calmly sitting there if this entrance to my refuge had been discovered.'

'A watch-rat, so to speak.'

'Kingsley, at this rate, you'll soon be auditioning as a comedian.'

She handed Kingsley the tiny electric light and rummaged in the fist-sized lumps of concrete and brick until one of them gave a most unrubble-like 'click'.

The rubble plug swung back. Evadne crawled through, waited for Kingsley, then pushed the camouflaged door closed behind them.

The only illumination came from the electric light Kingsley had in his hand. He held it up, but the shadows defeated its modest output. The sound the closing door had made told him that the space was large and so it proved when lights sprang up and he found himself in the antechamber that preceded Evadne's underground refuge. A series of doors – with excellent locks – and they were inside.

'Now,' Evadne said. 'Rest. You'll be safe here. I should be back directly.'

'Back? Where are you going?'

'I have some errands to run.'

'I'll come with you.'

'I'd rather not. This errand is of a personal nature, and I'm still not sure how much to trust you.'

Ah, trust. 'I suppose that's up to you, but I do my best to be trustworthy.'

She smiled at him and he felt as if he'd been poked in the stomach by a torpedo. 'I'm sure you do. Your upright character is one of your more endearing features, but it does tend to suggest you don't quite fit into the Demimonde.'

'I don't fit in?'

'The natural denizens of the Demimonde have a certain moral slipperiness about them. They're at ease with accommodating values that might, at first, appear contradictory. They can hold several different points of view in their head at the same time without any discomfort at all.'

'I know all about having different points of view, but I'm not so sure about the discomfort,' he admitted.

'This suggests you'd stand out in the Demimonde. You'd either be easy pickings for those looking for you or you'd be seduced by its blandishments.'

'I say.'

'I've seen many well-intentioned overworlders charmed by the Demimonde, becoming so tainted that there was no way back.'

'I could always put wax in my ears.'

'Like Odysseus? What about your eyes? And up your nose? You'd be a pretty sight.'

'And what about you? Are you tainted by the Demimonde?'

She gave a nonchalant flip of her hand. 'I glide through that world unaffected, serene in my sense of self.' She narrowed her eyes. 'Either that, or I've hardened myself to its temptations.'

'With the thought of Clarence to guide you, no doubt.'

'Who?'

'Clarence. Your beau.'

Her hand went to her throat. 'Clarence. Of course.

He's impervious to the goings-on in the Demimonde. Adamant of will, is he.'

'A model to us all. You know, I'd like to meet Clarence. I'm sure I could learn a thing or two from such a sterling chap.'

'He's a fine teacher, patient and wise, but I understand he's a little busy at the moment.'

Kingsley shook his head. 'Don't leave me here alone. I'd prefer to risk the Demimonde, really.'

'You wouldn't be alone. My myrmidons are here.'

'As much as I like rats, I'd rather be with you.'

'You're too kind.'

'With you by my side, I'm sure I'll be able to resist the call of the Demimonde.'

'Quite possibly.' She bit her lip, looked away, then faced him. 'I know I said that I'd help you find your foster father, but I have something I must do first. Perhaps you'd like to help me with it?'

Kingsley felt the same way he did at the crucial point in a magical routine. Choices. Many could lead to disaster, a few could lead to a winning outcome. He desperately needed to get back on the trail to find his foster father. The longer he left it, the colder it would become. But having the help of someone familiar with the outlandish world he'd fallen into would be necessary. He sighed. 'I'd be glad to be of any assistance. What is it?'

'I need to kill a band of immortal magicians.'

∽ NINETEEN ∾

While Kingsley wrestled with astonishment he followed Evadne straight to the largest steel cabinet in her workshop. It was vast and the no-nonsense grey colour favoured by the military when it wanted to be serious.

'Now,' she said. 'Before we confront these Immortals, we must prepare.' She looked gravely at Kingsley. 'I always prepare, don't you?'

'Of course. Preparation is the key to success – but wait a moment.'

Evadne flung open the cabinet doors with a crash and stood in front of them with her hands on her hips. 'Yes?'

'You want to kill these Immortals.'

'That's right.'

'The undying, evil, powerful, magical, vastly rich sorcerers?'

Evadne bit her lip. 'Kingsley, just come out and say it

143

if you don't want to go. You can stay here. I think I have the remains of a seed cake in the cupboard.'

'It's not that. I just think you're being a little precipitous.'

'Precipitous? This isn't precipitous. Yesterday was precipitous.'

'The Spawn in the sewers?'

'My temper had the better of me.' She closed her eyes briefly. 'Kingsley, I'm doing my best to approach this calmly, because the alternative is launching myself at those horrors in a mad rage, despite the danger.'

'Your crusade is that important.'

'Important? At times, it's overwhelming.' She bit her lip before continuing. 'I've known about these Immortals for a long time, Kingsley. Going up against them isn't a lark. They're murderous, deadly, and very, very powerful.'

Kingsley knew that Evadne was spelling out the peril for him. 'And yet you're determined to confront them.'

'I have no choice.'

Evadne turned back to the cabinet, leaving Kingsley in a welter of confusion. He wanted to find his foster father, but with events conspiring as they had, he knew he needed help. In addition, there was Kipling and his hints about the Immortals and their plans – unspecified, but assumed to be of dreadful import – concerning the Olympic Games. And here in front of him was an undoubtedly troubled Evadne, setting off to confront these selfsame wizards.

When trapped in the dark, manacled in a chest with water pouring in, Kingsley knew that the best thing to do was to decide on a single course of action and to stick to it. Trying to do a number of things at once was the way to a disastrous end. Here, his course was clear. He had to help Evadne, and by helping her he'd gain an important ally in the search for his foster father.

'What's in the cabinet?' he asked.

'Necessary equipment.'

She stood aside, and Kingsley had his first real look at what the cabinet contained.

The objects he was looking at must be weapons, for nothing else in the universe had that combination of elegance of design and utter deadliness in a neat, manageable package. Death-dealing in one hand. Or two, as he took in some of the larger devices.

Someone had taken the basic components of metal, wood and a smooth black substance like jet and constructed a few dozen weapons that glittered and smelled of oil and destruction.

'You've had firearms training?' Evadne selected a long-armed number that had more glass than Kingsley was accustomed to in a rifle. It also sported various knobs, chambers and levers that should have made it look ridiculous but instead made it look as if it could annihilate regiments once it warmed up.

'Some.' Kingsley fancied himself as a marksman and had once been a member of the school's Rifle Brigade, but he'd always preferred target shooting rather than the prospect of hunting.

'Good.' Evadne slid open what Kingsley assumed was the breech and inspected it. 'At least you'll know which end to point where. After that, you shouldn't have to worry.'

Kingsley reached for one weapon that was mostly brass, including a skeleton-like stock.

'Not Neptune's Trident,' Evadne said. 'It's for underwater use, and I don't anticipate we'll need it where we're going.'

'Neptune's Trident?' Kingsley blinked. 'Do you have anything rather less ... outlandish?'

Evadne shrugged. 'I didn't think I was being outlandish when I made them. I was just having some wicked fun.'

Kingsley had become well acquainted with astonishment in the last few days, so he recognised it when it jumped up and hit him between the eyes. 'You made these?' He surveyed the wreakers of mayhem in front of him. 'I thought you must have bought them from one of your Demimonde people. I was imagining a secret tribe of weaponsmiths, Brotherhood of Vulcan or the Hammerhead Boys or suchlike.'

'Oh, I had some help with some of the components, and there are some remarkably fine engineers in the Demimonde, but they're all my own design. They're all bespoke, you see.'

'Mmm.'

'I do hope you're not still judging by appearances.'

'Me? I'm more than happy to believe that what lies underneath the surface is important.'

'Good. I just happen to be excellent at engineering design as well as juggling.'

'Naturally. Of course. Makes perfect sense.' Kingsley ran his hand over the compact shape of what could be a handgun, if handguns were the shape of a seashell and as lethal as a cobra. 'These are works of art. What about this one?'

'Midnight's Kiss? That's fine. Just be careful of that button.'

'Which button?'

'That button. The one you just triggered and made the spike punch through the top of the cabinet.'

Kingsley saw no point in denying it, since the evidence was clear. 'That cabinet needed an airhole, anyway.'

Gingerly, he touched the button – just next to the safety – and the six-inch blade slid back into a neatly concealed slot. He hefted the pistol – which was really more of an elongated disc than a shell shape – and was impressed at how light it was. He hoped it would be enough to combat immortal sorcerers and their underlings. 'Do you have names for all of your weapons?'

'It's part of the fun.'

Evadne was once more entirely blithe, as if preparing for a Sunday picnic rather than a mission of mayhem, but Kingsley was concerned at the brittleness of her guise. 'What about ammunition?' he asked.

'For that one? Over there, fourth drawer, second from the left. The magazines are already loaded.'

Kingsley found the ammunition cabinet as Evadne had said. The smell of gun oil was heavy, and each of the many drawers was neatly labelled with numbers that were ominous in their anonymity.

He paused. 'You do seem to have expended much ingenuity on devices of destruction.'

'My weapons?' She gazed around. 'I suppose so. In the Demimonde, though, prominent means of self-defence are always useful.'

'Self-defence? All this is for self-defence?'

She shrugged. 'I became carried away.'

He didn't know what to make of Evadne. A juggler, a

wit and a genius? Any two would be overwhelming, and he had the feeling that three wasn't the end of it.

He found the correct drawer. The magazine was the size of an omnibus ticket, but heavy. He wasn't surprised when it slotted perfectly into the pistol. Half a dozen others were in the drawer, and he took them all.

'Don't forget to select a knife.' Evadne pointed at another cabinet, to the right of the ammunition store. 'Knives don't run out of ammunition.'

'You make knives, too?'

'Those, I buy. I know my limitations.'

You might, Kingsley thought, *but I certainly haven't found them yet.*

Evadne crossed the room and tapped at the bare wall. A door swung back to reveal a safe.

The safe was waist high and looked as if it had been designed to discourage burglars simply by its looks. *'Don't waste your time,'* the solid metal bulk seemed to say. *'I am impervious,'* its dull grey colour announced. *'Why bother?'* the many dials and knobs on the front insisted.

After a complicated series of twistings and turnings, the safe swung open. Evadne found what she was after and heaved it shut with a neat hip swivel that did alarming things to Kingsley. He looked away and concentrated on his knife selection. Far less dangerous.

Evadne came to his side. Her presence was, he admitted, agreeable. 'Take the one on the end.'

'The one on the end? They don't have names?'

'I only name that which I make.'

Kingsley was about to follow this intriguing delineation when a horde of small furry shapes shot through the open door and raced directly at Evadne.

148

He had his knife in hand before he saw that there were only six of the creatures – enough for a horde, in his mind – and that they were Evadne's myrmidons.

He relaxed and tucked his new knife away.

'I was wondering what was taking you so long,' Evadne said to her minions. They swarmed about her feet, some rising on their back legs in the ecstasy of seeing her. She crouched and patted them, distributing her affection evenly.

This time, Kingsley made an effort to study them, even though something deep inside him wanted to pick them up by the scruff of their necks and give them a short, sharp shake.

Each was the size of a cat, but after that they did conform to his notion of a rat, apart from half of them having three eyes. They had the snout, the scaly tail, the brown fur that suggested they were, indeed, descendants of those who were the Black Death's best friends.

'They're half-machine and half-animal,' Evadne explained. 'They're my first experiment with this sort of hybrid. It's a very difficult area.'

'So I'd imagine.'

'Not just technically, although it's a nightmare to mesh the biological parts with the non-biological. I meant that it's difficult ethically. These creatures are stronger, quicker, more intelligent than they were, but I'm still not sure whether I have the right to do what I have.'

'I'm impressed that you're troubled.'

'What do you mean?'

'I imagine inventing types lost in the enthusiasm of projects, not giving a fig for questions like this. I'm happier with someone who's thoughtful.'

Before she turned her head away, Kingsley was sure she blushed. It was only a soft pinkening of her cheeks, but he was certain he'd seen it.

'Kingsley, would you please fetch me some of the excursion biscuits? They love them. They're in the Huntley & Palmers tin.'

When Kingsley came back with the tin, the myrmidons had gone. 'Where are they?'

Evadne spread her hands. 'They were so eager to be off on their mission, they wouldn't even wait for a biscuit.'

'They have a mission?'

'Among other things, I've sent them looking for any signs of those inimical to the Immortals. The League of the Righteous. The Supplicants. The Aaconites. No-one has heard of them for years, but my myrmidons are persistent.' Evadne opened the tin and took out a biscuit. 'Almond ring. My favourite.'

Kingsley was dazed. Try as he might, he found it hard to keep up with Evadne. It wasn't an unpleasant sensation; he found himself wanting to rise to the challenge that she was. 'One thing that puzzles me . . .'

'Only one? What a happy state you must live in.'

'One thing will do for the moment: what on earth are you doing in the theatre?'

Evadne looked at him solemnly for a moment, then she re-racked her weapon of choice – a pistol that looked mostly to be made of crystal. She reached into a pocket of her riding jacket and produced a handful of brass cylinders – shells, of a sort, but where the bullet looked nothing like lead. Kingsley wondered if they were some sort of incendiary rounds, but at that moment, Evadne began to juggle.

Slowly at first, two, then three of the brass cylinders glittered, arcing from one hand to the other. They were joined by one more, then another. 'I enjoy the theatre,' she said.

Kingsley applauded, helplessly. He admired dexterity and when it was allied with grace, it was doubly impressive. 'You're excellent,' he said, 'but that's not what I mean. I understand the thrill of performance, the challenge of entertaining people, but when you have this –' he swept an arm around the cabinet-filled room – 'why wouldn't you devote yourself to inventing?'

She made a face and with three quick motions the shells disappeared back into her pocket. 'A question for a question. How many female inventors do you know of?'

'I don't know of many inventors,' he admitted.

'Scientists, then. Or engineers. What about your foster father's colleagues? How many women academics are there?

'Ah. I see.'

'And that's not to mention the opprobrium from my family.'

'Are you saying they'd rather have you on the stage than working in science?'

'I don't know. When it was clear that they wouldn't favour either, I left them to their own devices.'

'You ran away from home.'

'That makes it sound rather more rapid than it was. I walked away from home, head held high, with a thousand plans in my head and Montague Dobbs waiting for me.'

'Montague Dobbs. What about Clarence?'

Evadne touched the chain around her neck. 'Clarence never knew about Montague Dobbs.'

'I expect he wouldn't,' Kingsley said. Why hadn't Evadne spoken of this Dobbs fellow before? 'Well,' he said with an effort at briskness. 'I'll need some sort of rucksack, if we're to equip ourselves properly. And rope. Do you have any rope?'

Evadne laughed, but indicated a cabinet near the door. 'Rope is in that one. You'll find a selection of rucksacks in the drawers underneath.'

'Thank you.'

'Your face has the virtue of being wonderfully open,' Evadne said. 'Mostly.'

'And where is this Dabbs fellow?' Kingsley busied himself in choosing an appropriate coil of rope. Jute or manila? 'Why isn't he here to help you on this expedition?'

'Dobbs, not Dabbs.' Evadne stifled another laugh. 'He's not here because he's not real. I made him up, years ago.'

'I beg your pardon?'

Evadne had a hand over her mouth, but her eyes danced. 'Montague Dobbs is the holder of a number of lucrative patents and the owner of several companies. Since minors can't hold patents, sign contracts or generally do business, I needed someone who could.'

'What about your father?'

'Oh no, I couldn't let him know about my doings. I'd disappoint him dreadfully. He wants me to be dutiful.' She closed the gun cabinet. 'I invented Montague Dobbs. Quite a wealthy man, is Dobbs, but he's rather a recluse.'

'You can't just invent someone out of thin air. A company director must have meetings, needs to talk to bank managers.'

'I have an actor to do that. A discreet fellow. And he'll continue to be discreet if he wants the generous fees I pay him.' She opened another cabinet and paused in front of a collection of swords. 'Most of my business is conducted through the post. His Majesty's Postal Service is rather more reliable than even the best of actors equipped with the most superb of scripts.' She selected one of the blades. 'I do love a sabre, don't you?'

'I'm astounded.'

'I can tell.'

'So you paid for all of this through your patents?'

'I've licensed – sorry, Montague Dobbs has licensed – a number of patents useful in the optical industry.' She belted on her sabre then tapped her spectacles. 'I've also allowed them to be used in astronomical research.'

'You're rich.'

She rolled her eyes. 'Rich enough. The financial speculation helped.'

'Naturally,' Kingsley said desperately.

'Bonds, consols, that sort of thing. I'd rather have my money working for me than not. Daddy is enormously wealthy, but I wouldn't touch anything of his. After some lean times, I'm now wealthy enough to do what I want.'

'Which is to invent things and to go on the stage.'

'I couldn't have a retreat like this if I didn't invent things.'

'Of course not. It must have cost the earth.'

'It wasn't cheap.' She made a few ghostly juggling motions with both hands. 'Everything here is powered by a revolutionary source.' Small dimples creased the corners of her mouth. 'It's called phlogiston.'

153

'Oh, phlogiston.'

'You've never heard of it, have you?'

'Not in this context, no.'

'In what context have you heard of it?'

'None, really. I was just trying to give myself some time to cudgel the old brain to come up with something.'

She eyed him with cool amusement. 'Phlogiston was thought to be the vital part that materials released when burning, which explains why something burnt couldn't be reburned. And don't say "but". This was early chemistry, remember, and really has nothing to do with what we call phlogiston, which is a magical fluid that can be extracted from air.'

'Magic.'

'We're in the Demimonde, remember? Some magic works. Some of the time.' She wrinkled her brow. 'Phlogiston is tied up with the Immortals, strange to say. Neo–Platonism anyway. They say that phlogiston is the exhalation of the Earth. It's the outpouring of the supernatural entity of which our planet is only a physical manifestation.'

Kingsley looked at her blankly. 'That makes no sense.'

'It makes perfect sense, just not a sense that you're accustomed to.'

'So you use phlogiston to power this place?'

'I invented a neat little phlogiston extractor, much better than the stuff I could buy out there. It's hideously expensive, which is my point.'

'I'm sure.'

'Did I mention that it's also highly explosive?'

'No, but I have no trouble accepting it.'

'Wait here.'

Evadne went to her safe again. She returned holding a glass vial, the size of a finger and glowing red. She was smiling. 'Phlogiston.' Then she pulled another vial from the pocket of her robe with a flourish. 'More phlogiston.' Then she leaned over and, with a capable piece of sleight of hand, pulled another vial from Kingsley's ear. 'And more phlogiston.'

With another smile, a different one this time, rather more professional, Kingsley decided, she began to juggle them.

She began slowly, sending all three vials in an easy loop, then she began tossing them higher, plucking them out of the air, passing them behind her back, showering and cascading them, faster and faster until the glow was a blur.

Kingsley was impressed and alarmed. He hesitated, not wanting to break her concentration, but he had to ask: 'Didn't you say this stuff was explosive?'

'It's safe in the right hands, which mine are.'

With a toss of her head, Evadne launched all three skywards. She caught the first in her pocket, the second behind her back and the third fell perfectly into her upraised palm without her looking at it.

Her eyes were bright and she was breathing fast. She held up a finger, asking for a moment, then she answered. 'Under the right circumstances, it's highly explosive, which means with a correct detonator and such. With the right preparation, a hundred different effects can be achieved, thanks to phlogiston's remarkable qualities.'

'What happens if you drop one? The glass would break and then what?'

From the look on her face, Kingsley immediately regretted the fact that words didn't have strings tied to them so he could have tugged back the questions he'd just asked.

'Firstly,' she said, 'I don't drop things when I juggle. Secondly, these aren't simply glass. They're embedded with phlogiston itself for extra strength.'

'I've never seen a better juggler.'

She curtseyed. 'I thank you.'

'Remarkable stuff, that phlogiston.'

She leaned close in her enthusiasm and Kingsley could appreciate how fine her eyelashes were, as if they were extracted from the breath of snow. 'It's what I used to collapse those tunnels, the ones the Spawn were using to get to us, to make sure we are safe here.'

'Versatile stuff.'

'Even more exciting, I'm working with anti-phlogiston.'

'And why would you do that?'

'Apart from pure scientific rascality? It's exciting, that's why! Something that is equal and opposite to phlogiston must have enormous potential. Apart being extremely antagonistic to phlogiston, which is rather too obvious to be interesting.'

'So that's science. What about the theatre?'

She narrowed her eyes at the sudden change of topic, but replied. 'I love the theatre, but, to tell the truth, it serves another purpose.'

'I'm surprised. Everything else has been so straight-forward.'

'Another bon mot. You're rising to the occasion, Kingsley and I'm glad. I thought you might be becoming Byronic, swanning about all gloomy and handsome.'

'I tried being Byronic once, but it gave me a headache.' Kingsley was trapped inside a whirlwind, but he was determined to keep up. 'You were telling me how the theatre had a double purpose for you.'

'Most of those who exploit children end up in the Demimonde, so I needed access to it. The theatre was my entry.' She made an odd gesture then, putting both hands side by side, palms up, then bringing them together – as if she were closing a book.

Kingsley decided that it was clearly the end of the matter.

'This mission,' he said. 'Are you sure you're doing the right thing?

'Sure?' Evadne's lightness of mood fell away. 'Hardly. I'd love to live a life of certainty, but it's not for me. I live a life of maybes, perhapses and howevers. Nothing is certain.'

'Which gives room for hope.'

She touched his cheek. 'Now that, Kingsley, is just what I needed to hear.'

~ TWENTY ~

Kingsley felt exposed. He reminded himself again that this was part of the plan – he had to be visible. Attract attention at the Floating Market, and then track any Spawn back to the Immortals' hiding place. Simple, straightforward and with a touch of terror to make things even better.

As Evadne had explained it, the Floating Market floated in more ways than one. Its physical location changed, sometimes when authorities from the overworld roused themselves enough to do something about the state of repair in parts of their sewer network and other times when one of the bouts of periodic hostility erupted into outright warfare between the shadowy groups in the Demimonde. And physically, it was composed of ramshackle rafts adrift in the huge confluence of five lost sewer mains, a veritable lake, if only a few feet deep.

Evadne had found it without too much trouble this time, near Camden, as rumoured. Once night fell, they'd taken a roundabout route to get there, above and below ground. Every step of the way Kingsley felt eyes on his back. Evadne, as usual, was sure-footed in the dim light but he had to struggle and trust to her lead, something that frustrated him enormously. His frustration was only partly mollified by the time-honoured method of jamming his fists into the pockets of his jacket, something he gave up quickly when he nearly pitched on his nose after a misstep, due to not having a restraining hand ready to fling out.

Evadne had spun at that, her leather coat swinging about her litheness, the bright blue scarf a highlight at her throat. She'd laughed, not unkindly, and helped him up with such pragmatism that he couldn't object. Besides, the scent she wore was infinitely preferable to the stink of the tunnel his face had become acquainted with.

While they went, water dripping from the rotting brickwork above roused in Kingsley a dim memory and a pang of nostalgia, as if he were in the jungle where rain often continued to fall long after clouds had passed. It called to him.

In deference to its location, the Floating Market didn't deal with foodstuffs but otherwise the range of merchandise was eye-popping. After skipping across the freshly laid stepping stones on the south-east approach, Kingsley did as planned and made himself conspicuous. He moved from raft to raft and inspected the stalls, questioning store holders about the provenance of Renaissance artworks, arguing with the makers of weapons that were chained to tables, and simply wondering at the exact nature of objects that could be mere decoration or could be some sort of machine for lifting walls. Stalls abounded with items purporting to be magical and the matter-of-fact way they were presented and spruiked did more to dent Kingsley's scepticism than any mountebank's shouting could have.

The stallholders were as various as their wares. Kingsley had to strive not to stare at those who towered feet above the crowds and at the doll-sized merchants who called from atop their piles of velvets and satins, their voices shrill and piping. Others were even less human, and his wild self bridled at a cat-like thing, as tall as he was, upright and clothed, haggling with a huge woman clad in furs.

The Demimonde was diverse, if nothing else, he decided.

His task of being conspicuous was assisted by the garments that Evadne had insisted he wear. While she maintained that the canary yellow trousers with the royal blue top coat weren't out of place in the Demimonde, he thought he was a fop's dream of an ideal fop. To add to this eye-catching ensemble, she gave him a silver-topped cane. She reiterated that his job was to stand out, not blend in, so he acquiesced and donned the pale grey gloves and top hat that completed the outfit. Even the weight of the special pistol Evadne had given him in his jacket pocket failed to make him feel any less of a goose, nor did his careful hiding of his standard escapology tools in the jacket's lining, the seams of his trousers and the collar of his shirt.

Kingsley couldn't see Evadne, but that was part of the plan. She was moving around the outskirts of the market, staying close to the walls and keeping Kingsley in sight. She'd been concerned about the sparseness of the crowd at the market, an unusual phenomenon, she said, but since they were committed, she reluctantly patted Kingsley on the back before he strode off.

Kingsley took a deep breath and threw himself into his role, so much so that when the plan bumped into action, he was taken by surprise.

Kingsley was musing over a pile of scrolls. The stall-holder shrugged when he expressed doubt over the claim that they were saved when the Great Library of Alexandria was burnt. Kingsley was lamenting his lack of Aramaic when his shoulder was seized from behind.

Kingsley let his body do the work. He bent at the knees and brought his cane around as he whirled. He was happy when the silver knob plunged right into the midriff of the first of the Spawn, making it double over and become a perfect target for the shoulder shove that sent it sprawling.

The second Spawn didn't react at the fate of its comrade. It reached for Kingsley. 'Come with us.'

While the stallholder raised his voice in protest, Kingsley danced back a few paces. He swung his cane, snapping from the wrist, making sure to keep his animal side in check. It wanted to go for the throat, no subtlety, no plan – which wasn't what he needed.

The first Spawn climbed to its feet and for a moment the two stood and simply looked at him. They were almost identical. Thin, stretched features and garments that would have been at home on a parson in a particularly poor area: shabby black suits, too short at ankle and wrist.

The stallholder prodded Kingsley from behind and shouted. Kingsley ignored him and reached into his inner jacket pocket to find the weapon Evadne had given him. He brandished its unlikeliness but the Spawn advanced, unworried by its appearance.

It had an ivory handle and three brass prongs six or eight inches long. In between the prongs was a ball of what looked like steel wool woven with wires of brighter reflecting metal.

The leading Spawn reached out. Kingsley jabbed at it with the weapon. Instantly, a bolt of white light leaped out and enveloped the Spawn. It hissed, then collapsed bonelessly, smoke rising from its sightless eyes.

The babble of commerce around them immediately stilled. Kingsley gaped at the weapon in his hand. He'd almost laughed when Evadne warned him of its power.

The handle was warm. He held it gingerly. The second Spawn looked at it, then at him, before disappearing through the crowd that had gathered.

'I'll give you a fiver for him,' a voice at Kingsley's side said. It took him a moment to realise he was being made an offer for the dead (*deactivated*?) Spawn that was stretched in front of him.

'Done,' he said faintly.

~∞ TWENTY-ONE ∞~

The river was chill that night and the rain pitched down in slashes. Soames had managed to position himself in the wheelhouse because the captain was a hireling of his, one usually given to smuggling and illicit deliveries up and down the Thames, a time-honoured Demimonde trade. If the captain were asked, and if paid for his response, Soames was sure that he'd divulge that this was one of the stranger deliveries he'd ever made. The more he were paid, the more he'd expound on the various strangenesses, including the time of day (near midnight), the destination (just past Greenwich) and the passengers (brawny men – very brawny men – muffled, swaddled and hooded as if on a polar expedition and prepared to sit cross-legged on the open deck despite the rain and despite a perfectly good hold they could settle themselves in).

Soames had no intention of dispelling any of this. He'd

found that a reputation for the mysterious was almost as helpful as a reputation for violence. A combination of both, naturally, was the way to comport oneself in the Demimonde, if one wanted to maintain a level of pride.

It would do no good, for instance, to reveal to the skipper that his passengers hated the thought of river travel. Enclosing themselves in the hold – perhaps even below the level of the water – was the stuff of nightmare for them. Huddling on the deck was their way of coping with what they saw as the unnaturalness of this mode of transport.

Soames was proud of his capacity to work with the Neanderthals. Sporadic though his commissions from these most private of Demimonde denizens had been, he was confident that he could deal with them again and perhaps make them good, steady customers. He knew they hated humanity with a passion beyond words, which limited their interactions with outsiders. Many years ago, after tense and guarded negotiations, he had convinced the Neanderthals that he could be the trusted intermediary they needed. He had made the most of this opportunity. It had been much to his profit, even if he still had trouble with the way they looked at him, as if wondering how stringy he'd be.

There was no doubting, though, that they prepared well for any excursions beyond their secret lair. Underneath their heavy coats, each of the Neanderthals carried firearms of their own construction, each different from the one his comrades bore. They also had heavy hand-to-hand weapons. Most were clearly derived from clubs, but a few were more medieval – giant-sized axes and maces. They hefted these with ease, single-handed, even though

Soames was sure he couldn't have lifted them with both hands.

Soames had been delighted that the frivolities at the White City had acted like a huge plughole, drawing people from across London towards Shepherd's Bush. It meant that the river was quiet and the Greenwich area empty. All the craft tied up were dark. Soames had the warm feeling that signalled that things were falling into place.

The boat pulled in. The Neanderthals nearest the bow made her fast just in time to get out of the way of their comrades, who lost no time vaulting over the gunwales. For such bulky people, Soames noted, they moved quietly, landing softly and in a crouch, ready and alert.

In a show of her seniority and courage, Damona waited for him before she disembarked. 'Your captain,' she said to Soames, 'he won't leave without us?'

Soames looked back at the wheelhouse. The captain was relighting his pipe. The flare of the match threw light over his deep-set eyes and grey beard. 'Not if he knows what's good for him. And for his bank balance.'

'Greed.' Damona eyed the wheelhouse. 'Your people are different from mine.'

'Your people aren't greedy?'

'Not for gold.'

Soames let the matter drop.

The Neanderthal woman had gathered twenty of her kin for the attack and had looked askance at Soames when he asked if they'd be enough, and her disdain made him uneasy. Matters hadn't been helped when he overheard two of the brawnier youngsters mutter, 'Say what you like about Invaders – at least they're tasty.'

Business is business, Jabez, he reminded himself, and the thought comforted him. Business always did.

As the rain tumbled, he joined the Neanderthals on the jetty. They looked to him, eyes deep in their hoods catching the light. He was dressed sensibly in a mackintosh, but his top hat was suffering so he thrust up his umbrella and marched off towards the old Naval College.

The edifice was dark, with its Christopher Wren facade affording many places for shadows to flock and cling. Soames strode through the central courtyard, striving to give the appearance of someone who had every right to be there. Damona's band crept close to the sides of the building. Soames decided that if challenged, he would simply evince horror at being pursued by a horde of monsters and run for his life.

They skirted the Palladian elegance of the Queen's House and then it was the open expanse of Greenwich Park. This prospect had concerned Soames, but in the end the rain was of such tumultuous proportions that he was sure a battleship could have sailed across the sward without being seen.

The Royal Observatory loomed over the park. A few lights were on, but Soames wasn't concerned. His goal, after all, wasn't what lay on top of the hill, but what lay under it.

Long ago, the Immortals had extended some of the underground chambers that were part of the old tower standing there, a haunt of Henry VIII. They constructed a lair directly underneath, and made use of the many conduits, drains and tunnels criss-crossing the park, some of which originally joined the tower to old Greenwich Castle on the riverbank.

Whenever facing a customer, client or potential foe, Soames made it his duty to find out as much as he could about them. This meant that he knew entirely too much about bizarre practices, ceremonies and rites. He was also aware of at least twenty-seven currently operational plans to rule the world and fourteen to end it. This only included plans coming from the Demimonde, of course. Soames kept apprised of the politics of the mundane world, even though they were largely irrelevant to the true running of the globe.

Soames led his clients to the Conduit House. Damona stood aside while two younger Neanderthals busied themselves. The lock was circumvented. Directly, they were confronted by the trap door in the floor.

'Wait for five minutes, then follow me,' Soames said to Damona, enjoying her discomfort and inventing a few details to further disquiet her. 'You'll be faced with a corridor of about twenty or thirty yards. Do not look to either side, at neither the niches nor the intersecting corridors. Definitely do not look into any mirrors. The double doors come from an Egyptian temple and should open with a push. The chamber beyond has the throne of the Immortals, but they will be guarded by Spawn.'

'How many?' Damona demanded.

'I have no idea. They shouldn't be expecting anything. A handful.'

Damona eyed him for an uncomfortable, wet time before she relayed the information to the others.

A trickle of water fell from Soames's collar and went straight down his neck. He grimaced. He didn't like this place and he didn't care if it was a site of power. Once he determined the extent of the Immortals' organisation and asserted his control, he'd move the base much closer to the city. He had his eye on an office block in Westminster. He was sure that the Immortals' organisation could use some modernising. Premises would be a start, but Soames relished the thought of what else he could do with the Immortals' Spawn and their riches.

He shook himself and snapped out his reverie. *Daydreaming at night, Jabez? What next?*

First things first. Soames tugged on his gloves, settled his hat, furled his umbrella, and climbed into the darkness.

At the end of the tunnel he saluted to the statues of Seth and Anubis towering on either side, then he pushed open the door.

The piping voice of Jia hailed him. 'Soames! What are you doing here?'

Soames removed his hat and bowed. 'It's the Neanderthals. They're on the rampage.'

TWENTY-TWO

After the Floating Market, events ran helter-skelter. Evadne rushed up and extracted Kingsley from a crowd that had lost interest quickly, especially after the body of the dead Spawn had been whisked away by its anonymous purchaser. Together they vaulted across a floating bridge and scrambled up a ladder into a vast, echoing tunnel junction. The vaulted ceiling was lost in shadows overhead.

Evadne had a satchel over her shoulder and an object in her hands the size of a cigar box. 'That way!' She pointed at the fourth tunnel on the right.

Kingsley sighed. It was the only one with water coming from it. He pushed back his hair with one hand and glanced behind him at the floating bridge. 'Evadne,' he breathed. 'I suppose we should be getting used to it, but I think someone's following us.'

Evadne swivelled and touched her spectacles. 'It's that man who was waiting outside the entrance to my refuge.'

'Then I'd definitely say some accosting is in order this time.'

'We can't. We'd lose the signal.' Evadne held up her box. 'Hurry.'

She darted into the watery tunnel. Before following, Kingsley looked back. The man was slogging through a knee-deep drain, his coat bedraggled, his hat stuck on his head as if glued. He looked lost, but cast about with the sort of determination that Kingsley didn't like to see in someone who could be a pursuer.

Then he straightened, waved and called out, his voice echoing from the walls. It was enough to jolt Kingsley into moving, and he set off after Evadne with another worry added to his ever-expanding bag of troubles.

The tangled route the Spawn took was a nightmare. They would have lost it a hundred times if it weren't for Evadne's clever box. It was elegantly made of dark wood and brass, with two handles on each end and a featureless top. Evadne kept her hands on the handles and was rewarded with a vibration if she turned away from the direction of the myrmidon that was shadowing the Spawn.

When they finally dragged themselves through the manhole they were confronted by the night-time Thames and a view that Kingsley had last seen in a Canaletto. The imperial bulk of the Naval College stretched along the bank, the twin domes, the Queen's House behind, with the Royal Observatory in the distance.

'Greenwich.' Evadne said. 'This must be the Isle of Dogs.'

'What time is it?'

Evadne took out her watch. 'Just after midnight.'

'It's later than I – Look.'

The myrmidon was waiting for them, running circles in front of a small domed building. It rose on its hind legs, scrabbling at the air and generally doing all it could to attract their attention without actually building a bonfire.

'The foot tunnel,' Evadne said.

The ratty construct almost rolled over with delight when they approached and was ecstatic when it led them along the gloomy, echoing sub-river tunnel, its claws ticking along. When they emerged on the Greenwich side of the river the rain was heavy – which suited Kingsley. Despite its saturating him immediately, he was grateful that ordinary folk would be kept at home.

The myrmidon guided them north-west, paralleling King William Walk and keeping to the shadows as much as possible. Once it reached the openness of the park it stopped every ten yards or so, its ratty countenance peering back at them to make sure they hadn't become lost.

That was the moment when Evadne pointed at a furtive band crossing the park. 'Now, that's curious.' She threw herself on the wet ground, careful not to land on her sabre, and adjusted her spectacles. 'Very curious.'

Kingsley joined her, thinking that the mud might very well be an improvement on his popinjay garments. Yellow trousers. What had Evadne been thinking?

'I'm glad it's curious,' he said, squinting through the rain and dark, 'but a little more detail would be helpful. What can you see?'

'The Demimonde is abroad.' She dragged her satchel up so she could prop her elbows on it. 'Something is afoot.'

'Gangs roaming about Greenwich in the dead of night? I'd say so. Shouldn't we inform the police?'

'I doubt that the police would be able to help here.' Evadne touched her spectacles and peered through the darkness. 'They're Neanderthals.' She turned to him. 'They hate us, you know.'

Kingsley stifled a growl. 'Those brutish murderers? Here? For any particular reason?'

'I can't think of anything, apart from our ancestors' hunting them nearly to extinction.'

'Mm. I can see how that could lead to deep-seated, brooding enmity.'

'Indeed. And when you blend that with supreme mechanical artificing, humanity would have been in grave danger if not for their small numbers and their inability to work together very well.'

'You'll be telling me that you have dinosaurs in the Demimonde, next.' He waited. 'You don't, do you?'

'I don't know everything about the Demimonde, but I wouldn't wager anything on it.'

'I think I need to know more about these Neanderthals,' Kingsley muttered.

'True, but not now.' Evadne lifted herself. 'My, it's like Oxford Street out here.'

'Someone else?'

'A man, by himself. I think it's the one who was following us after the Floating Market.'

'Who could he be?'

'Someone of little concern, I hope. Did you see where the Neanderthals went?'

'You're not thinking of going ahead? Not with those Neanderthals hereabouts?'

'I'm not leaving.'

Even in the dark Kingsley could see her determination. She was a crusader, however much she might decline the title. 'Child abductors, you say?'

'It's worse than that, Kingsley, but I'm not sure if you're up for it.'

'Worse than abduction? What could be worse?'

'They're magicians, and they've lived for a long time. A *very* long time, through their magic.'

'So you say.'

She flared. 'It's not me who says it. The whole Demimonde knows about the Immortals, and fears them.'

'So they're nasty.'

She looked at him and then she dropped her gaze to her hands. She twisted the ring on her little finger. 'The Immortals are rumoured to be able to manipulate objects and minds, and even time itself. They are totally without conscience. They use whoever and whatever for their own ends.'

'Including children.'

'They use young children to help them stay alive. They wear them out, you see, and then transfer their essence to fresh new flesh after it has been prepared with secret magic. Again and again, over centuries.'

'I understand.'

'I doubt it.'

Kingsley was tired. He pointed. 'I think they went up there. Near that shed.'

Evadne rose, hefting the satchel over her shoulder. 'After this, we'll find your foster father. I promise.'

When they reached the shed – which was a rather more substantial brick building than Kingsley had thought – they found the door open.

Evadne nudged him. 'You still have the Incapacitator?'

'The steel wool weapon? Is that what you call it?'

'What's the good of making unique weapons if you can't give them gaudy names?' She shook her sleeve and produced a startling five-barrelled handgun. 'I have the Crushing Reply.' She reached behind her collar and plucked out a fine spray of steel and handed it to him. 'And the Scorpion.' She pushed aside her pleated skirt and reached into her boot. Something like an icicle crossed with a sickle emerged. 'This is the Life Changer.'

'Life Changer?'

'They take one look at it and start seeking another occupation.'

'Naturally.'

The tunnel led them downward. Kingsley held the Incapacitator in front of him in one hand and the pen light in the other. The silence had a weight of its own, pressing down like doom. The walls were tiled with black, shiny rectangles that caught the light and bent it in streaks along the arched way.

The tunnel ended in a five-sided door. It was guarded by two glowering Egyptian statues.

Evadne dropped to her knees and rummaged in her satchel. Kingsley was startled when she pulled out a tiny brass cylinder, hardly as big as his finger. 'Is that explosive?'

She tucked the cylinder behind the base of the female statue. 'It's a phlogiston-based material of my own devising. Very powerful.'

'That tiny thing?'

'If I can secrete a few more of these, I don't think the Immortals will be using this place again.'

'You can't,' he said, aghast. 'You'll destroy the observatory.'

'It's worth it to put an end to these creatures.'

'No it's not. The observatory is our heritage.'

'You'd put a pile of bricks against the chance of getting rid of the most hideous monsters in the Demimonde?'

'It's not just a pile of bricks. It's enlightenment, it's rationality, it's the first step in humanity making sense of the universe in a way that matters.' He ran his hand through his wet hair. 'It's Wren, it's Hooke, it's Flamsteed. It's solving the longitude problem, it's seeing the world clearly for a change.'

'You're serious,' she said.

'Of course.'

'Then what is the alternative?'

'Alternative?'

'We're here. If I'm right, the Immortals are behind that door. We have explosives, they have the Spawn. What are we going to do?'

'I suppose a good ticking off is out of the question?'

'Habits of millennia aren't likely to change due to a scolding.' Evadne's face became serious. 'Trust me. They need to be exterminated.'

Something ran deep in Evadne's set against the Immortals. 'What is it? Why are you so down on them?'

She twisted the ring on her finger. 'It's a secret.'

'We all have secrets. Some are meant to be shared.'

'I'm sorry.' She shook her head. 'I'm a solo performer, an independent operator, self-sufficient and complete.'

'If that's the case, what are you doing with me?'

'I . . .' She closed her mouth, then opened it again, perplexed. 'It was a whim, at first, but I think I became carried away by circumstances.'

'They can do that, circumstances.'

'You have a secret, too,' she said softly.

'Don't we all?'

'Yes, but I happen to know yours. That makes us uneven.'

Kingsley went to answer, but he was interrupted by a roar that came right through the marble door in front of them. He dropped to all fours and a growl tore from his throat.

Evadne looked at him, unafraid and with some satisfaction. He climbed to his feet, abashed, and wiped his hands together. 'Sorry,' he muttered.

'We all have secrets, but yours is one of the more interesting.' She glanced at the door. 'In the spirit of an open and honest working partnership, let's do what we can in there – without destroying the observatory – and afterwards I'll share my secret with you.'

She offered her hand. He took it. They shook, solemnly. Kingsley realised that for the first time, he'd met someone who he didn't mind knowing his secret.

∽ TWENTY-THREE ∽

Kingsley and Evadne lingered just inside the doorway, hidden in the shadows but with a fine view. They were confronted with an immense chamber composed entirely of pentagons. The five-sided ceiling was at least a few hundred feet overhead. Soft light fell from it, filling the entire chamber with a radiance that unsettled Kingsley, for it was a touch too blue for honest sunlight or gaslight. Evadne grimaced and quickly changed her spectacles.

Large, five-sided alcoves were set in each of the walls. Two of the alcoves hosted objects that rotated, as far as Kingsley could tell, while floating a few feet above the floor – a large cube and an equally large tetrahedron. They glowed, each side in turn, but in no rhythm that Kingsley could discern. Both shifted colour through the spectrum, attaining some hues that Kingsley doubted had names at all.

The Neanderthals had preceded them. Their flying wedge formation had been met by a chaotic wave of Spawn. Fifty or more of the soulless creatures were flinging themselves at the intruders, preventing them from reaching the middle of the chamber and a hideously ornate golden sofa.

The golden sofa was divided into three separate seats and it was a wince-inducing contrast to the classical restraint of the chamber. Curlicues ran rampant, unicorns and dolphins cavorted, and enough silk cushions were strewn about to lay waste to a generation of silk worms.

Kingsley allowed himself to gape, and not only at the hideous bad taste of the furniture. The golden sofa throne hovered a foot or so above the floor like a balloon. Three chubby, dwarfish figures sat side by side in it, shrieking and gesticulating while the battle raged in front of them.

He raised an eyebrow at Evadne. She shrugged and put her finger on her lips, somewhat needlessly as Kingsley had about as much wish to bring attention to himself as he had of parading naked down Bond Street.

A solitary figure stood next to the throne. He was dressed well and regarded the brawl uneasily, shifting his weight from foot to foot, with his hands clasped behind his back. Occasionally he mopped his brow with a red handkerchief.

With a mighty shout, two Neanderthals in the vanguard cleared a path. In a mass, the rest of them followed, putting their heads down and pushing the Spawn aside through sheer momentum. Weaponless, the

Spawn clawed and grappled but were trodden down or simply smashed aside. The chamber rang to fierce battle cries and howls of sheer bestial triumph as the Neanderthals took to their bludgeoning weapons. Thin, colourless Spawn blood sprayed. Some Neanderthals flung their weapons away and used their mighty fists. One young Neanderthal simply grabbed a gibbering Spawn and, with one hand, tossed him at a knot of other Spawn, while casually bludgeoning another attacker with a huge backhand blow.

The Spawn had abandoned any semblance of humanity. In ragged trousers and tunics, they slavered and leaped at the Neanderthals, clawing and biting, their skins grey and sullen like spoiled lead. As they attempted to bring the Neanderthals down with weight of numbers, Kingsley's wolfishness responded. The battle called and the smell of blood was exciting but he had to hold on. He watched, eagerly, and his nails dug into his palms. His heart thumped. His muscles quivered as he leaned towards the fray.

Yes! The pack hunts together, to tear and rend, to separate the weak and to wreak havoc on the others! Terror is our friend!

He became aware that Evadne was looking at him – not with horror, but with concern. Angry at himself, he bit his lip and looked away. He couldn't afford to surrender to his wild side, not now, not in this predicament. He needed all his wits about him, no matter how his blood sang.

The Neanderthals pushed towards the throne, roaring with triumph. The human darted away, disappearing through a five-sided door in the wall near one of the

179

alcoves. The Immortals squeaked and gestured wildly, full of rage and indignation, pointing at the floating cube in the far alcove. It glowed a sickly green, then faded, which appeared to enrage the Immortals even more, but just before the Neanderthals reached the throne all three of them sagged, falling back onto their cushions like rag dolls.

The Neanderthals didn't hesitate. Kingsley's civilised self wanted to look away, but his atavistic wild side was excited. In the end, he watched grimly as the Neanderthals tore the tiny bodies apart, howling and brandishing limbs like trophies.

A new surge of Spawn erupted from the direction the human had fled. They screeched as they ran.

The Neanderthals stood back to back as Spawn attacked. In the middle of the ring, half a dozen were using projectile weapons to pick off Spawn at a distance with darts, bullets, bolts, tiny whirring chains and – astonishingly – tiny balls of fire. The noise was punishing. The Neanderthals clustered around these marksmen, smiling grimly or roaring defiantly, according to personal preference. The floor underneath became slippery with Neanderthal blood mixing with the spiritless ichor of the Spawn.

'Please drop your weapons and turn very slowly.'

The voice was fussy, polite and human. Kingsley swallowed and shifted around.

A middle-aged man – Kingsley recognised him as the same one who had been standing with the Immortals – regarded them over the top of a decidedly ordinary revolver. In spite of it being ordinary compared to the exotic weapons Kingsley had been confronted with in the last few days, he had a healthy respect for the damage it could do. He took out the Incapacitator and dropped it on the floor. Evadne tossed her pistol aside, then the Scorpion and the Life Changer.

'The satchel, too, young lady. And the ... what is it? A sabre?'

With his striped trousers, cutaway jacket and topcoat, he looked exactly like a City stockbroker, if a little frayed around the edges and slightly dyspeptic. 'Keep your hands away from your pockets. I know you probably only want a handkerchief to cry into, but I'd regret it if you took out something and I had to shoot you.'

Kingsley was convinced. He held his hands well away from his sides.

'Wait.' The man widened his eyes at Evadne. 'You are delightful, aren't you, my dear?'

'Oh yes,' Evadne said. 'And harmless. Put down your revolver and I'll show you.'

'You're game, too. Excellent.' He glanced at Kingsley, then peered intently at him. 'Move into the light. Both of you.'

Kingsley and Evadne backed into the chamber. The noise of the battle behind them echoed around the hard angles of the pentagons, blurring and overlapping to become a veritable bedlam.

The man with the revolver stopped smiling briefly, then a broad grin spread across a face that looked unaccustomed so such extremes of emotion. 'You're the boy that Kipling is after, aren't you? Don't bother to deny it – my question was purely rhetorical.'

'Why's that important to you?' Evadne snapped.

'It's a matter of bargaining from a position of strength,' the man said, his grin widening, if possible. 'With you in my possession, boy, I'm now very strong indeed.'

TWENTY-FOUR

Jabez Soames was not a gambling man. He preferred activities where luck didn't enter into it. So he was unaccustomed to feeling as extraordinarily lucky as he was at the way things had transpired this evening. If this was how gamblers felt when the dice fell their way or their horse crossed the line foremost, then he could see the allure of Lady Fortune.

'I want the boy,' Damona said. She was sitting on a marble step in front of the rotating tetrahedron and looked satisfied. Smoke drifted about the grand chamber, left over from some of the more poorly constructed firearms.

'I guessed as much,' Soames said. The Spawn were heaped in a large pile near one of the vacant alcoves. They would rot quickly and unpleasantly. He took out a handkerchief ready to cover his nose in this eventuality.

Damona grunted. She was unhurt, and Soames thought

that the way she gazed at her fellow brutes as they laughed, slapped backs and recounted their various braveries was more like a mother benignly watching children at play than a warlord at the end of a battle. She jerked a thumb over her shoulder. 'What is that?'

Soames was careful with giving away information for nothing, but Damona did have the useful negotiating advantage of a horde of bloodthirsty savages at her back.

'The Immortals called it a Temporal Manipulator.'

'Time?' The Neanderthal woman looked at it over her shoulder. 'Magic stuff?'

'The Immortals are pre-eminent sorcerers, bending space and time to their will,' Soames said. *It didn't help them this time*, he added to himself and smiled.

'I can send people to study it?' Damona asked.

As the new landlord, and as someone whose plans had fallen into place so well, Soames decided he could afford to be magnanimous to keep a client happy. 'Possibly,' he said. 'In a month, say, once I've organised things here properly.'

The old woman croaked. It took some time before Soames realised she was laughing. 'A month?' she said. 'Much can happen in a month.'

'I'm sure it can,' Soames said, disconcerted by the woman's reaction.

'Now,' she said, turning her back on the Temporal Manipulator. 'The boy.'

'Ah, yes. The boy.'

Soames stroked his chin. The boy and the girl were an interesting problem. They'd refused to tell him why they were here, and he hadn't had time to question them properly. The girl's appearance was singular enough to make him think he'd seen her before, skulking about the

Demimonde. If nothing else, he could make a tidy profit selling her to one of the slavers. He'd get a good price for her rare beauty.

The thought warmed him to the point of chuckling.

'Funny?' Damona spat on the floor. 'Don't forget. You tricked us. This place was too well defended.'

'I? Tricked you?' Soames managed to look affronted. 'I hope, madam, that you are not going back on your word.'

Damona spat again, very deliberately. 'The place is yours.' She grimaced as she climbed to her feet. 'I will take the girl and the boy. Their equipment, too.'

'What?' Queasily, Soames tore his gaze from the spittle on the floor.

'Your face said you want her. So I want her.'

Soames bit the inside of his cheek, a tactic he employed whenever he had an impulse to shoot a customer dead on the spot. 'I was about to offer her to you, but you pre-empted me.'

'Liar.'

'A pleasure to do business with you. They're in the cells below.'

The Neanderthal woman signalled to two of her bully boys and they hurried through the door Soames indicated. Before Soames could instigate some polite small talk, one of them was back. 'They're not there.'

Damona cleared her throat. 'Soames?'

'I put them there myself,' he said quickly, before she could spit again. 'If your people released them, I bear no responsibility.'

A shout went up, and a Neanderthal staggered backward through a door. Another emerged holding the white-skinned girl by the back of her neck, her feet dangling off the ground. The boy flew through the air, rolled well enough and snarled as another of the Neanderthals closed on him, but all the fight went out of him when he saw the girl was helpless.

'One squeeze,' the Neanderthal growled. 'That's all.'

The boy stood. Soames watched keenly as he shook himself and straightened, becoming an altogether different person – less angry, far more collected. The way he shuddered, however, suggested that he was having to exert himself to maintain this demeanour. It was almost as if he were warring against an impulse to throw himself at the girl's captor, despite the odds.

'Tie them,' Damona said, 'then we leave.'

Soames adjusted his cuffs uneasily. He had the distinct impression that something was going on here, something of which he wasn't fully apprised. He hated that.

Jabez, he thought, *it may be time for honey instead of vinegar.*

Soames assumed his most charming aspect. 'I'm impressed with the way your comrades disposed of the Immortals.'

'It was good to do it.' She smiled, and it was horrible.

'They wouldn't be for hire, would they? I occasionally have need of muscular types to help negotiations along, that sort of thing.'

'No.'

'I thought not, but no harm in asking, is there?' He went to move away, but then looked back. 'Oh, one last thing, if you'd indulge me. Curious as I am, I'm interested in why you want the boy so much.'

Silently, Damona regarded him for a moment. Soames

was beginning to feel decidedly edible, and then she spoke: 'Our business.'

'Of course.'

Damona glanced at her bravoes. They had bound the boy and the girl. Soames was disappointed in losing her, but business was business.

And that, for Jabez Soames, was sufficient reason for nearly anything.

⌁ TWENTY-FIVE ⌁

Gustave greeted Damona. 'Good news, Eldest!'

'Casualties, Gustave.' Damona stood aside. Her fellow raiders dragged themselves up the ramp that led to the river. At the top of the ramp was the tunnel that took them home. It was good to see it. All were weary, but chaffed Gustave. That bluff heartiness that had been missing for years. Laughter. Jokes. The stories growing already.

She was pleased. Not just because she'd ended the threat from the Immortals. Combat bound people together. Useful soon, maybe. She took Gustave by the arm, explained. 'Holger has a broken arm. Others have bad slashes. Have to get treatment for them.' She rubbed her forehead. The night had been long. 'Is Ragnar still practising medicine?'

'Medicine?' Gustave grimaced, then his eyes went wide. Two happy raiders toted the pair of bound prisoners. 'Invaders?'

'Useful prisoners.' Would Dr Ward respond best if he saw the boy? Or should she threaten the boy separately? He might be able to convince his father, as long as he had an incentive.

She yawned. Not now. She needed rest and a clear mind. 'We need some attention. Stitches, bone setting, nothing serious.'

'You've been raiding?' Gustave said. 'I thought you were off looking for material for the project.'

Damona had done her best to keep the raid a secret. A failure would have been a disaster. Now, though, battle success on top of their engineering success? Times were good. 'We were. In a way. Don't concern yourself with it.' Damona laced her hands in the small of her back. 'What's this good news?'

'We've improved the extraction process already,' he said. 'Hilda had an idea about compression and dimensional pressure. Output is up by at least twenty per cent.' He beamed.

'Twenty per cent? Congratulations. Let me see this advance.'

'You'd rather see it than your time machine, ready for testing?'

'What? Already?'

'I have enough volunteers for us to work in shifts.'

'Together? Cooperating?'

'It's a miracle.'

The workshop. Clangour. The screech of metalwork. The smell of hot oil. Vibrations underfoot. More True People were working in one place at one time than Damona had ever seen before. Heads down. Passing tools to each other. Advising, listening, sharing.

The project had already grown far beyond Damona's expectations.

The large space was now divided into bays. Each bay was abuzz with industry. Workers were happy to explain their tasks. Small machines to make larger machines. Devices which would be components. Fabricators. Plotters. Lamination mills. The workshop was a machine itself. Interlocking parts each depending on the other.

A serious youngster with a squint told her that the time machine was in a workshop of its own next door. Then he told her of their progress with reworking water distribution throughout the complex. Smiling.

Damona clapped him on the back. He returned to working on the filtration unit. Looked disappointed that he couldn't spend more time explaining it to her.

Damona was thoughtful as she left him. Such diligence. Such concerted effort. Had she made a mistake in pursuing her dream alone for so many years?

Gustave caught her attention. 'Eldest! Over here! Our new phlogiston extractor!' The whine of cutting tools. Sparks from a grinder.

Damona made sure she didn't limp. Gustave gestured proudly. Her eyebrows rose.

Right against the rock wall. The machine was long and only waist high. It bristled with large bore input pipes connected to the floor. Three extremely careful youngsters were polishing brass curlicues where none seemed necessary. One of the technicians crawled alongside on hands and knees. He was painting thin, parallel lines on the flanks of the machine. His work made the machine look as if it were speeding along while it was standing still.

It was beautiful. A song of brass and mahogany. Fine materials. From someone's hoard? Damona hadn't seen any wood like it for years.

Behind the machine, on the rock wall: racks of metal canisters. The wall itself was smooth and painted a deep cream colour. A gridwork of wires and struts surrounded the canisters. An open metal lattice. Brass pipes along the top of each row opened directly over the canisters.

Damona was impressed and curious. This machine was nothing like anything in her plans.

Gustave grinned. 'Watch!' He pointed at the output pipe.

The machine quivered. A glowing vial the size of her thumb flew from the mouth of the output conduit. It dropped into a metal basket. The basket ran along a wire. When it came to the far end the basket hinged open. The vial dropped into a canister. The basket then buzzed to the lattice tower at the far end. It stopped. Settled. Waiting for the next vial, Damona guessed.

Gustave held up a finger. 'Wait!'

The vial that had just been deposited shot straight up. Sucked into the hole in the brass pipe directly above it.

Damona was so impressed she applauded. Gustave beamed, pointed at the ceiling. 'Pneumatic delivery system!' he shouted. 'Everything in here is now phlogiston powered!'

Damona gazed up. A maze of pipes. Phlogiston extraction must have increased greatly to warrant such a system. But driving machines directly via phlogiston would provide an enormous boost in power.

'Damona!' Gustave touched her shoulder. 'Hilda has news!'

Hilda was standing next to Gustave. She was short, even for the True People. Her coppery hair was tied in a braid that reached to the middle of her back. She wore dark goggles. Damona hadn't seen her approach. Hilda pushed back her goggles, remembered to wipe her hands on her white coat before she offered one. 'Eldest!'

'Phlogiston extraction! How long?'

Hilda understood the abbreviated question. 'We have enough for a test, maybe two.'

'The phlogiston is piped to the time machine?'

Gustave answered. 'Of course, Eldest. It is our first priority.'

Damona squeezed Hilda's shoulder. She paid her the ultimate compliment of the True People: 'You do good work.'

‿ TWENTY-SIX ‿

Kingsley and Evadne were finally bundled into what Kingsley decided was a cell, but only after some consideration. It had the requisite heavy steel door, but instead of an institutional dullness, the ceiling, walls and floor were lined with glazed bricks suffused with a gentle blue colour. The hue wasn't uniform. Darker in some places, lighter in others, it created a swirling, almost restful vista. Two o'clock on a summer's afternoon, Kingsley decided. Perfect for an underground prison cell.

While Evadne fumed under her gag – a result of a fearsome tongue-lashing she'd launched into after being dragged out of the Immortals' lair – Kingsley refrained from working on his bonds just in case one of their captors came back. He rested, Evadne subsided and before he knew it, he'd fallen asleep.

When Kingsley woke, he glumly took stock of his

situation. Evadne was still asleep, which was good, but he was still dressed in the outlandish clothes she had given him for his excursion in the Demimonde, which was distressing. The yellow trousers were particularly badly off. Mud-bespattered, grass-stained, they looked as if they belonged to a clown who'd taken to rolling about in fields.

He inspected the ropes wrapped around him. Most people had no idea about tying up a prisoner. Even sailors had a tendency to concentrate on knots and not on the firmness of the actual binding. The simplest method – where he took a deep breath, and expanded his chest while the tying was going on – was usually enough, but one of the younger Neanderthals had been alert to this and had thrust a steely knuckle into Kingsley's ribs. The action had made Kingsley lose his lungful of air, so the binding had thus been tight. As a bonus, he'd added another bruise to Kingsley Ward's Marvellous Collection of Bruises, Grazes and Contusions, something he could have done without.

No matter, he thought, *the Basic Principles of Escapology (Rope Binding Section) still apply.*

Some time later, he wriggled towards Evadne. Immediately, her eyes flew open and she glared at him.

'Now,' he said, 'I don't want you to gain the wrong impression from this.'

Evadne said something that Kingsley was glad was muffled. Her eyes widened behind her spectacles when he lowered his head to hers, his mouth slightly open. Her skin was fine, even and white. Her perfume was heady. He paused a moment, enjoying her closeness, thrilled by the way the skin over her throat fluttered with her pulse. Then, with a careful movement, he used his teeth to seize the large white handkerchief that had been stuffed into her mouth. A yank or two and he spat it to the floor.

She cocked her head. A ghost of a flush coloured her cheeks for a moment in an altogether appealing display. 'I suppose I should thank you.'

'It is customary in such circumstances. Or so I've read.'

'You must read different books from the ones I read.'

'Perhaps.' Uncomfortable for a moment, he looked about their cell. A single bed, with no mattress. A three-legged stool. The necessary ablutions equipment looked an odd piece of engineering, and Kingsley decided he'd need an instruction manual to use it. Which he hoped he had no need to. 'I was hoping you could tell me what we've landed ourselves in.'

Her shrug was muted by her bonds. 'I'd say we've become caught in a dispute of one sort or another. Common enough in the Demimonde.'

'Common enough in the ordinary world too, but such things don't usually result in open warfare.'

'Really? I must remember to tell that to the Boers next time I see them.'

Kingsley winced. 'So if we're incidental to their struggle, we should be able to slip away without too much trouble?'

'Apart from being bound and locked up.'

Kingsley stood, the ropes falling away. 'And now, for my next trick.'

She glared. 'You could have done that at any time. You didn't need to . . . to . . .'

195

'Remove your gag like that? Ah. True.' Kingsley extemporised. 'I heard someone at the door. Didn't want to give away too much.'

Her glare smouldered, dropping from 'surface of the sun' to 'interior of a volcano'. 'Unbind me.'

'My pleasure.'

Kingsley reached behind his collar and found the length of thin metal, one edge of which he kept sharp. Carefully, he sawed through the key ropes and soon Evadne was standing in front of him, rubbing her elbow. 'I'm assuming the door won't be a problem?'

Kingsley had his lock picks in his tie. The Neanderthals had been thorough in their searching, showing considerable interest in the numerous weapons Soames had found on Evadne, but – as most people did – they missed the various bits of wire and metal secreted about Kingsley's person.

'The Basic Principles of Escapology begin with three very fine suggestions,' Kingsley said as he assembled his tools. 'Take your time. Stay calm. Take stock of your situation. I find they help in situations like this.'

Evadne eyed him. 'Basic Principles of Escapology,' she repeated. 'By a well-known master of the trade, no doubt?'

'The Basic Principles are a fluid set of guidelines, subject to change, and they're vital to any true escapologist.'

'That doesn't answer my question.'

'Surely you don't answer all questions anyone asks you about juggling? The mystery is important, after all.'

'You're still avoiding the question.'

'Rather than discuss such things, let me demonstrate the principles by taking stock.' He put his ear to the door.

'Is it safe?' Evadne asked.

'In the heart of the lair of prehistoric people who eat humans? Probably not.'

'Wait.'

'What for?'

'To show you you're not the only one who has something up his sleeve.'

From the folds of her top coat, from the brim of her hat, from the hem of her scarf and from the heel of her boot she produced a quick succession of cogs, tubes and struts that she snapped together into a small, but lethal-looking, firearm. It was just larger than her palm, a combination of shiny steel and close-grained wood, and she regarded it fondly. 'I've been dying for a chance to try out Whispering Death. Pneumatic, accurate to fifty yards.'

'Poison darts?'

'Or soporific. Or simply painful, if you're hit in the right spot.'

Kingsley reminded himself not to volunteer as a target. He wasn't sure if the little pistol would be of much use so he simply nodded, with gritted teeth, holding his wolfishness on a tight leash. It wasn't happy, being confined in a cell like this. It was aching to get out and run free.

He held one pick in his teeth while he inserted the other. The lock was sturdy-looking, but its mechanism was straightforward, even though the way the pins were arranged did take some adjusting before he had it. 'There.'

'Stand back. I'll go first.'

His wolfish self reared at that, fearing a snub. His civilised self objected, too, but quickly subsided. It was the sensible thing to do, since she was armed, and his estimation of

Evadne's capabilities was continuing to grow. No shrinking violet, she. He'd be prepared to match her against any tough, bravo or bully boy, Neanderthal or not.

Then he saw the markings on the wall over the bed. The pretty blue bricks had been defaced with scratches, the traditional prisoner's tally marks, rough and crude, but some were also uniform and precise, evidence of different hands – and of different prisoners being incarcerated here. The hair on the back of his neck rose. In the corner, in scratchings that could only be called 'dainty', was a single, recognisable sentence amid the tallies, in French: *Le vrai Lavoisier se trouve ici.*

Without a word, he pointed at the wall. Evadne left the door. 'Lavoisier,' she said and looked at him. 'The scientist?'

'One of my foster father's heroes. He discovered oxygen and was guillotined in the French Revolution.'

'The true Lavoisier lies here,' Evadne read. 'Maybe he didn't lose his head.'

'In the chaos that was the revolution, anything could have happened.'

'Even Neanderthals abducting the father of modern chemistry? Why?'

'Lavoisier was a genius. The Neanderthals might have needed one.'

With another mystery on his hands, Kingsley followed Evadne from the cell.

Presently, he decided that whoever was in charge of this part of the Neanderthal warren could have designed hospitals or industrial kitchens. It was spotless. Underfoot, the glaze had been roughened to prevent slipping. Light spilled from roundels in the ceiling, white tinged with yellow, the promise of sunshine.

The corridor was military straight. It sloped upward fifty yards or so to where a central observation point was sited. From there, Kingsley guessed, it could monitor the radiating corridors. Simple, efficient design. He was impressed.

'I think one of the cells is occupied,' Evadne said, pointing.

The cell closest to the monitoring station, on the right, had a small white light glowing on the floor in front of it, inset, as if the moon had fallen to earth.

Thirty yards away. Thirty yards of corridor, totally exposed to anyone in the monitoring station. Kingsley rubbed his chin. No time for creeping about. This had to be done with authority.

He took a deep breath, summoned some of his stage presence, and strolled up the middle of the corridor. His wild self was alarmed, would have preferred flitting from doorway to doorway, seeking cover, looking for danger, but this was an occasion for a civilised approach. Ambling along, hands in pockets, exuding confidence and project-ing the total and utter right to be there was the best way. His gaze roamed from side to side, taking in the surround-ings with unabashed interest, admiring the helpful light in front of the last cell.

It may not buy him more than an instant or two of doubt if a Neanderthal came around the corner, but it was the best Kingsley could do.

The monitoring station was empty. With relief, Kingsley took in the circular bench, the two stools and the wheelchair, a few crates hastily stowed next to one of them. The station was dusty, but it showed some signs of recent activity. The section nearest the occupied cell had been hastily swept clean. The large hand marks were still obvious.

Kingsley waved, gestured at Evadne to join him, and while he was waiting he saw something – one of the crates half-shoved under the bench of the monitoring station wasn't as dusty as those next to it.

Curious, he vaulted over the bench. He squatted and spied Evadne's satchel sitting on top of her sabre and the knife she'd insisted he carry. The other weapons were gone. With a sense of increasing unease, he saw that underneath this hasty arrangement the crate was packed with books. Familiar books, books that had a smell that made his throat tighten.

I wish I didn't know what blood smells like, he thought numbly as he shuffled closer. The spines of a dozen books looked up at him, the gold lettering not as bright as he remembered. Two of the volumes were spattered with a distressing brown stain: *The Peoples of the Sindh* and *Creation Legends Among the Jain.* The name of the author was obscured by the stain, but Kingsley didn't have to see it to know that the books were authored by – and belonged to – Dr Malcolm Ward, his foster father.

Evadne joined him. 'What have you found?'

He handed the weapons to her without answering. She buckled on her sabre, but took in his distress. Nimbly, she leaped over the bench. She put a hand on his shoulder. 'These came from your library at home, didn't they?'

He plucked one of the books from the crate. The bookplate on the flyleaf confirmed it.

Kingsley remembered the kindness of Mrs Walters. She'd been a practical, busy woman. She complained about his magic paraphernalia and never understood his interest, but she was always ready with some sustenance between meals, saying she knew all about the appetites of growing young men.

'They killed her for books?' he said aloud. It was so petty. A flicker grew inside him, calling for vengeance against the brutes, but it was smothered by sadness. So pointless.

'So it would seem.' Evadne tugged on his sleeve.

'Why? Why did they do it?'

Evadne glanced at the head of the stairs. 'Think. It's not a random selection of books. What do they have in common?'

'My foster father wrote them all.'

'True. And the subject of the books?'

'People. Origins of people.'

'So they're either interested in your father or this theories about the origins of humanity. That's enough for us to speculate on. Now, I want to see who's in that cell.'

'So do I,' Kingsley said, 'especially since I have some idea who it is.'

The man on the bed opened his eyes. 'My boy,' he croaked, 'I'm glad you've come.'

Kingsley was at his foster father's side instantly.

The old man's face was bruised. His clothing, more suitable for a night at the opera than a prison cell, was rumpled and his collar was streaked with blood. Kingsley was grimly pleased. The old man had resisted!

Dr Ward had always been a big man. His limbs were strong, he had a long and muscular trunk, his hands were large, his head was leonine. His hair was long and silver, swept back but thick. His habitual mode of speaking was the boom, and it was a sign of his travails that it had been reduced as much as it had.

Dr Ward eased himself into a sitting position, leaving his legs still covered by the light blanket. He declined offers of assistance. 'I'm well enough,' he managed, then he saw Evadne and his dull eyes brightened.

'How extraordinary you are, young lady. Do you know that a hundred years ago you could have been queen of Benin just because of your eyes?'

Evadne raised an eyebrow and Kingsley hastily made the introductions. 'Father, I'd never have found you without her.'

'I'm not sure about that.' Dr Ward chuckled, but Kingsley wasn't happy about the wheeziness of the laughter. 'Regardless, you are most beautiful, Miss Stephens. I'm sure that in days gone by, thousands of men would have perished for a chance at your hand.'

'Sorry,' Kingsley said to her, 'Father does live in the past, somewhat.'

'Hah!' Dr Ward was seized by a mighty coughing fit. He went alarmingly red in the face and hammered at his own thigh with a fist before he brought it under control. Kingsley hovered helplessly, his foster father waving him away whenever he approached too closely.

Eventually, Dr Ward gathered himself. 'I was about to say – as you know full well, my boy – that I don't live in the past, I merely study it.' His expression darkened. 'Which is why the brutes brought me here.'

'Tell us later, Father,' Kingsley said. 'Let us get you out of here first.'

Dr Ward held up a hand. 'Always precipitous, my boy, always precipitous.' His gaze drifted upward. 'My, that ceiling is a long way away.'

'He's right, Dr Ward,' Evadne said, 'we can't waste time.'

Dr Ward frowned, then touched his wrinkled brow. For a moment he was amused by the shapes it made before he gathered himself to answer. 'Time. That's what it's all about, after all.'

'Father?'

'These brutes are building a time machine. That's why they wanted me. To help with their destination.'

While Kingsley rocked back at this revelation, Evadne leaned forward. 'What do you mean?' she demanded.

Dr Ward touched his cheek. 'My, I do need a shave. I used to have a favourite barber. Marcello. He was a maestro with a razor.' He blinked at the fierceness of Evadne's regard. 'I'm sorry, my dear. I'm finding it hard to concentrate after their questioning.'

Kingsley was dismayed. Dr Ward had been good to him, in his vague and erratic way. He'd spent a career as a professional wanderer, often working in more than one area at once, sometimes abandoning avenues of inquiry unfinished when a new one arose. His lectures were famous for finishing many miles away from their nominal topic.

Kingsley touched Evadne on the forearm and, with a look, asked for understanding. She glanced at him, then at Dr Ward and then she bit her lip and nodded.

Dr Ward didn't notice this unspoken conversation. He continued, as if talking to himself. 'You know, my whole career has been looking backward, really.' He chuckled. More wheeziness. 'Further and further back, further and further.' He cocked a bright eye at Kingsley. 'That's what they want to know, but I haven't told them yet.'

'What do they want to know, Father?'

'Them and us. *Homo neanderthalensis* and *Homo sapiens*. When we diverged.' He rubbed his chest. 'They want to travel back in time and exterminate us. While there are only a few of us around. If they're successful, humanity will simply cease to be.'

Kingsley went to laugh, but he was halted by the expression on Evadne's face. 'I'm sorry,' he said softly. 'He's muddled. He needs care.'

'No.' She shook her head and her silver hair flew. 'No.'

'Don't tell me you believe this?'

This time, Dr Ward was following. 'And why shouldn't she, my boy?'

'We have to stop them,' Evadne said.

'Surely you're not serious,' Kingsley said. *Another* crusade? Evadne was a young woman of principle, but it did seem to get in the way.

She put her hands on her hips and glared at him. 'After all you've seen, you still doubt? The Neanderthals are the greatest artificers in the Demimonde. They hate us. This is exactly the sort of scheme I wouldn't put past them.'

'Besides,' Dr Ward said and his voice was suddenly steady and irresistibly rational, 'think of it this way. If you act and I'm right, you've saved humanity. If you don't act and I'm right, we're all doomed.'

That was the end of the argument. Kingsley could see that he was outmatched. Evadne's knowledge of and experience with the Demimonde convinced her that the Neanderthals were capable of this extraordinary deed. She would not be shaken from it.

'I surrender,' he said. 'Once we get you safely out of here, Father, then we can see what we can do about this time machine.'

'I think not,' Dr Ward said. 'I'd say it's best for you both to leave me behind.'

Kingsley bit his lip. Had his foster father's ill-treatment addled his brain? 'Don't be ridiculous. Up on your feet. We'll have you out of here in no time.'

'Ah, but that's the point.' He pulled the blanket aside and gestured at his feet.

Evadne gasped. Kingsley was sickened by the black and blue, misshapen things on the end of his legs. 'What have they done?'

Dr Ward shrugged. 'It makes good sense, from their point of view, and it has many historical precedents. Some Viking leaders actually hamstrung their slaves to stop them running away, so I may have got off lightly.'

'They broke your ankles? Aren't you in pain?'

'I was, at first, but they dose me with . . .' He squinted at them. 'I say, you've both thought that I'm losing my mind, haven't you?' He shook his head. 'It's the opiate they force on me. I can't walk – they deposit me in some sort of wheelchair when they want to undertake another of their ghastly interrogations – but I'm in no pain. Just damnably foggy. Stupid arrangement, really. They need me to be sharp if I'm to advise them, but they did this to me. Sometimes seems like no-one's in charge around here.'

'If they can take you out of here, we can,' Kingsley said.

'Don't be silly, my boy.' Dr Ward reached out, took Kingsley's hand, and Kingsley was surprised. The old man had never been one for shows of affection. It had to be the opiate. 'Leave me here and I can string them along for months, I'm sure. I've so many stories I can tell them, after all.'

Kingsley hesitated, sought for words, and decided that mawkish euphemisms were the enemy of true feeling. 'They killed Mrs Walters,' he said. 'They'll kill you.'

The old man's face collapsed. 'Mrs Walters? Ah.' His closed his eyes for a moment. 'She was a good woman, Kingsley. A fine woman.' Unfocused, he gazed into the distance for a moment, his head bobbing, before he gathered himself. 'Quickly now. Do your tricks, my boy, lock me in and then stop these fiends.'

Kingsley swayed. He'd found his foster father only to leave him behind, in the clutches of monsters who were on their way to exterminating all humanity? He couldn't leave him, but he must.

'We'll be back,' he said in a rush. He glanced at Evadne. She nodded. 'As soon as we can, we'll be back.'

Dr Ward eased the blanket back again. 'Don't worry about me, my boy. I can take care of myself. Just do what you have to and then find that man. The writer.'

'Kipling?'

'That's the fellow.'

'We've already met him, Father.'

'Good man, Kipling. Met him in India, more than once. He'll believe you – he's come across things that'd make your hair curl – and he has connections. He'll convince the PM to do something.'

Kingsley paused at the door. If his father thought it

necessary to involve the Prime Minister then events were dire indeed. 'Stay safe, Father,' he said, and his voice was grim.

He closed the door and inserted his picks. Just before the last tumbler fell, he heard his foster father's voice. 'Kingsley?'

'Yes, sir?'

'I'm sorry I never came to see you perform your magic.'

~ TWENTY-SEVEN ~

Finding their way about the Neanderthal complex was a nightmare. Any expectations about dwellings, construction or simply places where people lived were defeated by the haphazard way the lair of the Neanderthals had been put together. Some levels eschewed straight lines entirely, with corridors curving back and forth, even twisting back on themselves. Other levels were clinical in their straightness and the transition between these sections was breathtaking.

There were no standards. Ceiling heights, widths of corridors, wall colours, shape of doors, all were random or up for argument. Even the notion of level floors was arguable, it seemed, with some parts undulating like sand dunes, for no apparent reason. It was as if the entire place were put together by teams of builders who were using entirely different plans.

The levels were connected by far more lifts and stairs than were needed. They were situated right around the perimeter of the levels and presented a swashbuckling variety of means of locomotion: hydraulic lifts, pneumatic lifts and one that Evadne concluded was an electrical traction lift.

One advantage of all this was the potential for hiding places. They found many abandoned rooms, as if the population had been much greater in past times, and some stairwells were dead ends – useful as a temporary refuge, but appalling as means of access.

In order to catch their breath and take stock, they'd secreted themselves in one of the vacant suites, a chamber set in solid rock. The walls were so rough that mounds of rubble were still strewn about, behind which Kingsley and Evadne sat – but not before Evadne had confirmed that the room had three doors leading to other parts of the complex. She wasn't about to be trapped in a room with no exit. Kingsley thought it an excellent idea, especially since the main door was broken and couldn't be shut completely.

'On the whole,' Evadne panted, 'I'd rather be at home.'

Crouched next to her, behind something that could have been either a miniature forge or a work of modern art, Kingsley struggled to reply.

His wild self was pressing hard and threatening to burst out.

'Somewhere far from here would do,' he said through gritted teeth.

Four Neanderthals ambled past, chatting. They carried tool chests, and one had a flaming blowtorch in one hand. His friends jeered when he gestured grandly and nearly set his own beard on fire.

'I have an idea,' Kingsley said.

'That's timely, because I'm baffled. This place is larger than I thought.'

'If we're trying to find a workshop, why not follow workers?'

'That, sir, is a fine piece of reasoning.'

'Glad to be of assistance.'

'Interesting and useful,' she mused. Then she pursed her lips. 'Laurence would like to meet you, I'm sure. He's interesting and useful as well.'

'Laurence? Don't you mean Clarence?' Kingsley climbed to his feet and slapped dust from his trousers.

'Clarence? Of course. Just testing how alert you are.'

The Neanderthal workers were loud, making them easy to follow. The task needed stealth, however, which appealed to Kingsley's animal side.

By watching the lifts the Neanderthal workers used and timing their approach carefully so that no-one was waiting in the awkwardly shaped cubicle where the lift arrived, Kingsley and Evadne were eventually able to make their way down to the industrial level of the Neanderthals' lair, deep under the ground.

The choice of doors was made easier by the stream of Neanderthals leaving and entering the far door, from which the sounds of machinery and construction also emerged whenever it was open. The nearer door was closed, but promised proximity to the site of Neanderthal activity. A few seconds' work on the lock and they were inside.

They emerged into a high-ceilinged workshop. Twenty yards away was the far wall, which had a single door. Overhead were festoons of electrical cables and pipes, while the steam ducts rattled on the wall to their right, near the floor. Benches and tool racks lined the walls to their left, right and opposite, only interrupted by a glass-fronted cabinet that was alive with red light. Inside were dozens of tiny glass vials that Kingsley had seen elsewhere.

In the middle of the room, however, was the feature that gave Kingsley pause and prompted a gasp of admiration from Evadne.

A round raised area displayed something that could be called a machine, if one were using language to reduce rather than describe. It reached forty or fifty feet into the air. To Kingsley's eye it looked like a descendant of a funfair helter-skelter but with embellishments and additions that defied comprehension. A disc at the apex anchored thousands of golden wires that hung to the ground and nearly obscured the spiral walkway around the inner tower. When the wires rippled in the slight draught, they emitted a sweet, gentle ringing sound.

Directly in front of the machine was a brass pedestal. The base was wrought to look like a stalagmite. The panel on the top was the size of a tea tray and was a riot of crystal and glass.

Evadne took two steps forward and tried to look at the machine and the pedestal at the same time. She clasped her hands and touched them to her chin. 'Can you lock the door?' she asked softly. 'And do something to the lift so we're not disturbed? I want to look at this. No.' She shook her head. 'I *need* to look at it.'

'It's the time machine?'

'It's beautiful.'

Working out a way to bar the lift took some time. The controls inside were basic in the extreme and impervious to tampering. He settled for jamming the door open with a length of pipe he found on one of the benches.

He was on his way to lock the workroom door when the tools on one of the benches took his eye. Impressed by the quality of the workmanship, he picked up a beautifully finished pipe cutter – and a number of things happened one after the other.

Firstly, Kingsley found himself thinking that he hadn't known that Evadne was a whistler, then a gravelly voice that wasn't Evadne's cried out, 'Who are you?' only to be followed by a rather ominous click, a hiss, and a snap, that led to an even more ominous heavy bodily *thump*.

Kingsley was halfway around the glittering machine before he knew it to find a dismayed Evadne pocketing her dart gun and running to crouch beside a white-coated female Neanderthal who was stretched out on the floor.

'I'm sorry,' Evadne said, but whether to him or to the young Neanderthal woman he didn't know. They made a contrasting pair, with the ruddy features and bright red hair of the stocky Neanderthal against Evadne's snow-white countenance. She looked up. 'I wasn't thinking. I should have questioned her before shooting.'

'I hadn't managed to lock the door yet. Stupid of me,' Kingsley admitted. 'What's that in her hand?'

Evadne uncurled the fingers. Gently, she removed a glass capsule. Its red glow suffused her features. 'Ah.'

She touched her spectacles. Immediately they became slightly purple. She cocked her head. 'I thought so. Phlogiston. Remarkable.'

'More over there,' Kingsley said, pointing at the glass cabinet.

Evadne stood. 'I think I have a way to disrupt their plans for quite some time.'

Undoing her satchel as she went, Evadne hurried to the cabinet. The red light from it touched her features as she stood for a moment, studying the racks inside. 'There's enough phlogiston here to make a Demimonder a king.'

With an abrupt but graceful motion, Evadne swept a hand along the racks, tumbling the vials into the open satchel until she'd emptied the entire cabinet. She buckled it up and patted it. 'This will set them back, at least.'

'Will it give us enough time to get help?'

Evadne put a finger to her lips and bounced it once or twice. 'Why don't you go and make sure the door is locked this time?'

The door didn't take much effort, despite the oddity of the spring plate mechanism. When Kingsley rounded the machine, Evadne was studying the brass pedestal. She glanced at him, looked back to the panel, then held up a phlogiston vial. 'I think this goes ... here.'

Before Kingsley could protest, she slid the vial into an opening on the face of the panel. For a moment, nothing happened and Kingsley was relieved. Then a rapid series of rattles came from the machine and overhead a bank of lights came alive. They made the golden wires even more radiant and the whole machine shimmered. Now that Kingsley was closer he could see that the wires weren't attached at the bottom. They hung free, making the whole enclosure more of a curtain than a cage.

If we're trying to be furtive, he thought, *we're not going about it the right way*. He ran his fingers through his hair with exasperation. 'What on earth are you doing?'

'I'm trying to work out if this is a time machine or not.' She scowled at the panel. 'And, if so, how it's calibrated.'

'By starting it up?'

'With all the noise next door, I'm sure no-one will notice.'

'I'm not.'

'Oh, Kingsley, I couldn't *not* try it.' Her eyes were bright. 'It's magnificent!'

'We don't have time for this.'

'It's just a test. A very careful, sensible test.' Her hand rested on the panel. Her forefinger bounced up and down, while the others remained still. 'I'd say that most of these controls are for settings. I wonder if they keep specifications anywhere.'

Kingsley shook his head. 'We're supposed to be destroying it, not worshipping it.'

Evadne looked stricken. 'But it's so wonderful! We could learn so much!' Then she gathered herself. 'Of course. I'm sorry.'

At that moment, pounding came from the nearest door. Kingsley jumped with what he hoped was aplomb. He cleared his throat. 'Are you finished?'

A hum rose from the golden curtain. The sharp smell of ozone made Kingsley wrinkle his nose. It was like being near an electrical substation in the rain. A series of sharp snaps ran around the upper rim of the machine. Sparks curved into the air and immediately flew upward before disappearing into the mesh above the gantry.

The pounding on the doors became hammering, with angry shouts as an underscore. 'Now,' Evadne said, 'you're the escapologist – what's the best way out of this pickle?'

214

Kingsley rapidly turned over the de-pickling options, opted for the lift, but discarded this when the door of the lift edged back, then rammed forward, dislodging the iron bar he'd put in place.

The lift disappeared upward.

Now, he thought. *That's unhelpful.* 'How many darts do you have?'

'A dozen.'

'And you're a good shot?'

'With these spectacles? I'm a marksman. Markswoman. I'm unerring.'

'Right. We climb to the top of that machine. You keep shooting until they stop coming. Then we get out through the doorway, using your sabre and my knife.'

'That's the best you can come up with?'

'It's better than being eaten.'

'All it does is put off being eaten while making them angrier.'

'True.' Kingsley looked around, hoping to spot a secret door he'd missed seeing earlier. 'The Basic Principles of Escapology.'

'I know. Stay calm, take your time. You've told me.'

'There's one I haven't shared with you.' He took her hand. 'Come on.'

He led her up onto the platform. The time machine was rotating. An almost musical hum was coming from deep inside it.

Evadne looked at it, then at Kingsley. 'You want to use the time machine?'

'One of the most important Basic Principles of Escapology: when there's only one way out, use it.'

TWENTY-EIGHT

Damona hadn't lost her temper for thirty-two years. She surrendered herself to it now.

'Who?' She stood in front of the time machine. She shook both fists in the air. 'Who can I punish? I will tear their throats out!'

The time machine slowed, hissed and crackled. Her people in the workshop stared. Uncertain, afraid. More edged through the far door, a crowd. Behind them, noise and shouting. Labour. Activity. Progress.

Hilda was in a chair. Two friends attended her. She had her head in her hands. Weeping. She raised it when Damona approached. 'The phlogiston. It's gone.'

'I know.' Damona's rage subsided, dwindled. The young woman looked sick. An angry red mark bloomed on the side of her neck. 'You were shot?'

'With this.'

Damona took the dart. It was well made for Invader stuff. Well balanced. A reservoir for refilling. Someone was good. 'How much phlogiston did the machine use?'

'Much.' Hilda gestured at the cabinet. 'But they have taken the rest. Our stockpile.'

'You moved our stockpile here?'

Hilda's face crumpled. 'It was the efficient place for it.'

It made sense, but it was a disaster. It would take months to refine that much phlogiston.

Damona hissed. She was impatient, now, after all these years. Revenge was close. She wanted it now. She studied the machine. 'How far back did they go?'

'I had the controls set.' Hilda's voice was choked. 'Two hundred and fifty years.'

'Do we have any more phlogiston?'

'Some. In the main workshop.'

'Enough for another test?'

Gustave bustled forward. 'They were the two young Invaders you brought in earlier, Eldest.'

Damona grunted. Invaders. Trouble, always. The world would be better off without them.

She gave the dart back to Hilda. She put her hands on her hips. Head back. She studied the time machine. 'Hilda?'

'Can the machine operate again?' The young engineer smiled, slowly. 'Maybe. How far back, Eldest?'

'The same.' She searched the faces. 'Rolf. Magnus. Assemble a raiding team. I have a special mission for you.'

Magnus flinched, Rolf looked thoughtful. They jogged off in opposite directions.

217

Days of labour. Brainwork. Effort. Years of planning. Years of toil. Alone.

Damona now saw her dream made real. A time machine. Made by the True People to right a wrong. When it was ready the past would be mended. No more dispossession. No more persecution. No more wandering, lost and hunted.

Signe, my great-granddaughter, this is for you. And for all those who were taken before their time.

A grim smile. About her, people muttered, wondering. Damona went to the time machine. Stood in front of it, proudly.

'All is not lost,' she announced. She lifted her arms. Made fists. 'We now know the machine works.' They brightened. Smiled. Cheered. 'We will succeed!'

Rolf and Magnus pushed back through the door with others. Armed. Eager. Ready.

'Rolf. Magnus. We will send you back through time. Take your team. Find the Invaders. Bring back the phlogiston we need.'

Rolf cheered. Magnus asked: 'And the Invaders, Eldest?'

Damona thought of Dr Ward. 'Bring them back, if easy. If not . . .' She shrugged.

Hilda pushed through the crowd. She held a bundle of metal mesh. 'Eldest! If they are coming back, we need to make preparations!'

'Quickly,' Damona said. She smiled at those assembled, together, as one. Her people. 'Go. Hunt.'

TWENTY-NINE

Kingsley nearly choked when he staggered up the stairs that led from the underground river. The air was thick with smoke. His eyes watered. He found it hard to breathe. Evadne blundered into his back, pushing him forward and out into the open.

'This is an escape?' She flapped a hand and adjusted her phlogiston-filled satchel on her shoulder. 'Out of the frying pan, I'd say.'

'Where are we?' Kingsley had trouble working his mouth. Since arriving in the stinking dark cave, his brain had felt as if it had been pumped full of water and squeezed. Thoughts were heavy and imponderable and he had trouble articulating the simplest thing.

In addition, his wild self was terrified – the smoke and the grinding, thunderous sound filling the air made him want to either flee or hide.

'I've no idea,' Evadne said. 'Keep your wits about you.'

'This way,' he mumbled.

Together they stumbled into a street of two-storey, half-timbered buildings that jostled side by side with each other. In the narrow gap between them was a churning sea of frightened people.

Men, women and children shouted and screamed, pushed and clawed at each other. Kingsley coughed, and grimaced at the dark and smoky air. Then he looked up.

The sky was orange, and black, and red.

'The world's on fire,' he muttered.

Evadne wrapped her scarf around her face, pushed back her satchel and then dragged at his arm. He nearly tripped, but shambled with her to a crooked lane between two buildings. They climbed over a pile of broken pots, then Evadne had to stop and cough.

Kingsley leaned against rough timber. Muck and cobblestones were underfoot. Low, old buildings leaned towards the middle of the alley like conspiring gossips.

Noise nearby – shouting and the roar of . . . artillery?

Without thinking, he took Evadne around the waist and, bent double and coughing, they hurried through the smoke. A terrified hound caught up to them and raced past, howling. Part of Kingsley wanted nothing more than to join it.

A bone-aching concussion rocked the ground nearby. They were nearly bowled over by a man and woman who were adopting much the same mode of locomotion as they were, but were simply much better at it. Their wooden shoes clocked on the cobbles as they fairly sprinted past, just ahead of a tide of ash and hot air.

Evadne cried out and dropped to all fours. 'My spectacles!'

Kingsley stopped dead, acutely aware that his next step could be the end of Evadne's seeing, at least for the moment. He held out his hands, ready to ward people off. 'You said you carried extra sets.'

'The Neanderthals took them,' she said, almost weeping.

Another roar, then Kingsley shuddered at the shrieks from nearby. Someone – man, woman or child, he couldn't tell – was both terrified and without hope, but unwilling to stay silent in the face of whatever was coming for them.

'I have them!' Evadne cried but when she put them on she made a sound of disgust. 'I must find water. I can hardly see.'

Kingsley was starting to think more clearly and had a notion that water might be in short supply.

Another explosion nearby. More people pushed into the lane behind them and hurried in their direction. Kingsley and Evadne pressed against the half-timbered wall and let them past.

'This is bad,' he said softly as a welter of details impressed themselves on him. They were insistent, demanding that they be taken together to make a whole, but he shied away from them and their implications. Of all the times in London to be sent back to ...

Evadne gripped his arm. 'What is it? I can hardly see.'

'Nothing.'

'As bad as that, is it?'

'What do you mean?'

'People only say "nothing" to a question like that when the answer is dire.'

Kingsley flinched as a gigantic crash reverberated down the lane. They both had to shy away as a wave of dust, ash and smoke swept past them. 'We seem to be on fire,' he said.

'I can tell that, even with only a tiny patch of unsmeared vision, but something else bit you. What is it?'

'The people hustling past us. Unless they were from a nearby theatre, their clothes are hundreds of years old. But they're new. If you see what I mean.'

More hot ash and embers were driven at them. Kingsley turned away again, shielding Evadne. He screwed up his eyes. When he opened them again, she'd tilted her head and was looking at him through one corner of her spectacles. 'Thank you. I couldn't see that coming.'

'We need to get away from here.'

'Follow the strange dressers. They seemed to know which way to go.'

'Good idea.'

'In an emergency, I don't care how people are dressed, as long as they're helpful.'

Kingsley would never have said that he knew every street and byway of London, but he quickly admitted to himself that they'd emerged into a district that he'd never been in before. In the smoke and grit whipped up by the wind he couldn't make out any landmarks, either, but the nature of the buildings and the clothing on the panicked pedestrians confirmed the conclusion he'd come to.

Evadne rebelled against her almost helpless state, but after smearing her spectacles even more badly, she gave up and allowed Kingsley to drape his arm and pull her close, steering the way through the panicked streets. Explosions continued to punish the air, sending up sparks, dust and a chorus of shrieks with every detonation.

Sometimes, Kingsley thought, *all it takes is one point to fix a bearing.* In London, a few marks were unshakeable and he saw two of them at once – the river and the Tower. Immediately, he knew they were north of the river, not far from the City. *If that's the case*, he thought, fending off a man who was carrying a rooster, *where are the Houses of Parliament?*

They weren't there. Instead, a rambling pile of buildings, grand enough but rather ramshackle, sprawled along the riverbank. Then his eye was dragged back along the river. 'Tower Bridge isn't there.'

Two men in gorgeous velvet knee breeches ran past. They were carrying a small barrel on a sling between them. Their hats were wide brimmed and dashing. Their hair was long, as were their cloaks, and their beards were pointed. Scabbards flapped at their sides.

A man dressed in a leather apron staggered past, singing with more gusto than talent. He had a tankard of beer in each hand. Hardly thinking, Kingsley pointed past him. When the drunkard followed the direction of the gesture, Kingsley relieved him of one of the tankards. 'That woman!' he shouted in the man's ear. 'She's calling you!'

The man clearly had trouble understanding Kingsley, so Kingsley leered, then winked. The man leered back and swayed off, swinging his shoulders and swimming through the crowd.

'Here.' Kingsley gave the tankard to Evadne. 'Use it to wash your spectacles.'

She made a face when she smelled it. 'Beer?'

'Ale, I'd say. It's most likely cleaner than the water around here.'

She made another face, but carefully dipped the spectacles in the beer before using her handkerchief. 'Better. Smelly, but it will do for now.'

'I want you to tell me I'm not dreaming.' He slapped at his shoulder, which had started smouldering, the victim of a drifting spark. He pointed. 'You see the Tower. What's on the river near it?'

'Boats. Lots of them.'

'Any bridges?'

Evadne put a hand to her mouth. 'Where's Tower Bridge?' She swung her gaze. 'Where's Big Ben?'

'Remember how you told me to keep an open mind? It's your turn now.'

Ash and embers swirled about them. The people in the tiny crossroads were undecided about whether to panic, to sing or to pray, so they were doing all of them at once.

Evadne looked at them and then at Kingsley. 'Tell me.'

'I think we've landed ourselves in the Great Fire. Welcome to 1666.'

'I'm willing to accept that the Neanderthals have a working, phlogiston-powered time machine that's shot us back almost two hundred and fifty years,' Evadne said. 'What I'm keenest to discover, though, is a way for us to get back home.'

They'd made their way across London Bridge, along

with thousands of others, in the hope that the river would provide a barrier from the fire beast that was consuming the world. From their viewpoint, on the walls of the dilapidated and rambling maze of buildings that a weeping man told them was Winchester Palace, they could see the explosions as the city authorities did their best to make firebreaks to stop the spread of the conflagration. The velvet-clad cavaliers that Kingsley had seen earlier were no doubt King Charles's men, running gunpowder for the desperate task.

Unlike all those around them, Kingsley and Evadne had the small comfort of knowing that the city would survive. From where they were, however, that appeared most unlikely. The entire vista was afire. Flame rolled across rooftops like a stormy ocean, wave on wave sweeping across London, devouring with a hunger that was unquenchable. Boats made the perilous crossing, ferrying passengers across the ash-laden water.

The wind roared towards the fire from the east, sucked into its greediness, but the fire itself outroared it, a vast grinding underlying a hissing and coughing that sounded like a great jungle animal. Nothing could stand in its way. It would consume and continue to consume until the world ended.

'Have you read Mr Wells's novel?' Kingsley asked Evadne as they gazed at the catastrophe.

'*The Time Machine*? Of course.'

'It looks as if we're living what he dreamed,' he said.

'Two hundred years.' Evadne put her satchel on the parapet beside her, then she stood with her arms wrapped around herself.

'Nearer two hundred and fifty.'

'A new London will rise from this.'

He gazed at the shabbiness of the old bishop's palace. The whole edifice had an air of neglect – tumbledown outbuildings, shrubs and small trees rooting in the cracks between stones, ivy questing indiscriminately. No-one had protested when they, along with hundreds of others, had mounted the walls to gaze at the inferno across the river. 'The old London looks as if it won't be missed.'

'It will be, but it will mostly be forgotten.'

'Time does that.'

'And what are we going to do?'

'I've never met a trap I haven't been able to find my way out of.'

'I'm reassured.'

'It's just a matter of thinking about basic principles, looking for weaknesses, taking opportunities ...'

'And multiplying platitudes?'

'I love a multiplying platitude,' he said solemnly. 'So fulfilling.'

She crossed her arms, then uncrossed them to cover her mouth when she yawned. 'I'm tired.'

'You should be. You haven't slept for two hundred and fifty years ... Negative two hundred and fifty years. A long time.'

'Then sleep would appear to be a solution.'

'And food.' Kingsley gazed across the city. Were they, indeed, trapped? He glanced at the wan Evadne. A small smudge of soot marred one cheek.

He saw how she was fingering the chain of her pendant. 'Are you missing Clarence?'

'Clarence?'

He gestured at her hand.

226

'Ah.' She drew out the pendant and clicked it open. She studied it for a moment before sliding it back under her collar. 'I was thinking that he'd enjoy it here. He's a scholar of Stuart drama.'

'A remarkable fellow, Clarence. I couldn't invent someone so accomplished.'

'What are you suggesting?'

'Far be it from me to suggest anything. I simply bow down in front of Clarence. Or his picture, in any case.'

'And so you should.'

Evadne gazed back at the spectacle of the fire and Kingsley turned to gaze at her. A thought came to him, unasked for and surprising. It wasn't hard to imagine, if things went sour and they had to remain in 1666, building a life here with this mercurial, accomplished and dauntless young woman.

He actually blinked at the idea. It wasn't one of those that sidled up edgewise. No, this was the equivalent of a mental blow between the eyes, but as he did his best to recover, he was already seeing its possibilities. Without Clarence – mythical or otherwise – together, surely, they could make something out of this seventeenth-century city with their twentieth-century knowledge and a satchel full of phlogiston. Besides, a city like this was bound to be less civilised than King Edward's London. He may have more chance to let his wild side run free. It could be a relief from constantly trying to keep it in check. He could, strange as it might sound, reach some sort of accommodation with himself.

As long as he didn't think about what was happening in 1908, he might be comfortable here – but he couldn't banish the memory of the plight of his foster father, nor the knowledge of the Neanderthals' plans.

It made his head ache to contemplate, but what would happen if the Neanderthals in 1908 went ahead and constructed their time machine, went back and exterminated the early humans? Would Evadne and he immediately be surrounded by a Neanderthal–populated London? Or would they simply disappear? If so, when? And did that last question make any sense at all when time itself had been turned inside out, or stood on its head, or twisted into something fiendishly knotty and impossible to undo?

A gust of wind from the east made Kingsley squint, but his eyes still watered from the windborne smoke. The scene across the river smeared, with the orange light becoming red and dire.

'The Immortals.' A notion had struck him with enough force to make his ears ring. 'You said they have time travel.'

Evadne's hands were on the stone battlements, white against grey. 'I said they messed about with time and space, whatever that means.'

'And that Neanderthal woman. When she was leaving the Immortals' place, she was talking with that man about what she called a Temporal Manipulator.'

Evadne yawned. 'I fail to see the importance.'

'If these sorcerers are actually immortal, that means that they might be here, now, in 1666. With a time machine.'

Evadne swung around to face him. 'Kingsley, that is an outstanding piece of brainwork.'

'D'you think so?'

'Indubitably. Here I was, thinking through the implications of setting up here with you while you, quite brilliantly, find an escape.'

'You were thinking about what? Setting up here?'

Evadne put both hands to her mouth. 'And I've had an equally brilliant addition to your plan. Do you remember my telling you about Demimonde groups opposed to the Immortals?'

'I – Yes, I remember.'

'I'm sure they were active this long ago. I'd say they'd know where the Immortals are in this time, and might be persuaded to help us.'

THIRTY

Soames revelled in being lord of the manor. Taking possession of the Immortals' lair was right and proper; it was a fitting place for him to reside and assume a position in the world that was his due.

At last, Jabez, a place worthy of you!

He explored, wanting to know his estate and its facilities. He found a complex of corridors and rooms leading off the main hall. Stairs led down to the cells beneath. Once he confirmed to himself that they were empty of the children his underlings had sent the Immortals, he promised to inspect them at another time.

The library was a happy find. It was windowless, naturally, but that meant all the more room for books. No concession was made to the decorative, either. It was simply a long, narrow room with books floor to ceiling. A line of back-to-back shelves ran down the centre of the room, to increase the intense bookiness of the place. It smelled of leather and paper, dust and knowledge.

Not many people would know what to make of this, Jabez, he thought and began to applaud himself. The echoes made it seem as if an enormous crowd were paying him homage. *You were born for this!*

Soames was both delighted and daunted. The key to the Immortals' longevity would be in here, he was sure, but where? Starting at 'A' and working his way around would be the work of a lifetime or two. He could hire assistants. He knew a dozen Demimonders who would leap at the chance, and would probably pay for the privilege, but did he want to share this treasure with anyone? Who could he trust?

No-one.

It was a shame, and he had much to sort out. The Immortals' time in India, for instance. What had they been doing there? The shipment he'd arranged for them would be well on its way. He was looking forward to seeing what they needed so eagerly.

And then there were the devices he'd had his underlings place around the Olympic Stadium. He really should get hold of one to see what was going on there and what he could make of it.

You're a busy man, Jabez, he thought, *but a busy Jabez is a happy Jabez!*

He continued his explorations.

Hours later, he came across a small room. It was cosy, carpeted and rather too working class for Soames's taste, but he took it as evidence that he wasn't the only ordinary human that the Immortals employed. He settled himself in an armchair, after carefully brushing it off, and appreciated the more human scale of the room. It would make a fine temporary office. He'd have a desk brought in, and some filing cabinets. When he was accustomed to the main hall, he could move everything out there where he belonged.

Soames was sitting back, looking about the small room and estimating where best to locate a bank of pigeon holes, when he heard the noise.

At first, he assumed it came from rats. He wrinkled his nose. He detested rats and their dirty, smelly ways, but he accepted that most underground – and many overground – domiciles were rife with them.

I'll get a cat, he thought. He laced his hands on his chest. *Maybe two.*

Soames liked cats. He understood the self-absorbed, clinical killers. Their complete selfishness appealed to him. Feed them, let them in and out, and they'd co-operate. Cross them, and watch out.

A plan that was clear, simple, straightforward. He liked it.

Soames stood, shook out his trouser creases, and went looking for signs of rats.

An hour later and Soames was puzzled. He couldn't find any signs of rats. No holes, no chewed books or furniture, no nasty droppings. He'd inspected the small room, the library, a dozen rooms in between and all their corridors as well.

Nothing.

He returned to the small room and shrugged. It may be a puzzle, but it was a small one.

Then he heard the noise again.

Plink, it went. Then *plink* again.

Soames exited the small room. He found the main hall and stood just inside one of the five-sided doors.

Plink. Plink.

This wasn't rats. Soames rubbed his hands together. His gaze darted about the vast chamber. No, nothing rodental about this noise, but he had no idea what it was.

Jabez, he thought, *this is a mystery of an unpleasant sort.*

Soames retied the laces on his shoes, then flicked a speck of mud from the toe of his left. He straightened, shook out the creases in his trousers, unbuttoned and rebuttoned his waistcoat, and made sure it was even.

Unexplained noises in what had been the lair of mysterious magicians. No, this didn't augur well at all. He was rapidly revising his plans to move his entire base of operations to the subterranean Greenwich warren. He might be called overly suspicious, but he'd learned that such an attitude paid useful dividends in the Demimonde.

Plink. Ka-plink.

In the morning of the following day, after a sleepless night caused by the irregular but remorseless noise, a red-eyed Soames made a cup of tea in the small room. He found a slightly stale digestive biscuit and ate it for breakfast. For a moment, he'd enjoyed the unexpected rush of memories – young Soames in his nursery – then he heard the noise.

Plink.

Soames jerked. The tea soaked his sleeve and he jerked again before flinging the cup away from him in disgust. It shattered on the sink. He uttered an oath that he thought coarse when others resorted to it.

He dabbed at his sleeve with his handkerchief, pursed his lips at the stain on his cuff and promised himself that he'd get Mrs Tollemache's Steam Laundry to go to work on it. Then he plucked his trusty Bulldog from his pocket, determined that *this time* he'd find who was intruding on his domain.

He edged out into the hall.

Ka-plink.

Soames stiffened then swivelled on the spot, taking in the whole chamber.

Ka-plink-plink.

He swept his Bulldog over the pentagonal floor. Nothing stirred in any of the alcoves apart from the two gently rotating manipulators. This time, he had it.

The sound came from below.

Soames's experience with the Demimonde had led him into much contact with magic. As a result, he rarely wasted time puzzling over the uncanny. It simply *was*, as the weather was, or hunger was, or destiny was. He'd seen enough to realise that the sounds leaking up from the nether reaches of the Immortals' complex were likely to be dangerous, but he also knew that he'd never be comfortable in the place until he'd investigated. Besides, in his quest to understand the Immortals' methods, he couldn't overlook anything. The smallest device or the tiniest phenomenon might be the key to unlocking their secrets.

His descent took him past cell after cell, all empty.

At first, Soames was horrified by the lack of parapet or guardrail, but after passing a hundred cells or more he became accustomed to the dizzying drop on his left. He smiled as he heard, repeated at long intervals, the *ka-plink* sound or its cousins, confident that he had an inkling or two as to its origin. Eventually, he found it a homely, reassuring sound, like glasses touching after a toast. He even amused himself by imagining a banquet in his honour, with kings and queens pleading for him to speak.

The final ladder led to the floor, a featureless black disc that Soames had no intention of setting foot on. It was ten or fifteen yards across, as black as any soul that Soames had met. He had the disturbing notion that it would eat him if he touched it, so he put his hand on his chin, balanced his elbow on the back of his other hand, and waited.

Some time later – he blinked when he realised he hadn't looked at his watch – he felt the sound rather more than heard it.

Ka-plink.

A glass vial hung in the air over – as far as Soames could judge – the centre of the black disc. It glowed with a light that Soames recognised and lusted after, as would anyone who did business in the Demimonde.

Phlogiston.

Soames reached for the glowing vial, almost before he realised it, but pulled back suddenly at the impression of overwhelming eagerness from the black disc. The vial shot upward, blurring with speed, leaving a trail that shimmered in Soames's vision, lingering red before reluctantly fading.

Soames waited, his excellent watch in his hand this time, to find that it was twelve minutes before the next glowing vial appeared. Seventeen minutes later, two vials appeared at once with a double-clink, shooting off like paired comets.

While waiting for the next vial to appear, Soames was doing some rough calculations. He was helpless not to, and the result suggested that at this rate, with this much phlogiston, he could be richer than the dreams of avarice, except that, in this one particular field, he was a very fine dreamer indeed.

He looked up when the most recent vial flew up. Overhead was nearly as black as the hungry black disc near his feet.

All he had to do now was find out where the flying vials were going.

THIRTY-ONE

Kingsley stretched as they left the inn. 'Rested?' he asked Evadne.

Her face was mournful. 'I enjoy my sleep. It's going to take more than a few hours to make up for what I've lost.'

'I'm just glad you found somewhere to take us.'

'Some inns like catering to the Demimonde.' She fitted a finger behind her spectacles and rubbed her eye. 'And the silver helped the negotiation.'

'Sixpence goes a long way here,' Kingsley said. In this case, it had extended to two rooms for the afternoon and a rough meal of what was either a thick vegetable soup or a thin vegetable stew. Regardless, it satisfied what had become a yawning void inside him.

He cast a look back at the inn, tucked away as it was in a street running south from the river. The inn was the epitome of inconspicuousness. He was sure he would have walked past it a dozen times without noticing it if it were not for Evadne.

'The innkeeper was so grateful for that sixpence that he was happy to answer a few questions,' Evadne said. 'He confirmed that some of the anti-Immortalists are about here and now and gave me a few suggestions as to where we could find them.' She adjusted the hood of the cloak she'd bought from the innkeeper. It hid her face, something that Kingsley thought a shame, but he understood the good sense behind it. While the panic and tumult of the fire may have allowed Evadne to go relatively unnoticed so far, there was no point in risking someone pointing at her because of her unusual appearance and blaming the whole disaster on her. A crowd was a fickle thing and dangerous when roused.

'So we're going to collar some of these anti-Immortalists and demand they tell us where these sorcerers are?'

'Nothing as crude as that. Let me think about it.'

It was barely a moment later, near the Pickle Herring Stairs on the river, that Kingsley saw the Neanderthals. Neanderthals in the open. Neanderthals among normal humans. Neanderthals dressed in garments from 1908.

Kingsley acted quickly and dragged Evadne behind a wall. She was startled, but didn't cry out. Her eyes widened when she followed his gesture and saw the reason for the precipitous action.

'I still have my dart gun,' Evadne breathed in Kingsley's ear, creating all number of extraordinary sensations.

'Hold onto it,' he whispered back and wiped his streaming eyes. The air on this side of the river was still abominable.

The Neanderthals were pushing through the crowd on the embankment and probably enjoying the sensation of being taller than those around them. They were also probably enjoying – if that were the word – the fact that their appearance wasn't causing alarm; the ordinary Londoners were no doubt expecting demons to cavort down the street at any moment, so a few broad-browed, thickset people were hardly cause for alarm.

The Neanderthals disappeared through a stone arch. Kingsley watched them go, fully aware that the dangerous surroundings had suddenly become even more dangerous.

On the southern bank of the Thames, with the theatres, bull and bear baiting, riotous taverns and eating houses, there was a general atmosphere of lawlessness that was only made worse by the End of Days scene on the other side of the river. Kingsley thought it was as if a bit of the Demimonde had given up trying to hide and simply lumped itself out in plain sight.

As they pushed through crowds that were both despairing and celebratory, sometimes at the same time, Evadne confirmed his suspicions. Holding tightly to his arm, she had to shout into his ear. 'The walls are thin here, between the Demimonde and the ordinary world! That's why I'm hoping to find our allies!'

'You're calling them allies already?' Kingsley danced them both around a man who was sitting the middle of the road, weeping. He held a puppet in his lap.

'I'm full of hope!' She smiled, and Kingsley was pleased to find no brittleness.

Evadne brought them to a gaunt edifice overlooking the uproar of Southwark and the fire on the other side of the river like a disapproving aunt. The church that would one day be Southwark Cathedral was now filled with worshippers obviously inspired – or frightened to death – by the catastrophe to the north.

Evadne pushed against the flow of worshippers, however, and they made their way to the rear of the church and out to the old priory buildings. Most of these were disused and in desperate need of repair, but Kingsley was intrigued to see people at glassless windows watching the milling crowd and leaning precariously to catch sight of the far bank and the fire.

Evadne led them down what may have been a narrow lane, but was more like a gap where two of the priory buildings had leaned away from each other. A drain had seized the opportunity, as drains tend to, and ran through the middle of it. Evadne moved nimbly along one side, but Kingsley had to straddle the horrible gutter. The stench made his ears ring.

'Here.'

Kingsley would have walked straight past the door. Not because it was hard to see, or obscured, or hidden in any way. It was remarkably ordinary, a wooden door set into bricks with no identifying features, but perhaps its ordinariness made the eye skate over it, kept the observer moving, because of its outstanding lack of interest.

Evadne pushed the door open and they were confronted with a grimy room only a few feet square, with no window but a set of stairs leading upward. A stool with only two legs was the sole thing in the neglected place.

The lean of the building became more apparent as

they mounted the stairs. Kingsley had to steady himself against the wall as they came to the first floor landing. Two rooms, only one with a door.

'This is the place?' he asked Evadne. He kept his voice low.

'So I'm led to believe.' She kept a hand in her pocket. She pushed back her hood, reached out with the other hand and rapped sharply. 'A Demimonde location for a Demimonde group.'

The door swung back. A woman studied them with no trace of surprise. She was small, with dark eyes, and she wore a coarse smock. Her feet were bare. 'What do you want?'

'You are the Retrievers?'

The woman cast a look over her shoulder. Kingsley heard movement. He glanced around him, searching for the best way out, as his wild side threatened to rouse.

Evadne put a hand on the door. 'Please. We understand you search for lost children.'

'And find them, when we can.' The woman's voice was thick, her vowels strained. 'We bring them home.'

'From the Immortals?'

The woman shivered. 'Aye. From them, or their agents, when we can.'

'We want to help.'

The woman swung back the door. As she did, Kingsley's eyes widened.

She was missing her little finger.

Three men and another woman were in the tiny room. A single shuttered window let light through in streaks.

A rough table, two benches and a raft of suspicion greeted Kingsley and Evadne when they entered.

'Who are they?' one of the men whispered. He wore richer clothes than the others – a velvet jacket with lace collar and cuffs. His voice was hoarse. Both his hands were under the table.

'We're from your future,' Evadne said. 'We need to find the Immortals' lair to use their magic so we can go home again.'

'Ah.' The man put his hands on the table. One held a wicked bone-handled knife. The other had only four fingers. 'So it is help you want?'

'We can pay,' Evadne said. 'Silver.'

Kingsley rocked on his heels. 'I'm sorry, but wait a moment.' He tugged on Evadne's sleeve. 'You simply came out and told them? Just like that?'

She shrugged. 'We're in the Demimonde. I'm sure they've heard more outlandish tales.'

The woman closed the door. 'People from the future? You are strange enough.' She gestured. 'Your garments. Your talk.'

The hoarse man glanced at the others. 'Besides, silver overcomes disbelief. Most readily.'

'Sit.' The woman said. 'Tell us what you want.'

Kingsley had accepted that his clothes were already a lost cause, with the smoke, cinders and general dirt, so the encrusted bench was hardly an obstacle. He sat next to Evadne, who hesitated not at all. 'You are few,' she said.

The hoarse man shrugged. 'We were more. The magicians kill us when they find us.'

'Yet you continue your work.'

'How could we not?' the woman said. 'They take

242

children and they use them most foully. Who would not rise to defend the innocent?'

Evadne's face was hard. 'Many.'

'But not you?'

'No. I want to stop them. If I can find them, I will do them harm.'

Kingsley put his hand on Evadne's. 'We want their magic to send us home.'

Evadne grimaced. 'Yes. Of course.' She took a deep breath. 'They have something in their lair that could help us.'

'When you go home, you will do them harm?' the woman asked, her eyes on Evadne.

'Oh yes,' Evadne breathed. 'Certes.'

The woman looked at Hoarse Voice. He nodded. The others followed, some more slowly than the rest. 'They are building a lair under Greenwich. Near the palace.'

Evadne stood and distributed the silver. The woman rose, went to the door and opened it. She saw the direction of Kingsley's gaze. 'We do it to ourselves,' she said, holding up her hand, 'to remind us of the foulness of the magicians.'

Hoarse Voice rapped on the table and held up his four-fingered hand as well. 'They do it to themselves for their magic. We do it so we will never forget.'

At the doorway, Evadne paused. 'You have all lost a child to them, have you not?'

The woman cast her gaze down. 'My daughter. Only eleven years, she had, but she was bonny.'

Hoarse Voice stood. 'We all have. Harm them for us. We will watch, do what we can.'

'And we will remember,' the woman said.

The door closed.

∽ THIRTY-TWO ∽

Just as evening exchanged places with night, the Neanderthals ambushed them in Deptford.

Kingsley was eying the inn on one side of the square. He could smell food and decided another tub of turnips and beans would hit the spot nicely.

Much to the consternation of the few passers-by, Evadne was up on the market cross, ignoring the rain and trying to spy out the surroundings, her satchel over her shoulder, her sabre on her hip. 'Everything looks different,' she called to Kingsley at the base of the monument, where he stood hands in pocket, his thoughts full of turnips and beans.

'A few hundred years of urban development will change a city,' he pointed out.

Evadne rolled her eyes and leaned to the east, but cried out just as Kingsley was admiring her agility. 'Kingsley! Neanderthals!'

Half a dozen of the brutish figures tumbled through a gap between the half-timbered buildings. They were led by one taller and even broader shouldered than his comrades – and with a bristling black beard to boot – while more were bowling out of a lane on the other side of the square.

Immediately and instinctively, Kingsley looked for avenues of escape around the muddy and puddle-strewn square, but they came too fast – and Evadne was trapped on the market cross.

Traps come in many sizes and shapes, he thought. The brutes pounded towards them and he had to admit they were all in the 'big and muscular' category. No weaklings here, no candidates for Professor Blumenthal's Physical Academy, which was a pity.

He bounced on his toes. He licked lips that were suddenly dry. *They must have a weakness*, he thought while his heart accelerated its beating. *It's just a matter of finding it.*

The first and most eager of the Neanderthals lunged. Kingsley caught him on the side of the jaw with a right hook that had all of his strength behind it – and immediately regretted it. It was like punching leather-covered stone. He let out a sharp oath and backed away rapidly, each step an adventure on the uneven, muddy cobbles.

The brute growled and pawed at him again.

Noted, Kingsley thought as he tried to stay upright, *the left side of the jaw isn't their weak spot*. He wasn't pinning much hope on the right side of the jaw either.

Kingsley had automatically thrust his throbbing fist under his armpit, but he dragged it out and jabbed at the Neanderthal as he advanced – not with any hope of doing damage, and with some hope of not connecting, but just to keep the blackguard at bay. The last thing Kingsley wanted to do was to wrestle with the barrel-chested brute. Grappling was a shortcut to being torn apart; nimbleness was the only answer. *Keep moving*, he told himself, *don't get caught*.

A *twang* came from behind him. His attacker blinked. He fumbled at his shoulder, then staggered and fell. 'To your right!' Evadne cried. Kingsley twisted just in time to avoid a shoulder charge that would have knocked him right over the dockyards and into the river, but was quick enough to launch a kick at the ham-like buttocks sailing past. The extra padding there meant that his foot didn't suffer the same fate as his fist, but it knew it had done a good day's work, nonetheless. The extra impetus sent the Neanderthal crashing into a pile of muck that released an odour not unlike hell. Undignified, but not seriously inconveniencing.

Another *twang* and a second Neanderthal fell. Kingsley saw then that his job was to keep the Neanderthals at bay while Evadne used her dart gun to dispatch as many as possible. The trouble was that the Neanderthals had come to the same conclusion and were swarming up the steps of the market cross. Two smaller brutes circled him, with a certain level of amusement at his more and more frantic glances to where Evadne was calmly shooting, reloading and shooting again.

'What, only two of you?' Kingsley tried. He bobbed and then drew back, retreating until he came up against the remains of a cart that had been left there. A huge fist whistled past and the Neanderthal laughed. 'Stand still, grub!'

'So you can break all the bones in my body? Of course!' Kingsley dropped his hands and came to attention, smiling.

Both Neanderthals frowned at this display, but obviously thought it too good an opportunity to argue with. They advanced, arms spread wide.

That's right, just a few more steps.

The puddle wasn't deep, but it was wet enough for both Neanderthals to look down at what they'd trodden in – which gave Kingsley time to produce the solid length of wood he'd been working at behind his back, thankful that the derelict nature of the cart meant quick and easy disassembly.

Kingsley wound up, spared a hope that he wasn't simply about to irritate his foes, and then swung.

He almost lifted himself off his feet with the effort, but the length of wood caught the first Neanderthal on the side of the head – the left, again – with a sound like a giant coconut shy. The blow toppled him against his comrade. They struck heads. The result was a double coconut sound and they both went to their knees, sprawling in the mud and water.

When they looked up, they'd stopped smiling. The first had blood dripping down his scalp and into his straggly, sandy beard. He wiped it away. 'I'll eat your heart for that, grub.'

Kingsley was shoved in his back, propelled towards the grub-hating brute who had thrown his arms out, ready for a spine-cracking hug. Desperately, Kingsley allowed his momentum to carry him forward. Ignoring a basic rule of hand-to-hand combat (*Don't go to ground!*) he threw himself to one side of the Neanderthal's grasp,

247

hoping that he could roll to his feet in time to meet any new attacker.

A heavy-gutted Neanderthal loomed over him for an instant, but his eyes rolled up and he crumpled, going to his knees and then falling. Kingsley managed to avoid being crushed, but when he bounced to his feet he was surrounded. A ring of four foes faced him. Three others were climbing the market cross and were reaching for Evadne, who had scrambled up as high as she could go. She had a leg hooked around the top of the cross. One hand held the dart gun and the other slashed with her sabre. In the middle of all the mayhem, Kingsley found a split-second to admire her swordplay, her aim and the quality of her taunting – her descriptions of her attackers' physical failings and her estimations of their family origins made them even more determined to drag her from her perch. She'd thrown back her hood and her hair flashed silver as she swivelled, keeping her attackers at bay with such elan that it was worthy of applause.

Despite this, Kingsley was under no illusions about their predicament. *Things could be going better*, he thought as he feinted right, then sprinted through the gap that caused, barely avoiding clutching hands. He leaped over another pile of muck that his pursuer opted to plough through.

Three Neanderthals were stretched out, slumbering, but they still had seven to contend with.

Kingsley reached the wall of the inn. He whirled. Kingsley essayed a jab at one of them, who instinctively pulled away, then advanced. Kingsley lunged one way, then the other, but they'd learned. They closed, flanking him to cut off any avenue of escape.

Kingsley swallowed. His teeth buried themselves in his lower lip. He knew, then, that he was standing on the precipice, in one of those moments that would determine the course of his life. If the Neanderthals took him, he would end up dead or worse – and he'd be unable to help Evadne. He could surrender and make sure of this fate, or he could continue to fight and end up the same.

His life's possibilities had narrowed to two equally unpalatable choices. He was trapped.

He blinked. Trapped? No answers? It was back to the Basic Principles. He remembered one of his favourites: *Take advantage of whatever is available in order to free yourself.*

What was available to him? Backed against a well-made stone wall with his only source of help under siege herself, he had little at his command.

Except surrendering to his wild self.

It burst free as if it had been waiting for this opportunity, and he threw back his head and howled. It had the unexpected effect of momentarily stopping the advance of the Neanderthals.

Suddenly, in the heat of the fight, Kingsley's world was richer. Sounds were more thrilling, smells were manifold and each told its own story. Removing the strictures of civilisation had allowed him to see what needed to be done. Decency, honour, mercy: none of them had any place here.

He was fighting for his life.

Fiercely, teeth bared, he lashed out and clawed at the eyes of the nearest of the advancing Neanderthals – not to do serious damage, but merely to distract. While that one snarled and staggered, Kingsley snapped a kick right at the groin of the fellow who was about to seize him from his left. He didn't take any time to revel in the agonised yelp that signalled a successful strike, or to marvel that the Neanderthals shared a classic weak spot with their cousins. He stooped and dragged up a handful of mud that he planted in the open mouth of his more wary third assailant, then raked his hand upward to plug the enormous nostrils. He clawed them into the bargain. The Neanderthal tried to shriek, but the intake of breath only meant he sucked the mud straight down his throat. Choking, he staggered away, eyes bulging, grasping at his own neck.

One left.

Kingsley moved on his toes, snarling, looking for an opportunity. The blood roared in his veins as he circled, the suddenly careful Neanderthal circling in the opposite direction, one hand extended. Hardly thinking, noticing details at a level beneath the conscious, Kingsley saw the sweat on the brute's brow and knew that his grip would be slippery. He saw the pulse beating in the bull neck and instantly knew the vein would be well protected. The boots on his foe's feet were solid — *stay away from a kick!* — but were extremely heavy. He'd be slow to move.

Kingsley danced to his right. As expected, the Neanderthal followed, but Kingsley had judged nicely. The pair of raised cobbles caught his foe's heavy boot. The brute went to shift his weight and Kingsley flicked his fingers at him. Not much mud was left, but the Neanderthal flinched as the patter struck his face.

It was enough. Kingsley crouched, took up a loose cobble, leaped and brought the stone down. Not on the Neanderthal's head, but on his neck where the pulse had fluttered.

The lout fell like a tree. Panting with effort and wild

exhilaration, Kingsley danced around him, growling deep in his chest. He wanted to take to him with his teeth, to rip at his throat, to feel blood on lips.

Kingsley took a step, then reeled away. He crouched against the wall of the inn, trembling, staring at his fallen foe, his breath coming in ragged gasps. There, in the mud and rain, he had a moment of clarity. He understood, at least in part, the allure of the wild, most especially in circumstances such as these. Throwing aside the conventions of civilisation was liberating. More than that, it was, thrilling!

Exactly like escaping from a trap.

Fighting for one's life was existence brought to its fundamentals. There was no time for niceties, no time for hesitation. Survival was a matter of split-second opportunities. A chance to defeat one's foe came in a heartbeat and had to be taken then, there, with all the force that could be summoned.

The trappings of civilisation were an impediment in a fight such as he'd just been through. It was like wearing a lead overcoat – an unnecessary, constricting burden. Civilisation was a countermanding voice, insisting that one couldn't claw at the eyes, that a foe should be given respect, that cunning was unworthy.

In such circumstances, civilisation was a shortcut to death. The pack who raised Kingsley, who saved him from death, had no need for civilisation. They were wild. They were free.

Kingsley heard its call and wanted to run with it. With the license granted to the wild, without the restraining influences of civilisation, ruthlessness wasn't just acceptable, it was laudable!

Still crouched, still panting, still with the heavy cobble-stone in his hand, he felt the rain begin to fall. It washed away the sweat on his brow. He tasted salt on his lips.

He was sceptical. He always had trouble with simple answers to complex situations. Life was rarely as straight-forward as his wild self would like it to be. The wild might be the natural state of humanity but, like it or not, Kingsley Ward lived in a civilised world. Besides, some of these layers that civilisation brought – some of these useless trappings, according to his wild self – were worthwhile. In a fight, the wild world had no time for compassion, or for mercy, but Kingsley knew that the world, and he, would be worse off without them.

Sometimes we can be better than our natures.

He dropped the cobblestone. He stepped over the Neanderthal and looked for Evadne, only to find her serenely descending from the market cross, the last of the comatose Neanderthals scattered around her like pagan worshippers prostrate in the face of the arrival of a goddess. The sight was so bizarre and so civilised – so *unwild* – that Kingsley was cheered.

He touched his ribs. They were hurting, even though he couldn't remember actually being struck there. Most of his muscles were trembling. His stomach was hollow, a gaping void inside him. The square was strewn with Neanderthals and Kingsley dully noted how Evadne had taken care of those he'd inconvenienced. With more interest, he noted how each of them, underneath their workaday jacket, was wearing an unlikely broad belt that sparkled as if sequin-strewn.

Adjusting the phlogiston satchel over her shoulder, she came to him, put a hand on his shoulder and peered into his face. Her hair was wet, her eyes concerned. 'Are you hurt?'

'Not seriously. Bruised ribs.'

'You did well.'

'Thanks. So did you.'

Evadne was looking at him over the top of her blue-tinted spectacles. 'Do you remember that secret you were going to tell me? I don't think you really have to spell it out for me.'

Kingsley looked down, looked up, looked around, looked anywhere but at this remarkable young woman who was still there, despite having seen – *knowing!* – the secret Kingsley had inside him.

'Perhaps,' he mumbled. Then he straightened. 'Which puts me at a disadvantage in our secret-sharing pact.'

'Don't worry. I don't intend to renege. A pact is a pact.'

Kingsley was spared from responding when the patrons of the inn began to creep out from where they'd been hiding. The first, the most curious, was a short man, even shorter than those behind him. He was young, with awkwardly cropped hair and a jacket that looked as if had seen better days a century or so ago. 'You beat the ogres,' he said, eyes wide, staring at the Neanderthals, then at Kingsley and Evadne. 'You and the ghost beat the monsters.'

At first, Kingsley had trouble understanding. The vowels were long and thick, the words stretched, but he put the sense together. 'She's not a ghost.'

The curious one and his friends – several with tankards in hand – chose to differ. 'White skin, hair. Ghost.'

Arguing wasn't likely to get them anywhere. Without

thinking, Kingsley took her hand. 'The ogres will wake up soon. They eat people.'

Kingsley and Evadne crossed the square while the patrons of the inn tried to see who could run the fastest in the opposite direction.

THIRTY-THREE

After spending the night in two small but clean rooms that Evadne found at another Demimonde establishment, it had been Kingsley's turn to lead the way. At the Royal Dockyards, he negotiated passage with a boatman who was more interested in Kingsley's silver coins than in his strange way of speaking and even stranger garb.

For a moment, as the boat neared Greenwich, Kingsley was convinced that they had been brought to the wrong place. The riverbanks were crowded with people. They clustered in small groups, on wharfs and along the water's grassy edge, looking upriver to the horror that was London ablaze, but it wasn't that which so disconcerted Kingsley. The entire shape of the park and its environs threw him akilter because the most familiar buildings weren't there. The palace renovations that would eventually become the beginnings of the massive Naval College were under way. The rest of the rambling old palace took up much of the bank, a tower was where the observatory should be, and the park itself was much more higgledy-piggledy than the one he knew – the one he'd seen only the night before.

The night before and two hundred and fifty years from now, he reminded himself.

Kingsley pushed through the crowd on the dock, while Evadne kept her head down, shielding her memorable face. The people displayed an odd mixture of attitudes. Many were that most recognisable of types: the ghoulish onlooker, the sort that Kingsley imagined had been on the outskirts of human disasters forever, probably standing near the ruins of Troy and commenting on the size of that horse. Others were praying for deliverance, either mumbling and downcast or wildly imploring the heavens. One wild-eyed fellow, bearded and surprisingly sprightly, was doing his best to convince everyone that this was the beginning of the Day of Judgement, it being the devilish year of 1666, so they'd be better off preparing themselves than gawking.

Kingsley shivered at his words, which were delivered with a chilling, matter-of-fact voice, as if the man were recommending a particular cut of beef for dinner. No beseecher, him.

Evadne gripped his arm. Standing at the back of the crowd was a tall, cadaverous figure in robes. It was by itself, a gap having opened around it as if it were blighted.

Spawn.

Kingsley had to steel himself to keep walking and not run. The Spawn couldn't be looking for them – Evadne and he didn't exist in this time, so to speak.

He needn't have worried. The creature didn't stir as they walked past, nor notice the way Evadne's hand tightened on the sabre under her coat. Its attention was on the distant flames.

They found a path leading up from the river between two garden beds alive with hollyhocks, foxgloves and masses of daisies. 'They'll observe and report, no doubt.' Evadne's voice was flat and deadly. 'The Immortals will want to know what's happening in the city.'

'At least we have confirmation that the Immortals are here, after all.'

'Mm.' Evadne's eyes tracked the Spawn. 'Let's not lose it.'

They skirted the Queen's House. It was new, to their eyes, and magnificent – and looked decidedly lived in. Smoke came from the chimneys and the grounds on the east side included what was most definitely a kitchen garden.

They lingered a moment at a low brick wall before they broached the Giant Steps that joined the upper and lower parts of the park. In the distance to the east, Kingsley was charmed to see a herd of deer cropping the grass in front of the woods.

On top of the hill was a dismal sight. As they drew closer, Kingsley could see that the tower was derelict. Weeds, rampant and lank, infested the area. The battlements were uneven where stones had fallen and not been replaced – or had been stolen.

Kingsley leaned against a useful fir tree. 'So the observatory must be built in the future?'

'Their future,' Evadne said. She rested a hand on her satchel. 'Our past.'

The observatory wasn't the only thing missing. The Conduit House that provided the entrance to the tunnel leading to the Hall of the Immortals wasn't there either. Evadne stalked about, her hands on her hips, glancing up at the unfamiliar buildings on the summit of the hill. 'Where's the entrance to the Immortals' lair?'

Kingsley gestured towards the remains of the tower. 'I'd be tempted to look around there. I'm sure a ruin would be a fine place to hide a secret entrance, aren't you?'

As fortresses went, Kingsley decided, the structure on the top of the hill would have been modest, even in its heyday. The property wasn't extensive, ranging barely over the summit of the humble hill. Even so, the walls of the two towers were still impressively thick. Kingsley ran his hand over the stone, damp from the recent rain, and imagined the long-ago stonemasons at work, levelling and settling the huge blocks with the barest of tools.

A gate lodge just outside the towers was in an awful state. The roof had collapsed and a fire had taken most of the timbers, leaving a skeleton of stone. Some of the outbuildings showed signs of recent habitation, with rubbish piles and rough cooking places.

The fortress still commanded a superb view over the surroundings – including a view of the inferno the city had become. Kingsley and Evadne stood for a time, helpless. In a trick of perspective, it was almost as if the angry black clouds above were reaching down to the city to smite it, so thick was the smoke.

People were gathered about the lower reaches of the

hill, looking towards the city. Kingsley had been puzzled as to why they weren't seeking the better outlook of the summit – or even from the tower itself, but when Evadne and he had pushed through their ranks, their expressions had plainly told him that they were afraid of the hill.

Three heavy, iron-bound doors in what must have been the cellar of one of the towers all promised access to the lower reaches. Each of them yielded to Kingsley's lock-picking skills while Evadne kept watch. When the areas under the cellars surrendered nothing promising, mostly having collapsed, Kingsley drummed the stone wall with a fist in frustration.

He looked for Evadne and found her brooding. She was using her sabre to scratch the ground in an aimless but deadly looking manner.

The passion she'd shown when talking to the Retrievers had diminished and Kingsley was concerned that her crusade was oppressing her. He started towards her, aiming to cheer her out of her brown study, but he pulled himself up short. He had a notion that good-natured jollying wasn't the sort of thing to work on Evadne Stephens. Anything that smacked of condescension could result in physical harm – something he was prepared to risk, as long as whatever provoked it had a chance of success, which he doubted condescension did.

However . . .

'When is a door not a door?' Kingsley asked aloud after he'd relocked the third of the doors. The walled courtyard had only two of the walls remaining. It was open to the sky that, directly above, was remarkably blue and innocent.

Evadne looked over the top of her spectacles. 'Are you saying we should be looking for a jar?'

Kingsley was pleased to hear some lightness in Evadne's voice. 'Not exactly a jar, but something that doesn't look like a door.'

She found a convenient block of stone and sat on it cross-legged, instantly resembling a classical monument as she put elbow on knee and chin in hand. 'Many things don't look like a door. Most things don't, if you think about it.'

'True, but many things function like a door, in principle. They allow access.'

'You mean like windows?'

Kingsley wanted to cheer. As he'd hoped, the puzzle had brought Evadne to herself. An intellectual challenge was her cup of tea. 'Yes, and chimneys, and hatches and all sorts of things like that. But what doesn't function in that way?'

'We've reduced the possibilities from millions to slightly fewer millions.'

'True.' Kingsley looked up at the sky. 'Do you know the very first Basic Principle of Escapology?'

'Please excuse my rudeness, but sometimes I feel as if you're making these up as you go along.'

'I won't deign to dignify that remark with a denial.'

'Ah, I see.'

He ploughed on. 'The First and Fundamental Principle of Escapology states: There exists a universal key to all traps and escapes.'

'I sense that I'm meant to ask what it is.'

'Thinking. Thinking is the key to every trap. And I've just had a thought.'

She pursed her lips. 'While I'm trying to articulate an adequate expression of my derision, why don't you tell me what your thought is?'

'I'm wondering how long those Spawn are going to watch before they report.'

Evadne raised an eyebrow. 'That is brilliant.'

'I'm just doing my best to keep up with you.'

She looked at him oddly. 'And that's the sort of remark that wouldn't be out of place at court. I'm sure you'd have the ladies swooning at your feet after such neat phrasing, if they weren't already.'

'The prospect of bundles of swooned ladies around my feet sounds positively alarming.'

'And now Normal Kingsley has returned.'

'I should hope so.'

'Never mind.' She tilted her head a little, studying him with that disconcerting, spectacled gaze. 'Doesn't it worry you to be seen with a female who's smarter than you?'

'Why should it?'

'It worries most males. Something about the natural order of things, they say.'

'What a load of rubbish.'

'I'm glad you agree. We'll make you into a suffragist next.' She took his hand. 'Come on. Let's play Spot a Spawn.'

The prophet of doom was still on the dock when Kingsley and Evadne made their way back there. He greeted Evadne with a wave of a finger, as if they were clerks who regularly met at a station before going to the office. He wasn't fazed by Evadne's appearance, and Kingsley wondered if the man saw equally extraordinary sights every day in his visions.

An hour later, Kingsley touched Evadne on the shoulder. A Spawn, almost identical to the one that hadn't moved from its position at the rear of the mob, was striding down the hill. Its long, black wool robes swirled about its bare feet. When it reached its colleague, not a word was spoken. For a moment they stood shoulder to shoulder, eyes on the distance, then the first spun on its heel and marched away.

The Spawn showed no uneasiness, no indication that it even contemplated being followed. It trudged across the grass, ignoring the paths and the steps, making a straight line towards the hilltop fortress. Kingsley's uneasiness at the dreadful creature increased as it went. He had trouble putting his finger on the source of this until he realised that the Spawn's arms and legs were not moving in time. Instead of its right leg and left arm swinging together, with left leg working with the right arm, its limbs moved independently, jerkily, with no rhythm or connection.

Kingsley shuddered, but despite its lack of coordination, the Spawn's progress was powerful. It had the crude unstoppability of a sledge hammer on its way down.

A few people were still in the park at the base of the hill. An old woman stared at Evadne, averted her eyes and made rough, stabbing gestures. She muttered either prayers or older, guarded chants of protection.

When the Spawn reached the forlorn gardens around the tower, Kingsley was surprised when it showed some awareness of its surroundings. Instead of marching straight through the flower beds it took the path to the rear. To keep it in sight, Kingsley and Evadne were forced to run until they were able to throw themselves behind a mound of large stones, the remains of a stable or barn.

They watched as it slipped through one of the gaps in the rear wall and into a courtyard. There, it stood a moment then it took a dozen ragged steps and leaped feet first into the well.

Evadne gasped, but Kingsley was already running. When he reached the well he leaned over the low wall and smiled. 'Misdirection,' he said softly. 'Nicely, nicely done.'

⧼ THIRTY-FOUR ⧽

The handholds began a few yards down the stone wall of the well. They were well spaced, obviously suiting the spider-like Spawn. Kingsley had had some trouble before his foot found the first of them, but once he had, he was easily able to clamber down to the platform he'd spotted some twenty or thirty feet down.

He was begrudgingly admiring the nerveless way in which the Spawn had eschewed the handholds and simply dropped to the platform when Evadne joined him. She'd had no difficulty with the climbing, simply finding crannies among the stones when the handholds were inconvenient.

The platform was tiny. They were forced to stand close together. Kingsley hardly had to tilt his head to meet Evadne's gaze, so tall was she. Above, the oval of light that was the outside world was distant and forgettable, a mere decoration in the heavens.

The arched tunnel that was punched into the wall of the well was dark. 'You lead,' Kingsley whispered.

He kept a hand on her shoulder as they crept deeper into the heart of the hill, crouched, her sabre occasionally knocking against his hip. His wild self hunched even more, unhappy at the closeness of the passage, fretful in the darkness. The tunnel sloped downward severely, and kinked from side to side, seemingly at random, but the further they went the more sound came from ahead.

When the tunnel ended in an elaborate stone arch, they stopped dead.

The light made it hard to judge distances. Small fires and lanterns punctuated the darkness, as though the stars had come down from the sky for a bit of a hobnob. The impression of vastness came more from the way the sounds of construction echoed, convincing Kingsley that this was indeed a cavernous space being carved out of the hill.

Above the almost comforting sounds of sawing and hammering was a constant, indistinct susurration, like wind whispering in a thousand trees, or a gentle shuffling on a dance floor, backward and forward, backward and forward. It was aural wool, muffling every other sound, wrapping them in blurriness.

A million monks in robes, Kingsley thought wildly, *scuffling along in socks.*

Evadne took his hand and led him to the left. They followed a flight of iron stairs down slowly, testing their weight with each footfall, fearful of drawing attention to themselves. Kingsley strove to remember the pentagon-based chamber of the Immortals, the one he'd seen two hundred and fifty years from now, but the light and the shadows defeated him. He relied on Evadne and her light-gathering spectacles.

She put a hand on his shoulder and made him crouch behind what he took in the dim light to be a pile of handmade bricks.

Kingsley waited, impatiently, while Evadne unslung her satchel full of phlogiston and gazed into the shadows. She touched the side of her spectacles once, then again, muttering. 'They're too far away,' she whispered to herself and then a long silence stretched. He was beginning to worry – *What if her temper broke loose again?* – then once again he had the uncomfortable and exciting experience of Evadne's putting her lips to his ear. 'The Immortals are out there, in the middle. Sitting on their throne. Hovering in midair. The Spawn we followed has stopped on the edge of an abyss.'

'Abyss?'

'The floor isn't finished. A large section is uncovered. Underneath is a huge space with walkways and rooms around the rim, arranged in levels.'

'How far down do they go?'

She touched her spectacles. 'At least ten storeys. Maybe more.'

'What's the Spawn doing?'

'Nothing. It's just waiting to deliver its report, I'd say.'

At that moment, Kingsley hissed and flung a hand up to shield his eyes. Evadne gasped and ducked her head behind the pile of bricks.

Light bloomed, filling the space and revealing the colossal construction site. Kingsley gasped at what had been making the eerie whispering noise.

Scores of Spawn clung to surfaces by their supernaturally strong fingers and toes. They moved slowly, lovingly polishing walls, floor and ceiling. The shuffling noise was the sound of hundreds of cloths and papers, smoothing, smoothing, smoothing.

Kingsley managed to look away from the unsettling sight – it was too much like a swarm of insects for his liking – to take in the rest of the gigantic chamber. The dodecahedron shape had already been carved out. Scaffolding, saw benches and metalworking lathes were scattered about in something approaching chaos. The pentagonal alcoves were already in place, but only two of them were occupied. One was a large cube. The other was the mysterious rotating solid that Kingsley had seen two hundred and fifty years from now, the tetrahedron that was the Temporal Manipulator.

Through the sliver of floor that was unfinished, it was almost as if he were looking down on an amphitheatre. He counted ten rings – vast rings – that descended into the heart of the earth, connected by stairways spaced around the perimeter. He even spied a stairway that led to a door in the wall opposite, right next to the Temporal Manipulator.

'Look at the bottom,' Evadne breathed.

The lowest level was a dead black disc, clearly visible against the grey stone that made up the walkways. It was impossible to tell how large it was with nothing nearby, and as he tried to make sense of it, his hackles rose; it was loathsome.

Kingsley hadn't thought much about black, assuming that black was black. As he tried to make out this slab of nothingness, he understood that he'd been labouring under a misapprehension. Not all blacks were the same. The black of a midnight sky wasn't the same as the black of a friendly cat. The black he saw when he closed his eyes wasn't the same as the black of the ink in his favourite books.

This black disc was different from all of them. It made all the other blacks look half-hearted. It had taken all other blacks, intensifying them, extracting and distilling them, doubling them and then doubling them again until it was the perfect, irrefutable, all-consuming black. This was the acme of blacks.

'It's throbbing,' Evadne whispered.

Kingsley went to deny this, for the continuous polishing noise tended to swallow any subtle sounds, but then he paused. He couldn't hear it, but he perceived a single pulse.

He peered at the almost void. He couldn't see anything, and was about to convince himself that he was imagining it when it happened again. A ripple as much as a drumbeat, he sensed it deep inside himself – a perturbation of the soul. He squinted, but saw nothing. He listened, but no sound emanated from the blankness. It happened again; he turned sideways and listened for the next trump of doom; his adjusted position was enough to confirm that the stroke came from the disc below.

'What is it?' he whispered to Evadne.

'It's the biggest phlogiston extractor I've ever seen. Ever *heard* of.'

'How can you tell?'

She touched her spectacles, then tweaked the bridge over her nose. 'On this setting, I can see the lines of disturbance in the ether that mean that phlogiston is being drawn to it.'

'Ether? You mean the anaesthetic?'

'A different ether. It's a name for the underlying substrate of reality, through which phlogiston and countless other exotic and no doubt magical elements permeate the universe.'

'I think I may have to unlearn everything I ever knew.'

'Not really,' Evadne said absently and Kingsley was pleased to see her absorbed in the mystery of the Immortals' device. 'Simply add another layer of understanding rather than throw out the old. It may come in handy one day.' Evadne tapped her teeth with a fingernail. 'So the Immortals have a giant phlogiston extractor under their headquarters. I wonder what for?'

'To power their whatsits. That cube and their Temporal Manipulator.'

'We can't use the Temporal Manipulator,' Evadne said slowly.

'I hope that's not the case,' Kingsley said. 'Otherwise we're in an appalling situation. Look, I'm sure you'll be able to work it out.'

'I meant that we can't use it right now.'

'You're not thinking of trying to destroy the Immortals, are you? Wait until we get back to 1908. We'll be able to equip ourselves properly, plan thoroughly –'

Evadne gripped his arm hard enough to leave bruises. 'Wait a moment.'

The tri-partite throne swivelled on its own centre and faced the waiting Spawn. Then it drifted to the rim of the yawning pit, coming close enough for Kingsley to see that the figures sitting on the thrones were substantially larger than the children he'd seen in the twentieth century. These looked like ten- or twelve-year-olds.

He felt ill. These entities – he couldn't think of them as people – thousands of years old, transferring their essence to a succession of young bodies? He now understood Evadne's desire to expunge them, regardless of their actions. Any humanity they may once have had was gone, drained by centuries of treating others as items of convenience – necessary for their survival, but hardly important beyond that.

He also saw, with horror, that the Immortals were almost completely swaddled in bloody bandages, right up to thighs and armpits, and they all had bandages wrapped around their heads. Making their army of Spawn had been costly.

Costly. Kingsley clenched his fists. Was this the wearing out that Evadne had spoken of? If so, it meant that the sorcerers would be needing new bodies to inhabit, and soon, if their dreadful current state was any indication. His horror grew as he realised that the streets of a panicked seventeenth-century London might be a fertile place to gather children. The Immortals may well have bodies ready and waiting for them.

How could he broach this with Evadne? He didn't want her rushing off precipitously, as she had in the tunnels near her refuge. He had to be careful.

He needn't have bothered. One look at her face told him that she'd reached the same conclusion he had. 'The cells down there,' she said. Her voice was like tempered steel. 'The Immortals could have children down there.'

'We're not in a good position to do anything,' Kingsley pointed out. 'We should fall back. Maybe we can find those Retrievers again, or get assistance from the Demimonde.'

'You can stay here, if you like. I'm going.'

❧ THIRTY-FIVE ❧

Kingsley decided that the Immortals had no truck with order and organisation. Their answer to a problem was to throw Spawn at it. The larger the problem, the more Spawn they lobbed its way. The giant size of their hiding place and the chaos of its building site was testimony to their approach. Kingsley was grateful, for it meant that his and Evadne's passage to the levels beneath the main chamber, while circuitous, would simply be a matter of flitting from cover to cover.

Kingsley did wonder, however, if the indiscriminate application of labour was one reason the bodies used by the Immortals wore out. Lopping off pieces whenever a ditch digger was needed couldn't be good for them.

Which made him even more curious about the Immortals' choice of bodies. Why children? Wouldn't adults be more useful? And why were the chosen bodies younger in the twentieth century than they were here?

He wasn't sure he wanted to know the answers.

The Immortals listened to the gossip from the Spawn Kingsley and Evadne had followed in, while other Spawn built, cleaned, polished and painted to make a home for the ages. The perfect balance of zero degrees longitude would one day run right through here, and Kingsley was sure this wasn't by accident.

He wondered where they had been before this place. Stonehenge? Lindisfarne? Or somewhere overseas, a place of great power like Mount Ararat, Olympus or the monasteries of Tibet?

A commotion on the other side of the great hall when a scaffold collapsed was the moment Kingsley and Evadne needed. They slipped through the five-sided door, closed it behind them and descended into the abyss.

Evadne was hard-faced as they came to the first cell. Through the small, barred window in the door they could make out eyes. Kingsley whispered through the bars and tried to gain attention, but the shadowy figures did not stir. When Evadne risked all and shone a beam from her pen light, there were more than a dozen ragged and sooty-faced children, none looking more than ten years old, sitting or slumped on stone. They had no spark in them, no curiosity, no eagerness for rescue. They sat, unspeaking, dull faced, resigned.

The next cell was the same, and the next. Each cell was full of impassive, almost somnolent urchins, forsaken boys and girls.

As they went, Evadne became more and more grim, and Kingsley feared for the pen light, such was the intensity of her grip. Again and again, she touched her glove over her little finger, the one that bore her silver ring.

When she'd spoken of her calling, Kingsley had seen sadness amid the righteous anger. Was the source of this sadness the secret she'd promised to share with him? He put his hand lightly on her shoulder as they neared the next cell, but she shook him off without turning her head.

This cell was different. Evadne shone the light through the bars and piping cries of joy erupted from it.

Evadne thrust the pen light on Kingsley. She gripped the bars and pressed her face against them. 'It's all right,' she whispered. 'We've come to save you.'

Kingsley struggled to shine the beam past Evadne. In the cell, two children had come to their feet and were leaping up and down, arms extended, crying for their mother with joy that soon became sobbing. They fell at the foot of the door, scratching at it feebly. Kingsley ached to let them out. It would only take a second or two, but then what would they do?

Evadne crouched by the door, speaking softly, promising comfort and safety, repeating herself until their despair dwindled into a soft and wordless lament. The faint sound floated through the barred window, hanging in the air and filling it with a plaintiveness that was as lost as the children themselves.

Kingsley understood, even if he couldn't share Evadne's depth of anger. His wild side added to his sympathy: young ones were to be protected – it was the duty of the pack. Rally to take care of the young. Distract predators with your own self. Sacrifice yourself to keep them safe.

He put his hand on Evadne's shoulder. This time, he refused to be shaken off. 'We can't stay here.'

She didn't look up. 'I can't leave them.'

'Someone will send one of the Spawn to investigate.'

'Let them.' She placed one gloved hand against the door. 'I'll destroy them. I'll destroy them all.'

He sighed. 'I know you will, but let's just see what we can do to improve our chances here.'

She knuckled tears away from her face. 'We should go downward, then.'

He helped her to her feet, until she was abruptly standing face to face with him. She wasn't ethereal, he decided. She was too earthy to be angelic. 'Lead on,' he whispered.

On the next level down, she flung her arms wide, nearly striking Kingsley, who was right behind her. 'Why didn't the others cry out?' she asked. 'Why only those two?'

'I hope they've just been daunted by their imprisonment,' he said. 'Imagine facing the Spawn as your captors if you were six years old.'

She shuddered, her shoulders trembling. 'But you think it might be something else?'

'They could have been given a drug, or potion, or subjected to some sort of magic ritual. I've no idea.'

Kingsley decided that the slight, sharp exhalation from Evadne might have been a laugh. 'Kingsley,' she said, maintaining a forward regard, 'at the rate you're taking aboard new concepts, you'll be a true Demimonder before you know it.'

Kingsley didn't reply. He was too busy pondering whether this was a good thing or bad.

The last level before the black disc contained a single, solid iron door. Kingsley spread his hand on it, felt nothing, and put an ear to it. 'I can't hear anything.'

'Another mystery,' Evadne said.

Kingsley didn't like having it at his back, blocking their retreat. The lock was more formidable than those on the cell doors. He thought he could open it quickly – but would that be a wise thing to do?

He touched the surface of the door again. It was cold. He shook his head. 'It's solid. Whatever is behind it will stay there for some time.'

Evadne looked away.

Just as they reached the black disc, a glass vial appeared in midair with an incongruous tinkling sound and hovered over the centre of the blackness. Kingsley stared at the glow, then glanced up to make sure they were well hidden by the overhang of the ramp above. 'Is that phlogiston?' he asked Evadne.

'Oh, yes.' She crossed her arms in a strange gesture of satisfaction when the vial rocketed upward, vanishing some way over their heads. 'We'll find a stockpile here somewhere.'

'I'm sure these Immortals wouldn't tolerate our sniffing about for their treasure store.'

Evadne crouched and held her hand a careful few inches above the surface of the blackness. 'Remarkable. If I'm not mistaken, this is an entirely different way to extract phlogiston. No moving parts at all. Just magic.'

'Capital.' Kingsley looked up. The thin slice of uncompleted floor overhead was growing smaller. 'While that might be interesting, I'm not sure if it's providing us with anything to improve our chances.'

'Mm?'

What we have here is a trap, he thought, *on a very large scale. So what's the way out?* It was back to Basic Principles.

'Thinking is the key,' he muttered aloud. Another glowing vial appeared and shot off. 'The back door.'

Evadne whirled, her coat swinging. 'Bravo, Kingsley! The Immortals wouldn't drag urchins through their perfect hall!'

He looked around at the iron door. 'I'm thinking that the old palace by the river and tower on the hill would have had a connection, something underground. It would have been easy enough to run a side tunnel off that. In fact, I'll wager that the park is criss-crossed with tunnels.'

'We can take them out the way they came in,' Evadne said.

Kingsley unlocked the door while Evadne stood to one side, pistol and sabre ready. When he eased it open, however, all that emerged was a soft gust of air, damp but fresh.

'I can smell the river,' Evadne said.

'That's good. If the children can make it down to the riverbank, they should be able to get away from there.' He knew they'd be frightened, but at least they'd be well away from the fire that was consuming London. They wouldn't be the only lost children. And anything would be better than being held by the Immortals.

She looked hopeful. 'Perhaps the Retrievers will find them.'

They worked from the top down. The children from the uppermost cells were lethargic but biddable. None of them questioned their surroundings, or the orders Evadne gave in clear, strained tones. As they worked downward, the children began to show signs of animation. A few essayed half-hearted queries and Kingsley had to deal with a case or two of strangely detached terror, staunching tears with a handkerchief that immediately became an item of distracted wonder.

Kingsley was dismayed by their demeanour. Even if nothing malignant had gone on, the children were well cowed, their spirits broken.

And who could blame them? he thought as he slipped the bolt on his next challenge. The Spawn were hard enough for an adult to face. Any child who wasn't daunted after being taken by the ghastly creatures would be a rare beast indeed.

Working down the levels, Kingsley had to remind Evadne to keep moving after he caught her consoling instead of shepherding. He was as gentle and as firm as he could be, but more than once she bit back a retort when he interrupted her ministrations.

'I'm sorry,' she whispered as she brought her latest charge to his feet. The pale-faced lad had been the last of nine in the cell to rouse. He rubbed his eyes with his chubby fists, then stuck one of them in his mouth.

'This is your crusade?' Kingsley asked Evadne.

'I never called it a crusade,' she said. 'And, anyway, it's more than that.'

'I'd guessed. And it's a secret?'

She bit her lip, but nodded and looked away. 'Don't worry about me. I can manage.'

Evadne peered into the face of one of the last children to be freed. One of the least affected and more self-possessed, she was a girl of ten or twelve years, clean-faced and wearing a well-scrubbed pinafore. She had long black hair and dark, serious eyes.

'Take this.' Evadne put the pen light into the girl's hand and curled her fingers around it. She pointed at the tunnel beyond the iron door. 'Guide the others out of here.'

The girl looked at Evadne, then Kingsley. 'Where are we going?'

'Away from here,' Evadne said firmly. 'Find the river. People will help you there.'

It was enough. Without hesitation, the girl plunged into the darkness.

Kingsley stood by the arch and helped the urchins on their way. *And from darkness shall come light*, he thought.

He was amazed at how the children didn't hesitate, how each one simply followed the one in front. Boys, girls, some on the verge of adolescence, some barely walking. Most of them were still docile, although some showed a flicker of fear as they approached the arch.

If they were placid, Kingsley decided, it was a placidity of a particularly troubled kind. They weren't sheep, despite displaying considerable sheeplike qualities. It was as if a damper had been placed on their thoughts and emotions, stifling them until they were manageable.

Kingsley wondered if, underneath, the poor children were screaming.

'It will wear off,' Evadne said as the last child – a lank-haired, limping boy – stumbled over the threshold and hurried after the others.

'They'll be themselves again?'

'At best, they'll remember this as a bad dream.'

Kingsley didn't really want to ask what the worst was. 'They're on their way home. Let's see what we can do about doing the same.'

She gazed at the arch, and she fingered her satchel.

'You can't use the phlogiston,' he said.

'I beg your pardon?'

'You look as if you're thinking explosively, so to speak.'

'And?'

'The Temporal Manipulator looks as if it could be our only hope of getting home. If you blow up this place, we're stuck here.'

'We may not have another chance to destroy the Immortals' headquarters.'

'True, but you know what they say about a time and a place for everything.'

The floor underneath the Immortals' throne was now almost entirely completed. Spawn were on hands and knees and actually stretching the substance of the floor as if they were laying carpet. A dozen or more were on one side of the pentagon, with an equivalent number on the other. Slowly, they were roofing over the abyss.

Kingsley and Evadne huddled under a pile of rough canvas they'd found next to a scaffold. His legs were aching from the climb, but Evadne was showing no signs of weariness. She was driven. The Immortals' throne was hovering near the rotating cube. Each side of the cube shone dully with one of the primary colours – red, blue or yellow – in a pattern that Kingsley gave up trying to discern when the cube pulsed and the arrangement changed. The faces were still primary colours, but the distribution was now different.

In midair a foot or so in front of the cube, a rippling black mat was appearing. The mat tumbled down over the two steps that led to the alcove and then became part of the floor that the Spawn were stretching across the cavernous space below.

The floor was being extruded out of the air.

Magic, Kingsley thought, and he shrugged at his newfound willingness to accept the evidence of his eyes. He wasn't foolish enough to keep insisting that there was a trick involved, that there had to be a man behind the screen. Being sceptical didn't mean refusing to acknowledge the evidence.

The Spawn on the far side of the chamber reached the stairs of the opposite alcoves. More stretching, some smoothing from side to side.

The lights went out on the cube. Its spinning began to slow until it resumed the stately rotation Kingsley had seen when they first crept into the chamber.

The river of black material stuttered, dwindled, and ended, the last of it falling onto the stairs like a black velvet drape.

Four Spawn leaped towards it. With sharp blades like sickles, they trimmed the join, smoothing it and making it straight. One of them staggered off with the offcuts of the black material that, to judge from the difficulty it had in gathering, was growing harder and less flexible.

'A phlogiston-powered Material Manipulator, I'd say,' Evadne whispered. 'It could explain why the Immortals don't have much to do with the rest of the Demimonde. They don't need to trade for materials.'

'So, a Time Manipulator and a Material Manipulator.' He pointed at the empty alcove. 'They have others?'

She shrugged. 'While I'm curious, I can wait to find out.'

'Can you wait two hundred and fifty years?'

'I'm a model of patience.'

THIRTY-SIX

Anger rarely sat well with a squeaky voice, Soames decided as he stood in front of the Immortals. He held his hat in one hand, ready to leave for his office, and his umbrella in the other, the most useless of shields in the face of Augustus's spittle-laced tirade. Soames took some solace in that umbrellas were at least the most British of shields. He was proud of that.

He had been astonished, dismayed and angered when the Immortals had been carried up from the depths of their lair by a brace of Spawn. How underhand of them to vanish like that and leave him as a mere caretaker! It was reprehensible!

He had an awful moment when he thought they'd come back to punish him, but they showed no signs of knowing that he'd conspired with the Neanderthals.

Of course they didn't know, Jabez, he thought. *Your plan was masterly!*

The Immortals were different. Still in the bodies of children, but *different* children. Which made sense, in an outlandish way, for hadn't Soames himself seen the Immortals torn to pieces by the Neanderthals?

Using his years of practice, he hid his feelings and welcomed the Immortals back, assuring them that he'd kept the place just as they'd left it.

It didn't stop the Immortals' ranting at him.

Augustus came to a snarling conclusion in his estimation of Soames's abilities. Jia took over, cold and hard and unstoppable as a glacier.

Migration of souls. In all Soames's scheming, all his planning, he hadn't really understood the extent of the Immortals' magic. He knew that they moved from body to body as they wore out, but he simply hadn't thought of the implications. That they had simply migrated out of their endangered bodies just before the Neanderthals descended on them and taken up residence in fresh bodies in a nearby, but undisclosed, location hadn't occurred to him.

It gave him a chill as he re-estimated the extent of the Immortals' abilities.

'Of course I understood that your dismemberment was a mere inconvenience,' he lied when Jia's ire subsided. 'That's why, once I discovered that those appalling Neanderthals were in residence, I brought my own band of bullies and bravoes to drive them out, clean up your ... remains ... and make the place secure for your return.'

In some ways he was glad to relinquish guardianship of the uncanny place, but he was irritated by the peremptory nature of their homecoming. They weren't even surprised at his presence.

'This cannot be countenanced!' Augustus snapped. Although their physical appearance had changed, their taste in clothing hadn't, much to Soames's relief as it gave him some indication who he was talking to. Augustus's feet dangled nowhere near the floor, the same as his equally incensed colleagues'. Jia had both tiny, bloody, bandaged hands clenched on the arms of her throne and looked as if she were barely restraining herself from leaping at Soames and biting him. Forkbeard was more subdued, but only in the way that an angry bear is more subdued than an angry wildcat. His chin was down and he looked at Soames from bloodshot eyes, his lids drooping and his breath a rough rumble. His feet were bare and bandaged.

Soames was wary of their anger. There was no dignity here, no gravity gained from millennia of experience. This was the fury of the elderly, the wrath of the frustrated geriatric. While most of Soames was devoted to remaining dignified in face of the anger directed at him, a small part wondered what sort of minds were couched behind those once sweet faces. Was mental decay a fact of existence that their bodily transfer couldn't overcome?

Augustus hammered on the arm of his throne with a chubby fist that was lacking a thumb and asked the question Soames had been hoping for: 'And you, wretch! What are you going to do about it?'

'It', of course, was the unheard-of situation in which the Immortals had found themselves. They had been driven out of their home and had to take refuge in another – unnamed – location, they had been bested by one of their many enemies, their slowly nurtured plans had been disrupted and, just before they had escaped, they had seen the boy they had been hunting for, there, in their own hall!

Intolerable wasn't a strong enough word. Everything about it had incensed the Immortals, but Soames suspected that it had also shocked them to be confronted with evidence that they weren't as infallible as they had thought.

Soames enjoyed that. It gave him some confidence.

'I? What will I do? I will endeavour to assist you in any way I can, as I always have.'

His plans for assuming the mantle of the Immortals would have to wait. This wasn't necessarily a bad thing, for his time as lord of the manor hadn't been as trouble free as he had thought it would be. Perhaps he could use the interruption to inveigle some answers from the creatures, perhaps a pointer or two towards solving the mystery of their power.

Augustus narrowed his eyes. 'Then find children for us. To replace those we have just used.'

'Of course.'

Jia startled him, then, as she leaned forward, her child's face suffused red. 'And get the boy for us, now!'

Soames blinked. 'Now?'

'We want his brain.' Forkbeard's voice may have had the shrillness of a six-year-old, but his essence made the child's throat grab the words, reducing them to a hideous growl.

Obscure as the Immortals' motives had always been, Soames was heartened by this insight. The boy's brain was important? Who would have thought? Soames started to think of the best way to approach the Neanderthals about the lad.

'Getting the boy back will take much phlogiston,' he said. 'For bribes.'

Augustus didn't answer. He sat with his arms crossed, looking away. Soames was no longer important to him. Jia glanced at her companion and hissed before addressing Soames. 'You'll have it.'

'And I will need time.'

Jia narrowed her eyes. 'How long?'

'A few days.'

She leaned towards Forkbeard and they had a rapid, whispered discussion. When they finished, she had to adjust her black wig. Soames noted that at least one of her ears was missing. Spawn production had been in full swing.

'Three days,' she said. 'Do not take longer. Find him. Do not bother us with minutiae.'

A Spawn trotted up and whispered in Forkbeard's ear. The fur-clad Immortal leaped to his feet, then toppled onto the cushions, howling. 'And don't forget the children! Fresh children! More!'

Jia and Augustus muttered to each other and glanced at Soames.

'Arrangements are under way,' Soames said, as soothingly as he could manage, quite happy if he could curry favour with two of the three Immortals. 'I have my eye on a particularly useful source of the items you're after and your cells will be stocked before you know it.'

Augustus sat up. 'That is what I like to hear. Go, do your work.'

Soames congratulated himself on his flexibility and quick thinking – and turned over the possibilities for wringing an advantage out of this curiously important boy.

Soames was sent to supervise the Spawn in assembling the phlogiston to trade for the boy. After some curt words from a bleeding Augustus, the Material Manipulator – the cube – glowed and spat green light at Soames. Terrified and doing his best not to show it, he found himself rising, along with a trio of newly formed – and quite dazed – Spawn.

Soames swallowed his fear and composed himself as he drifted up, high above the floor of the Hall of the Immortals. He had never been one for aerial balloon ascents, not seeing the entertainment gained by putting oneself in a state where setting foot on the earth again could be precipitous and fatal. He had trouble breathing as he rose.

A pentagonal hatch slid aside as he and his helpers drew near the ceiling. They rose through it and were gently deposited inside a chamber nearly as large as the Hall of the Immortals itself.

Soames was overcome.

He actually went to one knee. He bowed his head. He breathed deeply and tried to maintain his dignity, surrounded as he was with wealth of such a magnitude that he was light-headed, giddy, teetering on disbelief.

Jabez! This could all be yours!

Soames was forced to reappraise his estimate of the abilities of the Immortals. And their history. And their underground dominance. He was stunned by this evidence of their power, which was much greater than his already substantial estimate.

Each of the five walls that joined the floor and sloped away from him was embedded with slots, as were the walls that joined the ceiling. Most of the slots in the lower five walls contained a glowing phlogiston vial.

His brain stumbled in trying to estimate how long the Immortals had been gathering phlogiston. Centuries. Longer. The wealth here was immeasurable. With it, the Immortals could buy the world and have enough left over for a deposit on the moon and stars.

The prospect of immortality suddenly dwindled in importance. Riches, immediate and concrete; that was something much more worthwhile! Besides, if he could take this treasure for his own, he could easily overwhelm the Immortals and discover their secrets!

Numbly, he directed the Spawn to gather the requisite vials. He wasn't even surprised when a new vial appeared in midair and shot off to lodge itself in a slot on the far wall, evidence of the ongoing phlogiston extraction. Discovering the secret of the plinking noise simply wasn't important any more.

He did, however, wonder at the purpose of such a treasury. What were the Immortals doing with all this wealth? They must use some of it to power their magic – the manipulators, for a start – but what else? Did they spend time up here, gloating at their riches? Did they pile the vials in the middle of the chamber and dive into them, swimming about like pudgy pink otters?

The most ordinary of considerations took some time to nudge its way into Soames's bruised mind: the Hall of the Immortals must be buried deeper than he'd thought.

While the Spawn gathered the vials, Soames struggled. Simply by its vastness, the phlogiston treasury emphasised how inconsequential he – and every other mortal – was. In the face of the Immortals' might, ordinary earthly endeavours were meaningless.

Eventually, however, Soames remembered himself. He ran both hands through his hair. He straightened his jacket, took his tie pin out and reseated it.

If anyone is going to be in charge of such a wonder, Jabez, it should be you.

Jabez Soames was not one to be cowed.

THIRTY-SEVEN

Kingsley had never been as glad to see a band of Neanderthals as he was when two dozen of them thundered into the Immortals' unfinished lair. A diversion was what Kingsley and Evadne needed and a band of well-armed, pugnacious brutes filled the vacancy to perfection.

Instantly, the enormous space became a battleground. Spawn everywhere abandoned their construction work and hurled themselves at the intruders. The Immortals themselves waved their pudgy hands and shrieked orders that lacked tactical subtlety, but left no question that they wanted the Neanderthals chopped up and removed immediately.

The Neanderthals produced a bizarre assortment of firearms and set about laying waste to the charging Spawn. The hail of metal shredded the creatures mid-advance.

'The Neanderthals must want us badly,' he said. He peered at the mayhem. He recognised the foremost

Neanderthal as the leader of the band that had ambushed them in Deptford.

Evadne touched her satchel. 'They must be desperate for this phlogiston.'

'Or they have another reason.'

'It doesn't matter. Let's go.'

Evadne hurried off, bent nearly double, and Kingsley slapped himself on the forehead. *A diversion is worthless if you don't use it, Kingsley!* What magician wouldn't lift a dozen watches and purloin a handful of spectacles from an audience if a brawl broke out in the front row, only to dazzle the owners some time later with their return?

Evadne made the most of the building debris and tools that had been abandoned by the Spawn. She flitted from scaffold to wheelbarrow to workbench to coils of rope, waiting each time for Kingsley to join her before she advanced to the next milestone. The barrels of paint were the last before a dangerous open stretch and they paused a moment, judging the best time to go.

The Neanderthals had pressed close. Only a triple line of Spawn stood between them and the Immortals. The battle was awesome in its violence. The clubs of the Neanderthals swung with enough power to puncture metal, but the Spawn didn't back away. From all sides, they charged at the Neanderthal advance, seeking a weak spot, a way in, a misstep, but the juggernaut pushed on, snarling in a way that Kingsley couldn't help but respond to. His wild side was equally excited and appalled. It wanted to join the Neanderthals and to run away from them.

Kingsley's wildness was diverted, however, when the throne of the Immortals began to shake. It dislodged Spawn from its bottom step like a dog ridding itself of fleas, then it rose. When it was forty feet above the floor, the rotating cube sprang into life, bathing its alcove in bright green light.

A bolt of green lightning flashed, joining the cube and the throne for a split-second and rending the air in the chamber with an ear-punishing *crack*. The Spawn and the Neanderthals were bowled over like dolls.

When Kingsley's vision had cleared, the Immortals and their throne were gone.

'That is a truly splendid escape act,' he said, and he wondered if this were the moment the Immortals decided India was a more hospitable place for their particular needs.

～ THIRTY-EIGHT ～

Evadne was looking up with an expression of frustrated disappointment. 'Don't take my hand,' she said to
Kingsley. 'We can run faster if we don't.'

'Yes. Good point. Ready?'

She rolled her eyes and then she was gone. He had to
sprint to catch up to her.

For a moment, Kingsley had the hope that they might
be getting away unnoticed, but then a shout went up. He
increased his efforts and leaped into the alcove to join
Evadne. She was crouching and examining the rotating
pyramid.

Kingsley left her to it. He positioned himself on the
second stair of the alcove, between Evadne and the three
Neanderthals who were running towards them. 'Soon
would be best,' he called over his shoulder.

'I'm doing the best that I ... Oh!'

Kingsley didn't like the sound of that. He liked even less the flare of warm light that rolled over his back, briefly illuminating the hall and making the trio of approaching Neanderthals stop dead.

He risked a glance over his shoulder. Evadne was standing there, staring at her open hand. 'I had a vial of phlogiston. It ate it.'

'Now it's rotating faster.' Kingsley turned back to see the Neanderthals had resumed their advance, but they were more cautious, even hesitant, spreading out as they neared.

Another flare of light washed over him, then another. The satisfied 'Aha!' from behind made him look over his shoulder again, and while he took in the fact that the tetrahedron was whirling much faster now, it also gave the Neanderthal on his left time to charge.

Kingsley thought he'd been hit by an omnibus. Two omnibuses. The entire London fleet of omnibuses. He landed with the Neanderthal on top of him. As well as having all of the air driven out of his lungs, his head cracked hard on the marble plinth.

It was as if he'd taken a step sideways from the universe, which had then had all of the colour shaken from it, while all of the sounds had been passed through layers of wool to make them familiar in shape but utterly meaningless. Bright lights hung in his vision, which he vaguely thought appropriate. He saw more Neanderthals rushing and leaping over him. Four backed Evadne against the wall of the alcove. Her sabre flashed. More flaring light. A giant bell was tolling at the back of his skull and had been for some time.

He closed his eyes and it all went away.

'We're back home.'

Kingsley found he was lying down. He went to sit up, but he was made of rubber and couldn't. He made an effort to show he was coherent by repeating part of what Evadne said, but chose poorly: 'We're?'

Evadne loomed over him. She'd lost her coat, he noticed, but he did like the way it showed off her dove grey dress with the red ruching. Her arm snaked under his shoulders. 'Here, drink this.'

He sipped at the water and had a feeling he should admire the mug, which was made of gold, but he couldn't raise the energy. She studied him with concern. She looked tired, but determined and entirely, inappropriately fetching.

He was about to ask the standard orientating question when he took in the glazed blue bricks. *They haven't invented a prison I couldn't break out of*, he thought, *but I can't stop them putting me back in it*.

'You're going to feel nauseated, I'm sure. That was quite a knock on the head.'

It came back to him. He touched the back of his head and regretted it, but his astonishment and relief made the pain bearable. 'It worked? The Time Manipulator?'

'In a manner of speaking. Two Neanderthals tried to take me, but one of them put his hand on the tetrahedron. He vanished.'

'He activated the machine?'

She grimaced, an altogether wonderful sight. Kingsley wondered if she'd ever had her portrait done. 'It stopped glowing after he disappeared, so it would seem. But I have no idea where he went. I couldn't see any way to calibrate it, no controls to set, nothing. It's frustrating.'

'I imagine that's how our missing Neanderthal must feel. He's probably sitting around in the Renaissance thinking what he'd do if he had his time over again. So to speak.' He sat up, gingerly. 'So we've travelled back in time a few hundred years, then forward in time by the same amount. Quite an achievement. And then there's freeing a company of abducted children and avoiding the clutches of the Immortals.'

'I'd love to be in a position to marvel over our achievements,' Evadne said. 'I have a few people I'd like to consult about the mechanics of our time travelling. However, we have more pressing issues. Escaping from here, for one.'

'Wait. You said we didn't use the Time Manipulator. How did we get back here if we didn't?'

'We were taken through time in the not so gentle embrace of the Neanderthals.'

'I beg your pardon?'

'The sparkling belts they wore weren't fashionable accoutrements. They were part of their time travel equipment. One of them slung you over his shoulder and one held me tightly. The others surrounded us in a ring, then they linked their belts with fine chains so they were all connected. The black-bearded one took out two brass marbles. He fitted one into a slot on his belt, and as soon as he inserted the other into a different slot, we snapped out of 1666 and ended up here.' She gave a small laugh. 'Our arrival did some damage to their machine, I'm pleased to say.'

'What? How?'

'The argument was about someone forgetting to allow for the fact that you and I had temporal potential energy as well as our captors.' Absently, she made juggling motions with her hands. 'We snapped back with too much force and the dampeners hadn't been set to compensate, apparently. We've burned out some sensitive bits and pieces. They'll need remanufacturing.'

'I suppose they took your satchel.'

'Most greedily. And my sabre and pistol.' She cocked her head. 'Are you all right? You don't have a fractured skull, do you? Let me look at your eyes.'

'I don't think so. Just a bump and a nasty headache.'

She let go of the sides of his head. 'Your eyes look well enough. Your concussion must be minor.'

'You have medical training – no, don't tell me.' He held out a hand in the manner of a traffic policeman. 'Clarence has. He's an amateur brain surgeon.'

She opened her mouth, closed it again, reconsidered, then said: 'I note your heavy-handed irony and I'll endeavour, in future, not to bore you with Clarence's achievements.'

'He isn't, is he?'

'A brain surgeon? No, not amateur nor otherwise. He has worked on a voluntary basis, however, with doctors treating the poor and indigent.'

'I find it hard to believe.'

'I beg your pardon?'

'Achieving so much in one lifetime. Extraordinary chap.'

She looked at him closely. 'He's very busy.'

'So it would seem.' He stretched. 'We're in the Neanderthals' prison, aren't we?'

'Freshly dusted for our convenience. What is it?'

'What is what?'

'What is it you've just thought of? You went all squidgy there.'

'Squidgy?'

'You drew in your cheeks, narrowed your eyes, and moved your jaw from side to side. Something awkward or embarrassing has just occurred to you.'

Kingsley put a hand to his chin. 'I did all that?'

'You did.'

'And you noticed and you have a name for it?'

Evadne hesitated and nipped around the question in an expert flanking manoeuvre. 'What was it?'

'I don't think we're going to be here long. Otherwise they would have put us in two cells.'

'Ah.' She looked around. 'I'm not sure if the Neanderthals think like that.'

'You're right. I'm not sure what Neanderthals think at all.' He hesitated. 'Have you ever talked with one?'

'Kingsley, until the last few days I'd never even seen one. They're among the most elusive of Demimonders.' She poured herself a cup of water and drank it all. 'You're right, of course. I have no idea what they're thinking, apart from that they want to wipe us out or possibly eat us. And what we've just been through has shown that they can do what they're planning. I'd say they simply don't have enough power yet.'

'If we can stop their plans to destroy humanity, I'd like to see what makes them tick.'

'What makes a tiger tick?'

'They're people, not animals.' Even as he said it, he wondered if perhaps the Neanderthals were closer to the wild than Sapiens were – and if perhaps this could shed some light on his particular halfway state.

'Are they? Are they any different?'

Kingsley shrugged. 'You're different. I'm different.'

Evadne stared at him. She blinked, then stared again. Finally, she sat back and crossed her arms on her chest. 'You, Kingsley Ward, have done something very rare: you've made me change my mind.'

'I have?'

'Do you know how many people have tried to make me change my mind? Grown men have given up in tears, professors have taken up holy orders, judges have become hermits.'

'I realise that you're strong-minded.'

'My mind has had plenty of exercise. Of course it's strong.'

'But it's also flexible.'

'True. I see your point. I'm not sure where it gets us, but I see your point.'

'Most people are different from ourselves,' he said, 'so difference actually makes us all the same, if you see what I mean.'

'Now you're just being confusing.' She lifted her fore-finger and tapped it up and down on her arm. 'But if you're saying that these Neanderthals are just as human as anyone else, I might agree. It's just that anyone else, in this case, is a dangerous maniac.'

'That's fair. I'm not saying that they're likely to be saints, no more than we are.'

'Speak for yourself.'

'I beg your pardon. I mean to say that I'd still like to know how they think.'

'So that you can see how mass murder can be justified? No need to ask the Neanderthals. Look at history. The Crusades. Genghis Khan. The Inquisition.'

'Now it's your turn to be correct: it's easy to find justification for mass murder, as long as you're convinced you're right.' Kingsley put his chin in his hand. 'Say what you like. I want to stop these Neanderthals, but I can't bring myself to hate them.'

She paused and studied him again. 'As a project, Kingsley Ward, you are by far my most interesting.' Evadne reached behind her. 'Would you like something to eat? We have fruit, bread, cheese.'

'They've provided food for their prisoners? How very human.'

Later that day, when the six burly Neanderthals came to the cell door, Kingsley briefly amused himself by wondering if there was any other type.

It'd do me good to see a lanky Neanderthal with pipe cleaner arms.

One of the six was the black-bearded leader of the team who had pursued them across seventeenth-century London. Without a word they were marched to a room near the main workshop. Of course, this made it somewhat near the workshop that held the time machine, but Kingsley accepted that this was a moot point, guarded as they were.

The room wasn't luxurious. Kingsley was puzzled by the manner in which everything was curved, even the pillars that held up the roof. The walls were painted with murals, scenes of forests and deserts, acutely realistic in detail, as if one could take a step and be there.

A single old female Neanderthal that Kingsley recognised as the one who had saved him from the Spawn – then set out in pursuit of him – put down a saw she'd been sharpening and hung it on a rack over the crowded workbench. She wiped her hands on the sides of her overalls. Kingsley saw her age in the way she limped – one hip was troubling her, even though she tried to hide it. Her forearms were still muscular, however, and her eyes were clear. She looked as old as the mountains.

She studied him for a moment, in the slightly distant way a farmer would look at stock. She barely glanced at Evadne, who managed an 'I demand –' before one of the Neanderthals clamped a hand over her mouth. She resisted furiously but her captor was impassive.

'Is this him, Rolf?' the old woman said to blackbeard, ignoring Evadne's performance. Her voice was like a barrel filled with stones.

Blackbeard – Rolf – looked sideways at Kingsley with a mixture of disgust and anger, and Kingsley wondered if he'd been friendly with the Neanderthal who had vanished into the Immortals' Temporal Manipulator. 'Looks like him. The girl did have the phlogiston.'

'You had trouble?'

Rolf smiled. 'We ran into those sorcerers. Immortals. We couldn't resist the chance to do them some harm.'

'Harm in the past? Good. They are back in their lair now, which is bad.'

'What?' Rolf's eyes were wide. 'We tore them apart.' He looked puzzled. 'Here, I mean. Not back then. '

'Magic,' the old woman said sourly.

Kingsley felt as if he'd been hit with a brick. The Immortals? Alive? He'd thought his brain was safe from the Immortals seeing as they'd been torn to pieces, but now?

Evadne went rigid for an instant, then shook in a frantic effort to free herself. It was futile.

The old woman lapsed into silence. Kingsley went to speak, but she gestured and one of the guards clapped a hand over his mouth as well. Kingsley didn't struggle. He was too busy trying to read her broad face.

'Attend to me, young Invaders,' she said. She didn't look at them, which made Kingsley nervous. Her gaze was slightly over his shoulder, but he knew she wasn't talking to the row of Neanderthal bravoes behind him. 'Your fate has been determined. Make your peace.'

Kingsley struggled then, but was held tight by two pairs of hands either side. He jerked and managed to get in a good elbow jab, but it was like hitting a slab of well-seasoned timber.

'We have heard from the Immortals. They will leave us alone if we trade you to them,' the old woman said. Then as she turned away, she added in a mutter: 'The old man will break soon. I don't need you any more.'

Kingsley shook off the muffling hand and howled as fear and shock set his wild self free.

Panting and aching after regaining control, Kingsley remained impassive while they chained him up to take him to the Immortals, but inside he raged. The beasts! Torturing an old man! He wanted to rend the nearest savage apart.

But they had learned. This time, they used manacles, shackles and chains on Kingsley instead of ropes. They were of excellent manufacture, with every appearance of being bespoke. The linkages on the leg-irons, for instance, were significantly different from those on the manacles, while the finishing showed signs of hand polishing.

They wouldn't be a problem, he decided, even if they were heavy enough to lead a rhinoceros on a walk. Just strike the manacles on a hard surface, preferably a corner, right there where the hasp entered, and he'd be free soon enough.

They had been rough with Evadne, and Kingsley vowed to make them pay for that. She had made the mistake of resisting – to no avail, given the superior strength of the Neanderthals. Her glares made no difference either. They were impervious.

While being transported, Kingsley tried to talk to his captors. Through drains, shafts, a remarkably domed concourse, an overground stretch through a lane with merchants who specialised in Egyptian antiquities, and finally into a beautifully arched red-brick conduit with spectacular quoining, Kingsley strove to treat his captors as fellows. He put aside his rage and his embarrassment at being transported in a Neanderthal-sized wheelbarrow and asked them what they wanted, how they could be helped. They ignored him. Most did so with ease, as if he were simply a noisy farm animal, but a few of the younger Neanderthals had more difficulty restraining themselves. One finally burst out with 'Shut your filthy face, Invader!' and advanced before one of the more senior straight-armed him with a shove to the chest that would have put a hole in a stone wall.

Evadne, unusually, had been quiet during all this but soon after they reached a red-brick confluence of three tunnels, she mouthed, 'My turn.'

'Phlogiston,' she said quietly, as if to herself, and immediately she had the attention of the entire band, even though they did their best not to betray it. 'You've made some gains in phlogiston extraction.'

She went on as if they had answered, even though none of them had uttered a word. 'I thought so. The purity looked outstanding. I've had to triple refine to get that concentration.'

The silence of the Neanderthals was considerably strained.

'Of course, that would mean you'd have to double-baffle the fractionating column to avoid explosions,' she said.

A few furtive glances among their captors.

'Ah. You've learned that? I could have saved you the trouble if you'd asked.'

'We use ammonia-based refrigeration to get over the problem,' one of the younger Neanderthals muttered. At the disgust of his fellows, he looked down, abashed.

'Good idea,' Evadne said, nodding as much as she could with ropes up to her chin, 'but my approach means a more compact unit.'

'Enough,' growled Rolf. 'We're here.'

Evadne jerked. 'I can double your extraction rate!'

'After we hand you over, we'll have all the phlogiston we need.'

~ THIRTY-NINE ~

Soames knew Rolf, the leader of the Neanderthals, as one of Damona's trusted underlings. Rolf hadn't been happy at Soames's having half a dozen hastily grown Spawn with him, but after some patently ritual objections, his phlogiston greed took over.

'Is it all there, Soames?' Rolf growled.

Soames waved at the handcart. 'Two gross vials was the price agreed upon, but I managed to round it up to three hundred for you. Think of it as a gesture of good will.'

'Good will. Hah!'

Soames was interested in the attitude of the Neanderthals to their prisoners. He'd expected the disgust and anger – the typical Neanderthal reaction to humans – but as they left, was that a lingering look backward, at the girl, from some of the Neanderthals? Remarkable.

The girl struggled as the Spawn took her, but the boy's

attention was on the Neanderthals. He waited until they had disappeared. 'Don't take us to the Immortals,' he said to Soames.

Soames sighed. It was so predictable. 'Do you know how much pleading I've heard from people in your position? I've had offers of money, threats, prayers and promises. I haven't relented to any of them.'

'A man of principle,' the girl said. She'd stopped struggling. Her spectacles were dislodged, hanging from one ear in rather delightful disarray.

Soames straightened them. He admired the neatness he'd brought about, and her singularly beautiful face. 'We all have principles,' he said to her. 'Mine are rather more pragmatic than most, and they mean you won't be going to the Immortals, my dear. They're not interested in you.'

'But you are?' the girl said with no fear at all, which Soames found most extraordinary.

'You are my way of ensuring a nice profit out of this escapade. I know several slavers who'll be willing to bid for you.'

She laughed. 'And here I was, imagining that you had a lofty purpose in mind for me. Human sacrifice, some sort of ghoulish ritual.'

Soames adjusted his cuffs. 'Hardly. I'm not a sorcerer, I'm a businessman.'

'If you're a businessman, then you'll want to talk to us,' the boy said. Husky as he was, he was no match for the Spawn and had realised it. He wasn't struggling.

Soames appreciated it when someone was resigned to their fate. It made things much easier.

'I doubt it.' Soames motioned to the Spawn. Without

speaking, a pair took the prisoners head and foot. The girl looked angry, but the boy was strangely calm.

The boy waited, and just before the Spawn entered the tunnel he craned his neck and looked directly at Soames. 'If you don't talk to us,' he said, 'you'll miss an opportunity.'

Opportunity. Soames couldn't help reacting – hesitating, leaning slightly in the boy's direction – and he cursed himself for it.

⮜⮞ FORTY ⮜⮞

Kingsley summoned his stage presence and charged his words with sincerity. With as much conviction as he could summon he spoke to the oleaginous man. 'The Neanderthals are planning to exterminate all humanity.'

The man's face fell. 'It that all? The Neanderthals have been trying to do that for centuries. They always fail.'

'They're desperate now,' Kingsley said with as much composure as someone who was confined by a hundred-weight or two of chains could, 'and they're staking everything on an ultimate effort.'

'Who can blame them, after we hunted them to the edge of extinction?' Soames signed to the Spawn. 'It's of no matter. I'm sure I'll survive whatever attack they're planning and be there to pick up the pieces.' He put his hands together. 'There's money to be made in ruins.'

'I'm afraid I haven't quite explained myself adequately.'

Soames leaned and peered at him. Kingsley thought he could squeeze a few pints of oil from the man's hair alone. 'I must say, it's a pleasure dealing with you, young man, especially after some of the types I'm forced to associate with. You're so polite.'

'You beastly man,' Evadne burst out, 'you're dooming everyone if you don't listen to us!'

Soames raised his eyebrows. He straightened and examined his cufflinks. 'And there you have it. I think we need to be off.'

Kingsley shot Evadne a glance. She subsided, smouldering.

'A last word, if you don't mind,' Kingsley said carefully. 'You see, the Neanderthals are about to make every single human being disappear, including you.'

'What did you say?'

'It's the phlogiston, you idiot!' Evadne cried. 'The Neanderthals are powering a time machine with it and you've given them enough to complete their goal.' She grimaced. 'Sorry.'

'Put them down,' Soames said to the Spawn. 'Wait at the Hall. Now,' he said to Kingsley and Evadne after producing a nasty-looking little pistol, 'tell me more.'

Kingsley watched the man grow graver and graver as he stood in front of them and listened to Evadne's description of the time machine. She used their 1666 mishap to impress on him how advanced the Neanderthals' planning was. 'All that they need, really, is some calibration, some coordinates and enough phlogiston.' She shook her head. 'Why on earth did your masters give away so much?'

'They're not my masters,' Soames said quickly. He was sweating, Kingsley noted, despite the cool of the grotto. 'They're my clients.'

'I'm sure that's an important distinction to you.'

'Business is business. It also means that I need to decide how I can find a profit here.' He tapped the barrel of the gun against his cheek. 'What *is* the best way to use this information you've just given me?'

'What about by trying to stop them? If they're not stopped, you won't be around to cheat and cozen the likes of us, because we won't be either.'

'This *is* a wonderful story,' the man said. 'I must congratulate you. It's diverted me more than any I've heard for years. It hasn't worked, mind you, but it has drawn things out.'

Enough was enough, Kingsley decided. He could see that the man was hardly likely to be straight with them, not when he had them at such a disadvantage.

While Evadne had been talking, Kingsley had been readying himself, trusting to Evadne's urgency and the man's obvious fascination with her to hold his attention.

Firstly, misdirection.

Kingsley's hands were behind his back, something he'd managed to make sure of when the Spawn had bound him. Now, with his unobserved hands quite free, it was a simple matter to find a lock pick that he'd hidden in the sleeve of the jacket Evadne had given to him. After years of exercise, he knew his wrists and fingers were strong, but his next manoeuvre needed more than just strength: it needed timing and dexterity as well.

310

Without moving his shoulders, solely relying on his wrists and fingers, he flipped the lock pick up and over his head in an arc that took it across the cave. It struck the far wall and fell, tinkling all the way.

No-one human could ignore it. Kingsley was glad for confirmation of Soames's species status when his head whipped around to see what had caused the noise.

Secondly, effect.

Kingsley stood and already his manacles were falling away. He had his hands ready. He grasped the chains, then swung them at the ghastly man.

Soames staggered back. The chain whistled past his shocked face, and Kingsley was already in position. He knocked the man's arm upward, seized it, struck him hard in the armpit and then in the midriff.

Soames's eyes went wide. He made to cry out but, as Kingsley had hoped, the blow in the midriff had winded him. He doubled over and his knees gave way.

Thirdly, the flourish.

Kingsley squeezed Soames's wrist until he dropped the pistol. Kingsley caught it in his other hand. 'Now,' he said, his mind already leaping ahead to what needed to be done next. 'Are there any other tables that need turning?'

~ FORTY-ONE ~

The imminent demise of the human race didn't allow Kingsley time for second thoughts. 'I have a way to get into the Neanderthals' lair and destroy the time machine,' he said, ignoring the dangers that his plan entailed. *And to save my father,* he added to himself.

Soames, bound and at gunpoint, laughed from where he'd been propped against a decorative stalagmite. 'Preposterous. Nothing enters that place unexamined. Even my shipments are examined.'

'That's why I have to do it the buried alive way.'

Evadne frowned. 'I don't like the sound of that.'

'It's very impressive, if it's performed correctly.'

Evadne raised an eyebrow. 'I take it that "correctly" means you come out alive instead of dead.'

'It's all in the technique. And it's much safer than many other effects.'

'Such as?' Evadne asked, clearly unimpressed.

'Oh, the bullet catch, for instance.'

'The bullet catch trick?' Soames perked up. 'Didn't Otto Blumenfeld die trying to perform that?

'Er . . . I think so.'

'In Frankfurt, if I remember correctly,' Soames said. 'And didn't Michael Hatal suffer a similar fate in Brussels, attempting the same trick?'

'Hatal? I seem to remember the name . . .'

'A shame, really,' Soames said. 'Hatal had a capital twist on a magic cabinet disappearance. Quite the finest I ever saw.'

Kingsley couldn't believe it. Soames was a magical aficionado.

Before he could take this up with him, he saw Evadne regarding him severely. 'So your plan's being safer than the bullet catch trick isn't actually very reassuring.'

'The buried alive escape leaves much less to chance. Nothing can go wrong.'

'That's what Michael Hatal said,' Soames observed.

'The buried alive trick,' Kingsley hurried on, 'simply requires focus and discipline. Locked in a confined space, the escaper must breathe slowly and shallowly, making the utmost of every scintilla of air, until he emerges some improbable time later.'

Kingsley liked the idea of the buried alive trick, but had never actually been able to bring himself to try it. It perfectly encapsulated the principles of escapology, almost in the purest of forms. He knew the principles and he'd experimented with them – but without the additional complication of being confined and buried.

'How will you get out?' Soames asked with the sort of

313

fascination Kingsley had seen before in those who were attracted to the world of stage magic.

'It would be best if I have a few tools with me. I'll need a saw, and a pry bar would be lovely. I'd like a drill, too.'

'A drill?' Evadne asked.

'Double purpose. If something goes wrong, I can open some airholes. If it goes smoothly, I can use it to see outside before I emerge.'

'I don't like it,' Evadne said flatly.

Kingsley shrugged. 'What are our alternatives?' He gestured at Soames with the pistol. 'How do you make your shipments to the Neanderthals?'

Evadne stamped a foot. 'Kingsley! I wouldn't trust him with a penny!'

'Trust?' Soames chuckled. Kingsley had to admit that the man had considerable self-possession. 'No, I'm afraid you can't trust me. But you can buy me.'

'With what?' Kingsley said.

'I know that our Neanderthal cousins have a considerable amount of phlogiston, since I just gave it to them. I think, however, that they may have more. Am I right?'

'Go on,' Evadne said.

'If I have a way to get you to the Neanderthals' lair, then I want their phlogiston.'

After that, Kingsley was grateful it was merely a matter of details. Firstly, Evadne insisted on a dash across the city to her refuge. In the darkness, while Kingsley leaned against the fence under the Olympic stadium with a manacled and compliant Soames, she disappeared, returning with another satchel full of equipment she insisted was vital – and a device she gave to Kingsley, telling him it was even more important.

Soames then took them down the river to Wapping, where he was obviously well known. At the docks, he ushered them to a dry goods warehouse. 'It's mine,' he said to Kingsley's inquiring glance. 'A presence at the docks is useful for a man in my situation.'

'And you do business with the Neanderthals from here?'

'Foodstuffs mostly, a great deal of it. They do love to eat.'

Evadne waved his pistol in front of Soames's face before they unshackled him. He nodded at the unspoken warning and appeared to accept this as reasonable in the circumstances. Briskly, he negotiated with some under-lings, organising a cart, some barrels, and several navvies to take it all to the point where the Neanderthals would assume delivery.

'You're thinking of his masters, aren't you?' Kingsley said to her.

'You're practising a mentalist act now? "Kingsley the Reader of Minds"?'

'The set you have against them shows in your face.' Kingsley refrained from mentioning that she'd also been tapping the finger that wore the silver ring. Part of her mystery lay in that ring, he was sure, but he was also sure that a direct query would be rebuffed.

'That's unfortunate,' she said. 'I'd been hoping to build a reputation as inscrutable.'

Two navvies rolled a barrel across the warehouse. Kingsley rubbed his chin. The barrel was smaller than he'd thought.

'Kingsley.'

He turned. A myrmidon that hadn't been there a moment ago was at her feet.

'Here,' she said, and thrust Soames's pistol at him. 'Watch that man. I don't trust him.'

'What? Where are you going?'

'Outside. Someone wants to talk to me.'

'Here? Who knows you're here?'

'Someone who is now convinced who we are and who has also found a way to talk to my myrmidons.'

Kingsley undertook what he had to admit was one of the worst jobs of supervising since a foreman in Pisa glanced at some foundations and declared they were plenty stable. He kept flicking his attention between Soames, who seemed genuinely absorbed in the delicacies of organising and haggling, and Evadne, who was talking to an extremely nondescript man in the courtyard outside the warehouse.

Kingsley was sure the man was the same one who'd been after them for some time, cloaked in his utter ordinariness.

Divided as his attention was, Kingsley had no idea how long it was before Evadne came back. Ten minutes? Twenty?

'Kingsley,' she said. 'I want to tell you my secret.'

'Here? Now?'

'Yes.'

Evadne's sudden urge to share unnerved him. Her voice was as steely as her gaze. 'That man. What did he want?'

She smiled, but for once it didn't sit easily on her face. 'He had a useful message.'

'From whom?'

'From the past.' She took out her watch, glanced at it and put it away. 'Do you remember the Retrievers?'

'Those poor souls back in the Great Fire?'

'They certainly remembered us. They were grateful that the Immortals had left their London and the children were freed.' She glanced outside. A patter of rain touched the cobbles. 'They charged a law firm in their Demimonde with some information, to be kept for two hundred and fifty years.'

'For us.'

Another jarring smile. 'I'm afraid, Kingsley, it was for me. We didn't leave names, you see, and my appearance . . .'

'So that man finally found you. What did he tell you?'

'Something interesting about secret river gates and diversions at Greenwich. Without too much effort, I should be able to flood the Immortals' lair.'

'Capital! When I get back from this we can plan an assault, arm ourselves with some of those splendid weapons of yours . . .' He saw her face. He hesitated. 'You're planning something. Something dangerous.'

'What do you mean?'

'Telling me your secret. You're making a clean . . .' He stumbled. 'You're wanting to set things right before you do something reckless.'

'Nonsense.' Evadne did her best to affect briskness, but Kingsley could see how superficial it was – and for a fleeting instant he wondered how he'd come to know this surprising young woman so well and so quickly. 'I know your secret and, if we're to have a useful working partnership, you need to know mine.'

'I –'

'Don't interrupt, there's a good fellow. This is going to be hard enough as it is.' Evadne took off her gloves and tucked them into the pocket of her coat. She held up her right hand. The ring glinted. 'My story about leaving home to seek my fortune wasn't the entire truth. This belonged to my sister, Flora.'

Ah. 'I didn't know you had a sister.'

'I don't. Not any more.' Evadne's hands fell to her side. Then, she lifted them. Without looking, she made a few ghost throws with invisible juggling balls, but her pattern fell apart.

Kingsley took a step towards her, impelled by an instinctive urge to comfort the hurt, but she moved away. She clasped her hands and touched them to her chin, still not meeting his gaze. 'Let me tell you what happened.

'I was ten. Flora was five. We were playing in our garden. Naturally, I was in charge of my little sister but, as much as I loved her, I found her to be a terrible trial. I became absorbed in collecting pine cones.' She smiled at Kingsley, and his heart ached at the fragility of it. 'I wanted to make a battalion of pine cone soldiers. I didn't notice her wandering away.'

'She became lost?'

'She was abducted. Three other children in the district were taken that week. Flora was the first of them.' She took a sharp breath. 'Do you know the word *vendetta*?'

'The blood feud. The Corsicans practise it.'

'In some ways, vengeance is easy if you know who was responsible. Since I didn't, my *vendetta* is with all those who take children.'

'Like these Immortals.'

318

'They're the worst. Now that they're active again, I won't rest until I bring them down. With your help, I hope.'

'And the help of Clarence?'

Evadne pursed her lips. She took hold of the chain around her neck and withdrew her pendant. She opened it. It was empty. 'There is no Clarence.'

'I had an inkling.'

'I cut it out of a postcard. A comely chap.'

'And you keep him in your locket for a reason?'

'I've found him a useful defence. Certain people tend to leave me alone once I point out that I already have an intended.'

'You strike a blow in advance.'

'Precisely. It saves so much nonsense.'

Kingsley sensed that this was a time to leave well enough alone. 'I appreciate your sharing, but I insist that it still suggests you're about to do something dangerous.'

'Kingsley –'

He had it. 'Your rat. It came just before the nondescript man. It told you something.'

Evadne trembled. Just slightly, but Kingsley took it as a sign of the effort it was taking her to remain composed. 'Mrs Oldham's School for Girls has been burnt to the ground. All the children were abducted, according to Lady Aglaia. I'm going to rescue them and, finally, to destroy the Immortals.' She crossed her arms. 'There. Now you have it, go and ready yourself, prepare, sing a song, whatever it is you do.' She turned away and when she turned back she'd changed glasses. These were so dark he couldn't see her eyes. 'Please go quickly. I'm barely restraining myself at the moment. Every part of me wants to rush out and save Meg and the others.'

'I can't let you go alone. I'm coming with you.'

'Kingsley, there's no telling how soon the Neander-thals might act. They could have the dates and be ready to begin! You have to go and save the world!'

Kingsley sought for the appropriate words, and they were there so quickly that he hardly thought before he spoke: 'I'm not sure that a saved world would be worth-while if you're not in it.'

Evadne didn't reply. She remained still and silent. The world beyond them, with barrels rolling and oaths echoing from the rafters, was distant, as if behind a haze. 'Kingsley,' she finally said. 'That's the sort of romantic tosh that makes me ...'

'Melt?'

'Makes me want to throw something.' She smiled. This time, it was entirely Evadne – challenging, enigmatic and staggeringly fetching. 'But I've learned something from you.'

'How not to lose one's mind while being pulled in a hundred different directions?'

'I've learned something about control.' She patted him on the arm. 'You go and save the world, I'll go and save the children and afterwards we'll meet for tea at the Savoy.'

'I –'

Soames chose this inauspicious moment to stride towards them, clapping his hands together and rubbing them in anticipation. 'Now, what about showing me some of this escapology business, eh?'

With a wrench that could have torn several major muscle groups, Kingsley brought himself back to the task at hand.

He was almost amused at how interested Soames was. The man questioned him endlessly as Kingsley arranged himself at the bottom of the large barrel, asking his opinion of Herrmann and Devant. Kingsley realised that Soames had seen hundreds of magic perform-ances. His opinions were well-considered and informed. His enthusiasm changed him. His oiliness disappeared. His face became open, his voice direct.

The man has hidden depths, Kingsley thought. *Who would have suspected it?*

He braced his shoulder while Soames himself leaned inside the barrel and nailed in the false bottom. The noise was hurtful, and soon after Kingsley felt the extra pressure when the barrel was filled with split peas. Kingsley hoped that Soames had nailed well, fitting the bottom into the extra croze in the barrel. He didn't want to be suffocated by split peas, an ignominious end if ever there was one.

Kingsley's resting place smelled of dust and oil. He wrinkled his nose, not wanting to sneeze. He lay on his side, curled around so that his head and his knees were nearly touching.

He cradled the device Evadne had given to him as contribution to the plan.

After that, he heard a tap on the side of the barrel, the stave right near his head. Evadne's voice came to him clearly: 'Tea at the Savoy, remember?'

The barrel jerked. He was off.

Time became inconsequential. It *had* to be inconsequen-tial. Kingsley couldn't afford to pay attention to it. He needed to drift, to detach himself as best he could from his surroundings. It was something that he found extremely difficult – and his wildness found it almost impossible. Not pay attention to one's surroundings? That was the way to ending up in someone's belly.

He had to soothe his fretting wildness, calming it, sending it to sleep while he maintained his regime of leisurely, even breathing.

Dockside sounds, wheels on cobblestones, grunts and curses, all were irrelevant as Kingsley concentrated on the sound of his heartbeat. *Slow is good*, he repeated to himself over and over. *Slow is good*.

He retired from engaging with the world. He drifted. Every sound, every movement, every smell, was background, a mattress on which he rested.

Curled up in the dead space, nailed in under the consignment of dried peas, Kingsley knew that death was hovering nearby, waiting for the air to lose its goodness. He pushed the concern away lest it grow into fear, then panic. He deliberated instead on lying still and conserving what little air there was.

The blackness came closer as time stretched. When stray thoughts came to his attention he wiped them out, casually cleaning the blackboard of his mind. Every breath was long and flavoursome. He had time to welcome each one and to feel disappointed at its departure. Dimly, he became aware that the air in his tight space was growing thick, but he took it as comforting, like a blanket on a cold night.

His wild self roused for a moment and looked at the blackness for what it might contain. He could roam free in it, forever, if he chose.

322

Rest, he told it. *Your time is not now.*

A banging, a settling, a time of nothing at all – no movement, no sound. He had to remind himself – and it was difficult to stir enough awareness to do so – that Soames had said that the barrels would be delivered to a place from which the Neanderthals would take them. Breaking out here would be a disaster.

He slipped back into the drowsy embrace of torpor.

Guttural voices, heavy footfalls. The barrel lifted suddenly, shockingly. Movement, rumbling, travel – but irrelevant, a far-off tale, hardly real or bothersome.

He didn't sleep but he wasn't truly awake either. He breathed, his heart beat, and that was all. Savour each breath. Take all that it has to offer before letting it free. Repeat.

He knew his body was in pain, curled and unable to move as it was, but it was an abstract thing, as if it were happening to someone else.

He drifted.

Control.

If he couldn't control his actions here, he'd be lost. If he couldn't control his breathing or he couldn't control his wild self, he would die.

Control.

Rocking, halting, descent. Tipping suddenly, enough to startle. For a moment, his surroundings came to him, an urgent welter of sounds and smells. He was shaken, disorientated when the barrel rolled on its side. Up and down exchanged places with each other, again and again. His tiny, dark world spun.

In time, he was on his side again. He sipped once more at his tiny corner of air. *Easy*, he told his heart, *no need to run away. Easy.*

All was quiet. All was still. Kingsley existed until he knew it was time.

Move.

He opened his eyes, saw nothing but blackness. He found the hacksaw blade in his sock. He used the pry bar to ease the staves apart and he slipped the saw between them. He cut the chime hoop, the one nearest the base, then the quarter hoop. He was halfway through the bulge hoop when the barrel gave way. Kingsley spilled onto the floor in a tide of green split peas.

I did it.

Lying on the floor, surrounded by dried legumes, Kingsley breathed freely and counted his aching muscles. Then he revelled in his triumph. He'd succeeded. He'd kept death at bay simply through his self-control. His will had overridden his body's natural impulses and he'd survived.

He rolled over, aching everywhere, and regarded the ceiling, accepting what had happened. He needn't shy away from anything again. He could keep his wild side leashed. He could attempt the most dangerous escape. He could approach life squarely.

He rolled to his feet. He made a fist and shook it, bubbling with the triumph that came from success, but also from the exhilaration that came from understanding a little bit more about who he was.

Something ran into his boot. Kingsley looked down. He almost kicked at the furry shape before he realised it wasn't a rat but one of Evadne's myrmidons.

The creature circled at Kingsley's feet, chasing its tail, then it sat up on its back legs and blinked at him. At least, two of its eyes blinked.

Kingsley went to his knees, curious. The myrmidon must have followed the delivery, but what had Evadne been thinking?

The myrmidon dropped to all fours, then it wriggled. A tremor passed along its length, then it hunched and opened its mouth wide.

The creature shook its head, then spat out a tiny vial. It looked up at Kingsley, then it nudged the vial with its nose.

Kingsley picked it up. The vial was half the size of the phlogiston vials and it was dull grey, not glowing at all. He tilted it to the light and made out fine script etched along the side.

Anti-phlogiston.

Breaking in was a great deal like breaking out, Kingsley decided as he listened at the door he'd just slipped through. He'd kept the pry bar with him after freeing himself from the barrel. While he was ready to use it as a weapon, it was mostly for reassurance – and for some quick ingress when he had no time to pick a lock.

After so long being shuttlecocked around, it was good to be fighting back.

The Neanderthals' complex was even busier than the last time he was there. Anyone he'd seen was carrying tools or materials – and hurrying. The whole place had an air of urgency that Kingsley wasn't at all happy about.

However, this activity did mean that the focus of the Neanderthals was on things other than expecting an intruder.

With something approaching confidence, Kingsley called on his wild self, hoping that its wariness would be helpful. He crept around the disconcerting corridors, halls, chambers and galleries; on several occasions he sensed the approach of Neanderthals and hid just in time.

Meanwhile, his civilised self noticed the patterns of movement and gave him a destination. By and large, the Neanderthals were all moving in one direction, along corridors or via stairs and lifts.

The great project of the Neanderthals was drawing them all together.

The True People, Soames had said the Neanderthals called themselves. Kingsley wasn't surprised. Hazily, he remembered his wild upbringing and knew that there were only two sorts to the pack: us and others. Strangers were to be feared.

So many of the world's ills could be attributed to that sort of attitude. Kingsley wished that the Demimonde had a magic to change it.

Increasing pandemonium and an industrial cacophony of steel and steam told Kingsley that he was approaching the major workshop.

He waited, patience itself, watching eager, chattering workers come and go. He recognised one, the red-haired female Evadne had rendered unconscious with her dart gun. She spoke expansively to her colleagues, flinging her arms wide in her enthusiasm.

Inside his jacket, his fingers found the pocket watch and phlogiston device that Evadne had given him. In

Soames's warehouse she'd used jeweller's tools she'd brought from her refuge and constructed it with dazzling speed from her own pocket watch and some wire. He remembered how her juggler's hands had moved with grace and precision.

Listening intently, alert for any presence, Kingsley slipped into the workshop that was the home of the time machine.

He stared. The machine had changed.

The inner spiral was still present, but the disc from which the golden wires had hung had been removed. An airy framework was in its place, made of exceedingly thin wires radiating from the central tower, joining to an equally thin hoop supporting the golden curtain. The tower was now connected to the ceiling by a complicated arrangement of pipes and cables, all of them a bright silver that flashed in the light.

Near the control panel, had been Evadne's instruction. Directly underneath the control panel struck him as close enough, so he used the wire to lash Evadne's device around the pedestal, up high, as close to the underside of the control panel as he could make it. He took a step back and it couldn't be seen; not unless someone dropped on hands and knees and peered upward. He couldn't imagine the humourless Neanderthals engaging in a spot of leap frog or shamble-my-toe, so he congratulated himself on an optimum solution.

He went down on all fours, then reached up for the two loose copper ends and twisted them together. With the device securely anchored and well hidden, he stood. He straightened his jacket, then his tie, and had a wistful moment regretting that he had no gloves to straighten and thereby complete the set, ready for the next part of his performance.

Trapped deep underground, at the very furthest reaches of the Neanderthal lair, surrounded by brutish people who would soon have their cherished dream of revenge snatched away from them, he had one hour to perform his greatest escape while rescuing his crippled foster father at the same time.

He had to do it. He was *not* going to miss having tea at the Savoy with Evadne Stephens.

~ FORTY-TWO ~

Soames watched as his underlings wheeled the cart through the doors of the warehouse and into the night. The men were reluctant and it was only Soames's liberal payments that overcame their nervousness in taking the delivery to the crypt where the Neanderthals were waiting.

He was amused by the girl's damp sentimentality as she watched it disappear, and he decided the time was right to do something about the awkward situation. He cleared his throat. 'Now, my dear, I'll have to report to the Immortals soon.'

She didn't respond. She still had his pistol in her hand, but her attention was on the night beyond the doors.

'I imagine I'll have to concoct a story to account for the non-appearance of the boy,' he continued, hiding his irritation. 'Blaming the Neanderthals should work, but it will be difficult.'

At that moment, a rat scurried through the doors. Soames recoiled a step or two, but then became alert. The filthy thing might frighten her enough to drop the pistol.

She astonished him by reaching down to the rat. Soames couldn't believe it. The vermin was actually pleased to see her, running in circles and rolling over to expose its belly.

He was about to express his incredulity when she swivelled. Her face was ghostly, but calm. She began tossing the Bulldog from hand to hand.

He backed away. 'I say. That's a dangerous thing to do, my dear.'

She advanced, the pistol still looping from one hand to the other without her even looking at it. He collided with a stack of crates. He licked his lips nervously. Had the girl gone mad? Cuddling rats and now juggling firearms?

'Now, let me have it, there's a good girl.'

With a twist of her wrist, she spun the pistol at him.

Soames gasped and fumbled for it. The next thing he knew the girl had taken two steps and driven her shoulder into his throat, then cracked him under the chin with a sharply rising elbow.

With his skull ringing and his lungs empty, Soames had no choice but to slide to the floor of the warehouse. He lay there, whimpering.

When he was capable of making sense of what he saw, he realised he was looking at his Bulldog again, back in her firm and unwavering hand.

'Now my friend isn't here to stop me,' she said, 'you'll take me to the Immortals' lair and do what I tell you, otherwise I'll blow your head off.'

'I beg your pardon?'

'Don't mistake me, Soames. My seriousness is of the deadly sort.'

Soames swallowed. 'Strangely enough, I'm quite convinced of that.'

'Now, hand over your pocket watch.'

Had the girl gone mad? Soames had heard about albinos. Could her condition be affecting her mind? 'You're robbing me?'

'Take it out and throw it to me.'

He ached. His watch was a Dent quarter repeater with offset seconds; one of a kind, since he'd commissioned its building himself. It had a mirrored inner case and he'd trained himself to tell the time backward so he could know as soon as he cracked the case what time it was. An affectation, but he enjoyed it.

He lobbed the watch to the girl. She took it easily, glanced at it and tossed it up so it flipped over and landed in her palm. 'A Dent? Good.'

'I'm glad, my dear. Shall we go now?'

'We shall.' She gestured with the pistol. 'And one more thing.'

'Yes?'

'I'm not your dear. Not unless you have a desire for a permanent limp.'

They eventually reached the grotto in Greenwich. Soames paused just before the girl told him to stop. 'Here –' she added.

He turned and cried out to see his watch looping through the air towards him. Never good at games, Soames lunged and managed to catch the watch in both hands. He immediately froze. 'What have you done to my watch?'

'I've wired a special vial to it,' she said. 'It will explode if you tamper with it.'

Fear opened a trapdoor for Soames to fall through. 'What?'

'It'll explode in an hour anyway, but don't fiddle with it. You can't defuse it and you'll only make it go off.'

Soames liked a good watch, but an exploding one wasn't what he was after. He held it at arm's length. 'I'm afraid that I'm not in favour of anything that could result in my being blown to pieces.'

'You can't imagine how much that pains me, but a certain level of risk on your behalf is part of my plan.'

'I'd rather you spoke plainly, my d—' Soames winced at the Bulldog, which was looking far too eager for his liking. '— preference lies in that direction.'

'That vial is going to explode in an hour,' she said, with a touch more patience this time. 'All you have to do is to make sure it's near the Immortals' phlogiston stockpile when it does.'

Soames's jaw fell. 'But all that phlogiston! Greenwich will be destroyed!'

The girl cocked an eyebrow. 'They have that much?'

Soames saw he may have made an error. 'They have a considerable amount,' he allowed. 'Enough for it to be a disaster.'

'In deference to my absent friend, I've actually considered this eventuality. If this particular substance is released, it will seek to unite itself with any phlogiston nearby. It will dissolve vials and the harmless compound will then rejoin the atmosphere. With only a moderate explosion.'

'Not before I souvenir an armful or two, I should hope.'

'You'll have to be at a distance. A few hundred feet at a minimum.'

Soames was working this through, and he wasn't altogether unhappy with what he was concluding. 'They depend on phlogiston to power their manipulators. They'll be powerless if it works as you describe.'

'That's part of my plan.'

'And the other part?'

'Is something that I'll keep to myself.'

'I take it you won't be coming with me.' He rubbed his jaw. 'What's to stop me discarding your little device and confessing all to the Immortals?'

'I'm sensing that greed outweighs loyalty by a substantial amount in you.'

He bowed, slightly. 'I don't find it a weakness to admit to that.'

'You have the chance of assembling more wealth in your pockets than you could in a year.'

'A convincing argument.' He studied the explosive device gingerly. He was sure he could find a way to dispose of it once he left the girl.

She sighed. 'Greed and trustworthiness don't sit well together. I can see that you need another incentive to adhere to my plan.'

Soames was immediately cautious. 'I don't think so. You've been very persuasive.'

'Perhaps. But I have the feeling that once you're out of range of this delightful little pistol, all my persuasiveness will be for naught.' She reached into the pocket of her jacket and took out a glass disc the size of a sovereign. 'You've had some practice, now. Catch.'

Soames was growing tired of the demand, but this time he managed to bring both hands together and clap the disc between them. He held it up and immediately his poor, abused stomach lurched again. 'Where did you get this?'

'Never mind.'

Soames couldn't take his eyes away from the image. Small though it was, he could clearly see himself in earnest discussion with Damona, the chief of the Neanderthals.

'Here's another.'

Soames hardly looked at the disc winking its way to him, so horrified was he by the evidence of his double-dealing. Without thinking, he caught it single-handedly and brought it to his eyes.

Another image. Soames and the Neanderthal crew alighting at the Greenwich wharf.

His stomach rolled over, complained, and made a tentative push up his oesophagus. 'I take it that you have copies of these? And they'll make their way to the Immortals if I don't cooperate with your scheme?'

'Spoken like an experienced blackmailer. Of course, I won't just stop at the Immortals. I shall make sure most of the London Demimonde sees them. You'll never do business again.'

He blanched. 'Never do business . . .' He took a deep breath. 'And if I do cooperate, you'll destroy the plates?'

'My quarrel is with the Immortals, not you.' She peered at him over the top of her spectacles. 'I think.'

Instantly, Soames was very glad not to have this alarming young woman as an enemy, but he couldn't help himself asking: 'And what *is* your quarrel with them?'

'Of no concern to you, is what it is.' She gave him another thoughtful look that convinced him not to pursue this matter any further – nor to reveal anything about his more unpleasant business with the Immortals.

His shoulders slumped. 'It appears as if I'm about to do something dangerous.'

'It would seem to be the best option, but before you go, one last thing: why are the Immortals interested in the Olympic Games?'

'Hm?' Soames blinked. He'd been so careful. How had he ended up in such a position? His planning, his care, all outmanoeuvred by this upstart girl. 'I've no idea.'

'Time's wasting.'

Impertinence. 'It is as I said. I was instructed to emplace devices in the stadium, but for what purpose, I have no idea.'

'You didn't ask?'

'I'd like to see you confront the Immortals, missy. It might bring you down a peg.'

'Oh dear.' She sighed. '"Missy?" You really haven't come to terms with me yet, have you? I think it best that you go on your way.'

Soames took a step, then stopped, his fists clenched, teeth grinding. 'Those photographs! How did you get them? We were alone!'

'Let's just say that someone ratted on you.'

Soames was a salesman at heart, his mother used to say. In fact, it was the last thing she said before he sold her at the slave market.

335

With the girl's photographic discs heavy in his pocket, he was able to face the Immortals. He spoke with all the sincerity he'd learned to dissemble over his years of duping, cheating and betraying.

'And of course you understand how stubborn the Neanderthals can be, don't you?' he finished.

Augustus narrowed his eyes. 'Those animals. Once we finished our experiments on them, we should have eradicated the whole lot of them.'

'We learned all we could from their wildness,' Jia said absently. She was having difficulty jotting in a small notebook. 'So we still need the boy. The way he unites the wild and civilisation is useful to us. Get him from them.'

Soames pricked up his ears at that, but decided it wasn't the time to pursue this hint at the Immortals' interest in the boy. 'Twenty or thirty more vials should do the trick,' he said. 'I'll have him for you later today.'

Forkbeard grunted, then swivelled so he was looking over his shoulder. He barked a few words in a language Soames didn't recognise.

The cube of the Materials Manipulator glowed green. It began to rotate faster. A few seconds later a flash of green light burst from it and lanced at Soames, who automatically threw his hands up to ward it off, and the leather case he held in his hand struck him on the forehead.

The Immortals laughed. High, shrill giggles, child-like but with an edge of ancient mirth that was as far from innocence as could be.

Soames tried to adopt a dignified posture as he rose. He didn't touch his brow, despite its throbbing. They would pay. Once the phlogiston was gone, once they were helpless in their haunted hall, he'd send in his underlings. The more vicious the better.

Soames smiled.

Soames dawdled over the selection of vials. He regretted the waste that was about to occur, every vial a fortune. For a moment, he considered revealing the girl's plan to the Immortals. He was sure they could do something with the explosive.

He snorted and continued to fill the leather case, stacking in as many vials as he could. Such an action would be foolish. A perfect way to cripple the Immortals had fallen into his lap. If the girl's device did as she claimed, the Immortals would be without phlogiston. They would be helpless.

Soames snapped the case shut. He liked serendipity, especially when he could wring it for his own ends.

Soames had no idea what made him linger just outside the Hall of Immortals and wait for the explosion, after telling them he was off to fetch the boy. It wasn't a business decision. It had no real benefit for him in monetary terms. It wasn't even really an opportunity. He could only attribute it to sheer curiosity, a quality he'd forgotten he possessed.

Of course, it would provide him with an opportunity to gloat, which Soames always found to be one of life's great pleasures.

For the rest of the hour, ignored by the Immortals – who were engaged in quiet, intense discussions about harvesting the animus generated at the Olympic Games – he pretended to be busy in the small living room he'd found earlier.

Animus harvesting. That sounded like something he'd enjoy learning more about once the Immortals were gone.

Even secreted away as he was, and without his lovely watch, Soames knew when the girl's device went off. The round globes that lit the small living room flickered, then went out.

The darkness in the underground chamber was absolute.

Soames sat still, not daring to move, and from above came the sound of a great wind. He blinked, for the blackness momentarily shifted. It entered a region of sensation that was both more and less than emptiness, then it righted itself and Soames was alone again.

Wild screeching came from the direction of the Hall of the Immortals.

With infinite care, Soames edged out of the living room. One hand ran along the shelves of ledgers and accounts, some of the archives going back centuries, while he hefted the leather case with the other. He found the door after a few moments of throat-tightening panic, and made his way up the stairs by touch, guided by the hysterical anger of the Immortals, which had been joined by vacant, seagull cries from the Spawn.

Soames blinked when he crept into the Hall of the Immortals. He could see, dimly. The pentagonal ceiling was like a window looking out on a snowy evening, a dull grey that was fading as Soames watched. He wondered if the girl had anticipated this effect of the liberation of all that phlogiston, or if it was the sheer amount of the magical fluid that was causing this phenomenon. Regardless, Soames thought that he'd lingered too long. It was time to leave.

Before he could, he gaped, astonished. Three tiny figures were waddling on uncertain legs across the gigantic hall, their plump arms flailing.

The Immortals had left their throne.

It was upended on the other side of the hall. Then Soames saw that one of the Immortals – Jia? – had a single glowing vial in her fist. Cursing, the three reached the alcove that held the Material Manipulator. The cube was still rotating, but wouldn't be for long, Soames knew. As soon as its inner phlogiston ran out it, too, would die.

The Immortals flung themselves on the cube. Jia hammered at it with the vial she held. An eruption of green light and the Immortals were gone.

Soames was alone in the rapidly darkening Hall of the Immortals, apart from a few dozen Spawn who were blundering about mindlessly, crashing into walls and each other, mewling and croaking.

He'd overstayed his welcome.

Just as Soames was about to set off, he felt a rumbling underfoot. With a sense of dread, he remembered the girl saying she had a second part to her plan.

The doors opening into the hall crashed open. Roaring like a giant released, water cascaded through them, an irresistible flood sluicing through the openings, flinging streamers of spray high into the air and throwing the golden throne aside as if it were made of paper.

Spawn were tossed about like sticks.

Soames held the leather case to his chest as the water thundered towards him. He gaped, disbelieving.

Jabez! It can't end like this!

He wished he'd listened to the girl.

⇜ FORTY-THREE ⇝

Kingsley ducked just as the time machine came alive, crashing with colours that strained reality, singing with the sound of metal on metal. He flung his arm up to protect his eyes when the machine sizzled and the room crackled with caged lightning. He went to run, but the entire room shook and he staggered, only to be caught by a fist of displaced air as the machine flashed again.

Kingsley went to all fours and rose in time to see a stunned-looking Neanderthal standing above him on the platform of the time machine.

He rolled to one side but the Neanderthal toppled on him.

'Stay there, grub,' the Neanderthal slurred in his ear. A fist clipped Kingsley on the side of the head. The light that burst inside his skull didn't come from the time machine. 'You shouldn't be here.'

I may be the only stage performer ever to be twice flattened by Neanderthals, Kingsley thought, dazed as he was. He could hardly breathe, crushed under the weight of the creature, who smelled as if he hadn't bathed for a lifetime or two.

The Neanderthal stood, swaying a little, but dragged Kingsley up by his collar and delivered a slap that made his head ring. The Neanderthal held him at arm's length while, with his other hand, he fumbled around under his jacket and withdrew a glittering belt.

Kingsley's thoughts were foggy from the blow, but he stared. Could this be the Neanderthal who'd been lost in the Immortals' Temporal Manipulator? It was the sort of scientific puzzle that would drive Evadne into paroxysms of speculation.

The Neanderthal towed him out of the workshop and into the main activity site, which was heavy with the smell of hot metal and steam. Workers ran about, shouting to those operating the gantry cranes to move great sheets of metal around. Showers of sparks fell like shooting stars while teams worked on welding and cutting. Smoke wound towards the ceiling where five great exhaust fans strove to keep the heights clear.

The Neanderthal held Kingsley by the collar while he cast about, peering at the faces of those hurrying past until he saw one that made him cry out. 'Rolf!'

A black-bearded, leather-aproned Neanderthal wearing heavy dark goggles swung around. 'Magnus!'

The leather-aproned Neanderthal bounded over to Kingsley's captor and took him in an embrace that would have crushed an elephant. They pounded each other on the back.

Touching though it was, Kingsley wasn't about to miss his chance. He jerked his neck. His collar detached. With a duck and a slither, he was away, leaving his captor gaping at the sorry-looking piece of cloth in his hand.

Kingsley grinned at the shouts from behind him. They were meaningless in the general uproar where every second Neanderthal was raising his or her voice over the bedlam.

Shouting was one thing, seeing was another. Reactions varied. Some Neanderthals threw tools at him while others dropped them in disbelief at the sight of an Invader scampering loose in the heart of their home. Kingsley galloped along the rows of machines, changing direction at random whenever a hostile Neanderthal appeared ahead of him. The blood rose in his ears. His body fell into a state that could carry him for miles, alert and ready, muscles working smoothly. His lips parted, baring his teeth as he sought about for both his foster father and a way out.

He wheeled around a tall metal punch. His gaze fell on the pipes that rose from all the machines, connecting them to the ceiling. In this area of idiosyncratically designed and constructed machines, the constant was the network of pipes criss-crossing the ceiling.

Kingsley's random course became more deliberate as he traced the pipes to their source at the distant far end of the workshop and a plan started to evolve in his mind. He vaulted conveyor belts and slid under benches, swerving around Neanderthals who blundered out of clouds of steam. He avoided any fisticuffs and backed off rather than come to close quarters. *Keep moving. Keep moving.*

The source of the pipes was one and a half machines against the far wall of the workshop, underneath a complex delivery system of racks, tracks and containers. One of the machines was all brass and wood, a work of ornamental art. Its companion was still under construction and was more humble, composed mostly of gigantic rubber bladders strapped into a mesh of steel and pipes.

Phlogiston extractors. Just as Evadne had predicted.

Panting, Kingsley looked about for what he knew must be there. The pipework – where did it connect to the phlogiston extractors?

The racks, the containers. The glowing vial that shot out of the maw of the elegant machine confirmed Kingsley's guess. He wanted to cheer when it was dumped into a container, then was sucked into the network of pipes.

Kingsley had seen a pneumatic capsule delivery system before in the House of Commons. In front of him was an eccentric, handcrafted version delivering phlogiston to the dozens of machines in the workshop.

He had a target for Evadne's anti-phlogiston.

He didn't hesitate. He took the vial from his pocket and sprinted at the extractors, desperation driving him forward. As much as he might feel sorry for the Neanderthals, he couldn't let them proceed with their plan.

They moved to block him but he wove between them, ducking, rolling and coming to his feet, squeezing between shuddering metal uprights before reaching his target. With a bound, he was on top of the more elegant machine while Neanderthals cried out in alarm. He ran along its length and then hurled himself at the shelves. He clung to a canister with one hand while a metal basket buzzed back and forth just above his head like a wasp. With dismay, he felt the canister start to tear loose from the rock, but before it could give way he slammed the tiny vial into the hole in the brass pipe.

It disappeared.

Within seconds, a vast metal press nearby where two Neanderthals were cutting a sheet of corrugated iron began to turn red. An instant later, it became a blazing white and started to melt. The operators fled, crying out in alarm.

Then the giant extraction fans in the ceiling exploded, sending sparks and a hail of hot metal flying through the air.

The Neanderthals working on the half-completed extractor gaped for a split-second and then downed tools more quickly than a well-organised strike. As one, they ran. The biggest grabbed an iron bar and hammered at anything in his path to raise the alarm, shouting, 'Run! Run!'

Kingsley had already dropped to the abandoned extractor, landing lightly. He dashed for the nearest stairs.

Overhead, the feeder pipes were changing colour. The brass deepened, becoming ruddy, and a low hum emanated from them as they started to vibrate. The ominous change spread as the anti-phlogiston sought phlogiston to annihilate.

Kingsley reached the stairs and risked a look back. The machines nearest the phlogiston extractors were shaking, rattling and casting parts about in the same way dandelions lose their fluff. They looked like children's toys as they vibrated, torn apart from the inside.

The chaos spread. Neanderthals were crowding the lifts and moving stairways, but the more wary ones avoided them knowing that they, too, were phlogiston powered and would be caught in the wave of phlogiston–antiphlogiston antagonism. Some were stampeding in Kingsley's direction and he saw that even though his nimbleness would keep him ahead of the relatively ponderous Neanderthals, he shouldn't tarry.

He counted accurately and left the stairwell to find himself, blessedly, in the prison level. He sprinted up the slope, vaulted over the counter of the monitoring station and dragged the wheelchair out from under the desk. His hand trembled uncharacteristically as he worked at the lock; he couldn't block out the unnatural screaming noise that was coming up through the floor at his feet, which was vibrating so hard Kingsley thought it might come apart.

His foster father struggled gamely until he was sitting up. 'Hello, Kingsley. Have we found a propitious moment?'

'To escape? We certainly have. I have an appointment for afternoon tea.'

~❦~ FORTY-FOUR ~❦~

The Olympic Stadium was a vast bowl full of noise. It was the noise of 80,000 people enjoying the afternoon sun, a crowd that had already had a fine day's athletic entertainment but was looking forward to what promised to be a splendid awards ceremony. The band of the Grenadier Guards played what was meant to be selections from the national anthems of the competing nations, but which became, by force of repetition, a compote of brassy tunes. On the east side of the track, the second and third placegetters were assembling, readying to march to the Royal Box and receive their awards, many nations mixing in camaraderie unhindered by differences in language or background.

It was an entirely civilised scene, but one that Kingsley was far too busy to bask in. 'Screwdriver,' he said to Evadne. 'The short-handled one.'

She passed the screwdriver over his shoulder. The access panel was awkwardly placed behind one of the pillars that supported the banks of seating overhead, but this location made it unobtrusive, something that Kingsley was sure the Immortals had planned.

The covered way that ran beneath and behind the banks of seating allowed access to dressing rooms, refreshments, committee facilities and offices, and also provided a full perimeter around the huge stadium. A perfect location, Evadne had calculated, for the Immortals' harvesting devices to absorb the outpouring of positive animus that the culmination of the Olympic Games would produce.

Kingsley gingerly removed the last screw and eased the metal plate aside. 'You're sure this is the last one?' he asked Evadne, without taking his eyes from his task.

'My Ether Disturbance Monitor says so.' She put a hand on his shoulder, leaned, and waggled a shiny object in front of his nose.

'I still think it looks like a tobacco tin with some holes cut in it.'

'It may once have been a tobacco tin, but Westminster Abbey was once a heap of rough stone lying about in a marsh.'

'I withdraw my observation. It's a cathedral among monitors. Now, if you'll just take it away I'll be able to see what I'm doing here.'

A wave of applause and cheering came to them, but Kingsley didn't look up. He was secure in the fact that almost everyone in the vicinity was out watching the parade and readying for the award ceremony – and any who were left would hardly notice them in the Demi-monde accoutrements Evadne had provided. When he'd finally helped his foster father to her refuge, exhausted and filthy after their flight from the Neanderthals' home, he'd wanted nothing more than to sleep, but she had thrown these clothes at him and dragged him out – leaving Dr Ward under the medical care of the mysterious and stately Lady Aglaia, who Kingsley would have enjoyed questioning about Evadne's past.

He didn't like the way the grey flannel coat fitted him, while the cloth cap was itchy on his sweaty brow. Evadne, however, looked a treat with her hair tucked under the cap and the sleeves of her coat folded up. The outfit was a veritable guarantee that they could work away unnoticed and undisturbed, especially with the toolbox each had, and the sheaf of forms that Evadne tucked into her coat pocket. Brandishing these would be certain to turn away any half-interested official or policeman, convincing them that they had more pressing business elsewhere.

He leaned the metal plate against the wall and peered into the space he'd revealed. The tangle of wires was almost familiar after the four other devices they'd removed. It was more like a nest than a logical array of elements, and sitting in the middle of the nest was a fist-sized dodecahedron, its pentagonal sides glowing a baleful red.

Kingsley licked his lips. Inside, his wild self was wisely insisting that he cut and run. He soothed it by promising himself that was just what he'd do – making sure Evadne was ahead of him – if the object moved, changed shape, or started talking.

A shocking thought pushed itself on him. Could the Immortals have been planning to take advantage of the extraordinary gathering by turning it sour, setting troublemakers loose in the crowd, sowing discord and ill-will, setting spectator against spectator? Could that provide an outpouring of hateful animus ready for gathering?

Music seeped through the stands: 'See the Conquering Hero Comes'. Sprightly, happy, greeted by cheering and a rolling wave of laughter. No hateful animus there, just the bonhomie of people assembled to give thanks and acclamation to the strong, the fleet and the nimble from all around the world.

No, whatever the Immortals had been planning, it wasn't something as vile as that.

Satisfied, fingers extended, he gently plucked the dodecahedron from its surrounds. It came away easily, and immediately the blood-red glow began to fade, exactly as had happened with the other four.

'All safe?' he asked Evadne.

A pause. Then: 'The ether has calmed. All is steady.'

Kingsley sighed. Unwilling to leave a job half-done, he screwed the access plate back. He stood and gave the inert harvester to Evadne. She took it solemnly and placed it in a bag in her toolbox.

'I think I know what they were collecting,' Kingsley said.

A roar shook the stands above them. Had Queen Alexandra arrived?

'High spirits?' Evadne guessed. 'Good nature? Jollity?'

'Civilisation. It's as Kipling said: this is the greatest expression of the influence of civilisation of this age.'

'Civilisation? What on earth for?'

'They want whatever they think is inside my head because it might tell them something about civilisation and the wild. I'll wager that this is connected with gathering the concentrated essence of civilisation.'

'And not in a way that's likely to lead to good times for all, I'm sure.'

'No. Not good times for all, but even if they're still around, we've stopped them for now.'

Evadne adjusted her hat. 'In that case, would you like to watch the parade?'

'Why not?'

～∽ FORTY-FIVE ∽～

For three days Damona wandered through the sanctuary of the True People. Sometimes, she stopped to pick up objects. She admired their craft. She contemplated murals and carvings. She remembered who lived in the dwelling spaces and workshops. She found additions she never knew existed.

Three days. She had barely slept since the disaster. She had hardly eaten. She was aware that she had eased into a state only lightly connected to the earth.

She coughed. Grimaced. Her throat was raw. It rasped in the air, which was still smoky. Sour.

She took a corner at random. It didn't matter. She was adrift.

Her people had gone. Every machine connected to the phlogiston grid had melted. Almost all the lighting had failed. Their sanctuary was dark, foul-smelling, badly made.

A few oil lamps lit her way. Quickly made after the disaster. They worked. More or less.

Alone. Damona was determined to visit every part of their sanctuary. A pilgrimage? An expiation? Was she apologising to a place she had hurt?

She stopped. Looked around. A workshop? She didn't recognise where she was. It didn't worry her.

She rested on a bench. Put her lantern on the parquetry floor. For a moment she studied the inlaid wood. Good patterns. Fine toolwork. True People stuff.

She shifted. Ignored the pain. Ran a hand over the bench. It was wood, too. A waterfall? Water, waves rolling down a stony slope. Every curve, every ripple smoothed by the long-ago maker's hands.

It was supremely comfortable.

The room was small. Damona could not remember who had lived here. Or when. Not a family place. A one-person place? A basin, cooking facilities, a small bathroom opening off the main area. For sleeping and for work?

A lathe, bandsaw, both rusty, against the far wall. Damona looked up, tried to find their power source. Cobwebs. Dust. Electricity? Could she turn them on? See their sturdiness in action?

'Eldest?'

Damona shifted her weight and her hip complained. The title was a burden. On the wings of pain, she eased herself around. Gustave stood at the door. 'What is it?'

'The last of us are on the ramp. About to set off. I came to see if . . .'

'If I've changed my mind?'

Gustave shrugged. He had stitches in his forehead. His beard was ragged from the fire. 'If you want to join us.'

'You'd have me?'

'We don't want to lose you.'

Damona grunted. No-one had been hurt when the end had come. Gustave and his friends were brave, organised. They had arranged an evacuation to the furthest reaches. Then they went to fight the fires. Two long days. Then Gustave braved the main complex. Inspected it. Declared it safe enough.

Safe enough to begin their departure.

'You have a destination?' Damona asked him.

'Far away, I think.' He leaned against the doorframe. Damona felt his exhaustion. 'Rolf and Magnus went out into the Demimonde, with the last gold we could scrape together. They say we can get a ship.'

'Ah.'

'We're tired of underground, Eldest. We want to feel the sun again. We'll risk a sea voyage.'

'It's a brave plan.'

'Won't you come?'

'Not just now.'

Gustave left. It took some time before Damona realised.

Her lamp flickered. She knew that it needed more oil. Without it she'd be left in the dark.

She was comfortable.

Damona had striven. She wanted to give her people a future, but she had failed. The Invaders had won.

She lay back. She remembered Signe. She remembered the songs she sang. She wanted to apologise to her but words were heavy on her tongue.

The lamp went out.

~ FORTY-SIX ~

Evadne poured.

The glass cupola of the Thames Foyer alternated between brightness and gloom as clouds and blue sky exchanged places. Kipling had chosen an alcove with window seats and red cushions, with plenty of room for Dr Ward's wheelchair. A violinist played, waiters wafted about, and Kingsley enjoyed the absence of being chased, beaten, sold, exchanged or abducted.

'Muffins!' Dr Ward exclaimed as a waiter uncovered a silver dish. 'Just the thing!'

Evadne finished pouring. 'I couldn't agree more. Hot buttered muffins and tea is a wonderful way to remind one that one is alive.'

Kingsley had a high regard for Evadne's aplomb. She chatted, made a quip or two, and charmed both Kipling and Dr Ward with her wit and steady cheerfulness.

Kingsley ate half of his excellent muffin and admired Evadne's light blue dress. She'd pointed out, when she joined them at the Savoy, that it was chiffon and the lace jacket thing was a bolero. All by himself, he could tell that the hat had roses all over it, but she emphasised that it was a broad-leafed chip hat.

Just so, Kingsley thought. He'd come out in a blazer and flannel trousers, topped with a boater, all well kept and hardly smelling of mothballs, despite having been stored away at Porchester Terrace since he'd left the place to pursue a life on the stage.

When Kipling found them at the Savoy, he had been overjoyed. Kingsley's telephone invitation had reassured the writer that they were alive and well, but it was a different thing, seeing them in the flesh.

The first half an hour of their reunion had been devoted to informing Kipling of the events since they had parted. It was a measure of the writer's imagination and patience that he remained silent while Kingsley and Evadne bounced the story between them, with a few solemn interjections from Dr Ward – and he expressed no incredulity.

'And so we're staying at the hotel, here,' Kingsley finished.

'We couldn't stay at Porchester Terrace,' Dr Ward murmured. 'Not after what happened there.'

'And I'm simply enjoying the luxury,' Evadne said. 'My refuge is comfortable enough, but I wasn't about to pass up a room at the Savoy.'

'That's a major disadvantage of the subterranean life,' Kingsley said, 'the lack of view.'

Evadne and he shared a look. She challenged him with a smile that he returned.

'We're grateful to you, Kipling,' Dr Ward said. His colour was better, and if it weren't for his still-recovering ankles, Kingsley was sure he'd be up and about under his own locomotion. 'Your efforts at the Yard have smoothed the way.'

'I did what I could, Dr Ward, but it was your reappearance and the testimony of Miss Stephens that convinced the authorities that Kingsley here couldn't be responsible for the death of Mrs Walters.'

'And who do they think is?' Kingsley asked.

'"Investigations are continuing," I think the phrase is. At least, that's what I was told, but I have the impression that a few of my more senior sources know more than they're letting on.'

'The PM, Kipling?' Dr Ward asked. 'Did you inform him?'

'Not the PM, Dr Ward, not yet. Once I was sure Evadne and Kingsley were safe, I did have a meeting with the Agency.'

'The Agency? Of course. Should have thought of that. And do they think the Immortals could still be out there?'

Kipling cast a rueful look at Evadne. 'I'm sorry, my dear, but we must consider the possibility that the torrent you unleashed didn't finish them off.'

'I had,' Evadne said softly. 'The world would be better off without them, but I fear that may be easier said than done.'

Kingsley couldn't help himself. He reached up and touched the back of his head. He preferred his brain intact, and was determined to keep it so, immortal sorcerers or not.

Evadne caught his eye and nodded, emphatically, just the once.

It was enough.

'It's remarkable, you know,' Kipling said. 'I thought I knew a thing or two about the shadowy fringes of the world, but you've certainly opened my eyes. I'll never look at a manhole the same way again.'

'The Demimonde is vaster and more mysterious than a few manholes,' Dr Ward said.

'And how long exactly have you known of it, Father?' Kingsley asked.

'My work introduced me to it years ago.' Dr Ward closed his mouth and frowned. Kingsley knew this was a matter for another day.

A three-tiered stand of small cakes and elaborate biscuits was placed on the table. Evadne plucked a pink concoction from the top level. 'Superb,' she adjudged after taking a small bite.

Her lipstick was subtle and suited her, Kingsley decided, and was very evenly applied. He wondered if she'd invented a device to do it for her.

'And what are you going to do with my son's story, Kipling?' Dr Ward asked.

'It remains a fine and private thing, Dr Ward.' Kipling took out his notebook and started to read. His voice was low, but carried perfectly to the three listeners at the table.

Waters of the Waingunga, the Man-Pack have cast me out.
I did them no harm, but they were afraid of me. Why?
Wolf Pack, ye have cast me out too. The jungle is shut to me
and the village gates are shut. Why?

> As Mang flies between the beasts and the birds, so fly I
> between the village and the jungle. Why?
>
> I dance on the hide of Shere Khan, but my heart is very
> heavy. My mouth is cut and wounded with the stones
> from the village, but my heart is very light because I have
> come back to the jungle. Why?
>
> These two things fight together in me as the snakes fight in
> the spring. The water comes out of my eyes; yet I laugh
> while it falls. Why?
>
> I am two Mowglis, but the hide of Shere Khan is under my
> feet.
>
> All the jungle knows that I have killed Shere Khan.
> Look—look well, O Wolves!
>
> Ahae! My heart is heavy with the things that I do not
> understand.

When Kipling finished, he looked at Kingsley. 'I don't have to write your story, my boy, because I've written it already.'

'But that's not me. I'm not Mowgli.'

'I know. I meant that I understand your predicament. Caught between two worlds cannot be the easiest place to be.'

'Perhaps,' Evadne said. 'But being alone would make it worse.'

'"Things that I do not understand",' Kingsley repeated. 'There are so many of them, still.'

'Such as?' Dr Ward asked gently.

'You told me of my parents. My real parents.' Kingsley bit his lip, then rushed on. 'But all you said was that my father was a mysterious man who worked for the government.'

359

Kingsley couldn't fail to catch the sharp look that Kipling shot Dr Ward. 'Mr Kipling?'

The writer grimaced. 'A number of mysterious agents have been working in India over the years. The place is full of them.'

'From the little I know, Greville Sanderson was a hero,' Dr Ward said.

Kipling cocked his head. 'Greville Sanderson was your father, my boy? Extraordinary.'

'Dr Ward is my father,' Kingsley said firmly. 'This other man is someone I've never known.'

Dr Ward reached over and patted Kingsley's hand. 'Troubled and troublesome as you might be, Kingsley, you're a good lad.'

Kingsley warmed to his foster father's words. The old man was often preoccupied, occasionally forgetful, but he was always generous.

'Mr Kipling,' Kingsley said, pushing that thought away for later. 'You obviously know something of my father. My other father. Would you tell me of him? In exchange for my telling you my story?'

'That, young Mr Ward, is an offer a writer could never resist.'

Dr Ward leaned in the other direction. 'And you, Miss Stephens, what are your plans?'

For an answer, Evadne held up a finger. Then she picked a small silver dragee from a cake and balanced it on the end of the handle of a teaspoon that was resting on the damask table cloth. With a tilt of her head, she tapped the bowl of the teaspoon and launched the silver sugar ball into the air. It landed, with a tiny splash, in Kingsley's glass of lemon squash.

'We have an audience waiting for us,' she said when the applause died.

Kingsley had been listening. 'We?'

'I've been thinking that while juggling is all well and good, I'm looking for something new, something innovative. I thought a two-handed act might do the trick.'

'I don't follow you,' Dr Ward said, on the verge of floundering.

'Stephens and Ward: Juggling and Escapology.'

Kingsley sat back in his chair and crossed his arms. 'What about Ward and Stephens: Escapology and Juggling?'

Kipling tapped his glass with a fork. 'I have a suggestion.'

It was perfect.

~ FORTY-SEVEN ~

Kingsley's heart drummed, but he was pleased to see his hands were steady when he held them up in front of his face. He allowed his wildness some rein so it could take in the surroundings. The smells and sounds were disquieting, but he exerted himself and his wolfishness settled, satisfied that it was safe, especially when the scent of gardenia came to him from nearby.

Evadne emerged from the darkness, a portrait in silver and ruby. Her sequined headdress framed her face, and beads hung on either side, intertwining with her hair. Her dress continued the sequin and beads theme, which was made consistent with her slippers and her rose spectacles. She cocked her head, sending the beads swaying in an enchanting fashion. 'All set?'

Kingsley glanced at his equipment. The Chest of Terror was ready. The Cabinet of Doom was in place. The chains, the ropes, the manacles were in position. The stagehands were attentive and prepared, on their best behaviour since Kingsley had had a quiet word with each of them. A half-sovereign did the trick with most of them, but one troublemaker had needed some assistance falling over and getting up again – a small, physical discussion – before he understood the importance of cooperation.

'All set,' he confirmed.

Kingsley tugged the lapels of his dinner jacket. No turban this time. Lorenzo wasn't needed any more. After all he'd been through, Kingsley didn't feel much like hiding. Let the world see Kingsley Ward for who he was.

The orchestra began tuning. In a dressing room, a dog barked. Just the once, but Kingsley was sure its companions would have poked relentless fun at the offender for premature performing.

Evadne stood by his side, her face serene. She'd managed to do more than calm Mr Bernadetti. With Mr Kipling's help, she'd negotiated their way into a London show. Near the bottom of the bill, but Camden was undeniably a step up.

The orchestra, obviously deciding it had something better to do than tuning, banged straight into the overture. Kingsley took Evadne's hand and squeezed it. She squeezed back, but didn't let go.

The curtain rose and the announcer gave voice: 'Ladies and gentlemen, it gives me great pleasure to present, in their debut performance, please welcome The Extraordinaires!'

Hand in hand Kingsley and Evadne stepped into the limelight that was their world.

ACKNOWLEDGEMENTS

One of the joys of writing in this mode is the researching I have to do. In an effort to get my details right, I comb through many volumes and innumerable web pages. I inevitably stumble on titbits that amuse and entertain me, as well as making me think of narrative possibilities.

I'd like to mention a few that were particularly helpful, as their contribution to my story was immense.

For help with the Edwardian period in general, I appreciated Roy Hattersley's *The Edwardians*, as well as the extraordinary *Lost Voices of the Edwardians* by Max Arthur, which was a captivating collection of snippets from those who lived in these times, with details ranging from the mundane to the regal. Wonderful reading. In addition, *The Big Shots* by Jonathan Ruffer was important in adding to my coming to terms with the Edwardians and their ways.

For details about the 1908 Olympic Games and the Franco-British Exhibition, I was grateful for *The First Olympic Games* by Rebecca Jenkins. Full of lively anecdotes and tantalising photographs, this was extremely helpful.

For down to earth material about London, Roy Porter's *London: A Social History* was invaluable, while Peter Ackroyd's magisterial *London, the Biography* is unsurpassed in detail and scope.

The internet, of course, was a treasure trove. From actual street maps of 1908 London, to weather charts for the period, to the actual 330-page 'illustrated review' of the Franco-British exhibition, I had a wealth of material to work with. Edwardiana lives!

Naturally, the scholarship and diligence of all the writers and compilers I've listed cannot prevent a storyteller from getting things wrong. If I have, please accept that it is my fault, and not theirs.

ABOUT THE AUTHOR

Michael Pryor has published more than twenty-five fantasy books and over forty short stories, from literary fiction to science fiction to slapstick humour. Michael has been shortlisted six times for the Aurealis Awards, has been nominated for a Ditmar award, and six of his books have been Children's Book Council of Australia Notable Books, including three books in The Laws of Magic series. His most recent series are The Chronicles of Krangor, The Laws of Magic and The Extraordinaires.

For more information about Michael and his books, please visit www.michaelpryor.com.au

The Extraordinaires Book Two:
The Subterranean Stratagem
is available now

HAVE YOU READ

There's a magical and political storm brewing – and Aubrey Fitzwilliam is making sure he's right in the centre of it. Set in a world similar to Edwardian Britain, just before World War I, this fantasy series is full of magic, manners, conspiracy and intrigue, politics and personal trial – not to mention good old-fashioned fun. The Laws of Magic stars Aubrey Fitzwilliam, the son of a prominent ex-prime minister. He's brilliant at magic, but he's still stuck at school. At least he has his best friend, George, there to back him up. George would follow Aubrey anywhere – and with Aubrey's talent for thinking up impulsive and daring schemes that will get them both in trouble, that's no easy thing to do.

From golems to top-secret submersibles, soul stealers to ghosts, The Laws of Magic is a cracking good read.

AN EXTRACT FROM
THE LAWS OF MAGIC BOOK ONE:
BLAZE OF GLORY

Aubrey Fitzwilliam hated being dead. It made things much harder than they needed to be.

'When you're quite ready, Fitzwilliam! We haven't got all day!' bawled the pimply-faced Warrant Officer. Aubrey stood up straighter and glanced at him. The WO was Atkins, a fellow sixth-former, a newcomer to Stonelea School. He had an Adam's apple that made him look as if he'd swallowed a melon and he was taking great pleasure in his small position of authority. 'Two laps of the Hummocks, full pack.' Atkins paused to gloat. 'Lovely weather for it, cadet, if you enjoy heatstroke.'

Aubrey said nothing. He lifted his chin, stiffened his back and stared straight ahead to study the rounded hills of the Hummocks. The pounded earth trail he had to follow wound its way up and down through the sparse growth of the training course. Heat haze made the air ripple over the farthest reaches, obscuring the fence that separated the training course from the school playing fields.

Two miles, more or less. His task was to complete the circuit twice, at the double – in early afternoon heat that had already sent the tennis players from the courts and the birds to drowsiness in the trees around the fence line.

Before his accident, Aubrey knew he would have completed the challenge without difficulty, even though, at the age of seventeen when many others were filling out and taking on their adult strength, he was still slight. He had pale skin, black hair and dark-brown – almost black – eyes, and he looked frail, a poet rather than an athlete. But he'd always managed to surprise people with his determination in running, boxing, or games. Boys much larger than him had learned that provoking skinny Aubrey to fight could be a poor idea. He could drag himself over broken glass if he set his mind to it.

But since the disastrous magical experiment, things were different. Balanced on the edge of true death as he was, physical strain – even emotional strain – could tip him over. He only kept the semblance of a normal existence by a combination of arcane spells and strength of mind. If his magic failed, it would be the end for him.

I'll just have to make sure I don't let that happen, he thought. He adjusted his shoulders.

'Step lively, now!' Atkins said. 'The clock's running! Don't keep us waiting! Remember, no magical assistance!'

Aubrey set off, grinding his teeth. *Steady on*, he told himself. *He was probably bullied by his older brothers. And sisters.*

The heavy woollen uniform itched, but Aubrey had no time to scratch under the khaki. With the weight of a full field pack on his back, it was all he could do to retain his balance as he shuffled along as fast as he could in a shambling gait that resembled a drunken sailor more than a well-trained soldier.

Heat hammered down from the cloudless sky and radiated from the hard dirt path. Aubrey staggered up the first hill that gave the course its name. His breath rasped in a throat that felt as if it was made of sandpaper.

Dimly, he could see Atkins and his cronies standing in the shade of a row of elm trees. They were sniggering and pointing, but Aubrey was pleased to see that they became more circumspect when George Doyle sauntered over. With his massive shoulders and height, George looked more like a wrestler than a student. For years, Aubrey had seen George stop arguments and make fists drop simply by appearing on the scene. It was an ability that Aubrey had used, on occasion, to his own benefit. After all, what were best friends for?

Aubrey's forearms ached as he held the heavy Symons rifle in front of him. The wretched thing was thirty years old, if it was a day, but – thanks to Aubrey's meticulous maintenance – was in perfect working order, even if it hadn't seen live ammunition in decades. Aubrey had even replaced the bolt action, using a spare part he'd found in one of the outbuildings at Maidstone.

Whatever gets me there, Aubrey thought and he gritted his teeth again.

He felt the webbing straps of his pack cutting into his shoulders and decided, not for the first time, that his desire for promotion to Warrant Officer was one of his more stupid ambitions. He'd sailed through the written examination and the interview from two army majors was straightforward. All that remained was the physical test.

Aubrey reached the next hill and stumbled. He heard laughter. 'Come on, Fitzwilliam! You want to fail, like your old man?'

Uneasy laughter greeted this jibe. Aubrey tightened his grip on the rifle and slogged up the slope, cursing the varying height of the hummocks that made it hard to maintain a rhythm. His pack threatened to topple him backwards, but he was prepared. He leaned forward, bent at the knees, and forged up the hill.

When he reached the summit, Aubrey tried to shake sweat from his brow, but just managed to make his helmet slip. It hung there askew, and he tried to nudge it back with his shoulder.

For a perilous moment, he was on the brink of going headfirst down the slope. He caught himself and fought momentum as he descended. His boots threatened to skid out from under him and every step jarred his teeth, but he made it to the bottom.

The next hummock was a short trot away.

Through a combination of doggedness and good decision-making, Aubrey endured for nearly half an hour, but by then he felt as if he was wandering in the bowels of a furnace.

His rifle was a mass of hot iron and wood. He could feel blisters sprouting every time he moved his grip. His helmet seemed to think it was an oven and his head was the Sunday roast. He could feel the sunlight on his back as an actual weight, as if it were heavy rain. His breath was ragged, each sip of the hot air searing his throat.

His head sagged. His gaze was on the yard or so of the path directly in front of him. *If I can manage this step,* he thought, *and the one after that. Then the next . . .*

That was all he had time to contemplate. The ground suddenly fell away from underneath him and he realised, a little too late, that he'd reached the top of another hummock and he should have been easing down the other side.

By then, his balance was completely upset. His right foot insisted it was still climbing, while his left knew perfectly well that it was time to start heading downwards. The weight of the pack, however, had no time for Aubrey's feet to sort out their dispute, so it took over.

Aubrey had time for a startled yelp, then he pitched forward.

There was a fraction of an instant, a moment where all the forces conspiring against him were in balance and he knew that if he could angle his hip left, and flex his right knee while striking the ground just *so* with his heel, he could catch himself and all would be well.

Then his helmet slipped over his eyes and gravity was in charge.

Aubrey flew forwards, somersaulted once, then landed on his chest. He slid the rest of the way down the slope on his chin, his arms stretched out in front of him, still holding his rifle with both hands, according to regulation.

Atkins and his cronies were helpless with laughter. 'Oh, lovely style, Fitzwilliam! Lovely! Do it again!'

Despite the heat, a shiver ran through Aubrey. The perspiration drenching his body turned chill and he closed his eyes. The blackness behind his eyelids rippled and he knew that he was in trouble.

His control was wavering. The heat, the exhaustion, the physical strain had taken their toll. He was on the verge of losing his grip.

Hold on, he thought and he looked within himself for strength.

A voice nearby came to him. 'Aubrey.'

'George,' he said without opening his eyes. 'Wait. I must concentrate.'

'Your shadow,' George said. 'It's fading.'

It's worse than I thought, Aubrey decided. He breathed deeply, carefully, looking to stabilise his condition. He muttered one of the web of spells that was keeping him from the true death. He strove to pronounce each element as crisply as possible, particularly those dealing with duration, trying to re-establish their power. The strain of preventing himself from dying was a constant pressure, and he was still searching for the best combination of spells to counteract the implacable tugging on his soul. If the spells collapsed, his soul would pass through the final portal into the great unknown. Not for the first time, he cursed his own foolishness for putting himself in this perilous position.

Heavy footsteps made him open his eyes.

George was squatting next to him, shading him from the sun. Next to George, Atkins stood, hands on hips, a silhouette against the blue sky. His cronies stood around him, a straggly group of supporters. 'On your feet, Fitzwilliam,' the WO growled. He nudged Aubrey in the side with his boot. 'Your old man isn't here to help you now.'

Aubrey didn't move. *A minute*, Aubrey thought. *That's all I need. Then I'll stand, brush myself off, salute, apologise for my poor form . . .*

374

George straightened and dusted his hands. 'I don't think you should say things like that,' he said to Atkins, his voice low, his face mild. 'It gets him angry.'

'Hah!' one of Atkins' cronies said. 'So?'

'You should be afraid of getting him angry,' George said. '*I* get afraid when he's angry.'

The guffaws died down as they waded through what George had just suggested. Aubrey could see their laboured brain processes as they squinted and took in George's size, and wondered what on earth could make him afraid ...

Atkins cleared his throat. His slender grasp of military authority and decision-making was apparent on his face. He was groping for the best course of action that would allow him to keep his dignity, while maintaining that Aubrey was a worthless piece of cadet trash unsuited for officer training.

'I think I should get him to the infirmary,' George suggested.

Atkins nodded. Slowly at first, then more vigorously as the idea took hold. 'Yes. Quite right. See to it.'

He tried to gather his cronies with a glance. They stared at him, then he pushed the nearest in the direction of the gate. He strode off; they trotted in his wake.

Aubrey lifted his head and tried to prop himself on an elbow. After three attempts, he was successful. 'George, can you get this bloody pack off first? Might make things a little easier.'

George slung the pack over one shoulder. Balancing the load, he reached down and helped Aubrey to his feet. For a moment, Aubrey's head swam and his knees threatened to buckle. George slipped an arm under his. 'Ready?'

'Of course. I should be, after that nice lie down.'

Blood dripped from Aubrey's chin and onto his uniform. He took a half-hearted swipe. It smeared.

They limped to the gate, past the glowering Atkins, past the snickering cronies.

'He's failed, you know that!' Atkins called. 'All his father's influence can't change that!'

Aubrey let out a bitter snort of laughter. 'That's the last thing in the world I want, favours from my father.'

George sighed. 'I know, Aubrey. I know.'